JESSICAZ.

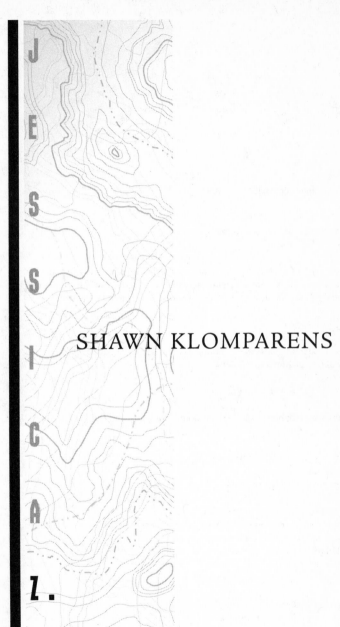

JESSICA Z.

SHAWN KLOMPARENS

DELTA TRADE PAPERBACKS

JESSICA Z.
A Delta Trade Paperback / July 2008

Published by Bantam Dell
A Division of Random House, Inc.
New York, New York

Book design by Carol Malcolm Russo

Delta is a registered trademark of Random House, Inc., and the
colophon is a trademark of Random House, Inc.

Library of Congress Cataloging-in-Publication Data
Klomparens, Shawn.
  Jessica Z. / Shawn Klomparens.
    p. cm.
ISBN 978-0-385-34200-1 (trade pbk.)
1. Single women—Fiction. 2. Terrorism—Fiction. 3. Identity (Psychology)—Fiction.
4. Psychological fiction. I. Title.
PS3611.L65J47 2008
813'.6—dc22

                    2008006622

Printed in the United States of America
Published simultaneously in Canada

www.bantamdell.com

BVG   10 9 8 7 6 5 4 3 2 1

FOR
JULIE

JESSICA Z.

PART

1

1

The morning is not quiet. There is no extra rest. The construction on my street begins, like it has every other workday morning this spring, at seven a.m., but even that is preceded by an hour of the workers drinking their coffee and talking so loudly that they may as well be in here with me four floors up. Today they seem to be discussing one of their coworkers.

Carlos almost got in big trouble last night, they're saying.

Carlos nearly got into a fight with some soldiers at that bar.

Did you hear about Carlos?

I pull a robe over my shoulders, and, in the apartment above me, I can hear Patrick moving around. The construction noises have him awake too. I listen to him up there, doing this, doing that. Footsteps. There's the sound of him turning on his shower, the rush of the pipes and the gurgle of the drain rumbling through the mysterious space between my ceiling and his floor. I go to my own bathroom, start my own shower, and get in. With the water running, I can't hear the jackhammer on the street.

Patrick comes down, as he has almost every day before work for the past two and a half weeks. He enters without knocking, while I'm making toast, with a pair of bowl-sized mugs filled with brownish foam. Since I knew he'd be coming, I'm toasting two slices of bread.

"I think I got it, Jess," he says, handing me one of the giant mugs. "Finally. I really think I got the milk-frothing thing. Got it down. Try. Try it."

I take a sip, and it isn't so bad. "This is ... a cappuccino?"

He seems a little disappointed that I'm not sure what it is. Patrick had a restaurant-grade espresso-making device installed in his kitchen a week ago today. "I was going for latte."

"It's a little strong, like, the coffee is strong," I say. "It's a strong flavor." Patrick frowns. "But it's good!" I add, to make him happy, and he sits down at my kitchen table and pokes at the foam in his mug with an index finger.

"Maybe it's the grinder," he says.

"You want toast?"

"What? Oh, sure. Please." There's a foam stalactite on his finger now.

"How much did you pay for that thing, Pat? The espresso maker machine."

"Does it really matter?" He's not angry. He's been doing well at work, and the purchase of new kitchen stuff lets him show it.

"Well, how many lattes could you buy at Tommie's before you equaled what you paid for it?"

"You're missing the point," he says. He holds the mug

out toward me and almost smiles. "It's not about money, right? It's about the pleasure of making something. It's about quality control."

I raise my eyebrows and peer into the coffee. "This is quality?"

"You suck. Did you hear about Carlos?"

"Sounds like Carlos nearly got into some trouble."

"Sounds like Carlos nearly got his ass kicked."

"Which one is Carlos, anyway?"

I place a piece of toast on one of my old blue plates on the table in front of him. He smells like soap and morning, and I can't help putting my hands on his shoulders to knead the muscles there.

"Wait, wait, wait," he says.

"What?"

"This violates the rule, for sure." He shoos my hands away.

"A neck rub?"

"Total violation."

"Seriously?" I slap my hands down at my sides. "Damn it, Pat, you're impossible."

"You made it, Jess. I'm just adhering. I know what neck rubs can lead to."

Rules get made, I suppose. Maybe they are made too hastily. Out of necessity, though, they are made.

My rule has been in effect now for almost three weeks, and, by all standards of measurement, it appears to be having its intended effect. Patrick has not spent the night in my apartment in all of that time, and it's been even longer since I've gone upstairs to sleep at his.

The rule is working. Shouldn't I be happy with this?

Though nothing has been formally written out, we've silently agreed that normal visitations during standard daytime and early evening hours are permissible. Dining together is allowed, as is morning coffee. We watch the news, and sometimes cooking shows, together on my TV, and we go out to movies and bars and restaurants. Sometimes, when we stumble home, we hold hands. But sleeping together, or any other activity that might *lead* to sleeping together or to any of the multitude of activities that can occur in bed, is strictly forbidden. This is the heart of the rule. And as the creator of the rule, I guess I should stick to it.

Now toast is finished, coffee is finished, and Patrick takes his two big mugs and goes upstairs to get his computer bag. I wait for him on the landing in front of my door, and then we go down the steps and out of our building together. There on the sidewalk in front we lean in close like we're almost going to kiss, like we're almost something, but we don't, and we aren't. There's a rule, after all.

"Talk tonight?" he says.

"Of course."

"Dinner? I can cook."

"Yes. Should I pick anything up?"

He shrugs. "I'll call you today. We can figure it out." Then we lean in again and he smiles, and he turns away and heads up the hill to get his train and I go off the other way down to my bus stop.

The ride to my office is lurching and sleepy, and at one of the stops a kid with a messenger bag takes the seat next to mine and immediately starts exchanging—with a completely bored look on his face—sexually explicit text messages with someone on his phone. He has no idea I'm reading them, and I try to remember some of the more choice ones to e-mail to my sister.

I make it to my office about ten minutes after nine. Mike, my boss, is there, as is Laurie, the new intern who hasn't yet figured out that Mike doesn't care too much about worker punctuality. I spend some time responding to e-mails, printing documents, moving paper. Doing nothing. I start to compose a message to my sister to tell her about my texting bus mate, but I'm interrupted by my e-mail program chiming to let me know there's a new message from one McAvoy, Patrick. The subject reads: "CLARIFICATION?"

He wants to know if neck rubs should, in fact, be exempt from the rule. I laugh at this, but then I stop: there's a thump, a boom, far away but still the kind of sound you feel inside your chest. A moment later my boss runs past my desk shouting, "What the hell was that?" Laurie follows him, and peeks into my cubicle with a startled look on her face.

"What was that?" she asks. "Did you hear that sound?"

Of course I heard it. Already, in the sound, I know that the day is going to be not quite right. We all know what it was.

2

After my bag drops and my shoes are kicked off, and my coat is thrown to the floor and the blinds that I didn't pull up this morning are opened and then closed again, the first thing I see when I'm back home is the blinking number on the answering machine.

Thirty-seven. Thirty-seven. Thirty-seven.

I've come to expect, after things like this, that a sizable percentage of everyone I've ever known will call and leave a message, hope I'm okay, and ask me to call when I get a chance. My mother will call. My absent father will too. College professors, former coworkers, and ex-boyfriends not seen since forgotten dormitory romps will leave messages letting me know they're thinking of me and wondering if I'm okay.

Am I okay?

They just want in on the action, I think.

The first couple messages are from early, before things turned not normal. The machine announces the time. Eight fifty-one, and my friend Amy is planning a birthday party for Alexei. Nine-ten, don't forget your dental appointment tomorrow. Nine forty-nine, Amy remembers to tell me that I should bring a bottle of wine tomorrow night. I delete the messages, stabbing at the button with my index finger, until the machine announces message six, left at ten twenty-two, which, as I've gleaned from conversations with everyone else walking home after being stranded by all transit shutting down, is seven minutes after it happened.

As expected, it's my mom.

"Jessica, honey, I heard something's going on out there, please call me when you can. I love you, call me soon, okay?"

My mother "hears" about things going on in roughly the same way a buzzard "hears" an antelope or something might be keeling over soon on the savanna: she circles the news channels, constantly, looking for some misery to feast on. She's a glutton for fear, my mom. And if I'm involved, even just by proximity, it becomes so much better than the garden variety tidal wave or child stuck in a mine shaft; now she can say to her friends: "Well, my daughter says...my daughter says...my daughter Jessica who *was right there* said..."

And just like that, she's part of the action.

She does sound a little afraid, though. And on messages seven, eight, ten, fourteen, fifteen, seventeen, and twenty through twenty-four, she sounds increasingly frantic.

"Jessica, honey, Jessie, please, please call me, your cell goes right to voice mail...."

Cell phones are a joke when these things happen. On the walk back from my office, in the shuffling crowd that had spilled off the sidewalk and onto the street, I had an interesting conversation with a very large man who claimed to be a telephone engineer. He was bald and black, and, by the way he was breathing, seemed unused to walking any significant distance. He told me that during events like this the cellular network gets shut down, "for security reasons, man." He said that "they" close it down to keep "them" from coordinating anything further.

I don't buy it, though. If a city of a hundred thousand is sent walking home, that means—and I know this is a rough estimate—at least a hundred thousand moms calling, jamming every circuit and rendering all wireless communication systems useless.

Now a message from my old college roommate Carrie plays (are a hundred thousand former roommates calling too?), and through squeals of "ohmigod, Jess, are you okay, ohmigod!" I hear helicopters fly over our building. Then I hear someone running up the stairs.

"Hey, Jess?" It's my downstairs neighbor Danny yelling through the door. "Your mom called me, she was trying to find you."

"Thanks, Danny." Then, by force of habit, survivor's etiquette, I guess, I ask: "Are you alright?"

"I didn't even know it happened until your mom told me. I was asleep."

"I'm sorry."

"It's no problem." Then he pounds back off down the stairs and I hear his door slam below me. Danny grew up in Israel, and I suspect that the tone of the call he got from his mom was somewhat different. She's had enough action.

Then I think: my mom has Danny's number? I ponder this as the phone rings, and the caller ID renders a greeting unnecessary.

"Mom."

"Oh, Jessie," she sobs. "Jessie, you're okay, oh honey, you're okay."

"I'm fine, Mom. It wasn't…It didn't happen anywhere near where I was."

"I kept trying to call—"

"I know, Mom. They shut the city down. I had to walk home." She just cries for a little bit. I feel bad for her, and a little embarrassed. She's really upset. "It took a while to get back here," I go on, "but I'm staying put."

"I don't know where anything is there, one of them could have been close, they showed all four places but I don't really know where your office—"

Four places.

"Four places? What?"

"The four places. The buses, there were four that blew up. Big . . . the buildings . . . the bombs were big and the fronts were all smashed in on the buildings."

"Four?"

"Simultaneous. Coordinated. On CNN they said they were detonated within seconds of each other." Mom calms down as she gets into the details.

Four buses? I start to feel a little sick. We only heard the one faint boom at my office, and all morning I—and everyone else I walked home with—was under the impression it was only one bus, with a little bomb, that got hit on Van Ness. One exploding bus I can deal with, sort of. Four blowing up at the same time seems stranger, scarier, like falling in a dream or tripping on a step in the dark. It's an insult to my security.

"Four?" I say again.

"And Fox is saying at least a hundred people—"

"Mom, stop." My forehead and cheeks feel cool and my own breath feels rushed through my nose.

"That number may not be right. It could be less."

"Mom," I say, then nothing else, because I can feel puke rising up with my words, my breath coming too easily through my throat. "I gotta go," I manage.

"Check in tonight? Call me?"

"I gotta go."

I don't bother to put the cordless back on its base before crawling, literally, through my kitchen to the bathroom at the back of the apartment. The toilet seat is closed, and I kneel, resting my head there on crossed arms.

Exhale. Inhale. With my eyes closed, each time I take a breath I'm willing it to pass. I take my left hand and pull the hair back from my face, and as I do I peek and see my freckled arm and the spot of condensation that has spread beneath it on the cream-colored lid. Better. The phone rings and I listen to the machine pick up.

"Hi, Jessica. It's Adam. Hey, we're thinking of you back here. Hang in there. Bye."

I don't even know who Adam is.

The bra I'm wearing is the itchiest, lamest piece of crap I own, but I'm too cheap to throw it out, and right now I feel too weak to remove it entirely. I reach back and fumble to unhook it for immediate relief, then pull a bath towel out of the basket under the sink and roll it up to use as a pillow. For some indeterminate amount of time, kneeling here with my head on the toilet and palms flat on the floor, I feel blank. Something like rest, something like sleep.

When finally I lift my head from the toilet and pull away a hair that's gotten stuck to the corner of my mouth, I feel as though I've slept a couple hours, but the toothpaste-splattered alarm clock to the side of my sink tells me it's only been about twenty minutes. Aside from a stiff neck, I feel much better. My pajamas are where I left them this morning, draped over the hamper at the end of my beloved claw-footed, cast-iron, pre-earthquake tub, and since I know I won't be going anywhere else today I change back into them. The phone rings as I'm pulling on my sweats and again I don't bother to answer, but when I hear the message begin I scramble out to the kitchen and pounce on the phone; this is the one call I do want to take.

"Katie," I say. "Katie, I'm here, don't hang up."

"Jess, you're there." It's my sister, calling from the other side of the country. "Are you scared?"

"I wasn't, but I am."

"I know you are. I am too."

We speak in a breathless rush, our own staccato creole born of a shared childhood room and what our friends have always regarded as an unnaturally close sibling relationship. Katie is two years younger than I am, but, as the family academic, she's always seemed older to me.

"I was fine," I say, "until Mom—"

"I know, Mom."

"She gets too into it."

"I know. She did the same thing—"

"After the club bomber?"

"She's crazy," Katie says. My little sister is finishing her master's in Boston, and after somebody blew both a nightclub and himself up there a month ago our mom spent a week insisting that she quit school and come back to live with her in Seattle. This, in spite of the fact that it happened on the other side of the city from where Katie lives, and she doesn't go out to clubs. Mom doesn't care.

"I hate this stuff," I say.

"I hate it too."

Feeling her there, through the phone and miles, has settled me enough to slip into the familiar. "Are you still seeing tall doctor guy?" I ask.

"Tall doctor-to-be guy, yes, still in the picture, picture getting hazy, though. He's going to start his residency—"

"Ooh."

"Yes, very hazy, he's looking to do it maybe in Salt Lake City."

"Well, that sounds like a safe place for you to go," I say, and feel stupid the moment I say it. Is this all we can think about now?

But Katie laughs.

"Probably very safe. But also, the Woods Hole people called."

"The boat!"

"The boat," Katie says. "I'm going for a third interview

Friday." Katie's research, which I sort of comprehend, has to do with geology and the ocean, the way crashing waves turn rocks into sand. She has explained to me, with tremendous enthusiasm, how, by carefully measuring the sizes of the grains of sand on a beach, she can determine the age of an island. All spring she's been working at getting an internship on a research boat in the South Pacific, where, apparently, there are many beaches and islands of various ages where she can study this wave-rock-sand phenomenon. I was a little dubious when she first told me about it, but I now believe that this boat may likely end up being the safest place—immune to both bombs and tall doctors—on earth. So I'm pretty enthusiastic about her taking the trip now, even if I fail to see the value in knowing exactly how old an island is.

"I want to know how it goes," I say. "Immediately."

"I'll tell you. How is Patrick?"

I sigh, and it isn't an overdramatic sigh, either. "The only thing I know for sure about Patrick is that he still lives above me. Beyond that, nothing is certain."

"Oh, Jess."

"But I wish he was here right now." I really do.

"Won't he be home soon?"

"He works out in Mountain View, and all the trains are stopped. He'll probably spend the night at his building. They have a gym there, that's where they slept the last time."

"What a pain."

"I wish he was here."

"Can you call him?"

"Maybe. I'll try later. The phones are, you know. Down."

"Has Dad called yet?"

"I didn't finish all my messages, but I don't think he did."

"He will," she says. "Eventually."

I can feel that the conversation is going to end soon, and the thought of my sister hanging up bothers me so much that I hold the phone to my ear with both hands. Katie senses it.

"I don't have to go," she says.

"No, it's fine. I'm just going to go sit and look out my window. I don't know. It's cloudy."

"Don't turn on the TV. No news. Get a bottle of wine."

"I was thinking something like that."

"I love you, Jess Z."

"I love you, K." And she's gone.

I'm usually reluctant to drink so early in the day, but it's now half past noon and the city has been shut down and my sister says I should, so why not? There's nothing in my apartment, though, and I don't want to get dressed again to go up the hill and see if the corner store is open, so I grab Patrick's key from my dresser. He'll have something. Since tech perked up and he's gone back to high-paying work, Pat has stopped drinking beer and become something of a wine snob. He even bought one of those stupid little wine fridges, which I plan to raid at this very moment.

Patrick's apartment has an identical floor plan, but I always feel disoriented when I go in. He has philodendrons strung everywhere, and he's set up the room I use as a living room and office as his bedroom. Where my dresser lives, Patrick has a cello propped up next to a music stand. And in his kitchen, the spot where my rolling cutting board should be is occupied by a short stainless-steel wine refrigerator with a digital temperature display and glass front. It (along with the espresso-making machine that now dominates his counter space) looks out of place, humming there, surrounded by all the old linoleum and chipped Formica, but every shelf inside is occupied, and I fully intend to exploit this bounty. I look at the bottles and try to determine which one is the least expensive—that's just what he'd love, after spending a shitty night on the gym floor at his office, to come home and discover that his sort-of-not-quite girlfriend had swiped his bottle of Château Something or Other that he had been saving for twenty years from now. There are a couple of screw-top bottles on the bottom shelf, red table wine, and I grab them both.

My sister told me to. And Patrick says those screw-tops can be very good.

3

I'm in my bedroom, sitting cross-legged on a pillow in the bay window, holding my one good wineglass with both hands and watching the people still walking home through the now abandoned street construction four stories down. It's just after three when I finish off the last of the first bottle. The wineglass is huge, more like a goblet, really, and I always drink too fast when I use it. But I'm not really feeling it today. I don't think I am, anyway.

I see a woman walking, barefoot, carrying a pair of pumps in one hand and a laptop bag in the other. There's a man behind her; he has one little girl on his shoulders and another little girl walking next to him, holding his hand. The one walking tugs at the front of her pants like she has to go to the bathroom.

Behind them, there's a man pushing a fat woman in a wheelchair. They're laughing about something together.

Another man trips on the curb and looks around quickly to see if anyone was watching.

I'm watching. Up here.

Without taking my eyes away from the window I reach down to the floor next to me for the second bottle. The cap makes a metal scraping sound as I open it, and I pour myself another full glass. The phone is in front of me, and I pick it up and dial Patrick's cell for the sixth time and there's a half ring and some tones before the kind woman-robot voice tells me, like she has all the other times, that all circuits are currently busy. If I try his office directly, I'll hear the same thing. And as I take the first sip from the new glass, I'm quite suddenly consumed by what I had, up until now, been holding off.

What if he needed to come into the city today?

What if he needed to take a bus?

What if he was just walking *by* a bus?

It's stupid. Stupid. I really can't let myself think this. It's the wine, that's all. I pick up the phone and hit redial, then I hang up before it even connects. He never comes into the city for work. This is stupid.

Here with me on the window ledge, clutched alongside my pillow and my wineglass, I have possibly the most beloved item from my childhood: a Rand McNally North American Road Atlas, publication date 1980. The year of my birth. My best friend Amy has a lumpy stuffed dolphin named Tippy, and I have this book of maps. The cover is gone and the stapled spine has been reinforced with masking tape, and printed across the top of the exposed index page in purple-marker little-girl letters are the words "Property of Jessica and Katherine Zorich."

Katie really, really wanted this when I left for college, but right now I'm very glad that I'm the one who got to keep it.

Almost every page is covered with some sort of notation left years ago. Routes are traced in yellow highlighter or smudged number-two pencil. Trips to be taken, mileages calculated, locations marked where dream homes could be built. Katie might someday be married on this page, on this dot, or I might go to college on this other one. The latest imagined location of our father was plotted; where is he now, where is he going, where will he be after that?

Where will I live someday?

California takes up two pages, and I sit cross-legged with my pillow in my lap and set my wineglass to the side and look, look, where is Pat? There's a Katie–pencil trace down the coast highway (a trip to be taken; we'd dreamed of a convertible), but following it with my fingertip there is no clue, nothing, I can't see him; Mountain View is only a speck on the map insert and where could he be where could he be *Goddammit where could he be?*

Just as I'm about to lose it, for real, I look up and out the window and I see him, coming up onto the end of our street at the top of the hill. It's so obviously him, the short hair and funny way he kind of holds his big shoulders too far back and bounces when he walks, even from this far away I can be sure and I am completely happy about it. I come up to my knees and lean against the window, sending the pillow and the map to the floor and nearly knocking over the wine bottle as I do, hoping he'll look up so I can wave at him and see him wave back. But he's looking ahead, and even when he looks up at our building he doesn't seem to see me until I pull up the peeling window sash and stick my head out.

"Patrick! Pat!"

"Hey!" he shouts up, and now he waves. "Buzz me in. Or throw me your keys."

I grab my keys, then let them fall and I'm afraid like always that they're going to hit him in the face like they hit Danny last summer and he needed stitches to close up his cheek. But Patrick makes a neat one-handed catch, and in a moment I hear him running up the stairs. I meet him at the door and he wraps his arms around me and we stand there, door open, for a long time until he asks the obligatory question:

"Are you okay?"

"Yes. No?"

"I know how you feel," he says.

We go sit on the couch, and Patrick rubs my neck.

"How did you get home?" I ask.

"They ran a couple trains. Soldiers with big fucking guns all over. You got frisked before you got on. No bags allowed, no phones. All my shit's still in Mountain View. Laptop, keys. What a mess."

I point to the window. "There's wine," I say. "I helped myself." I'm half expecting him to say something pissy about me taking the bottles, but instead he stands up and says, "We can do better than that today."

"I don't think I'll appreciate the good stuff," I say. "At this point."

"I will. My key?"

"The dresser."

He goes, and I hear his steps as he moves around upstairs, hear his little wine cooling unit open and shut. Then I hear him start his answering machine, hear the unintelligible messages, and I listen, as I lean over and rest my head on the arm of the couch and draw up my knees, to the muffled voice that must be Patrick's mom, calling over and over again.

The next thing I know, Patrick is trying to move me on the couch to make room for himself, and I snap upright.

"I'm not drunk," I say.

"Sure you're not. Come here, you can lie back down."

"I just fell asleep."

"I know, come here. Lie down." He pulls me back down so my head is resting in his lap, and pulls the afghan from the back of the couch and arranges it over me. I close my eyes and hug my knees, and as I adjust myself I can feel with the back of my head just how lean Patrick has become. He's lost a lot of weight since he went back to work, exercising at the gym there and sloughing off the hard-party gains of what he calls "the severance year." He's also been running, almost every morning, with Dana, the dyke triathlete who lives in the building across the street from us and motivates him, he claims, by shouting things like, "Move it, you fat fucking breeder!" I don't know Dana that well. She kind of intimidates me.

"How much weight have you lost, Pat?" I mumble. I don't want to open my eyes.

"Just about enough."

"How much?"

"Thirty pounds? Maybe a little more."

"Skinny boy."

"I can go back."

"I like skinny boy better."

Patrick plays with my hair, and I think about how long I've known him, how many times we've been on this couch like this. He had come down to help me carry boxes up from the rental truck the day I moved in almost five years ago. He seemed nice enough and funny enough and cute enough, and, above anything else, harmless enough. As in: completely nonthreatening, almost disappointingly nonthreatening. We carried boxes, I ordered pizza, he brought down a six-pack of beer, and after we finished he said good night and went back upstairs. See you around sometime.

Harmless enough. Right.

"Do you mind if I turn on the news?" he asks.

"I'd rather you not. I don't want to hear it."

"I'll mute it. You don't have to hear it."

"I don't want to see it, either."

"Keep your eyes shut, then."

He fidgets around under me as he hunts for the remote, and I hear the electric zing of my old television coming on. As he promised, Pat kills the sound immediately, but of course I have to look.

By a quarter 'til nine, Pat has made two more trips upstairs to his little steel refrigerator. Each time he goes up, I hear footsteps, thumping, bottles clanking. I hear his voice, too, on the phone: sometimes urgent, sometimes quiet. No matter how hard I try I can't make out any words through my ceiling and his floor. Each time he comes back down there's a new bottle in his hand, and by now we're both feeling it. I've had a couple strong cups of caffeinated tea, too, so I'm edgy and awake on top of being drunk.

I warm up some leftover takeout I have from last week and we share it from the folded paper container, dueling with our forks as we watch the silent news footage rotated through every half hour: the same smoky aerial shots, the same shirtless guy rescued from a rooftop, the same torn bus lying on its side. The bottom of the screen has a news ticker, and it's starting to drive me crazy.

SF SUICIDE BOMB TOLL 108; EXPECTED TO RISE
CA GOV TO TOUR BOMB SITE TUES.
LUCKY CAT RETURNS HOME AFTER CROSS COUNTRY TREK

Viewed against everything else, the last one seemed almost funny the first hundred times I saw it roll by, but on pass one hundred and one it makes me very angry. I stand up, clumsily, maybe a little too theatrically, and drop my fork into the paper container in Patrick's lap.

"I can't watch this anymore," I say. "I can't take it." I stomp through the doorless opening into my bedroom, sit on the bed, and cross my arms. I'm not really sure what I'm trying to accomplish by doing this, but now I'm here, and, for nothing but the principle, I stay seated on the bed. Pat continues to eat. Slowly. And I sit.

"I know what you're doing," Patrick says.

"Oh. So?"

"You don't have to."

"Okay."

Patrick turns off the TV and rises from the couch, losing his balance a little, then comes and sits next to me on the bed.

"Will you stay tonight?" I ask. "I need you to stay tonight."

"Only to rest," he says. "The rule."

"The rule. Right."

He looks at me and raises an eyebrow. "You have to promise."

"I promise," I say.

"I'm serious."

"I promise."

Naturally I'm not promising anything, and my fingers don't even need to be crossed. I'm not going to play coy, either; circumvention of this rule involves deception, the deception of the ordinary. So rather than slink around and give Pat sideways looks, I stick to routine: brush teeth, wait my turn to pee, cast off sweats, jump into bed. And as soon as Patrick turns off the light and slides in under the covers, I'm on him.

"Oh come on, Jess," he says, moving out from under me. "We aren't doing this."

"Why not?"

"We said we wouldn't. This was your rule in the first place, remember? And you promised."

"Can't we? Just tonight?"

He groans.

"Can't we? I need to feel close to you." And I'm not lying when I say it. "I need to *be* close to you."

"We can't." He puts his arm around me as he says it, and that wounds me more than if he had just turned away.

I play the "O" card. "I could tend the garden," I say, letting my voice trail off.

"No, Jess," he says. "Come on." Somewhere, over the evolution of our strange relationship, "tending the garden" has become the secret code for the performance of oral sex. I have no idea where it came from, or what it means exactly; something about raising crops maybe? Pat swears I came up with it, but I know it had to be him.

"I really will," I say. I thought this would be it, this rare irresistible deal-maker. It's not the act I'm so opposed to, it's the tedium. Well, that, and the disconcerting feeling sometimes that I can't breathe. But I'm drunk, so why not?

"You don't have to do that," he says, and I think, I have him! Then he rolls away from me. "I don't want you to do that."

And then I sigh and give up.

But there is one thing that's been bothering me. I listen to him breathing for a little bit, his slow exhalations, then I roll toward him and touch his shoulder. "Hey, Pat?"

"Hmm?"

"Were you trying to call someone?"

"What?"

"Those times you went upstairs, for the wine, were you trying to call someone?"

"I was trying to call everyone, Jess."

"Oh." And I leave it at that.

Pat's breathing slows and winds down into a wheezing drunken growl. After an hour or more of listening to it I can't take it or anything else, and my hands move down toward myself. And that great habitual tonic against sleeplessness and anxiety I've depended on—and only been able to achieve alone—since the ninth grade works its magic once again.

Patrick snores right through it, and as I close my eyes and my pulse settles down and the shuddering slips from my shoulders and neck, I wonder in that sleepy, senseless way: if a shirtless man is saved from a rooftop a thousand times, is he saved forever?

4

Pat leaves for a long run before I get up. I thought I'd have a rare chance to sleep in, but my rest is interrupted when Mike calls to see how I'm doing. I'm fine, I tell him, and he's fine too, for the most part.

"The girl who rents from us hasn't come home yet," he says. "The police came by, they didn't really tell us anything. We'll just keep waiting, I guess."

"Mike, I'm sorry."

"All we can do is wait." Mike says this with the gravity of a real-live grown-up. Suitable trait for an employer, I think. "Listen," he goes on, "I think everyone should just stay home this week. I mean, maybe we can all get together and catch up and have lunch at the office on Friday if the buses are going. You're doing the Cippoletti project, right? Work on that at home, if you can, and we'll play it by ear for Friday."

"Just let me know, Mike."

This Cippoletti thing involves me writing three para-graphs of promotional copy for a company that makes women's bike shorts—it's a job that should take all of twenty minutes, but I've stretched it out into a two-week project. And now that I can do it from home, my workday will be spent searching Google, reading catty blogs and online comic strips, and shooting instant messages to Katie in her lab at BU. This isn't really so different from what I do at my office anyway; I just won't need to be covert about it now.

The TV stays off while I work, and I intentionally avoid reading news sites. I'm feeling a little blocked, so I surf around online and hope creativity will strike. I check my fa-vorite blog, the PitchBitch, but there hasn't been a new post since last Friday, which isn't so surprising with everything that's gone on. Written anonymously by a girl here in the city who works—just like I do—in advertising and PR, it's read ob-sessively by everyone in my office. I've been accused by my coworkers of actually *being* the PitchBitch, which is more than a little flattering but in no way possible because: (a) I'm nowhere near clever enough to write like her, and (b) She's been pursuing some new guy, Jazzboy, she calls him, in seri-ous online detail over the past few weeks. And he refuses to give in. How could this man—this idiot, we've all con-cluded—resist the obvious intellect and charm of the Pitch-Bitch?

Is it strange that I hope this person, whom I've never met and probably never will, is doing okay?

I finally start to type, and by the afternoon I've got the copy done, for the most part. But I'm having trouble coming up with a tagline for these shorts. Even looking at the home pages of every cycling apparel manufacturer on the planet fails to inspire, and I don't think Mike would appreciate out-right plagiarism. I see Katie is online, so I open up a chat window.

"Women's cycling shorts," I type. "Need a tagline. It's for a trade show. Wow me."

"You're asking me to come up with one?" she types back.

"Yes. Client wants to hype the woman aspect."

"Are they cushy?"

"I haven't actually tried them on, but they look like they are the cushiest."

"Hold on." A long pause. "How about, 'The Spot for the Twat.' Would that work?"

This makes me laugh out loud. "You rule, K."

"I know. Bye bye."

That night Patrick makes me a passable interpretation of pad Thai for dinner up in his apartment. I try to care—really—about the wine he carefully pairs with it, but even my feigned interest in Riesling doesn't prevent him from wanting to spend the night in his own bed, alone. Back downstairs, I'm tipsy and restless under my covers, so action is once again taken, and action leads to sleep.

Wednesday is basically a repeat. Limited train service has resumed out to the valley, so Patrick leaves mid-morning, mostly to check in and see how people—the team, as he calls them—are doing, but also to get his little MacBook and phone, which he seems to be going crazy without. He surprises me by stopping in and kissing me before he leaves, a friendly sort of see-you-later kiss, nothing more, but he shakes his finger at me when he sees the look on my face after.

"Rule's a rule, Jessica," he says. And he leaves.

I sit down and stare at the Cippoletti logo on my desk. Everyone at work has taken to calling it "the ass," because, well, it's basically a swooshy yellow and blue line drawing of a woman's ass. It takes two hours for me to whittle my notes down to a list of eleven possible slogans for this stupid line of bike shorts. "The Spot for the Twat" is not one of them. Nothing on the list seems any good at all, so, in desperation,

I open my robe and pull on the shorts, half expecting that, as I do so, a beam of God-sent light will emerge through a crack in the ceiling and shoot right down to illuminate the proper choice on my list.

There is no beam of light. No flash of inspiration hits my head or the padded space between my legs. And when I see myself, and the shorts, in my mirror, I immediately pull them off and throw them onto my bed.

It's another hour before I almost come to a decision. "Her Sport. Her Motion. Cippoletti" is my number one, and "Cippoletti—For the Way She Moves" is number two. Even ranking them seems a little too hopeful; they both suck. But I find comfort in the knowledge that, when we finally meet with the Cippoletti people, they will graciously nod and thoughtfully hold their chins during my presentation before suggesting we go back to the Italian tagline they've always had and that no one understood in the first place. So either way, I'm covered.

I e-mail everything to Mike, cursing myself as soon as I hit the send button because I should have waited another day so he'd think I was still working on it. In any event, the job is done, and with this minor feeling of accomplishment I decide to actually get dressed for the first time in two days. But as soon as I get my jeans and ratty sweater on, I lie down on the couch and fall asleep.

I'm awakened sometime later by Patrick coming into my apartment and banging things around in a less-than-subtle way. I'm groggy and angry that he woke me up, but all is forgiven when I see that he's brought me a chicken salad sandwich from Mario's. This divine creation on light rye bread might be my most beloved culinary treat in all the Bay Area. If I'm ever to be blown up on a bus, or anywhere else for that matter, I hope one of these will have been my last meal.

Patrick sits next to me on the couch with a sandwich of his own in his hands and a wad of paper towels in his lap. We eat and watch the news on mute, since the pictures say enough and the anchors are a local joke.

"How was Mountain View?" I ask.

"They acted as though nothing happened," he says. "It was all like, 'project launch date in t-minus three weeks and counting, sir.'"

The TV is showing footage of the mayor riding, in a smiling display of confidence, on a Muni bus. It looks like the 71 line, but it's hard to tell. I'm watching him gesture with his hand as he silently talks to someone out of the shot, and then, over his shoulder, a scruffy crackhead peers into the frame. The guy disappears for a moment, maybe shooed away by one of the mayor's handlers, but then he's back, giving a wide smile that shows his few remaining teeth. I'm trying not to laugh as I watch. The mayor seems unfazed, though, and keeps talking, even as the crackhead starts a spastic dance behind him. Now I'm really trying to keep myself from laughing, but when I look at Pat I see he's biting his lip, transfixed, and I start to giggle. This turns into full-bore laughter, and Pat starts to lose it too.

The cameraman is obviously into it also, and he opens up the shot so we can see more of this dancing freak. Unable to ignore the guy anymore, the mayor turns and claps, feigning delight at his ruined photo op. Now it's the all-crackhead show, the camera fully devoted to his jerky efforts, and Pat unmutes just in time for us to hear the guy shout: "I love dis bus! I love dis may-YAH! Yahhh!"

The bizarre spectacle of a dancing homeless man next to our mayor has triggered some sort of necessary release, and I'm laughing so hard that tears are coming down my cheeks and there's chicken salad spilled on my jeans. Pat stands up and raises his arms and yells, "I love dis bus! I love dis may-YAH!"

Then he sits back down and we lean together and laugh, and every time it feels like we are about to stop, another wave of it comes and we lose it again, until finally it dies away for good, and my stomach muscles are sore from laughing so hard. We lean against one another for a long time, and I let out a long, happy breath.

I needed this. We both did.

Pat still chooses to spend the night upstairs, though.

Thursday is spent alone, and the solitude isn't such a bad thing. Patrick has some meeting in the evening, so I get takeout and mentally prepare myself for the following day's commute to my office. The bus ride Friday morning *is* mostly fine; the driver is too cheerful and welcoming and all of the passengers sit and quietly smile at each other. I join in and smile too as I take my seat, not really knowing why I'm doing it. Would a potential suicide bomber be so overcome by this collective effort of happiness that he might decide to abandon his mission? I think it's just that we're all so scared we want to pee in our pants. That's sort of how I feel, at least, so I keep smiling. Whatever it is, I'm happy when I get to my stop, because my cheeks are getting sore.

It's actually a great relief to be back at my office. We work primarily with outdoor-oriented companies, just a six-person shop, and I feel a strange comfort in the fact that I have to climb over three kayaks—the same kayaks I was *so* angry about no one taking care of last week—in our reception area to get to my cubicle.

"Hello?" Mike calls from the back.

"Hey, Mike, it's Jess."

"I got the Cippoletti stuff, looks great."

"Thanks," I say.

"Those tags are both so good, I don't know how we're going to decide."

Well isn't that something?

There's a dry erase board in the room with the coffeemaker and our mailboxes, and taped to the upper left-hand corner of the board is my very own fifteen minutes of mortifying fame, my picture on the cover of a two-year-old Cooper & Greaves Pacific Northwest Outfitters catalog. It's become a running competition here for people to try to come up with the funniest caption for the photo, and, thanks to an office filled with creative people, I'll admit that some of them have been pretty clever. The latest one is not, though; it says: "I'm not bad, I'm just drawn that way," and I can tell by the handwriting it's been put up by our creepy sales guy, Grant. This disposes me to hate the caption, regardless of what it says, so I wipe it away.

That I ended up on the cover of a catalog that my mother buys clothes from was a little unexpected. It certainly was not a planned part of my stumbling career arc, anyway. Amy and I had met up to grab lunch one day, and as we waited in line outside the little deli down the street, two guys came up to us, one with a giant camera and the other with a notepad. "We're scouting for a catalog shoot," the one with the notepad said. "Can we take your picture?" Amy rolled her eyes, but we did it, standing in the sun on the sidewalk, one shot from the front, one from the side. Notepad guy took our numbers (Amy, being a suspicious type, gave them a fake one) and told us we'd hear in a couple days if they were interested.

I acted indifferent and laughed along at the office jokes made about budding modeling careers, but I made sure my phone was on me at all times. And when it rang, I was secretly thrilled. They faxed me a photo release to sign and asked where the van should pick me up Saturday morning, and the weekend was basically spent walking around a vineyard having my picture taken in different combinations of conservative tops and shawls. Then they gave me five hundred dollars and dropped me off at home. When none of my pictures showed up in the next catalog, I figured they'd decided not to use any of my shots, and I forgot about it. Until Katie called.

"Jess!" she screamed. "You're on it!"

"On what?"

"Have you seen the latest Cooper & Greaves?"

I didn't even know I had it, there in the stack of catalogs to the side of my important mail. And when I searched through the pile and pulled it out, I gasped.

"Oh no," I said. "Oh no, no, no." There I was on the cover, but I was hardly myself: lips parted, dreamy eyes, with a shawl wrapped around my shoulders and a tendril of hair blowing across my face. All blemishes and ugliness Photoshopped away.

"Yes," Katie said. "You're the proto-lass, rising from the heather."

The cover only increased my already bad enough self-consciousness to severe levels. There are few things more ick-inducing than hearing a drunk frat boy in a bar shout: "Whoa! Dude! Check it out, she's the . . . Hey, I used to have your picture up in my room!"

The Cooper & Greaves people actually called me about a year ago to see if I'd do another shoot for them. Apparently they had gotten quite a bit of feedback on my cover. I declined. I think my sister would be more appropriate, anyway. People say she and I (and our mother, for that matter), look so alike, but it isn't the case. I'm nothing like them. My mother's body looks too fragile to have carried two children, and her breasts look too small to have nursed them. Katie got Mom's slight build and refined face, and we both got her red hair and fair freckled skin. My body, though, the odd one of the three, seems made up of too-broad hips and too-big boobs, blue-veined globes bearing pale bull's-eye nipples, with a rash of freckles painted down the center of my chest toward my other target, that red-haired exclamation mark that Katie calls "the Zorich pubic flame."

I look at the cover taped up on the whiteboard and get a marker and write "proto-lass, rising from the heather" beneath it.

It's nice to be back behind my desk. I power on my computer, and find that Patrick has sent me an e-mail with a picture of the snaggle-toothed crackhead on the bus attached.

"Aw, Jess!" I hear someone saying. "Jess." It's Grant, and I reflexively cross my arms over my sweater as he peers into my cubicle.

"You took down my quote," he says, pouting.

"Oh shoot, Grant, I'm sorry. I thought it had been up there for a while."

"What does 'proto-lass' mean?"

I just smile and shrug, telepathically willing him to leave. And he does, so maybe there's something to it. Another e-mail from Pat comes in, and this time it's a little animation someone's made of the bus guy dancing, moving his hips and raising his arms, looping over and over and over. Apparently he's become a local phenomenon. A third message arrives a few seconds later, this one blank except for a subject line that says: "CALLING NOW." Moments after I delete it, my extension rings. It's Patrick himself, letting me know he's going out with some people from his office tonight. He asks if I want to meet up with them.

"Come on," he says. "We aren't staying out late. You can go easy."

"Going easy" with Patrick usually ends up meaning "just as drunk with twice the remorse," and the place they're going is too far away. I'm not really excited about another bus ride to get there, or a staggering walk home, so I pass.

"You're sure?" he asks.

"I'm sure. And what's up with all the bus guy e-mails?"

A pause.

"They're funny?"

I say nothing, and can tell that my lack of a response hurts his feelings a little. "I'll stop sending them," he says. "You really won't come?"

"I'll see you later," I say. "Have fun."

5

The message machine is flashing a red number one when I get home, and, what do you know, Dad has called.

"Jessica," he says in the slow and oddly formal way that Katie imitates so perfectly, "it is your father. It is Friday afternoon. I will try you Saturday."

Whether this means tomorrow or some unknown Saturday in the future is anyone's guess. Raymond Zorich has spent the past couple years, flush with cash from royalties on his engineering patents, traveling around the country in a battered (and enormous) RV. Katie tells me he's been rolling with a companion named Wilma for the past couple months. He refuses to pay for a cellular phone, so communications with him have been somewhat sporadic. It's not like that's anything new, though.

Our father left home when I was twelve years old and

Katie was four days away from her tenth birthday. They had been fighting for a while, my parents, and when Mom called Katie and me down to the living room and I saw her, standing so severely with her hands on her hips, I had a pretty good idea what the news would be.

"Your father isn't coming home tonight," she said.

The melodramatic possibilities of my parents' impending divorce had been almost exciting; the potential attention and social elevation I saw my seventh-grade self receiving in the wake of such a family tragedy seemed almost too good to be true. The realization that it was actually happening, though, was another thing entirely.

"Is he coming home tomorrow?" I asked, pressing my lips together and clenching my teeth to try to stop the tremor in my chin, as if that would hold off the breakdown I could feel coming on.

"Your father isn't coming home tomorrow, or any day after that. Your father isn't going to be living here anymore."

My vision went blurry with tears, and I looked to my right at Katie, the skinny, little-girl Katie who I still see in my dreams sometimes, holding the book she'd been reading when Mom called us down. She turned to me and shrugged, giving an "oh well" look before she went back upstairs to her room. Mom didn't volunteer anything else, so I followed Katie up the staircase and went to my own room, where I curled up on my bed and cried and cried. If the foundation of my parents' marriage could be destroyed, I thought, surely everything else would be falling apart soon as well; probably an earthquake that would rip the earth open beneath us and swallow us whole, or maybe a distant volcano in the Cascades would erupt and bury our house in thick ash.

It was a while before I lifted myself, sniffling and hiccoughing and spent, from the wet spot of tears and snot on my pillow. And when I rose up, there was Katie, sitting on the floor at the foot of my bed, her book propped on her knees.

"When did you come in here?" I asked.

"A while ago," she said, closing the book. "Do you want to move into my room with me?"

"Alright," I said, and we spent the rest of the evening quietly dismantling my black lacquered bed frame with a screwdriver and worn pair of pliers from Dad's still-resident toolbox. Katie and I slid each piece down the hall to her room, where we reassembled it in a spot hastily vacated by her two enormous and outgrown dollhouses. Mom never suggested that I go back to my own room, and that was where I stayed, every night from that point on, until the day I left for college.

Remembering this makes me want to call Katie. She doesn't answer, and I don't leave a message. She'll see that I called, and that will be enough.

I consider the delicious idea of locking the door and taking a hot bath with my own book when the phone rings again. This time it's Amy, who says she's going out with her friend Susan to Brenneman's and do I want to come too? The place is close, it's a mellow bar, and she swears it's going to be an early night, so this time I say sure.

"See you at seven," she says.

Danny is crossing the street toward our building as I'm heading out. I wave at him and he waves back, and he puts his other hand on his hip and makes a butt-wiggling pirouette before jumping up to the curb next to me.

"You are such a complete freak," I say.

"I know, Jess," he says, and he kisses me on the cheek. "But the world would not be the same if I wasn't this way, right?"

"You have a point, Danny."

He's working to get his key in our building's front door. "I'll see you tomorrow night?"

"Tomorrow night, what?"

"Patrick's party. Duh!"

"Oh," I say. This is the first I've heard, but I go ahead and say: "Right."

"Later," he says, and the door bangs closed behind him.

I'm pretty sure Patrick hasn't mentioned anything about any party tomorrow night. I take out my phone and dial him as I walk along on the mostly empty sidewalk, and he answers almost as soon as I have the thing up to my ear.

"Jess!" he shouts over the bar sounds behind him. "Did you change your mind?"

"No, no," I say. "I'm meeting up with Amy for a little bit."

"Ah, I see how it is, you can make time for Amy, but not for Pat."

"That's right." I almost ask him outright about the party, but I opt for subterfuge instead. "Hey, do you want to do a nice dinner out tomorrow? Like the Danube, maybe? I could make reservations..."

"We can't do that, I've got people coming over, remember?"

"What?"

"I'm doing that little party for the artist guy, Joe and I know him from back in...I know I told you about this."

"I don't think you did."

"Well, okay, we're doing a party at my place tomorrow night. Now you know. You sure you don't want to change your mind and come out here?"

"I'm sure. Talk to you later."

Did he tell me about this? Was I just so preoccupied with everything going on last week that I missed it? I try to forget about it, but it nags me until I'm inside Brenneman's and my eyes adjust. Amy's not sitting with nice Susan, the sweet, shy travel-marketing person I was expecting, but instead it's skanky Susan there in the booth, the girl with weird teeth and a bad boob job who sells ads for one of the alternative papers and has just finished dealing, Amy has told me, with a case of chlamydia. I force a smile when I see her, but I already know how the night will unfold: Susan will dominate all conversation, say bitchy things about every other girl in the bar, then get grossly drunk and go home with some big bellied, former-life fraternity boy.

"Hi, Jessica," Susan says as I take a seat, and she gives me a hug and makes a face—I suppose it's a smile—that looks like she's just sucked the juice from a lime.

"Hey, Jessie babe," Amy says, reaching across the table to squeeze my hand. I'm fairly certain she's the only person on earth who can get away with calling me "Jessie babe." "Did you bus it today?" she asks.

"With a grin all the way to Leavenworth," I say.

"Girls. Girls," Susan says, leaning forward and raising her hands, palms forward. "Do we *have* to talk about this? Haven't we had enough?"

This girl is unbelievable. Yes, Susan. We've had enough. Let's just forget about this. Let's just try very, very hard, and pretend it never happened. Pretend it *isn't* happening.

I can tell Amy's thinking the same thing. "You're right," she says, giving me a little eye roll that Susan completely misses. "I did get my hair cut this week." I know it's not true and I try not to laugh when I hear her say it, and I wonder: how is it that Amy considers this Susan person one of her friends?

"It's great," Susan says, and she makes the citrus expression again. "You have just the face for that look." She takes a sip of her whatever it is she's drinking and turns to me. "So who is this Gretchen woman I keep seeing Patrick with?"

"What?" I'm so surprised by this I don't know what else to say.

"Yeah, Gretchen, I think, I always see them having lunch at that, what's that place in Palo Alto? Cheng's." She looks at Amy. "Her name is Gretchen, right?" Susan doesn't seem to pick up on the look that Amy gives her, but I do.

"Yes, I think her name is Gretchen," Amy finally says, and I can't really figure out her expression now that she's looking at me.

But I'm pretty sure she knows exactly what I'm thinking.

You know he's with some Gretchen person? And you haven't told me?

"I think she works with him," Amy goes on, quietly. "Or something like—"

"She's cute," Susan cuts in, fishing a chunk of fruit out of her glass with her perfect nails. "Sort of short, but she's a cute girl."

"I heard it might warm up this weekend, finally," Amy says weakly. Now I understand the look on her face; it's that I'm-so-sorry-Jess-please-let-me-die-now look. Susan is oblivious.

"God, I hope it warms up," Susan says. "I'm so over the big chill." She shuffles toward me on the bench seat. "Can I get by you, Jessica? I need a potty break."

I get up to let her slip by, then jump back into my spot across from Amy. "Why didn't you tell me about this Gretchen person? You knew about this and you didn't tell me?"

"I thought they just worked together, Jess. I'm serious. She works with him, I never thought there was anything—"

"You're supposed to tell me these things. You're supposed to, you're my eyes in Mountain View."

"I didn't think there was any*thing* to tell you. Would I tell you if he was out to lunch with some guy?"

"I would have told you."

"Told me what? My boyfriend's going out to lunch with people from his office?" Amy leans back and crosses her arms. "I thought you were finished with waiting for him anyway. What happened to bad timing? What happened to 'I give up'?"

"I still would have said something. You're not stupid."

Amy doesn't say anything, and we just sit and look at each other until Susan gets back.

I probably should have stopped drinking after I got the Gretchen news, or non-news, or whatever it was. Now, on my way back home, I'm drunk and angry and I'm squeezing my keys as I try to stomp my footprints into the concrete of the sidewalk.

I'm an idiot. Of course he didn't tell me about this party.

Of course this Gretchen is going to be there.

Do I know her? Have I ever met her at one of Pat's little functions out in the valley? Has she ever been up at his place?

I climb the stairs to my floor and pause for a second, then continue up the fifth flight to Patrick's door. I almost knock, but hold myself back, and I put my ear to the door instead. Nothing. It's only a little bit after eleven; he won't be back for hours. Or *they* won't be back for hours? No, no. Maybe?

Goddammit.

I do knock, finally, and wait for a moment. Then I go back downstairs and don't bother to turn on the lights in my own place, just undress in the dark and get into bed and hug my big down pillow. And I sleep.

Sometime later—the clock by my bed says two thirty-two—I hear keys in my door, and my living room is momentarily illuminated from the hallway. I see Patrick's silhouette coming into my bedroom, and suddenly I'm wide awake and furious. Right, I'm thinking, as I listen to him drop his clothes on the floor next to my bed, right, you go out and get loaded and hang with your little friend Gretchen and *then* you think you can come home and get sweet Jessica to go back on the rule? If you could so adamantly refuse it Monday night, I can stonewall just as well now. You're looking at the impenetrable Fortress Jessica under these covers tonight, pal. This rule is standing like the Great Wall of Vagina.

And then I've got it: as soon as he gets in bed and comes to me with those drunken paws, I'll pounce. "So who is Gretchen, Patrick?" I'll ask. "Can you tell me about Gretchen?" My delivery will be so vicious, so icy, he'll wordlessly jump up and run away. Or beg me for forgiveness. Or both.

But no paws are forthcoming as I lie there, breathing, pretending to be asleep. Patrick just sits on the edge of the bed. Then quietly, almost cautiously, he eases in under the covers and reclines. A moment later he rolls toward me and nestles in against my back. An arm slips around my waist. And nothing more.

"What are you doing, Patrick?" I whisper.

"I needed to be close to you," he says.

"What?"

"I knew you'd understand."

I roll so I'm facing him and put my hand to his cheek. "Can we stop the rule?" I'm still whispering. "We don't have to do it anymore. Can we finally just be—"

Patrick sighs, but he keeps his arm around me. "Tomorrow," he says. "Let's talk about all this tomorrow."

6

Patrick leaves to run—again—before I'm awake, and when I do get
up I wonder if it was fitness or guilt that drove him out
the door. I make some coffee, try not to think of names
beginning with "G," and boot up my computer to check
e-mail. My computer isn't even that old, but the thing
gets slower every time I use it, I think.

There's a message from Katie, dated yesterday afternoon, in my in-box. "Can't answer phone, proctoring
exam for Dr. Kurtz," her mail says. "Thinking of you
too."

I check the news online, and the big story today is
that they've identified all of the bus bombers. Their photos are posted, there on the cable news home page, lined
up in a two-by-two grid. Two of them look white, one
looks black, and the other has Asian features, maybe
Filipino. The first picture, one of the whitish guys, looks

serious, like a mug shot. He's angry in his photo. The others seem to have been taken from snapshots. In the black guy's picture, he's smiling, and you can see he had his arm over someone's shoulder, a woman cropped away. You can barely tell that he's wearing a Raiders jersey, and the other white guy is wearing some sports shirt too. Maybe they met at a game? The Filipino guy looks really scrawny. I bet he was scared before he pressed the button.

I click on the story and read some more. There's a blurry surveillance picture from Monday morning in there, shot from a mini-mart security camera or something. Somebody's paying for his beef jerky or his gasoline, and in the background, wearing a hoodie and a backpack, is the black guy walking really purposefully. There are some quotes from one of the mothers. She can't believe it, she says. He was such a shy boy. He loved his Xbox. There must be a mistake.

Well, sure it's a mistake, lady. What kind of a mom are you?

I get more coffee and settle in to check the PitchBitch. I'm thrilled to see she has a new post, even if it is pretty brief and almost totally devoid of snark. Everything is fine at PB HQ, she writes, thanks for all the e-mails, she's okay, her cat, Blanco, remains calm as usual, things are fine. She writes about how she had to pitch a spec campaign *the day after* the bus bombing because the client was in town and was flying out that night; apparently it was a total disaster because she was hungover on top of being an emotional mess, but it ended up being no great loss because the product was some weird treatment for dry skin and the client was, as she puts it, "a complete raging giant puckered asshole." She goes on to describe an evening out with Jazzboy: the place was lame (she doesn't mention where; I want some dish), he seemed preoccupied (with work obligations; cryptic, but she claims to understand), and she ended up leaving early and not being really mad about doing so, because, she says, "the big big big chance comes tonight."

I know how she feels. And despite the fact that she generally works with fluff consumer products and I'm doing kayaks and bike shorts, I think she's my online long-lost twin. I'm pulling for the PitchBitch. I really am.

My phone rings as I sit there at my desk, and the ID says: "UNKNOWN CALLER—JACKPOT NV." A name like "Jackpot" gets me curious, so I pick up.

"Hello?" I'm struggling to recall if I know anyone in Nevada.

"Jessica, this is your father speaking."

"Oh, hi, Dad. How are you?"

"I am well. And how are you?"

"I'm doing okay." It's really pointless to say anything else. After these pleasantries are completed, my dad can get into what he does best: talking about himself. I hear him draw in a long breath, and then he lets it rip.

"It's been quite an adventure traveling through this nation's western states…" he begins, and I seriously wonder for a moment if he's reading to me from a prepared text. I wander back to the kitchen, not really listening. There's barely any coffee left, and it's starting to get that burnt smell, so I pour it out and start another pot. A kid's riding his bike in a circle down on the street, and I watch him through the window while Dad's voice drones into my ear. And just as I refill my mug with fresh coffee, there's a little shift in his tone that signifies he's wrapping up, so I tune back in.

"And I must say," he says, "Wilma has been a splendid companion, wandering over these highways and back roads. A splendid companion."

"That does sound splendid, Dad."

"Well, I shouldn't take up any more of your morning, Jessica. Do take care of yourself."

Having looked back upon their marriage through the somewhat clarifying lens of my own adult relationships, I'm not surprised that Mom divorced Dad. If anything, I'm proud of her. What does surprise me is that they got together in the first place. And even more startling is the fact they were, at some point, physically intimate. Katie and I do exist, so it's safe to assume there were at least two episodes of parental sexual intercourse. How did that happen?

Someday, I'll ask Mom what the hell she was thinking.

It's hard not to feel as though Patrick is avoiding me for the rest of the day. I hear him, more than once, running up and down the stairs in our building, and every time I try to duck out and catch him he's lugging something like a case of wine or flat of Danny's handblown martini glasses and tells me hold on, just a couple more trips to go, he's getting ready for the party. Finally I just go up and sit on his couch to wait for the next ascent, and it isn't long before I hear him running up the stairs two at a time. He looks a little surprised as he comes in and sees me there.

"Hey," he says. He's carrying one of those wooden wine crates, filled with bottles of differing heights and colors. "You want to help?"

"I want to talk," I say. Why do I always feel scared and clumsy at times like this? Sober times, anyway.

"I know." He's pulling the bottles out of the box and arranging them on a folding table.

Why not just get to the point? "Who is Gretchen?" I ask.

"Christ, Jessica." Patrick stops with the bottles and turns toward me. "Where did you get that? Who said something about Gretchen?"

"Who is she?"

"She consults for us. She's great, she's fun. Super nice. She'll be here tonight. You'll like her."

This is what I hate about Patrick sometimes. He sounds so sincere, so far from defensive, it's hard not to feel like I'm completely disarmed. In fact, I do almost look forward to meeting her. But there's something more I need to ask.

"Have you slept with her?"

"What? Where the hell did that come from?"

"Have you?"

"Not— No. I haven't." He turns back to the bottles.

"Were you about to say 'not yet'?"

"Come on."

"I can't believe you sometimes." I stand up and put my hands on my hips. "I want to stop the rule. It's not even the rule . . . I want to be . . . I want to be us. Why can't we just—"

"I can't do that right now, Jess." He's holding a big bottle of some whiskey-colored liquor by the neck and resting it on his thigh.

"What do you mean?"

"I mean, I can't do this. I can't, I sat around, and sat around, while you waited for what's-his-name from college to move out here or whatever—"

"His name is Jason."

"I don't care what his name is. I was ready to wait, I knew that fucking guy would flake. I was trying to be nice. And what the hell's up with you, sleeping with me while you're still waiting for your supposed true—"

"Shut up," I say, and now I'm squeezing my fists and can feel myself shaking.

"You shut up." Patrick sets the bottle on the table, and he's so calm it's infuriating. "You make this dumb fucking rule—one that you don't seem very prepared to live with, I should add—but okay, I'll respect that, timing's not right, whatever. I respect that. But then you get mad at the idea of me hanging out with someone else? What's up with that? What exactly are you expecting me to do here?"

He's right, and I hate it.

"I just think I'm ready now" is all I can make myself say.

"I'm sorry, Jess, but right now I'm not."

I don't want to fall apart, and if I do, I don't want him to see it. So I turn and hurry out through the still-open door and run down the stairs.

"Hey, Jess," I hear Patrick call. "I told everyone to show up around six-thirty tonight."

There's a knock at my door at five 'til seven, and I open it to find Danny, arms crossed and smiling. He's wearing a tight black shirt and a scarf, and he might be the only man I know who can pull off that look while avoiding the appearance of arrogant desperation that it seems to paint on anyone else.

"I was told to escort you upstairs," he says. We can hear footsteps and laughing and music through my ceiling.

"I don't know," I say. "I think I may just stay here."

Danny raises an eyebrow and makes an exaggerated show of looking me up and down, then he steps into my apartment and slips his arm through my own. "I see, you always dress up like this when you plan to stay in? Do you need to grab anything?" He's guiding me to the door.

"I'm set."

"You know how much I love that dress," Danny says. I'm pulling my door shut and about to thank him for the compliment, but he manages to slip in: "Did you get it from that catalog you were on?"

"Don't you remember? I got it the same time you ordered that girly scarf."

"Ha, ha," he says. "Ouch."

We're walking slowly up the stairs, and he still has my arm. I used to go on walks with my grandfather like this, arm in arm, through my grandparents' orchard, and climbing the steps with Danny this way brings a ghost of that old comfort. Danny lets go when we get to Patrick's floor, though, and the phantom is gone.

"Listen, you and Patrick, you need to—" Danny stops himself and holds up his hands. "No. This is entirely none of my business. I'm sorry for even starting."

"What? Danny, tell me." There's a shriek of laughter above the sound of the party behind Patrick's door.

"No. I'm saying nothing. You are my sweet friend, and you don't need my opinion. My little sister."

"A big brother would finish his sentence."

"No, a big brother would punch Patrick in the face for trying to get his hands on you. But serious, Jessica, this is none of my business."

Danny opens the door, and he touches my shoulder and slips away. There are a lot of people in the apartment, making it pretty warm inside despite Patrick having opened all the windows. I hear someone say "Hi, Jess" as we come in, and I sort of raise my hand and say hi back, even though I'm not sure exactly who it is I'm greeting as I look around and get my bearings. Everyone is nicely dressed, except for the usual freaks who try to outdo each other by acting like they don't care, and it seems like everyone is having a good time.

Someone has printed up a big picture of the dancing bus guy and taped it into one of Patrick's picture frames, and hanging over it is a printed banner that reads: "Bennie G. for Mayor (or council at least)!!"

I look around and try to find Patrick; I'm also looking at every short woman in the room to see if she looks familiar. Someone calls my name and I look over toward the folding-table "bar" and there's Patrick, holding up an empty martini glass and raising his eyebrows as he wags the glass from side to side. I nod and shrug to indicate "make me whatever," and he nods and shrugs and goes to work. It's a well-practiced ritual dance we have, and, through its performance, all of the day's earlier friction is pushed out of mind.

I feel a hand on my elbow, and turn and find a diminutive—and I mean tiny, like less than five feet tall—short-haired girl standing next to me.

"I think I know you," she says. "Did you ever work at MG Communications?"

"You're Gretchen," I say. *Of course* this is Gretchen. And of course I know her.

"And you're . . . Jennifer?"

"Jessica."

"That's right, sorry, Jessica. How are you?"

Gretchen had interviewed with us maybe a year and a half before. She was high energy, confident, and funny, and her portfolio was incredible. Everyone in the office loved her, and we told Mike he'd be crazy not to offer her the position. Mike did offer her the position, but, for reasons unknown, at least to me anyway, she had to decline, and we hired someone else, quiet Franklin, instead.

Patrick was right, she is great, and I feel a little cheated because how am I going to be able to hate this great person who is now, apparently, my rival?

"I'm good," I say, maybe a little reflexively, because I'm not so good, but I *am* happy to see her. "We were really sad when you didn't take the job. What happened?"

"You have no idea how hard it was to say no. I was very torn." She takes a little sip of whatever it is she's holding there, wrapped in a cocktail napkin. "But I had a huge chance to do a consulting gig. Very scary, big jump, big client, but it turned into so many incredible opportunities. You guys were the coolest shop I've ever seen, though, seriously. It was very hard to say no."

"Mike's such a great guy to work for."

"Seems like it. You guys still just do outdoorsy stuff?"

"I am ruled by bike shorts lately."

At some point while we're talking, Patrick ferries my drink over and silently hands it to me. He looks at me and then at Gretchen, and it almost seems like he's going to say something but he scoots away before I can thank him for the cocktail. Gretchen laughs at this, and I do too, but we keep our conversation going. She's much more funny than I remember, and prettier too (it was an interview environment, after all). Looking at her stretchy black top with thin straps, I can't stop mentally comparing the perfectly tanned skin of her shoulders to the freckles and splotches of my own.

"Hey, Gretchen!" calls a boy in the front room. He looks like one of Patrick's geeky little programmers. I've probably met him at some point, but they all look the same after a while.

Gretchen waves to him, then she looks at me and sighs. "I have to make an appearance. Ugh." She makes a little show of finishing her drink in one gulp for fortitude, and touches my elbow again. "Find me before you leave, okay?"

I nod, and she goes.

I don't really know anyone here, and Patrick is tied up in a conversation, so I look around the room for Danny, my favorite arm to hang on in social situations. Amy was supposed to be here, but she opted for a date instead.

A few people say hi as I push through the throng, and I feel a hand on my shoulder and gasp when I turn and see who's touching me. It's our old neighbor Sarah who used to live one floor down before she moved away to San Diego last summer. I had no idea she'd be here, and I'm pretty happy to see her.

"Jessica, honey, how are you?" she squeals, and she gives me a hug that almost makes me spill my drink.

"Hey, what are you doing here?" I ask. "How are you?"

"I'm great, things are great. I had business up here and Patrick told me about this party; I was hoping I'd see you." She glances around the room and lowers her voice. "How *are* things with Patrick?"

I guess I'm a little flustered by the Gretchen development, and I don't know where I'd begin to explain it, so I go for simple. "It's complicated."

"What's new?" Sarah frowns. "Things are always too complicated."

We chat for a while more, I catch up on her new girlfriend and what she's doing down south, then someone I don't know starts to talk to us and I break away to go find Danny. He's not in this room anywhere, and then I see him through the doorway, seated on the edge of Patrick's bed. A thin guy with sandy-colored hair is sitting with him, and they're both leaning in toward each other and gesturing as they talk.

"...But that vote does count," I hear Danny saying as I get closer. "It absolutely counts. You aren't going to change the system, you aren't going to take power from the right un-less—"

"You are kidding yourself if you believe that," sandy-haired guy says, and he's pointing at Danny as he says it. "The same money is behind both sides, and you know it. There's no real difference between the two..."

Danny looks up at me. "Hey, Jessica," he says, and he almost looks relieved that I've interrupted their discussion. He gestures toward the sandy-haired guy. "This is Josh."

Josh stands up, an act that never fails to impress me. "Hi," he says. "Jessica?" There's something odd about his eyes, they're gray, and I realize he's not blinking as he puts out his hand, just staring.

"Yes, Jessica, well, ah, Jess is fine too." It's not quite withering, the way he's looking at me. Critical? Penetrating? I can't read it. Then he blinks.

"Jess!" I hear a gravelly voice say, and then I feel an arm around my waist. "Ohh, Jess." It's Patrick's friend Joe latching on to me, wearing a floral print shirt and thick tinted glasses that make his eyeballs look huge. "You met Josh."

"I did," I say, trying subtly to twist out from his grasp. Joe used to be one of the funniest, kindest people I knew, but he's become one of the scariest. He was laid off—with a huge severance—around the same time as Patrick, but instead of straightening himself out and going back to work when his money ran out, he's slipped deeper into meth-fueled weird-ness. Apparently he's been selling his books and furniture lately for money to score.

"Josh is an artist," Joe growls. I can tell he's drunk on top of being tweaked, and it feels like he's using me to keep him-self from falling down.

"Really?" I ask. "What medium?" Now I'm actively trying to peel Joe's hand from my hip. Josh sees this, and grabs Joe by the shoulders and pulls him away from me.

"Come on, Joe, sit down."

"Ah," Joe says.

"I'm a lithographer," Josh says. "I make prints—"

"Of giant monster cocks!" Joe shouts. A few people around us laugh, but I want to kick him in the teeth. Josh doesn't laugh, though. He just looks at me.

"I know a lithographer, actually," I say. "Have you ever heard of Greg Murrant?"

"You know Murrant?"

"I went to high school with him. I have a couple of his prints. Older ones, before he got...you know, whatever famous is in the lithography world." Danny is looking up at me, bemused, from his seat on the bed.

"He's super famous. I teach him in my class."

"Your class?" I ask. "Just what do you do?"

"He takes monster cocks, and makes them art!" Joe slurs.

Josh turns and looks at Joe, and this time the look is seriously withering. Even in his state Joe gets it, and he mumbles something I can't understand as he pushes himself up and staggers away.

"I've been living in the U.K. I teach in London," he says, and suddenly I can hear that little difference in the cadence of his speech picked up from living abroad. "But I was missing my parents. I'd never really met my sister's kids and all that. And I had a chance to teach a course at the Art Academy here, so—"

"Your family lives here?"

"Oh no," Josh says. "They're back east. In the Midwest. So east of here, anyway. But it's easy enough to get around." Patrick comes to stand by my side.

"You guys need anything?" he asks. "You doing okay?"

"I'm fine," Josh says. Danny stands up and hands Patrick his glass, and I realize my own is empty. I give Patrick the nod-and-shrug, and he takes my glass and walks away.

"I'd love to see those Murrants sometime," Josh says. He's giving me that stare again.

"Sure," I say, wishing I had even my martini glass to hide behind. "Whenever, I mean, I live one floor down. Whenever."

"Alright, then," he says.

I get away and orbit the room. Josh keeps looking at me. I can feel it. Patrick is busy tending bar and playing DJ, so I can't go hide by him. I see Gretchen talking to him for a moment, and they're laughing together about something. So I go around the room again, saying hi, saying hi, and after a while I see Gretchen again, by herself. When our eyes meet she makes a funny face and laughs and we walk toward each other.

"Good time?" she asks. She looks down at herself, side to side, and picks at some speck on her top, just above her hip. "Cat hair. Gets everywhere. White cat, black top. No good." She holds up her index finger and thumb, pinched together like they're holding something. I don't see it.

"It's alright," I say. "I love to see the usual crazy folk. They always show up at Pat's little festivals."

"Who's the one in the glasses? Really messed up guy."

"That's Joe. He's a wreck. Unemployed, laid off with lots of money. Now, not so much money left."

"Like ten thousand other guys in this city. And the light-haired one?"

"He's an artist, I guess. A printer."

"He's watching you," she says, and she looks at me and raises an eyebrow.

I play dumb. "Is he?" I ask, and Gretchen rolls her eyes.

"Hey, Jess!" Patrick calls, holding up my now-filled martini glass in one hand and the Jaco Pastorius CD he asked me to get him for his birthday in the other. Is he asking me if he should play it? I do the shrug-and-nod again; I don't know anything about that music. My musical appreciation is stuck somewhere in the world of Sarah McLachlan and U2, while Patrick, who kindly has never teased me about my own musi-

cal tastes and actually *is* a musician, comprehends classical music and jazz and—

Jazz? White cat? Jazz*boy*? Blanco?

I quickly look back to Gretchen, and even before I'm fully thinking what I'm saying, I ask, "Do you write the Pitch-Bitch?"

Gretchen lets out a tiny gasp and her cheeks go pink. "I," she starts, then grabs my hand and comes close to me as she looks at the people around us. "You can't tell anyone," she says, and she actually seems really frightened there, looking up at me. "Please. I could lose my work. It would be...I've said stuff, really bad stuff, about clients. About everyone." She's whispering now.

"No, no," I say, and I'm squeezing her hand as I say it. "Honestly, I wouldn't—"

"How did you know? No one has ever..." We both look across to Patrick working over the stereo, and Gretchen gasps again. "Oh my God. I am so sorry."

"No, stop, you didn't know. It's not like...how would you have ever known?" This is, admittedly, pretty new territory for me, and I'm having a hard time thinking what I should say. So I say the first thing that comes to my mind: the truth. "I love your blog. I read it every day. Everyone at MG does."

"Really?"

"Serious. I was worried too, last week—"

"I got so many e-mails. You have no idea."

"I bet. You're popular. Do you ever get creepy people?"

"Honestly, no. I thought that would be a problem when it started to take off, but it's not like I have a picture up or anything, so no weirdos. Yet. The funniest thing is when people write me, like, thinking they know *for sure* who I am, you know, they can be kind of mean about it." Gretchen smiles and rolls her eyes.

We're still standing close and talking in low voices, and

our clasped hands lend a silly feeling of conspiracy that I kind of like. "Mike accused me of being you, once," I say.

"Is that good or bad?"

"I took it as a compliment."

Someone bumps Gretchen walking from behind, and she makes a "whoa!" face as she grabs my arm for support. "Jazzboy," she says, giggling as she keeps herself upright. "Mixing doubles."

"Doubles, triples," I say. "He's a gentleman, though."

"Maybe he's a little too much of a gentleman. So you said you're doing bike shorts."

"It's a women's clothing line. Active wear. They're trying to branch out from just the bike thing. Cute running tops. Not just black Lycra. They're more than bike shorts, you know." This drink is going down a little too easily, and seems maybe a little too potent. "Branching out. Building presence in U.S. markets. Markets worldwide."

"But you'd say," Gretchen says, "that you're familiar with the active lifestyle demographic."

"*You* could say that. I'd say I'm just pretending."

Gretchen laughs again, and I'm envious of the easy way she opens her mouth and shows her perfect teeth and lets it come out *ha ha ha!*

"We should talk more," she says, smiling. She's still gripping my hand.

7

Things are hazy as I'm waking up, and I'm blinking against the not quite daylit room as I take stock of my condition. Whoa. I'm in my own bed, even though I'm not sure how or when I got here, and I'm in my pajamas. Katie, in such a situation, would say something like, "Thank you, PJ Fairy!" I'm alone too, and the undisturbed covers on the left side of my bed suggest I have been all night. Maybe I should give thanks to the PJ Fairy for this as well.

I'm not sure what time it is. I sit up to look at the clock, but this motion disturbs whatever equilibrium I've been maintaining in my stomach, so I lie right back down again. There's a strange hissing sound coming from the back of my apartment that probably should be investigated, and I need to pee too, badly. I'll take care of both of these things, if I can get up.

Closing my eyes, I begin putting the pieces together.

Remembering laughing hard, laughing really hard about something with Gretchen. Must have been funny, whatever it was.

The hissing sound is starting to concern me, so I slide off the bed to my feet and shuffle back through the kitchen. It's definitely coming from the bathroom, and when I get there, I see the cold water tap has been left on full blast and my toothbrush is resting in the bottom of the sink. I turn off the water and grab the toothbrush, then scrub my teeth as I sit on the toilet to pee.

I know already that nothing significant is going to be accomplished today, so I go straight back to bed. Maybe I'll be successful at a little more sleep, but I doubt it. I never sleep well with a hangover. Katie claims that she doesn't suffer from hangovers, but I know it's a lie; I can think of several occasions during our teens when she was curled up in bed with a greenish complexion, swearing she'd never touch something or other again.

Katie and I never really partied in high school. We—well, maybe not so much me, but certainly Katie—had the "good girl" reputations around our necks; the valedictory stances we publicly maintained kept us from getting too crazy, and we kept each other in line. This is not to say we were never drunk, though.

Our father, when he left, left *everything*, including a well-stocked bar. I couldn't exactly tell my friends that he moved out because nothing was ever moved. He just left. His dresser remained filled, and his shirts and slacks stayed behind, hanging like paternal ghosts in what had been his side of the closet. Eventually, Mom hired some men to come and take these things away, along with the engraved wineglasses from the kitchen cabinet and the glass paperweights and weird lamp and stacks of textbooks and engineering journals that filled his study. She was practical enough to keep certain items of convenience, though: utilitarian things like heavy,

cluttered toolboxes and the lawn sprinkler, and his old electric carving knife remained and became ours.

Our suburban home was modest and not quite middle-
aged, and I came to understand that, in the terms of their
separation, things were set up so that the place would be
paid for by Dad though only we would continue to live there.
I loved our house. Two maple trees grew in the front yard,
and on clear days you could just barely see the far-off snowy
cap of Mount Rainier from our bedroom window. The basement had been finished at some point when we were very little, dressed up with fake wood paneling and textured ceiling
tiles and some mottled brown carpet that promptly got
damp and still vaguely smells, I'm sure, like moldy bread. A
bar was constructed as well, and its shiny varnished surface
was reflected by a Schlitz beer mirror hanging behind it.

The bar made a great play set for Katie and me when we
were small. It handily stood in as a kitchen or a store check-
out or an operating table, depending on our imaginary
needs of the day. The contents of the cabinets beneath the
bar seemed insignificant, just old boxes rendered limp by the
constant basement moisture, and it wasn't until the summer
before my sophomore year in high school that we actually
got interested in what had been stored down there.

The number of unopened liquor bottles we found in
those decaying boxes astounded us. Dad never really enter-
tained, and neither of us could remember him drinking anything other than wine with dinner, but the amount of spirits
stored in the bar seemed more appropriate for a busy restaurant, not some musty basement playroom. Our explorations
were cautious at first; we only sampled from bottles of clear
liquids where missing contents could be replaced by tap water. Any knowledge of the strange art of mixology gained
that summer came through trial and error: Coca-Cola mixed
with vodka, we learned, was fairly palatable, but gin and
Coke was certainly not.

We found a nice routine on those summer nights. Wait for Mom to go to bed, experiment with new drink mixture, curl up together under a blanket, and watch cable movie channels until asleep. Repeat on following night. We were obsessed with Cinemax, and we discussed the soft-core skin films with drunken, yet critical, eyes.

"I think the brown-haired girl is the killer," Katie would say.

"The one with the pointy boobs?"

"Yes, that one."

Katie was always more daring with her drink creations. She was, after all, the one responsible for gin and Coke. I remember pouring mine out after the first sip, but she refused to let it go to waste and later I rubbed her back while she hung her head in the toilet.

I'm not quite to the point of throwing up, lying here, but I have the feeling if I *did* throw up I might feel better. I don't want to make myself do it, though. But I do want to call Katie, so I roll over to the left side of the bed to stretch and reach and grab the phone. I dial her number and tumble back, closing my eyes as I listen to it ring.

"Katie," I croak when she picks up.

"What did you do?" She knows me too well.

"My stomach."

"Culprit? What was it?"

"It was pink, and served in a martini glass."

"The sweet drinks kill you every time, Jess."

"I'll never learn." I roll to my side and close my eyes as I hold the phone to my ear. "It wasn't as bad as gin and Coke."

"I learned from that pretty quickly. Did you get my message?"

"No? Your message? I didn't check."

"I left one last night." She pauses. "I got the call, I'm going on the boat." I can hear her smiling as she says it, and I sit up.

"You got on? They, you're accepted?"

"I did. I am."

"That's so great!" I'm thrilled, and for the moment, my hangover is forgotten. "When is it? When do you go?"

"Beginning of August. New Zealand first, South Island, ten days there for an orientation thing, then we fly to Tahiti. Then all around the islands for two months. Beaches galore."

"K., that's so great." I almost feel like I'm going to cry. She's going. She's safe. "I'm so happy for you. But how will we—"

She knows. "The boat has satellite Internet," she says. "We can send e-mail."

"What about the doctor friend?" I ask.

"We'll see where all that goes," she says, not very positively, and then she laughs. "I guess I can e-mail him too, if I need to."

I lie back down and close my eyes again. "I met an artist guy last night who knows Greg Murrant."

"That's a name I haven't thought of in forever. Was he cute?"

"The artist guy? Cute's not the right word. More like composed. Serious. Distinguished maybe."

"He's older?"

"Not older, just different. Not a boy."

"You like him," she says, and I'm not sure if I can hear another smile in her voice. "You're curious."

"I didn't say that."

"You think he's mysterious."

"There was an element of mystery there, yes."

"Be careful."

"There's nothing to be careful about."

"Yet," she says, and it doesn't sound like she's smiling now.

"Yet."

"What about Patrick?" she asks.

"Oh, right, him," I say. "I think his new girlfriend and I

are best friends now. Seriously." I need a drink of water. "Oh God, my stomach."

My sister sighs. "You always love to injure yourself, Jess."

I do manage to sleep a little more, and when I wake up I'm craving something fizzy and nonalcoholic to soothe my abused stomach. I know there's nothing like that in my fridge, and Patrick never buys soda (and even if he did, I'm not exactly sure I'd want to see him right now). But some fresh air would be positive, I think, and it's not such a long walk up to the corner store, so sure, I'll make the attempt. With jeans and a fleece pullover and Mazzy Star on my iPod, I think I can manage this voyage.

It's a foggy day, and the droplets of mist feel cool and perfect on my cheeks as I come down the front steps. Ours is the only building on our block that survived the big earthquake—a fact that makes it apparently more desirable and allows my landlord to charge me a higher rent than if I lived in the identical-looking structure next door, but I still love it. I love my neighborhood too. It's not quite gentrified, and not quite run-down; freaks and families and semi-wealthy techies have all found their way here and seem to live together with little friction.

I have to walk past Joe's apartment on my way to the store. He lives right at the crest of the hill in a ground-level unit, and even though I'm scared he'll see me and drag me into some nonsensical conversation, I still look in his window as I go by. And there he is, vacuuming his carpet with nothing but a bath towel around his waist and a cigarette hanging from his mouth. He just looks at me through his thick glasses and nods, and then returns to pushing his vacuum cleaner.

The corner market is seriously tiny, and I'm the only one currently shopping here. This place is known to everyone in the neighborhood as the MacGyver store because, inexplicably, a faded poster of Richard Dean Anderson hangs over the magazine rack against the wall. The proprietor, Nabil, is seated on a stool behind the counter in his usual pose with his chin in his hand as he watches the little TV back there. Today it looks like a golf tournament.

"Hey, Nabil," I say.

"Hey," he says, not looking away from the screen.

I pay for my Sprite and head back, and Joe is no longer there when I pass his place on the way back down the hill. As I'm breathing in the moist air the haze breaks and the chilly blue sky shows for only a moment, but just as quickly the fog closes up and the street is gray again. Today, I think, I like the gray better.

Climbing back up the stairs in my place, I can hear someone above coming down. The speed of the footsteps suggests it's Patrick, and I'm trying to think what I'm going to say when I see him. But halfway up the stairs to the third floor I see jeans, and Patrick never wears jeans; when I reach the landing I find myself looking up at Josh from last night.

"Hey," he says, and he's half smiling. "I was looking for you."

"Me? Well, hi? You weren't looking for Patrick?"

"He's not there, either." Josh leans his hip against the railing and nods up to my floor. "I wanted to see your Murrants. If the offer still stands. If you remember making it." More of that smile.

"Oh, I do. It's . . . Sure," I say, and the plastic Sprite bottle, wet with condensation, slips in my hands and I nearly drop it. I can feel my cheeks flushing. "My place is a mess."

"I'm used to messy places." Josh nods toward my hands as I come up next to him. "You know that stuff will kill you, right?"

I hold up the soda bottle as he's climbing alongside me. "This? Will it kill me faster than mixed drinks? I might be pretty close already."

He seems to think that's funny. I work the key into the lock. I'm struck, when my door swings open, by how warm it is inside. Did I not notice this temperature before?

"It's nice," Josh says.

"What?"

"Your apartment. I like it."

"It works."

Josh walks around the room, peering down at my things, my books and photos. I straighten the afghan on the back of my couch and try to ignore the way he's looking at my belongings.

"You had fun last night," he says. He picks up a framed picture of Katie and me and looks at it closely. It's almost aggressive the way he inserts himself into my space.

"Did I? I mean, are you asking if I had a good time?"

"No, I'm saying, you and that dark-haired woman, you two looked like you were having fun." The way he says it makes me wonder if I made a complete ass of myself. He holds the picture frame toward me. "Sister?"

"Yes. That's Katie."

"Are you twins?"

"No, no. She's younger." And before I think about it, I say, "She's prettier than I am."

Josh laughs as he sets the picture back on my shelf, and I wonder if he's laughing because I've said something stupid. Or does he not believe me? He keeps moving around the living room. I feel tense as I watch him examining my things, and I kind of want him to leave.

"No," he says. "You guys could be twins. Are you close?"

"Very." I half sit on the arm of my couch. "Are you close to your sister?" Josh just looks at me when I ask him this. "You mentioned her," I say. "Last night. She has kids?"

"Oh, yeah. No. We aren't close at all."

"I'm sorry."

"Don't be." He pauses. "I think she feels my positions on some things are a little extreme."

"Your positions are extreme? What positions? What things?"

Josh just looks at me, and I shift my weight on the arm of the couch. "Lots of things." Then he looks away. "Emily and I are not close."

"Um."

"I still love her, though."

Josh crouches down in front of my bookshelf, and I can see him cock his head when he sees something there. When he pulls my road atlas from the end, my heart goes tight in my chest.

"Wait," I say. I even lift up my hand. "That's—"

"Check this out," he says.

"—kind of personal."

He doesn't respond to this, just squats there and thumbs methodically through the tattered pages. I'm actually wringing my hands as he does so.

"Please," I say.

Josh looks at me, stares at me; I think he can tell I'm pleading with my eyes but I have no idea what he's thinking. Then he closes the atlas and slides it back into its place on the bottom shelf, and he rises back up to his full height.

"May I see the Murrants?"

"What? Right. Sure." I'm flustered and relieved. "In here," I say. He follows me into the bedroom and I pull the rumpled duvet flat as I nod up to the framed print on the wall. "That's the big one. The little one's over the dresser."

Josh puts his left knee onto my bed and leans in close to the frame. "Oh, wow. This is—" He squints at it and turns to me. "How old is this?"

"He gave it to me when I graduated from college. So, seven years, at least?"

Josh moves his fingertips in front of the image, not touching the glass. The print is a series of fanned-out shapes, like leaves or feathers, printed in a dusty green and gray. "Just incredible," Josh murmurs. "This guy is...these errors in registration, they're intentional. They give it...you know, that suggestion of depth." He looks at me again. "Do you know anything about this print?"

"It's pretty?" I shrug. "It looks like a peacock?"

"I mean, did he tell you anything about how he made it?"

"Oh, no, nothing like that."

Josh slides his leg off the bed and walks to look at the print over my dresser. This one is smaller, simpler, just a mottled blue sphere. "It's older, isn't it? You can tell he was just learning here."

"I can't tell that, but apparently you can."

He's holding his fingers close to this one too. "You can see it." Josh stands up straight and looks at me. "Hey, I'm doing a seminar Tuesday night at the Art Academy, if you'd like to come," he says. "Eight o'clock. It's like intro to litho. Basically I'm doing it for donor wives, but some fun people might be there too. And there's a studio session Thursday if you're—"

Donor wives? "I don't know," I say. I don't want to be rude. "I'm not sure what I've got going on this week."

"It's up to you. I'll put you on the list; come by if you want. You know the Academy, right? Go to the Graduate Center." I follow a few steps behind as he goes to the door. "Thanks for letting me see those prints."

When he's gone, there's an absence created, as well as a feeling of relief. Order is restored again. I go to the shelf in my living room and pick up the photo that Josh had held, the picture of Katie and me. It's from a hike we took in New Hampshire—some stranger on the trail snapped it for us—and we're sitting on a fallen tree, side by side in shorts and sport tops with the sleeves of our sweatshirts tied around our waists. We're smiling big, toothy smiles, and Katie has her arms around me.

The bottle of soda is still in my hands, getting warm. I twist it open while I look at the picture, and with the crack of the top opening the sticky stuff inside fizzes and overflows and splatters to the hardwood floor. Shit.

8

The kayaks are gone when I get to work Monday morning, and Mike's two sons are playing in our little lobby area. They're four and seven, I think; both of them spastic and adorable towheads. They're kneeling over some toys, and they both look up at me and shout, "Hi, Jessica!" before returning to stomping their plastic dinosaurs over the old magazines on the coffee table. Carol, our receptionist-slash-reference-librarian, looks up from her desk and smiles.

"No school today, Walt?" I ask the older one.

"It isn't starting again 'til tomorrow," Walt says. He's driving a toy car up and down his leg. "And butt face didn't want to go to daycare."

"Don't call me that!" cries James, the little brother.

"Butt face."

"Walter!" Mike shouts from the back. "I don't want to hear you talking like that anymore."

"Butt face," Walt whispers.

James starts to cry, and I leave because Mike is coming and I'm about to start laughing and don't want to send the wrong message. Mike is wearing a tie, which is unusual, but he's looking pretty serious as he walks past so I don't say anything about it. I sling my bag onto the canvas chair in the corner of my spacious cube, and slip off my shoes as the computer boots up. Katie opens a chat window, saying "Hey" almost as soon as I'm logged on.

"What's up, skipper?" I type.

"Nautical jokes getting old already," she types back. "But aye, aye. There. Said it. Now, beware: Mom's on the warpath. Has she called you yet?"

"What? No?"

"She's going to call to ask you to move. She's worked up about that memorial thing."

It takes me a moment to remember that Katie is referring to the hundred and eighteen seconds of silence planned by the city for ten-fifteen this morning. One morbid second for each victim, precisely a week after the fact. I think a better memorial would involve two minutes of noise, but I was not consulted on this.

"Christ," I type. I can hear Mike talking in his calm but firm dad voice out in the lobby.

"...both of you to find a place and spend a little time apart, and think about this," he says. "Okay?"

"Is she being hysterical-Mom or angry-Mom?"

"Mostly hysterical, with some indignation thrown in. Expect to hear from her after the TV coverage ends."

"Great. Thanks for the warning. Going to work now."

I'm not really going to work, though; I close the chat and open a browser window to see if Gretchen has updated the PitchBitch. There's a new post, but I don't have a chance to read it because I look up and see little James staring at me from the entryway of my cube.

"What's up, Jimmy?"

"May I please sit in here while I draw?" he asks in his wisp of a voice. "I promise I'll be quiet."

"Of course you can." He's so cute and polite, how could I say no? I reach over and pull my bag off the chair and he hops in and gets right to work with some crayons and a legal pad.

The subject of Gretchen's latest, posted at 8:19 this morning, has me a little confused. "THE ENEMY OF MY ENEMY IS MY FRIEND?" it says. The rest of the post is equally confusing: "Or is the friend of my friend my enemy? Help, help. Working new tagline, trying to breathe new life into a tired slogan. It's hopeless. By the way, Saturday w/ Jazzboy et al. was kicking. Updates TK."

I read the post again, and again once more. Is that enemy/friend thing somehow referring to me? I should call her, but I feel not quite right about it. Is there some plan, some significance, regarding her pursuit of Patrick?

Am I the enemy, or the friend?

I really should call, but not yet. And anyway, as I'm sitting there, I sense I'm being watched. I turn and see James looking at me, unblinking, with his hands resting on the pad of paper in his lap.

"Do you need something?" I ask.

He holds the pad out toward me. "I need help drawing hands. Can you draw hands?"

"Sure, I can try." I slide off my chair and kneel down next to him to take the pad. "Wow, Jimmy," I say. "You did these?" He smiles and nods as I look at the line of smiley faces he's drawn. They're crude circles with scribble-dot eyes and crooked mouths and big loops for ears, but I'm impressed, and not just because it's my employer's child, either.

I hold out my hand for a crayon. "What color do you want them to be?"

"Brown," he says. "No, green. This green. They can be stick hands." I draw a pair of green hands on one of the circles, and he signals approval by shaking his head up and down.

"Who are these people?" I ask.

He points to the leftmost face. "That's Mommy. With the hair. That's Walter. That's Walter again. He's happy Walter, and that one, this one is mean Walter. That's Daddy. That's Danielle. She's got hair too."

I'm finishing the last set of broomstick hands as I'm about to ask James who Danielle is, but I remember, suddenly, that Danielle was the girl who rented the apartment over Mike's garage and didn't come home a week ago. And in that instant my face feels cold and my palms go wet and my stomach seems to drop away, and I feel like I need to get to the bathroom immediately.

"Here, James," I say, handing him the pad. "I'll be right back."

"Thank you."

I get to the rear of our office as fast as I can without breaking into a full run, and thankfully no one is in the bathroom. I click on the fan but not the light and lock myself in, and sit on the toilet and put my head down between my knees and close my eyes and breathe. She was at Mike's Christmas party, she was plain and sweet and she had a little acne on her chin that she tried to hide with cracking makeup. She was taking a year off from school to figure things out. Mike's kids and Carol's daughter followed her around all night, and James sat in her lap when we had dinner. She read them books and brought them down in their pajamas to say good night to everyone at the party.

Don't think about this. Stop. Breathe.

I open my eyes after a bit and stare at my gray-stockinged feet on the tile floor and the shadows from the light coming under the door. My eyes have adjusted enough that I don't need to turn on the light as I rinse off my face in the sink, and I flush the toilet to throw off Grant, who is probably listening at this very moment and wondering what I'm doing in here.

Mike is returning to his office from the front as I exit the bathroom, and he points over toward my cube.

"Is he bugging you in there?" Mike asks.

"What? Oh, James? No, Mike, he's fine. He's a sweet-heart."

"Well, if he does, just tell him to come back here."

"He's fine, really."

"Just tell him if you need to."

"I will. Hey, Mike?" I ask, and he raises his eyebrows. "What happened to your . . . that girl? Your tenant?"

Mike shakes his head. "She was on the crosstown. Bad. Bad. Her uncle is staying with us to pack up her stuff."

"I'm so sorry."

"It's terrible. She was . . . God, the kids loved her. We loved her. Sherry wanted to hire her as a nanny, but she needed to get back to school. That's where she needed to be." Mike sighs and leans against the wall, and looks toward the lobby. "And James can't . . . he doesn't understand what's going on. Walt does, he realized it even before we let ourselves believe it. He's been sleeping with us all week."

"Poor guy," I say, and something about the idea of tough little Walter jumping into his parents' bed makes me feel like I'm going to start bawling, but I hold it off.

"Her mom and dad got in yesterday. Meeting her father was maybe the most difficult experience of my life. He's wrecked. We're going with them to that memorial in the park today, that's why this is making an appearance." He grabs the tie and flaps it against his chest. "It's just terrible."

"It is" is all I can say.

Mike straightens up. "I want to talk about that Cippo-letti stuff this afternoon when I'm back. You have anything going on?"

"I'm free," I say.

Back in my cube, James is still working away. He's flipped to a new page and seems eager for me to see his latest piece.

"It's you," he says with a big smile, and the red crayon tangle encircling the smiley face to represent my hair is proof.

"That's great," I say, holding the pad. "May I hang it up in here?" James smiles and nods his head furiously, apparently so thrilled at the thought he can't speak.

James is silent for the next half hour, drawing away as I respond to some actual work e-mails. Patrick sends me the word of the day—"perambulate" (duh, strolling, is this on every word of the day calendar?)—as I'm composing, and I promptly delete it. There's no need to hunt for hidden meaning in the daily word anymore; he forwards them every morning and usually I delete them immediately. I'd tell him to stop, but I like seeing his name in my in-box.

Mike peeks in at about nine-thirty, wearing a sport coat, and raps on the metal frame of the cubicle. James doesn't look up. "Come on, bud," Mike says. "Let's get going."

"Okay." He slides off the chair and walks to his dad.

"Anything you need to tell Jessica? About spending time in here?"

"Thank-you-for-letting-me-spend-time-in-here-Jessica," James says in a sad monotone, staring down at his feet. I give Mike one of those "aw" looks.

"You're welcome," I say. "And you are *always* welcome to come visit me when you're here." He looks up at me and smiles, and he grabs Mike's hand and they go.

I am so glad I'm not going with them to the memorial.

A few minutes later my phone double rings, and Carol tells me there's a Gretchen calling on line one. I punch the extension without thanking Carol.

"Gretchen. How are you? And what's up with that new post?"

"Lame, lame, lame, *lame*," she says. "Company sells destination golf vacation packages. I'm trying to hit the friendly competition note. You know, old college buddies, wealthy now, throwing down for a week of cutthroat action on the links by day, fucked up in the bar by night. I'm flailing, Jessica. I'm lost. But this account is so huge."

I feel better now. "So, 'enemy of my enemy'?"

"I told you, I'm flailing. And you should see the photos. The models look like they should just be back in the hotel room sucking each other off, not anywhere near a golf course. It's like it should be the leather golf vacation or something. Biker dudes golfing? Maybe I could pitch that. But the account, I can't even tell you. So huge. How were you feeling Saturday?"

"A little rough. You?"

"Not so bad. Tired mostly. Hey, do you want to meet for lunch somewhere?"

"Today? Sure?"

"Gram Bistro? I'll buy. I want to ask you something. About something we talked about."

Oh really? Now I'm really wishing I could remember more of Saturday night. I do want to see Gretchen, though, and I'm very curious. And I can walk to the Gram from my office, so I'm in. "Sure," I say. "You don't have to buy, though. What do you want to ask me?"

"Come on, think about it, you know. We'll talk there. Are you watching the memorial?"

"I cannot handle any kind of memorial," I say, rubbing my eyes.

"Ditto. Putting this shit on television is like, ugh." She pauses. "How about one-thirty for lunch. Everything can settle down in the city."

"I'll see you then," I say, and we say good-bye and hang up. I do some more actual work, and am so successful at putting the memorial out of my head for this little bit that I don't look at the small atomic clock on my desk until it's fourteen minutes after ten. Nothing changes when the minute flips to fifteen; the fan in my computer continues its perpetual sigh and I still feel the subliminal hum of the fluorescent lights above me.

What are Walter and James doing right now?

I'm staring at the clock now, watching the seconds accumulate, and my palms are flat on the desktop. Sixteen after.

Seconds and more seconds, they hit fifty, fifty-eight, and a new sound starts: I hear a car horn outside, then another and another; church bells start ringing and car alarms howl and the mess of rising sound positively invades my cubicle. Apparently I wasn't the only one wishing for noise. I drum my hands on the desk, not hard, in line with the racket, and Grant walks by and gives me a very confused look.

"What's going on?" he asks, and in the time he takes to say it, the sound goes away.

"It's the—" My hands are flat on the desk again. "It's nothing." He stares at me for a moment and walks away. Clueless.

I grab my bag and fish around inside for my cell phone to prepare for the coming-any-minute call from Mom. I consider turning it off to vex her, but she'd just call the office anyway, so I switch it to vibrate and set it next to my keyboard.

Sure enough, at exactly ten-thirty the phone begins to buzz and shimmy on the desktop.

"Mom, I'm not moving," is the first thing I say after flipping it open.

"I'm not asking you to move, Jessica."

"Oh."

"Did you watch any of the—"

"No, Mom. None of it."

"You don't need to be short with me. It was very tastefully done."

"I'm not being short," I say, and I switch the phone to my left ear so I can click my e-mail in-box button. Nothing there. "It's just been a weird morning."

"I know, honey. Maybe, maybe you'd just like to come stay with me for a while."

"You said you weren't asking me to move."

"I'm not, Jessica, I'm saying, just a visit."

"How long?"

"Oh, I don't know," she says, but of course she does know. "You can stay as long as you like. A month?"

"Uh, hello, Mom? I have a job? An apartment? Bills?"

"I'm sure we could handle all that."

"Mom. I'll come up." I hear her draw a surprised breath, but I stomp it right out of her. "For a weekend. I could manage that. When were you thinking?" She doesn't say anything. "Mom?"

"Well. That isn't exactly what I was envisioning. But." She pauses again. "I'm sure your sister told you about her program at sea—"

"Of course she did. It's very exciting."

"Well, I was thinking we should have a going-away party for her. Here. You could help me plan. It would be a nice surprise for her."

This intrigues me. I'm not so interested in the party thing, but I'd love to see Katie before she goes. And if Mom is willing to pay for me to get up to Seattle, what's not to like?

"Let me think about this, Mom."

"Maybe you could stay for a week?"

A week with Katie? "Maybe I could do a week. Depends on work."

"You know I love you, angel." Her tone is a little different now, not condescending or desperate like it can seem sometimes. "Please be safe. Please."

"I will, Mom."

"I mean it."

"I will."

The Gram Bistro is maybe a little trendier than I'd normally choose for lunch, but the midday rush is just about over by the time I get there and I'm hardly concerned with looking great or being seen, so no big deal. Gretchen isn't worried, either, apparently; she's seated in a booth with her back to me, and I can see as I come up behind her she's wearing a plain dark knit pullover and her hair has been sloppily pulled back. Sloppily perfect, I guess. She's pretty in a way that seems unfair, and it's hard not to feel a little twinge of envy when she looks up and smiles at me.

"Hey," she says, still smiling as I unshoulder my bag and slip into the booth. "Did you walk?"

"I did. Fortunately it's mostly downhill on the way back." Gretchen is leaning forward drizzling honey into a cup of tea, and she's so tiny it seems like her chin is barely above the edge of the table. I think for a moment about suggesting we get a booster seat, but I don't know her so well and it is a pretty stupid joke so I bite my lip and try not to laugh.

"What?" she asks as she shakes the spoon over her teacup. "Oh right. I know. You're thinking booster."

"Oh God," I say, and I laugh and cover my mouth with my hand. "I'm sorry."

I'm relieved when she laughs too. "Don't worry, I've heard it more than once. If a girl says it, it's kind of cute. If a guy says it, there's no second date."

"Patrick has never said it?" I feel weird asking, but Gretchen gets the conspiratorial smirk and everything is okay.

"Patrick has never once commented on my stature," she says. "I do hear some lame stuff sometimes, though. From other guys."

"Like?"

"Like how about, 'Bet you don't have to kneel to give a blow job, huh huh.' That one doesn't earn points. Or blow jobs, for that matter."

"That's so—"

"Yeah. I know." She takes a sip of her tea and licks her upper lip. "Mmm, but, speaking of such things, did Mr. Artist come over?"

"What?"

"To your place? To see those paintings, or what was it?"

"How did you know about that?"

"Are you kidding me? It was about the only thing you talked about Saturday night. Every time you saw me."

I feel my cheeks getting hot and know my face must be deep red. "Really?"

"You seriously don't remember? You hardly seemed drunk."

"It doesn't seem to take that much anymore," I say.

"I know what you mean," Gretchen says.

But I don't think she does.

The waitress comes and Gretchen and I both order the mountainous Bistro house salad, half of which I'll most likely box up and lug home for dinner tonight.

"To answer your question," I say after the server walks away, "he did stop by on Sunday."

"And?"

"And . . . it was weird."

Gretchen tilts her head. "Weird how?"

"He was a little bit intimidating."

"I can see that. He's got that alpha thing going on. The way he was looking at you at Patrick's, it was kind of whoa."

"Yeah," I say, but I'm not really recalling it.

"So what happened?"

"Nothing, really, he was only there for about twenty minutes." Gretchen almost looks disappointed when I say it. "He just kind of walked around and looked at my stuff, he looked at my friend's prints, which he loved, and then he left. Oh, and he invited me to some class he's teaching tomorrow night."

Gretchen raises her eyebrows. "And? You're going?"

"I don't know. It was just weird when he was there."

"Weird. Define weird."

"He was walking all around. Looking at my stuff?"

"Maybe he was interested."

"Like looking at my life. Into my life."

"Isn't that the way artists are? You should go to his thing."

"I'm just, I don't know."

She smiles. "You should."

"I'll consider it," I say. "So what is the big question?"

"Okay," she says, squeezing her hands together. "There are actually two questions. When we were talking about how fun it would be to work together—" I must look blank, because Gretchen cocks her head and stares at me. "You don't remember."

I shake my head, and I can feel my cheeks going warm again. "I remember really laughing about something," I say, and for an instant I feel very frightened about blanking, and then the feeling passes.

"We were laughing at Patrick," Gretchen says. "That dance he was doing. You really don't remember? It wasn't like you had any more than I did."

"Should I be worried about this?" I feel so stupid, but Gretchen's shaking her head and I can tell by the look on her face that she's been there too.

"No, come on, it's been a weird week, I'd try to forget most of it too if I could. You were probably just emotional with everything going on."

True. And she doesn't even know about my little fight with Patrick before the party. I almost tell her, but I stop myself.

"Anyway," I say. "Working together. Would be fun, yes."

"So fun. What if we did it?"

"What do you mean?"

"I mean, I've got this golf thing. It's more work than I can handle by myself. I'm already saying no to other clients on stuff. Would you want to help?"

"Are you serious?"

"Yes, I'm serious. You already do the outdoorsy stuff, it would be perfect, you know? And their budget, oh my God, Jessica, they want to do a six-month full-page run in all the in-flight magazines. Do you have any idea how much a full-page in a seatback goes for?"

I do, actually; it isn't cheap. I think about this as the salads show up, and Gretchen and I look at each other over two heaps of lettuce, avocado, and seared tuna and start to laugh.

"I'll be working on this for days," Gretchen says. "So. Interested?"

I am, but it's scary. Consulting on my own? "I don't know," I say. "Things are pretty good with Mike. I need to think about it."

"Okay. Good. Do."

"What's the other thing?"

"The other thing," she says between bites, "involves my alter ego. Do you want to do some guest posts on the Pitch-Bitch? Anonymously, of course."

"Are you serious?"

"Of course I'm serious."

"Gretchen, I don't think I'm quite that . . . caliber?"

"Come on, you don't give yourself enough credit. That story you told me about the bike shorts, I was dying. That would be so perfect—"

"I told you about the bike shorts?"

"Ha ha, you're kidding, I know."

I swallow and evade. "It is a pretty funny story, but I couldn't tell it on there; it'd be, you know, kind of a big deal at my office."

Gretchen smiles. "Not if you're working with me, it wouldn't."

I tell her I'll think about it.

9

I don't change out of my work clothes when I get home Tuesday night. Gretchen called me twice at work today to ask if I was going to Josh's seminar thing, and Katie, whom I've been messaging with all day, has been pushing me to go as well. I don't want to admit it to myself yet, but yes, yes, I'm going.

Goddammit.

I told Katie everything about my lunch with Gretchen yesterday, and the meeting I had later with Mike. The Cippoletti people, he informed me, have been asking preliminary questions about "expanding the relationship." If we do, and Mike thinks we will, he wants me to take over managing the account.

Golf land, bike land. Could I somehow do both? Right, Jess, that's pretty funny.

I'm thinking I look maybe a little too casual for this

seminar, or class, or whatever it is, but I'm having trouble coming up with an outfit that would hit the right note. The thought of mingling with donor wives is troubling; they'll probably all be rich, and I'll be flustered. I keep the black pants I'm wearing and swap out my top for a dark gray button-down; with this combination I can be elegantly dull or simply invisible. It all depends on who's looking, I guess.

It's quarter after seven and the thing starts at eight, and with my bag and my toggle coat I'm down the stairs and out the door and into the fog and to the bus stop with time to spare. No one else is on the crosstown, just me and the driver and the harsh bus light, and I only have a little walk to get to the Academy when I get off.

I've only been here once before, and never at night. The buildings are all oddly shaped and illuminated from the inside, and the light fans out in rays through the misty darkness. I walk around for a little bit before I ask a girl in a knit hat how to get to the Graduate Center. She points me back to a building I had already passed, and once I'm in I ask the very pierced guy at the reception desk where I need to go to find Josh.

"Josh?" he asks.

"He's a printer?" I say. "Doing a seminar?"

"Oh, Dr. Hadden's class."

Dr. Hadden?

Pierced guy looks at a paper. "What's your name?"

"Jessica. Zorich." I don't think I ever told Josh my last name. The guy looks down the paper and laughs.

"Are you 'red-haired Jessica from Pat and Joe's party with the two Murrant prints'?"

"That's, yes, that's me."

"Studio 1411," he says. "Almost all the way back there, before the atrium." When he points down the hall, I see a constellation of scabby track marks on the inside of his skinny tattooed arm.

It's just a couple minutes after eight when I slip into 1411, and Josh hasn't started yet. He looks at me without looking

at me when I come in and take a seat in one of the high con-
cept wooden chairs, and I think I see him smirk as he works
on setting up a laptop with a projector on one of the studio
tables. He's wearing jeans, again, and a dark cable-knit fisher-
man's sweater. Seated around the room are maybe twenty
well-dressed older women—donor wives, presumably—and
I'm at least fifteen years younger than the youngest of them.
They turn their scarved necks almost simultaneously and
watch with vague contempt as I take my seat, but a couple of
them do cock their heads and give me that "where have I seen
you before?" look that doesn't surprise me so much anymore.
Two well-groomed men, the only men in the room aside from
Josh, sit on the opposite side of the room and speak to each
other in low voices. They're good-looking, stylish even, both
with black hair and olive skin. One is wearing a dark ribbed
sweater, and the other has on a sport coat over a plain white
shirt wide open at the collar.

Josh stands up straight behind the laptop and looks
around the room. "Alright," he says. "Are we ready?" Something is projected on the screen but the room is too bright to
make out what it says. Josh holds up a little remote control
and aims it into the high open ceiling and presses a button.
"Is this? That's it." The lights dim, and now on the screen I
see an old print image of an orchid next to the words "DR.
JOSHUA HADDEN: Merging Traditional Lithographic
Techniques with Modern Imaging Technologies."

Oh God, I'm in for it. No, it's only an hour, I can manage
this.

"Thanks for coming," he starts, pressing his hands together. "I'm Dr. Josh Hadden. I'm a lithographer and I am
currently the Academy's Staynor Visiting Scholar in the
Print Arts, visiting from the Camberwell College of Arts in
London, England, where I'm a member of the faculty and
principally teach lithography and design." He's pacing, com-
fortably, as he speaks, and the women's heads follow him
back and forth like a flock of dumb birds.

"Before I begin," he goes on, "I'd like to take this opportunity to give my thanks to the Academy, and especially the Staynor Endowment, for supporting this program." The ladies clap and glance at each other, pleased with themselves, and Josh smiles at them, then he looks back at me with the most fleeting eye-roll expression of "don't worry, I understand how cheesy this is too" and I almost laugh as I look back at him and clap my hands together three times slowly. The two guys across the room just sit with their arms crossed.

"As I said," Josh continues, "I'm a lithographer, a print maker, and tonight I'm going to give you a quick introduction to the lithographic process. I'll give you a little history, show you some prints, show you what can be done with this very old technique, how people working with it right now are taking it in some very exciting directions. And Thursday night we'll get our hands dirty and make some prints of our own. Sound good? Alright." The women are rapt, almost quivering, as they listen to him, and it's sort of funny to see the way they lean toward him as he speaks. It's pretty easy to believe that any of these donor wives would like to take this handsome, well-spoken young artist home and make him a trophy.

But I'm the only one who will.

No, I did not just think that!

Did I?

Josh presses a button on the remote and the image on the screen changes; now it's another orchid in that old style, washed-out colors with a curlicue Latin description to the lower right. Josh turns and looks at the projection.

"Lithography was invented in 1798, in Germany, by a guy named Alois Senefelder. It's one of those great accidents of history that the reason Senefelder came up with it was because he was a writer, a terrible playwright, and no one would publish his work. He figured if no one would print his stuff, he'd come up with a way to print it himself, and in trying to do so he invented the whole lithographic process. Sort of the original vanity press." The women titter and Josh smiles as he brings up a new image. This one is a map, printed in black and white, and says "München—1860" across the top.

"I love these old maps," Josh says. He looks at it for a moment before pressing the remote again, and now it's a picture of Josh in a studio, working over a square slab of rock. He's wearing a tee shirt and surgical gloves and a heavy apron, and he has some sort of paintbrush in his hand. "Traditional lithography is a flat process, a chemical process, using polished limestone to hold and transfer the image. An artist, or failed writer, can prepare the image directly on the stone instead of needing to rely on a craftsman to prepare an engraving, as in other styles of printing...." He goes on, using words like "etch" and "intaglio" and "offset," but I'm not listening so much anymore. Just looking at the pictures. I'm mesmerized as he flips through them on the screen, and I'm trying to make up a story around them.

They're all taken in a studio, his studio in England I'm thinking, and it's autumn; the trees outside the many windows are almost overpowering in their reds and yellows and oranges. He's showing a picture now where he's lifting one of the rock slabs, and I can see the muscles in his arms and the strain in his neck carrying through his chin into a little grimace. They can be kind of heavy, he's saying. Care must be taken.

In the next picture the slab is in some printing press–type contraption, and Josh, photo-Josh, points at it, mouth open in mid-sentence. His dark blond hair is messed up and his other hand rests on his hip near a black smear of ink on his apron. There's a girl in the background, seated on a counter before one of the great, golden leafy windows; her hands rest on her knees and she laughs at whatever Josh has said. Girlfriend? Student? I'm thinking student. She has a crush on him.

Now the screen shows a young bearded guy with a serious look on his face, definitely a student; he's pulling a lever on the press as Josh looks over his shoulder. Easy there, take it easy, photo-Josh is saying.

More photos. Rollers and ink and brushes and gloves. Leaves of paper lain in place and peeled away, negatives and positives. A crack through the center of one of the slabs of stone, and the bearded student with his hands thrown in the air shouts *well fuck it all* while the others laugh.

"And a crack like that is really the worst case scenario," real Josh says. "But they do break sometimes, it does happen." He presses the button and now the room is confronted with a print of a grinning skeleton wielding a sword beneath the words *"LA MORT."* Josh crosses in front of the projector, and as his shadow passes over the screen the image of the skeleton is projected for a thrilling instant on his body. The effect is so perfect I wonder if he planned it, but he doesn't linger and continues right away with his talk.

"So," he says, "the lithographic process caught on in Europe just as a real explosion of understanding in human anatomy was under way. You've all seen a copy of *Gray's Anatomy*, I'm sure, those plates are chromolithographs, nicely executed, but pretty dull. A hundred years earlier than *Gray's* you had artists and anatomists collaborating on these just incredible atlases, the work is almost unbelievable. This guy"—he points at the skeleton—"is from the frontispiece of an 1831 French atlas. I study a lot of these. They've been a pretty big influence on me." He takes us through some anatomical prints and again I watch, the bones and dissections and fetuses flash by, real but not real. Josh shows a print of the human circulatory system, and then with a press of the button it's an 1899 map of Poland; the transition is stunning as veins turn to roads and arteries become rivers. He jogs back and forth between the two a couple times to drive in the effect, and then it's forward again, maps and more maps, colors and squiggles and topographic demarcations. He shows a detail from a corner of a map, a dusty red rose, and flashes from this to a full-sized illustration of roses and zinnias and poppies beneath the words "Lannier's Seed Catalogue—Philadelphia, 1902."

"These seed catalogs, as you'll see here in a bit, have been a pretty big influence on me too. They really represent the peak of American commercial lithography, traditional lithography anyway. It's a shame, these guys were working mostly between 1880 and the outbreak of the First World War, and we have no idea who most of them were." He zaps through pages from the catalogs, colorful varieties guaranteed to grow, flowers tomatoes cucumbers eggplants all flashing by. And suddenly, the image shown is very different: a jagged pale spiral, centered a little to the left of the image, winding down into something that looks organic, but isn't quite. The almost garish text from the earlier catalog pages is gone, and there's something very familiar to it.

"This," Josh says, "is a modern piece by a guy named Greg Murrant, and while it looks pretty different from the older prints I've shown you, Greg's work, his merging of sources, really ties those styles into the work I'm doing today. Murrant takes digital sources—in this case, it's from a digital map of the Hudson River—and arranges them into novel presentations bearing very little resemblance to the original material." Josh moves through a few of Greg's prints on the projector until he gets to one that makes me sit up: it's a bunch of leaflike forms arranged in a fan shape, just like the print I have over my bed. This one is different, though, a little bolder, a little more certain. I think Josh looks back at me while it's up there, but it's hard to tell in the dark.

"Now, any of you who have seen my current work might wonder how this relates," he says, and someone up front laughs. "But bear with me." A new slide is projected, just text that says: "JOSHUA HADDEN—NORTH AMERICAN FLORA." "These chromolithographs debuted in an exhibit last summer at the Whitney Museum of American Art, and were made from digital source materials I collected four years ago while traveling from Canada to Central America. I know we're running a little short on time, so I'll just advance through these without commentary and anyone with questions can come up and speak to me after. So. Right." Josh thumbs the remote and there's an audible gasp from the front of the room; what shows on the screen is so unexpected I almost gasp myself. It's a print of a giant, uncircumcised penis, but presented in a perfect imitation of that hundred-year-old seed catalog. The image is framed by a leafy border, and in the lower right, in that florid, old-style lettering, it says: "Denys, Calgary. Hardy Root System!" A new image, another penis: "Arthur, Vancouver. Easy to Grow!" Now a bulging vulva: "Marcia from Boise, Resistant to Frost!" And on and on, the cornucopia of genital varieties moves southward: Janice from Denver, spread wide open. Harold from Las Vegas, slightly erect. Leticia from Juárez has a pelt of black fur, and Ramón from San Salvador bends to the left. And by the time we get to Antonio in Panama City ("Pendant Fruit! Big on Color and Flavor, Low on Heat!"), I don't know whether to laugh or cover my face. The images are an assault, almost too much; fifteen minutes of these grotesque representations with their ridiculous descriptions have worn me out.

There's no other way to put it: the prints are undeniably brilliant. What does this make Josh, though? Pervert? Genius? Both?

I must confess that I'm curious.

Josh aims the remote into the ceiling again and the lights slowly come up to reveal the shell-shocked women in front of me. "Thank you all very much for coming," he says. "And don't forget, Thursday night, in here, same studio, we'll be making some prints. Be sure to wear clothes you don't really care about; the materials can get a little messy. Thanks again."

The two men stand up and leave the room without looking back. Everyone else rises slowly and a few of the women go up to talk to Josh while the rest file out, some looking titillated as they giggle and chatter in twos and threes, others looking weary as they shuffle toward the door. I bend down to get my bag from the floor, and when I rise I come face-to-face with a stooped, silver-haired woman.

"You were on that catalog, weren't you?" she asks.

Sometimes I act stupid about it, but this time I don't. "Yes," I say.

She grabs my wrist with a trembling hand. "You're a beautiful young woman," she says, then she lets go and walks away, leaving me with an odd, unsettled feeling. Maybe I should just deny it all the time from now on.

There are only two women left with Josh as I stand there against a work counter with my bag hanging down by my knees. They're leaning in to him, listening closely, nodding ferociously at every word out of his mouth. I could leave, now, while they talk, just slip out the door and go home and give him a call later and say thanks, it was very interesting.

But I don't.

One of the women is asking Josh about his plans for the future, is he doing any big projects while he's here in the States? Josh gestures with his hands as he speaks to them, and they listen so intently it looks like they should be taking notes.

"I'm interested in going back to doing something with maps," he says. "That old cartographic style, you know, work it into something. The Academy has some imaging equipment that I don't have at Camberwell, so I'd like to take advantage of that while I'm here. We'll see." They chat for a little bit more and the two women thank Josh profusely; they don't even look at me as they leave.

Josh clicks his laptop shut and walks over. "Well?" he says, with a half smile. He loops his thumbs into his pockets and shrugs, and the ropy collar of his sweater rides up to his

chin. "I guess I do take monster cocks, and make them art."
We both laugh.

"I thought Joe was just being Joe," I say. "I didn't think
he meant it, he says weird stuff all the time. He's kind of—"

"Yeah, he's a freak," Josh says, and we laugh again. "Did
you like it?"

"Yes," I say. "Yes, I did."

"Some people think it's kind of a gimmick. Kind of pre-
cious."

"No. It's . . . it turns everything on its head. It's weird, it's
like, you can't look away from it, it's so in your face. It's con-
frontational."

"Thank you," Josh says. "Thank you. That feels better
than a thousand good reviews. Or any bad one."

I'm blushing, I think, so I turn to pull my coat from the
back of the neighboring chair.

"Have you eaten?" Josh asks.

I could say yes. I could say I have plans. I could say I need
to get to work early tomorrow.

"No," I say.

"There's a Salvadoran place just off campus. Have you
ever had Salvadoran food?"

"There is such a cuisine?"

"You'll like it," he says. He grabs his laptop and slides it
into an orange bike messenger bag, and we head out. The
reception desk is unmanned now, and it's still foggy outside.

"I'm staying in that place up there," Josh says, pointing
to his left at a building that I can't really see.

"They have housing here?"

"Guest housing. It's plush. Private studio too."

We walk along, through the mist; my hands are jammed
down into the pockets of my coat and Josh's messenger bag
bumps into my side every few steps.

"How long does the visiting scholar thing last?" I ask.

"It's a full year."

"Does your school in England have a problem with that?" I guess I'm not too clear on how this academic stuff works.

"It's a sabbatical. It all fell into place pretty nicely, actually."

We only walk a little farther to get to the restaurant, which is called, appropriately enough, El Salvadoreño. The restaurant is next to a Laundromat and has similar decor; the cinder-block walls are painted robin's-egg blue and the tables are chipped and mismatched. An older couple is seated toward the back, and there's a faded poster of a palm-lined beach taped up on the wall by the cash register. A short mustachioed man wearing camouflage pants and a baggy tank top waves as he comes from the kitchen with some laminated menus.

"*Hola,* Yosh!" the man shouts as he comes over to us.

"*Hola,* Miguel," Josh says. He pulls out a chair for me, and he and this camo-pants Miguel person launch into a rapid-fire conversation that my eighth- and ninth-grade Spanish classes have in no way prepared me to follow. I do pick up on a couple words, and I keep hearing *novia* . . . *novia* . . . girlfriend?

"Miguel, this is Jessica," Josh finally says in English, and Miguel reaches for my hand.

"Nice to meet you," Miguel says with hardly any accent. "You guys take a look at the menu, I'll be right back."

"Who is the *novia*?" I ask after Miguel leaves.

Josh raises his eyebrows and smiles. "You speak Spanish?"

"Hardly. But I know a few words."

"Miguel misses his girlfriend. She's back visiting her family in San Salvador. She's the *novia.*"

"Gotcha. How do you speak it so well?"

"I studied in Mexico City for a couple years."

"You sound pretty fluent for only a couple years."

"I guess some people have a thing for languages."

"I guess. I'm not one of those people."

Josh shrugs and smiles, and holds up the menu. "You want me to order for us? It's all good here."

"That's fine," I say. "So where are you from, originally?"

"Originally?" Josh takes a sip of ice water from one of the blue plastic cups on the table. "Originally I'm from Ohio. But I don't like to admit it."

"Is it that bad? I always confuse it with Iowa."

"Everyone does. And I left as soon as I graduated from high school, if that says anything." He drinks some more water. "No, really, it's not that bad. It's just dull. I grew up in Columbus. Did you know it's the most demographically average city in the country? Everything is test-marketed there. Red state, blue state, minorities, just enough crime, just enough population growth, just enough city, just enough suburb. It's the ideal marketing lab."

"You'd think that would make it interesting," I say.

"Maybe, but who wants to live in a lab?"

He's got a point. "Do they have beer or wine here?" I ask.

"I think so," Josh says. "I've never ordered it."

"Do you not drink?" I ask, and my cheeks get hot. "Sorry, that's none of my business."

"No, it's fine. I do, just not very frequently." He lets out a little embarrassed laugh. "I get too charming when I drink. It's bad news. Dangerous."

"Uh huh, right." Now I take a sip of my own water, just to have something to do with my hands.

"I'm serious. Maybe only a little serious. Where are you from? Originally."

"I'm from Seattle. Well, west of there. I grew up drinking coffee."

Josh laughs. "That's good. Get that out preemptively, before anyone else can make the joke."

"It's a reflex."

Miguel comes to take our order, which Josh gives in Spanish; they go back and forth and Miguel smiles and looks at me and says, "Oh that's good, that's really good," in English before he walks away.

"So, I have a question," I say.

"Shoot."

"How did you get into your subject matter? Not just anatomy, but..."

"But?"

"Well, the detail. The close-up."

"I don't really know. It just sort of happened. I mean, it's not really erotic—"

"Not at all," I say.

"But I think people are maybe...I don't know, conditioned to respond to those, those parts in a certain way. It's like, the images are everywhere, online, wherever you look, you know? Naked women, dudes, everywhere, all really sexually charged. So I wanted to present it differently. Clinically. But clinical is dull. So why not make it a parody of clinical, right? And they aren't even realistic representations, but they push the right buttons because of how we've been conditioned to respond. It just kind of works, somehow."

"It totally works. But don't you think people are pretty desensitized already?"

"Sure they are," he says. "But that's where the seed catalog thing gets you, right? The context tricks you into looking at it a different way."

"It does. It's a pretty nice effect."

"I want to try the same thing with maps. See if it works. But not just those parts, something a little different. I'm still working it out in my head." Josh looks at me, suddenly serious, and his expression makes my face feel warm again. "Hey, now I want to ask you something," he says. "And it may sound a little weird, but you just got me thinking."

"What?"

"And you can feel free to say 'no thanks,' I'm not going to be offended or anything."

"What is it?"

"May I draw you? Tonight? Or whenever ..."

"Ah," I say, and my cheeks feel like they're about to ignite.

I could say no.

I could say I have plans.

"I guess so?"

10

The Academy's guest housing is indeed plush. And, in the case of Josh's residence, cluttered. It's modern and high ceilinged and open—mostly studio space, but there's a little kitchen at the far end and steep steps going up to a sleeping loft over what I assume to be the bathroom. Books and magazines are piled everywhere; stacks on the worktables, stacks in the kitchen, stacks on the floor, and art supplies seem to be tucked into every space where there aren't any books. Three enormous prints of flowers hang on the back wall, but none of Josh's other work is anywhere to be seen.

"Can I take your coat?" Josh asks.

"What? Oh, sure."

"We don't have to do this, you know, it's not a big deal if we don't."

"No, no, no," I say as I hand him my coat. "I'm fine."

Josh hangs my coat from a hook behind the door and walks to the kitchen. "Do you want something to drink? Water? I think there's a bottle of wine somewhere around—"

"Wine. Yes. Please," I say.

Dinner, after Josh made his drawing request, was mostly a blur. We talked, and we ate. There were little, doughy tortillas filled with some kind of stewed meat. All fine. Nothing spicy. We talked some more. It didn't matter, though, I wasn't thinking about food or conversation, just about the fact that I'd agreed, maybe too quickly, to pose for a man I really barely know who creates giant images of human genitalia. What was I thinking? Maybe, I don't know, maybe he just wants to draw my face. A nice portrait for my mom. But then there's the potential of everything else, the thought that this act of being drawn might lead to a multitude of other acts.

"Here you go," Josh says as he comes back, handing me a heavy water glass filled to the top with dark wine. He starts to move some of the books off a table. "Why don't you get undressed now," he says, and I take a big slug of the wine.

"You okay?" he asks.

"I'm fine. Should I do this?"

Josh shrugs, and a little smile comes across his face. "Should you?"

"That's no answer. Is that your bathroom?"

He nods. "There's a robe in there, if you want it."

"Yes. Maybe." I go in and close the door, and don't do anything but make stupid scared faces at myself in the mirror for a moment. I look through my bag for my phone and turn it off. What am I doing? I could stop. I don't have to do this. I don't have to unbutton my shirt, but I start, and the release of the topmost button by my shaking hand leads to a chain of events that culminates in me being totally naked and every one of my garments being neatly folded next to the sink. I look at myself in the mirror again and squeeze in my upper arms to create the effect of cleavage, but when I release, all parts fall back to their more natural, widely spaced positions.

I'm excited and I'm terrified, and I put on the robe and head back out.

Josh has taken his sweater off too, and now in his tight gray tee shirt he's kneeling on the floor and digging through an open toolbox filled with art supplies. "Just have a seat up there," he says without looking up.

Josh has cleared everything from the worktable and spread a red and white quilt out over it. It's a tall table, and I have to make two little jumps with my palms behind me on the edge of it to lift myself up to the surface. The motion of scooting myself back causes the robe to fall open, and I quickly pull it closed again, even though Josh is too busy looking at a slender piece of charcoal to notice. I have a drink from the glass of wine, then another, while Josh gets a large pad of paper from the other side of the studio and brings it back to the table.

"You ready?" Josh asks, and I nod. "You're sure?"

I nod again. "Yes," I say.

Josh reaches forward and pushes the robe off my shoulders. I watch as his eyes look down my body, as he tilts his head to the side when he sees my appendectomy scar, as he touches his fingers to the dark blemish left on my knee from when Katie wrecked Mom's car and I hit the dashboard. My legs are crossed, tightly, and I pull my arms from the sleeves of the robe and wrap them around my stomach under my breasts, clutching myself. Josh bends down to get the pad of paper from the floor.

"Why don't you lie back," he says. I do, and my legs are still crossed, hanging off the edge of the table. "Knees up. You need to scoot back a little. Get your feet up there. There you go."

I'm looking up at the white-painted ductwork in the ceiling, pressing my knees tightly together.

"You're going to need to open up," Josh says. I take a breath and hear my pulse in my ears, and then I feel Josh's hands on my shins, easing my knees apart.

"Oh God, I don't know about this," I say, and I sit up very quickly and cross my ankles and put my hands in my lap. I can feel my heart pounding, and my embarrassed flush has spread down into a blotchy smear across my chest.

"It's fine," Josh says. "It's not a problem."

I take another deep breath, and a long drink of wine. "No, just give me a second."

"Jessica, seriously, why don't you go get dressed. We don't have to do this right now."

I'm starting to feel the warmth of the wine spreading out through my skin. "I'm fine," I say. "I'm okay." This is just clinical. A parody of clinical. I lie back and look up into the pipes and ducts and pendant light fixtures again, and lift up my knees and let them fall open. Josh puts his hands on my feet and pushes them up closer to my butt. My mouth feels dry and I try to swallow, and I feel a tremble in my rushed breathing. Are those ducts white or off-white?

"Do you want a pillow?" Josh asks.

"I'm fine."

I hear the charcoal scraping over Josh's pad of paper.

"Can you kind of rock your hips back? Just roll them back a little . . . That's it, right there. Right there, Jessica. Perfect." More scratching charcoal. "Oh wow. Nice. Very nice."

Wow? Nice? I feel myself starting to shiver, and I wrap my arms over my tummy again, grabbing my elbows while I listen to charcoal on paper. Scratch, scratch, scratch.

"Perfect," Josh says. "Perfect."

I close my eyes and resist the urge to close my knees; this examination is driving me crazy. I don't even like to look down there myself, and now I'm allowing a virtual stranger to examine the wrinkly pink asymmetry that lives between my legs. I'm happy to handle it, manipulate it, play with it daily or more; just don't make me look at it. I've never even let Patrick look down there.

Wrong thought. Don't think about Patrick now. Just don't.

"How is it going?" I ask. Josh doesn't say anything, and when I lift my head to look down at him he shakes his head and keeps scribbling, looking from me to the pad and back again.

The wine has moved into me more; I feel it in my limbs and in my head. A far-off rumble comes from somewhere in the building, and a rush of air begins to flow from the vents in the ductwork suspended up in the ceiling. I see a cobweb being whipped back and forth, it dances up and undulates like a tiny serpent before stopping and drifting back down into the breeze again. I feel the furnace-pushed heat on my face as I'm transfixed by the motion of the little dusty floss, and as I'm distracted by this, something changes. It's no longer just Josh's eyes on me, but now his hands are too, on the insides of my legs, opening them farther.

"Is something wrong?" I say, and I'm not even sure why. Josh shakes his head again and goes back to drawing. I can still feel where his hands were on my legs, close, and I'm sort of surprised at myself for not being startled by the touch. They were there, and gone, and wish—do I really?—that they were there again.

I let my knees shut, just a little. Then that warmth again; his hands are there and they stay, and when they do move, it's not away from me, but closer. His fingers begin a motion that is almost jolting, but instead of sitting up or pulling away I close my eyes and push myself into the feeling.

Josh's fingers move, and move, and I turn my head to the side and breathe.

I'm lifting my hips, buoyed by warm air and wine, and this almost involuntary cooperation on my part brings on another transition: just as eyes have turned to fingers, now fingers have turned to mouth.

I have never, ever, let anyone do this before.

For an instant I think I should recoil, pull away, sit up, run. This is too close. Too intimate. Too fast. Josh has his whole face pressed into me, and I glance down and see that his eyes are closed before I look back up into the ceiling. The furnace stops, and in the sudden absence of its hum and rush the only sounds left are the wet noises coming from be-tween my legs.

I don't know if I can do this. I don't know. I don't.

I push myself closer to Josh, and reach down and touch my fingers to his hair. I'm breathing harder now, and he is too; every few breaths I let out a little "oh!" sound and feel stupid about it. That worry passes, though.

I don't know if I can do this. I don't know if I can let go.

I'm trying to lift myself higher now; I don't know if I'm trying to move closer to this feeling or if I want to get away from it. Josh has his arm wrapped around my left leg, he's holding me down by pressing on my hip bone. This is good, because I'm starting to feel like I might flop off the table.

I'm so close, Josh. Oh my God. I don't know. I don't know.

I look down again and see the blur of sandy hair, then I reach above my head with my left hand and grab a handful of the quilt and pull it down over my eyes. He keeps hitting a trig-ger, again again again, and every time he moves it my body shakes with an involuntary convulsion. He's focusing a little too much, it's oversensitive, too much like being tickled too hard. Damn it, I'm not going to make it, I'm not going to.

If you could, just a little lower, oh God please, just a little, yes, there, right there, there, that's it, there!

I reach up with my other hand to press the balled-up wad of quilt into my face to muffle the guttural nonsense that's shrieking out of my mouth. My hips rise up off the table and I sort of fall back down to my side, and somehow he manages to hold on and keep going as each wave of it comes over me and I push my legs out straight. The feeling rises and falls and finally passes, and he's pulled away and my legs are pressed tightly to-gether again because there is NO WAY I could handle anything else. Then I feel him jumping up onto the table and curling in next to me; his arm is around my waist and he's kind of trying to pull the quilt off my face, but I don't let go because I'm too worried I'm going to laugh or burst into tears or maybe both. What has just happened here?

What have I done?

We lie quietly, on the hard table, for a long time. I slide the quilt up and see Josh looking at me as I'm forcing my breath to slow down.

"That's never happened before," I say.

"What do you mean?"

"I mean, that's . . . I've never had a . . . you know."

"You've never had one? Come on, seriously?"

"No, I've had them. Lots." I pull the quilt down over my face again and sort of laugh. "Just never as a result of something done to me by another person."

"You're kidding."

"I'm not."

"I guess I'm honored," he says.

I peek out from under the quilt and roll my eyes. I've sort of come to the conclusion that we're going to have sex now; that intercourse would be the next logical act, but the transition isn't happening. The feeling is somewhere between resignation and expectation, and I have a pressing, silly desire to run to the bathroom to call Katie for some kind of direction. Josh just lies next to me with his hand on my stomach and his head resting on his forearm.

"This table is getting a little uncomfortable," I say.

"Do you want to go up and lie down?" he asks. I nod and we sit up, and I pull the mass of the quilt over my body as Josh hops off the table.

"Want to see the drawing?"

"I think I'll wait 'til morning."

He throws the dead bolt on the door and turns out the lights, and the room is illuminated from outside by the diffused sodium glow of the city in the fog. He walks back and takes my hand, and I follow him across the studio and up the steep steps to the loft with the quilt held up against my chest. There's a futon up there, and I drop down onto it as Josh undresses and feel suddenly very tired. Josh slides in next to me and we kiss, and I find myself thinking about how his lips feel different from Patrick's and his beard, or lack of it, feels less harsh. There's a bittersweet saltiness to his mouth too, and I'm a little startled when I realize that the taste is my own.

"What?" Josh asks.

"Mm, nothing," I say, and roll onto my back, still with the quilt around me. "So, is this a hookup?"

"That's kind of an undergrad way of putting it, isn't it?"

"Is it, though?"

"I don't think so. Do you?"

"Remains to be seen," I say.

"I'd like it not to be." He leans toward me and we kiss again. "Do you have to work tomorrow?" he asks.

"What, are you trying to get me to leave?"

"No, no," he says. "I want you to stay. I was just wondering about your job."

"They are surprisingly flexible. But if my boss wants to can me, I've got another offer."

"It's good to have options, I guess."

Isn't it?

"So, tell me about Iowa," I say. My hand is on Josh's chest, and I'm sort of fixated on the way he feels different and new. Less hair. Bony ribs. I should stop making comparisons to the one other male body I've become so familiar with, but I can't.

"Ohio," Josh says. "Beautiful Ohio. It's very flat. There are many suburbs. Many malls."

"It's like that Pretenders song."

"Yes, we had to learn that song in school. All kids in Ohio do. Fourth grade. No, I'm kidding. You aren't gullible, are you?"

"I'd like to think I'm not so easily fooled," I say, and now I'm feeling very, very sleepy. My body is trained, I think, to fall into post-orgasmic slumber. "Do things blow up in Ohio?"

"What?"

"Like buses. Malls. Do the bombers go there?" My eyelids are sliding shut, and I can't stop them.

"God no," Josh says, and he gives a sort of laugh. "No one rides the bus there anyway. And this is how pathetic that place is, a friend of mine sent me this thing from the paper in Columbus. It was an article about the top-ten potential terror targets there, almost hopeful, basically an invitation to blow stuff up. It's like, 'Hello terrorists? Would you please blow up the state capitol building to give us a little validation here?' So pathetic."

"It is, kind of."

"Those assholes deserve to explode, just for being so stupid." There's an iciness to the way he says it that makes me open my eyes.

"That's a little harsh, Josh."

"No, I don't want that to happen. My folks are there, my sister, my nephews. Well, maybe it could happen to my brother-in-law, that wouldn't be such a loss. I'm kidding. Kidding. People need to wake up, though. It's coming. For real."

My eyes have closed again, and waking up is the farthest thing from my world right now. "I'm sorry, Josh," I mumble. "I'm so tired all of a sudden."

"It's alright," he says. "You sleep. Sleep well."

11

The crosstown is full when I catch it the next morning, and I end up having to stand for the whole lurching ride back to my neighborhood. I overhear people talking about something happening last night, something blowing up, and I look over some woman's shoulder at the newspaper she's reading and see that a car bomb went off at the Dallas–Fort Worth airport. Only one person was killed, apparently; the thing went off too soon, not even close to the terminal, and it isn't clear if security stopped the guy or if he just went off prematurely.

In either event, I'm glad it didn't happen here. We've had enough stress. And maybe it's a little selfish of me, but I don't think I could handle another call from Mom.

I never ride this line, and I accidentally get off one stop before I should, leaving me with a three-block walk to get to my apartment. Shit. The walk will give me enough time to call Katie, though, so I power up the phone and speed-dial.

She answers quickly. "Jess, where were you? I tried to call a million times last night."

"I was . . . busy?"

"You stayed with the artist guy."

"I did."

"All night?"

"I'm on my way home right now."

"Jessica!"

"I know." I'm blushing.

"Did you?"

"Not everything."

"But something."

"Something. You were right about something. Very right."

"Wait, which something?"

For some reason I can't bring myself to say it out loud, so I make an embarrassingly stupid lip-smacking noise.

"No! Jessica! Are you serious?"

"Serious."

"Did you reciprocate?"

"This morning, yes." It wasn't really any sort of quid pro quo; I just felt like doing it. So I went down on him, he enjoyed it, I enjoyed it, and that was that.

"You vixen."

"I'm bad."

"No. What about Patrick?"

"God, Katie, you had to say that."

"But what are you going to do?"

I sigh and sidestep the legs of a panhandler who growls something at me as I go by. "Okay, he's seeing Gretchen, or almost seeing her, so I have some justification here."

"Right. Good."

"And he's at work now, so I won't have to see him until

tonight. I mean..." Why should I feel guilty? "I'll talk to him tonight."

"Things are over," Katie says, in that buck-up way that makes me love her so much. "Moving on to something new, right?"

"Right, yes. Thank you."

"So it was good?"

"What was good?"

"You know what."

"It was very good."

"Big 'O'?"

"Katie, you're making me blush and I'm walking by homeless people. Stop it."

"I told you so."

She's doing this to make me smile, and it's working. "I know you did. Now stop."

"Love you, Jess."

"Love you too, K. Bye bye."

I keep smiling as I walk past the MacGyver store, and even on past Joe's apartment. No lights are on in his living room, but I can see the glow from his computer's screen saver at his desk. And as I start down the hill I look up at my own place, see that I left the blinds open, see the pane in my bay window that's still cracked, and then I see something that makes me gasp.

Just above my place, Patrick is standing in his own window, looking out. He lifts his hand and waves, but he's not smiling.

I'm not either, anymore. I lift my hand and let it drop, and look straight ahead to the door of our building and wish I had an umbrella or something that I could hide under to get away from his stare. I dig for my keys as I'm going up the front steps, but Patrick buzzes me in before I even have them in my hand. I wait for a moment in the entryway.

Should I go up and talk to him?

No. Not yet. I run up—like, *run* up—the stairs to my door, and I'm inside my apartment with the door closed behind me in record time. The phone rings, and I'm so sure it's Patrick I don't check the ID; maybe I shouldn't be picking this up?

"Hello?" I say, sort of feebly.

"Jessica, where were you last night?" It's Gretchen. "Was your phone off? I tried to call—"

Jesus. "Hey, Gretchen, this might not be—"

"Were you with Josh?"

"—the best time for me to talk." My answering machine is flashing the number eleven, and as I take note of this I hear footsteps coming down outside my door.

"Will you call me later? I've got—" There's a slow knock at my door.

"Yes, later. Bye."

I take a long breath and go to the door, then another breath as I open it. Patrick is standing there, shoulders slouched, looking miserable. He knows.

"Hi," I say, and I try to smile.

"Hi."

"Come in?"

He walks in but doesn't sit down. I want to hug him, but I don't; I want to tell him it's his fault, but I don't do that, either. Maybe it's my fault. Maybe it's no one's fault.

"I heard you went to that class that Josh did." The way he says it makes me feel suddenly less sympathetic.

"Yes?"

"Gretchen told me."

"Okay."

"You didn't come home last night."

"I know."

"I was worried."

Right, just try to play that card. "Well," I say. "Thank you."

"Did you spend the night with him?"

"I did." I cross my arms and take a step closer to him.

"Did you sleep with him?"

"Excuse me? Are you kidding me? Are you seriously asking me this?"

"I just want to know."

I could say no, tell him nothing really happened, and he'd believe me and feel better. But now I'm angry, and I don't want him to feel better.

"It's none of your goddamn business," I say, and now my hands are on my hips. "Are you maybe missing the irony of this? That your girlfriend or whatever she is—"

"She's not my girlfriend. She's not anything."

"—whom I'm supposed to be all buddy-buddy with now, tells *you* that *I* am doing something with someone, and you get weird about it? I'm supposed to be happy that Pat is fucking Gretchen, and then when I'm with someone, you come down here and get all weird and jealous? Am I missing something here?"

"I'm not fucking Gretchen, nothing has happened—"

"That's not the point!" I'm shaking, and I hate how my voice gets so shrill when I'm mad.

"This isn't the way things are supposed to be."

"Oh? Really? I'll tell you how things are supposed to be, then." Maybe I'm acting a little over the top here, but I'm going with it. "I'll tell you how things are. Patrick is leaving my apartment. That's how it is. Get out. That's the way things are supposed to be. Out."

"Wait, Jessica."

"Get out!" I yell, and Patrick steps to the still-open door, looking shocked. "Wait," I say.

"What?" His eyebrows lift just a little hopefully.

Just like Katie said, it's over. Keep telling yourself this. Keep telling it to yourself, and maybe it will come true.

"Give me my key."

"Come on, Jess."

"I said give me my key." He takes his keys from his pocket

and works mine off the ring, and then he looks at me and sets the key on the little bureau by my door.

"I want my key, then," he says, not very convincingly.

"Fine. Here." I grab the key and fob from my dresser and throw it at him, thinking I'll hit him with it, but it goes past his head and right through the door and clatters out on the steps.

"You throw like such a girl," Patrick says, and the way he says it makes it sound like the saddest thing I've ever heard.

"Just leave. Please." He'd better, before I lose my nerve.

Patrick shakes his head and pulls the door shut, and it's a long moment before I hear him go back up the stairs.

PART 2

12

By the beginning of summer, I've developed a new workday routine for the mornings that I'm home:

Get up.

Turn on computer to start (slow, slow, slow) boot up.

Make coffee.

Return to computer, check e-mail.

The first message that comes through this morning is from Gretchen, linking to the latest mock-up of the golf resort Web site. My first task, as her new little helper, has been to write copy for the entire site. I have a love/hate relationship with Web copy—it's so easy to write (lower standards), but it's also so tedious (a lot of filler). It's all billable time, though, and the golf people pay us very, very well and offer lots of praise, so we're both happy about it.

The second e-mail is from Mike, my *former* boss, for

whom I am now managing the Cippoletti project as a consultant. Somehow, with guidance from Gretchen, I've managed to arrange a deal where I work fewer hours and with less stress, and I end up making more money.

So I sit at my desk and listen to the early-day sounds from the street below, and I write Web copy in my robe and sweats.

There is no friendly coffee in the mornings anymore. Patrick does not come by. In fact, Patrick and I have not spoken since the key-throwing incident, just over one month ago. I thought it would last for maybe a week before one of us cracked, but then a week became two, and then two became three. And three became habit and so on and so on, until we got so good at avoiding each other that things just stayed that way.

Today there are no sounds from above. Either Patrick is being very quiet, or he didn't come home last night. I'll never know for sure, because Gretchen and I have come to an unspoken pact whereby intimate encounters with one Patrick McAvoy will never be discussed.

It's our own rule. She understands it, I understand it, we don't talk about it, and that is that.

On some days, working at home, I will motivate myself enough to rise from my chair and walk the block and a half to Tommie's Coffee Shop for something to get me going. Most days, though, like today, I just make a big pot of my so-so supermarket blend and that works well enough. I do still have one of Pat's giant mugs, and the old chipped thing with painted-on flowers has become his surrogate.

My task today in golf land is to write a bio piece on one of the course designers, a former pro who also, I've learned from my Googling, shares a name with a food writer in Portland and an orthodontist somewhere in Florida. I've never held a golf club in my life, but I've put myself through virtual golf boot camp so I can write with at least the illusion of authority. These golf people seem unnaturally obsessed. They dress kind of funny too, and it's become a running joke for Gretchen and I to e-mail the most ridiculous golfing pictures back and forth to each other. Sometimes she adds hysterical captions. She never puts them on PitchBitch, though. We can't threaten the gravy train.

A chat window from my sister pops up as I work. Her little icon, now, is a sailboat. "Are you still there?" is the message in the box.

"Still here," I type back.

"I thought you were leaving for . . . Nevada? New Mexico?"

"Nevada. Not 'til tomorrow."

"And artist guy needs what?"

"Artist guy needs slabs of rock for his new printmaking thing. Which, apparently, I am now going to be a part of."

"Nevada and slabs of rock go together how?"

"There's some special quarry there. I thought you knew everything about rocks, anyway, Ms. Geologist? And aren't you working or something?"

"Working, yes. Also: bored. Summer session gang is dutifully taking its first exam while I pretend to monitor. Are you working? Or should I say, 'consulting'?"

"Fully consulting. Trying to. I need to be disciplined, K. Seriously."

"I won't bug you. Bye. Call me before you go to Nevada."

Josh and I, in Patrick's absence, have become a something. There have been more dinners, more drawings, more nights spent over. Lately, many nights spent over. And, even though I have no recollection of us explicitly discussing it, I've somehow agreed to become the subject of his next big project.

The something that we've become has never been openly discussed, either. It's comfortable, being together, but uncomfortable too, because it never seems real. For a while, at the beginning, the lack of definition was easy to justify: I liked the feeling of getting back at Patrick somehow. It didn't take long, though, to begin to feel less like I was the one doing the manipulating, and more like the one who was being pulled along.

Josh is a force of will, and I've just been going along. Any decision to be made is done so—regardless of my input—by him. We will dine out, or we will dine in. We will have sex, or we will sleep.

We will have more sex. This I know. On this subject, Josh and I are of the same mind.

It's funny to think how following along can become a habit. I suppose there's a comfort in not needing to find your way. So I keep following.

One thing I do avoid is any sort of political discussion with Josh. He can talk, and talk, about the oppression of the lower classes, disenfranchisement of minorities, U.S. imperialism in Latin America and beyond, or any other of a multitude of leftist arguments. It's not that I disagree with what he's saying—he often makes a lot of sense—it's more that I've learned anything I have to contribute will be, more or less, ignored. It's not such a loss. I don't care so much about politics anyway, and there are better things to do than argue.

There is comfort and art, good food and great sex. Politics are avoided. This is, in summation, my relationship with Josh. Things could be worse.

Katie's online status switches to "Away," and I close the chat window so I can get back to work. Her message has reminded me, though, that I still need to get my things together for this little road trip Josh and I will be taking. He's told me we'll be "camping," so I suppose I should take my backpack? I'm not even sure where my backpack is.

I'm also not sure just what I'm getting myself into.

13

Nevada, on the return from our rock-gathering mission, is beginning to feel like it may be the biggest state in the Union, and I'm so happy I'm not the one driving through it. It took us two days of travel to get to the quarry, and after we got up this morning Josh went in and hunted through the rocks while I stayed back and read a book in our borrowed pickup. We loaded up the slabs and started back home almost four hours ago, and the sign we just passed says another 187 miles of dry mountains and sagebrush to the border. The truck is moving a little more slowly than it did on the way out—Josh got almost a thousand pounds of this special limestone for his new project—and every one of these hills turns into a crawl going up and a rush coming down.

I've gotten out of having to drive the entire trip; I don't know how to operate a stick and I'd be way too terrified about the pop-up camper we're towing, anyway. Neither of us is insured, and I don't even know the guy at the Academy who loaned Josh the truck and little trailer. I've decided that he can deal with the moral burden of being an uninsured driver, and that seems to suit him just fine.

So my job, while Josh drives, is to check maps and control the iPod hooked up to the stereo. Josh is mostly easy to please, music-wise, and only rarely suggests that I skip over any songs. I don't think he's really listening, anyway. He always seems to be off somewhere, thinking about something else.

It's hot in the pickup, but Josh won't turn the air-conditioning on because it slows us down too much on the climbs. So both windows are open and the vents are up full blast, filling the car with an airy roar. My hair keeps whipping into my face, and I remind myself to check in my backpack—now resting on half a ton of limestone in the back of the truck—for a ponytail holder the next time we stop.

I grab my Nalgene bottle from down by my feet and take a long drink of tepid water.

"You want some?" I shout over the wind and the music, wagging the bottle over the shift lever. "Josh?" He's driving one-handed, looking off up the road, with his other arm resting in the open window. "Josh?"

"What?" He blinks and glances over at me. "Oh. Sure. Thank you." He takes a sip, then another, and with water dripping from his chin he hands the bottle back to me.

I want to call Katie, here, on the road in the rolling middle of nowhere, but Josh had badgered me into not bringing my cell. His argument was that we needed to get capital-A *Away,* but one apparently cannot get *Away* when everyone you know comes *With* in the form of a stored contacts list.

Maybe he has a point. I'd still like to talk to my sister, though, if for nothing more than to fill my ear with something other than the sound of rushing air.

We bottom out on a descent and begin another long

climb on the highway, and I can feel the way the weight of the trailer slows us down. I lean forward to look at it in the side mirror, but what I see makes me let out a little yelp: there's a dark car with flashing lights right behind us.

"Josh! Josh! There's a—" My chest is tight and I'm pointing at the mirror like an idiot. "Josh!"

He just looks at me. "Huh?"

"There's a . . . it's the police!"

Now he leans forward and looks into his own mirror. "Oh yeah," he says. Then he holds his arm out of the window and makes a lazy waving motion, and keeps driving.

"What are you doing?" I ask. I'm simultaneously feeling frantic about the no insurance thing and hating that this reaction is inherited completely from my mother.

"We'll stop at the top," Josh says, and the two minutes it takes us to get to the next crest feel like a year. Josh coasts to a halt on the wide shoulder and pulls the parking brake, then he turns down the stereo and grabs his battered leather day planner from the storage console between our seats.

"See if there's any registration or anything in the glove box," Josh says to me as he unzips the planner. He's taking out his passport and a folded-up piece of paper just as the trooper comes up to his window. The cop is younger, and cute, but he has his hand resting on the black pistol at his hip, which makes me nervous and kills any impression of cuteness.

"Afternoon," he says, leaning down to peer in at me before straightening up to speak with Josh. "Sir, are you aware you were going eighty-eight miles an hour back there?"

"You're kidding," Josh says as he hands over the passport and paper. "This truck goes that fast?" The cop laughs as he unfolds the paper and looks at it.

"What is this?"

"That's my U.K. driver's permit," Josh says. Complete calm. "I live in England."

The cop cocks his head and looks at it for a moment.

"Can I see your registration, Mr."—he squints as he looks at the paper again—"Hadden? Proof of insurance?"

"She's looking," Josh says, gesturing toward me with his chin. All I can seem to find in the mess of papers in the glove compartment are service receipts and fast food napkins and junk mail addressed to a Mr. Huai Liu Wang. "This isn't actually our truck."

"This isn't your vehicle?"

"I borrowed it from a colleague."

There's a long pause, and the cop looks at Josh's passport.

"You know I was behind you there for a while," he says.

"Yeah, I couldn't stop on the uphill, we'd never get going again." Josh looks over his shoulder. "Heavy. Heavy load."

"What have you got in there?"

"Limestone," Josh says. "I'm an artist." As if that explains everything. "You want to take a look?"

"Sure," the cop says, moving his hand back to the holster. "Why don't you step out."

Josh opens his door and gets out of the truck, taking his open planner with him, and he and the cop walk to the back of the truck, leaving me with only the steady ding-ding-ding of the door-open chime. There's a thump as the topper hatch is opened, and I glance back to see Josh gesturing as they talk. The chime is driving me crazy, but I can't quite reach across to the driver's side door, so I pull the key from the ignition and hope the sudden quiet doesn't somehow disrupt whatever Josh is doing back there to talk his way out of the trouble we're in. I hear the murmur of their voices, manly and low, punctuated by occasional laughter and the rush of a passing semi.

After ten minutes of distracting myself by reading the owner's manual and looking at more of Mr. Wang's mail—sometimes he's addressed as Harry Wang—the hatch to the topper bangs closed, and Josh wordlessly climbs back up into the driver's seat and pulls the door shut behind him. He leans forward and looks in the side mirror as he starts the engine, and waves as our trooper pulls past us in his dark patrol car. I see the cop raise his hand to us as he speeds off down the hill.

I'm almost holding my breath. "How bad is it?" I ask.

"What?" Josh puts the truck in gear and we slowly creep forward before the hill grabs us and starts to pull us along.

"Ticket? Citation?"

"No ticket. I took care of it."

"What do you mean?"

"I mean I took care of it."

"How?"

"How about, there was a transaction conducted."

I think I know what he means, but I can't believe it. "Explain?"

"I paid him off."

"Are you kidding me?" My mouth is hanging open; the ease with which he's accomplished this is like a weird magnetic force. I'm pulled and repelled at the same time.

"No," he says, and he glances over to the mirror again as a big truck passes us. "You've never paid off the police before?"

"You're serious. You just bribed that cop."

Josh looks at me and laughs. "You're just like my sister."

"What is that supposed to mean?"

"You're just—" There's a pause.

"What?"

"Naïve isn't the right word," he says.

"I'm not naïve." Unless "naïve" means being unfamiliar with paying off people of authority. I can't believe this.

"I didn't say you were." Josh downshifts as we start up the next hill. "That's just, you know, that's how the world works, Jessica."

"Through bribes?"

"Pretty much. Goods and services. We both had something the other wanted. Monetary exchange. Bribery is like the perfect form of capitalism. The most refined. That's why the Republicans love it so much."

I think this is going to lead into one of Josh's big political diatribes, but he doesn't say anything else, and the only sound left in the absence of his voice is the whine of the truck's engine as we struggle up the hill with cars blowing past us.

"Well, how much was it?" I ask. "What did you give him?"

"Two hundred dollars."

"Josh!"

"Easier to swallow than being arrested for driving a car that isn't mine with no insurance," he says, and he looks at me and lifts his shoulders into a little shrug. "And who would have driven you home?"

I shake my head. "You're nothing like *my* sister," I say.

We stop for the night at the same forest service campground we used on the way out. The perfect campsite we had the first time has been taken by some survivalist type and his dog, so we drive a little farther on the seriously washed-out dirt road to another vacant fire pit and Josh gets busy setting up the trailer. We're in the shadow of a big pine-covered hill, and I sit on a splintered picnic table with my fleece jacket pulled down over my knees as I watch him work. He pulls levers and turns cranks and adjusts jacks, and soon the wings of our tiny borrowed home fold open and that's that.

I hop up the pull-out step and climb inside to start putting the kitchen together while Josh pulls our stuff out of the back of the truck. Maybe Dad is onto something with this whole RV lifestyle. In spite of the dank old canvas smell, I've found myself starting to like this thing. My eyes adapt to the dusk, and I just stand in the darkness with my arms folded and listen to the rush of the stream running next to our campsite.

The flimsy camper door clatters behind me and I look to see Josh stepping in with a sleeping bag in each hand and a backpack slung from his slender shoulders. I take one of the bags from him and raise my hand and click on the camper's little overhead lamp, but Josh reaches up and turns it right back off and we stand, facing each other, close in the dark. I hear the gurgling noise of the stream and my pulse in my neck and a mosquito keening around somewhere close to our heads, then his arms are around me and mine around him and we fall together in a controlled descent to the slide-out bed closest to the truck.

Josh's stubble from three days of travel burns my chin as we kiss, and I'm cold as he pulls up my jacket and tee shirt. His hands are on my chest, and I'm sure he can feel me shivering.

"Sleeping bag?" he asks.

"Yes," I say, and I undress in the chilly night air while he works at pulling the bag from its nylon storage sack. He throws the unzipped bag over me and climbs under too, and I help him play catch-up with the removal of his clothes.

Sex with Josh is not like anything I've experienced with any other man. Not better, really, or worse; just very, very different. Well, maybe it is a little bit on the "better" end of the scale. Physically, anyway. Sometimes there's a startling aggression to his movement; not meanness, really, but a frenzied spasm that usually leaves me hunting for a headboard or wall to push against for support. Emotionally, though, there's always a sort of detachment that intrigues me and infuriates me; there are no hints to what he's thinking or feeling in the grunting breaths in my ear or the scratch of his beard on my neck and cheek. But by wrapping myself around him in every sense—legs, arms, and everything else—I've learned to give myself the advantage in this embrace. Josh can only push away from me so much before giving up and pushing back in again.

And again, until, with a gasp, it's over.

"Did you?" he asks, with his face pressed into my right shoulder.

I shake my head, and he kisses my neck and jockeys his weight to begin his dutiful downward journey. I wrap my arm around him, though, and don't let him go; his weight and warmth on my body is perfect right now.

"Don't," I say. "I don't always need to."

"You sure?"

"It's nice to be right here. Just lie with me here."

Did you? They've become my two favorite words. This anticipated, postcoital question is the window, the one moment of insecurity I ever get to see in Josh. Hearing his vulnerability in this nightly, breathy query is climax enough. A real one will never happen—not like that, anyway—and if it did, I wouldn't tell him.

If I lost that little window, what would be the point?

Besides, I'll take care of that later, myself, when Josh is asleep. For now, though, we've got the stream, the intermittent whine of a mosquito, and the plastic crumple of the sleeping bag as it lifts and falls with our breathing. Josh is three hundred miles west, thinking about his rock and paper and ink, and I'm here, with my own thoughts.

It's hard not to make comparisons. I think of Jason, my boyfriend from school. Maybe he fell a little lower on the scale. He didn't have much experience, I guess, and maybe, maybe he seemed to care too much? Lots of pausing, lots of staring in the eyes; many, many are-you-okays and is-that-alrights. Like every night was prom night. But he was sweet, and funny, and smart, and I guess he did love me for more than the fact that I liked him too. So we did it, and did it, and he got better (though I never had the heart to tell him that in the end, a few times, when I wasn't doing it with him, I was doing it with someone else). Until the night when, after days of subtle suggestion on my part, he finally made a determined attempt at being "rough" and "adventurous" and the ohh-babys and you-like-that-huh-do-yas became a little too much to bear.

It probably did hurt him a little bit when I started to laugh. Jason, I'm truly sorry for that.

And then there was Patrick.

Oh, Patrick.

I shouldn't think about him right now. I really shouldn't. And I won't, because Josh is sliding himself out from under the spread-open sleeping bag and pulling on his pants.

"You ready for something to eat?" Josh asks.

"Yes," I say, sitting up and feeling around by my feet to try to make sense of the clothes tangled up down there. "Will you have some wine?"

"You're corrupting me."

"Right."

"You're fogging my mind."

"Ha."

"Yes," he says, and I can see in the dark how the whiteness of his tee shirt slides over his head and down his body. "I will have some wine. Are you ready for the light?"

"Hold on," I say, and I hold up a wad of sleeping bag to cover my eyes. "Okay, ready."

The switch snaps on, and I slowly pull away the sleeping bag and blink my eyes open. Josh crouches down to get something from the storage cabinet under the sink, and a moth flits in a crazy orbit around the light above his head.

"Hey, Josh?"

He doesn't look up. "Yes?"

"If you took a picture of that moth, like a long exposure, a really long exposure, what would it look like?"

He stops banging around in the cabinet and turns his head to look at the moth. He looks at me and goes back to feeling under the sink. I can see him smiling.

This smile, I think, means approval. And I think I'm pleased by it.

He finally pulls a dented pot from the cabinet and begins

filling it with water from the little hand-operated pump over the sink. Josh is, without question, the most unimaginative cook I've ever met. He's completely fearless dining out—he'll order anything, and always actually seems to enjoy it—but when it comes to making his own food, I've only ever seen him wrap something in a tortilla or boil something and cover it with sauce from a jar. We've had spaghetti the previous two nights, and I'm not going out on a limb when I predict we'll be having it again. Out here, though, on our adventure, the pasta works and, with the addition of wine, it makes a nice, rustic, camping-trip-appropriate meal, I guess.

I straighten the inside-out sleeve of my jacket and pull it on while Josh works at igniting the burner on the tiny green campstove, and I jump down from the camper and dare myself to take a step beyond the feeble ring of luminescence we've cast and out into the real night. It's seriously *dark* out here, and cold, and my hands are clutched in a prayerful way up under my chin with my forearms tight to my chest as I shuffle toward the truck. I'm expecting a bear or mountain lion or guy who lives in his truck to pounce on me at any moment, but I make it to the back of the truck and get the topper hatch unlatched without being murdered. Crawling around inside, there's a warm density to the limestone under me as I hunt for my backpack and the duffel bag with the last two bottles of wine; if it was a little softer I think I could curl up and go to sleep in here. Instead I transfer the bottles into my pack, and before I crawl all the way out of the bed of the truck I stop and spy on Josh for a moment through the mosquito screen and vinyl window haze of the camper. His arms are crossed and he's holding a really long wooden spoon, but he's only staring into the pot of not-yet boiling water.

Back in the camper, it's my turn to feel around in the cabinet under the sink until I find two plastic party cups with the words "OSWALD'S KAMPER KORNER" printed on them, and then I get one of the bottles from my backpack and unscrew the lid. I've become a screw-top convert, I think.

"Does the 'K' make it more appealing?" I ask out loud. "Is it so outlandish to spell campground with a 'K' that a weary traveler would choose Oswald's over the many other campgrounds nearby?"

Josh continues to stare into the now-steaming pot of water.

"It's like that with used car lots too," I go on.

Finally, Josh speaks. "You write copy, what do you think?" he says, without looking at me. I believe this signals disapproval, but I reply anyway.

"I think it's absolutely stupid." Pretty much like I'm feeling right now, so I nearly fill both cups and set one by Josh on the counter and take a substantial slug from the other as I slide myself into the tiny dinette bench seat.

We don't say much more as Josh cooks the pasta; he takes sporadic drinks from his cup, and I take more frequent ones. When I unscrew the bottle again for a refill, Josh turns to look and gives a half-smile.

"Maybe I need to catch up," he says. Does he feel bad about that copywriting remark?

"Get working," I say.

"Dinner first. Dinner. I need something in my stomach if I'm going to keep up with you."

He brings two paper plates covered with noodles and smears of bright red sauce and sits down across from me. We eat, and talk, and drink, and he does indeed work on catching up—catching up so well that by the time we're finished eating, I'm reaching for the second bottle.

"So," I say as I crack open the cap, "just what is happening Monday?"

"Well, if they have the scanner moved into my studio, we'll figure out how to use the thing, and we'll start to take some pictures of you. It should only take a few days. Maybe a week. Are you sure you're in?"

"I'm sure," I say. Josh's new project, or at least as much as he's described to me, is something nebulous involving maps and the human body. My human body. And apparently my body needs to be imaged in three dimensions for it to work.

"We'll start with your foot, or your leg, or something."

"Whatever," I say.

"You sure it's okay with your work schedule?"

"Work is very flexible for me now."

"I'm so glad you're doing this, Jess." He smiles. "Really. You're perfect."

"Thanks?"

"You are."

"Well, thank you," I say, and I'm sure I'm blushing a little. "Now, there's something that I want to know."

"What's that?"

"How exactly am I like your sister?"

"Jessica, you're not—" He laughs—a small laugh, almost bitter—as he stacks my soggy plate on top of his own and puts them into the plastic grocery bag we're using for trash. "You're not really like her. Not at all."

"What made you say that, though?"

Josh smiles and shakes his head. "I'm going to get myself in trouble no matter what I tell you," he says. His cheeks, I've discovered, turn crimson when he drinks, and they're gaining color as we speak. "Emily has kind of a simple view of things—" I open my mouth to respond, but Josh holds up his hand. "I did not, did not say you were simple. See? I told you I'd get into trouble."

"Just how are we alike, then? I want to know more about Emily."

"Well, you are certainly unlike her in that she is not a cynic."

"I'm a cynic?"

"I'd say you have a highly tuned sense of cynicism, yes."

I smile. "I think you may have just complimented me. Was that a compliment?"

"You are what you are," Josh says, and I pour him some

more wine. "She's very caring. Really, really kind. Maybe to a fault."

"Am I like her that way?"

Josh smirks and says nothing, and I stick my tongue out at him.

"Okay," I say. "More. Emily. She has kids? A husband?"

"All of the above." Josh gets his backpack from the camper floor, pulls his day planner from inside, and takes out a photo. "This is them," he says as he slides the picture over the table to me. It's a cheap studio photo; the four of them are wearing matching white polo shirts. The kids, a pair of blond boys who look younger than Mike's sons, are adorable, and I'm surprised by how pretty and young Josh's sister looks. The husband is blond too, with a square jaw and a toothy smile and a softening build that has former-high-school-football-player written all over it.

"Really cute kids," I say. "But hubby looks a little—"

"He's an asshole," Josh says, and his voice goes hard. "Complete, fucking asshole." Josh rarely swears, and hearing the sharpness in his voice is a bit of a surprise.

"How so?"

"He's so . . . they're so right-wing. Tim's crazy. That's him. He thinks I am a freak." Josh finishes his wine in two big gulps.

"Not a good freak."

"Nooo. Like, deviant. Like, should be in jail. I didn't even tell Em about my last show." He starts to laugh. "You want to know a good way to get the crap beaten out of you?" I don't, really, but I suspect Josh is going to tell me anyway, and I am correct. "Suggest to your right-wing brother-in-law that you might want to take nude photos of him. That went over really well, like, almost-got-me-punched-in-the-face well." He sighs. "I just don't know how she got sucked into it."

"Is it really so bad?" I ask.

"He's a . . . they're just . . . He's such an asshole."

"She must see something in him."

"No, Jess, no." Josh has his elbow on the table and he rubs his temples with his fingers as he talks. "I just don't know how Emily got . . . how it even happened."

"There are relationships like that, Josh. Just because it doesn't make any sense to you, or because you can't see why she's so into him—"

He takes his hand away from his face and stares at me with reddening eyes. "He treats her like shit, Jessica. He treats her like an idiot. They're into that whole 'a woman's place is in the home' thing. Tim is the head of the household. Undisputed. He makes the paycheck, she takes care of the house and kids. Why? Why? She dropped out of college to marry him, you know? Can you believe that?"

"Is she happy, though? Does she love him?"

Josh rubs his face with his hand again. "How could anyone be happy in that situation? My sister? Would you be happy like that?"

"I'm not her, Josh. I can't say."

"Yes. Yes." He rests with his face in his hand for a long time, looking deflated.

"Okay," I say. "Let's talk about art then." This has the intended effect, and Josh perks right up.

"Art? That's something I can talk about. Which art?"

"Your art. Your prints. This new project. And my place in it."

"Your place. So. This scanner, the scanner we're renting . . . we had to rent the really good one from the university. The one at the Academy didn't have a high enough resolution. So this other one, this very expensive, very precise machine, it's going to take pictures of you."

"Okay."

"But not like, pictures, exactly . . . ?" Josh rests his chin in his palm again, and he's gesturing through the air with his other hand. "It records your shape. It's a three-dimensional scanner. So it's like, you'll be there…" His eyes are closed, and his hand, out in front of him, is still. He's quiet for a long time, thinking, or maybe passed out.

"I'm so tired," he finally says. He puts his hand on the table and opens his eyes.

"We had a long day," I say. "You did. All that driving." I get up and come around to help him stand. "Let's go to bed."

Josh lurches to his feet, and we brush the purple stains from the wine out of our teeth and off of our tongues, zip the sleeping bags together, and turn out the overhead lamp. It isn't long before snores and the sound of the rushing water are my last companions in the night, and I try not to shake the camper too severely as I get myself to sleep.

14

The scanner is not yet set up Monday morning. Gert, Josh's Dutch and very tall grad student, is next to me in the studio, leaning over the table I'm sitting on and reading a thick manual in a three-ring binder while some men behind him uncrate what I'm assuming to be parts of this very expensive scanning machine.

"I think we scan the foot first, Doc," Gert says as he looks up from the pages. "Or maybe the knee. Doc? You seen the doctor, Jess?"

My name, spoken with Gert's severe accent, comes out sounding like *Chiss.*

"He was just here," I say.

"We find the doctor," he says, and rises up like a big spindly insect and makes his way around the men with the crates and out the door. If I had to guess, I'd say Gert is about nine or ten feet tall, but I might be exaggerating.

He's thin like a stick with his tight tee shirts and sloppy Euro-hair, and I sometimes wish he would wear a fanny pack—even just once—to complete my perfect mental image. But he's always been nice to me, if maybe a little stern, and I think the way he calls Josh "Doctor" is sort of sweet.

I need to catch up with Gretchen about the press release I wrote last week for the golf vacations people. Normally I'd step out of the studio to make the call, but since Josh is not here to lecture me about my phone, I get it from my bag and dial. It rings long enough that I think I'll be leaving a voice mail, but then there's a fumbling, windy crackle in my ear and I hear Gretchen's voice.

"Hey, Jessica," she says, and I can hear her breathing and the sounds of traffic. "How was your rock expedition or whatever it was?"

"Mission accomplished," I say.

"Were there artistic encounters? Encounters with the artist?"

"That mission was also accomplished."

"Multiple missions? I want details. Was the camper wobbly?"

I can hear Josh and Gert and some other person talking in the hallway. "There was some squeaking," I say. "Details later."

"That means I get to see you? Today?"

I look down at the men kneeling next to the pallets and torn-away shrink-wrap and white metal scanner parts. "It's going to be a couple hours before they need me here, at least. Are you at HQ?"

"I'm just going up the stairs now."

I look over and see Josh and Gert are standing in the studio doorway. Josh is talking to someone I can't see in the hall.

"Yes," he says, gesturing at the men and parts on the floor. "Okay. I'll call you when they have it put together." Gert nods, arms crossed, and I hear the person in the hall say something I can't make out. I feel Josh looking at me, probably pissed off that I'm talking on the phone in his sacrosanct little workspace.

"I'll be over in a bit," I say. "See ya." Josh raises his eyebrow, walking toward me, as I snap the phone shut and drop it back into my bag.

"Important?" Josh says, and the tone of his voice makes me feel like *I'm* the one who needs to be pissed here.

"Just my job, which you may or may not consider to be important."

"I wasn't questioning the importance of your job."

"Right," I say, and I reach in the bag again and almost pull out the phone just to make him angry, but I don't. "Mmhmm. So, how long are these guys going to take? Do you really need me here right now?"

One of the guys working on the scanner has noticed our little spat, but he's trying to act like he doesn't.

"Well?" Josh says to him.

"Maybe, probably set up by lunchtime," the guy says.

Josh turns back to me. "I was thinking I could do a few sketches while they finish."

"No," I say, and I grab my bag and slide off the table. "I'm going to do some work."

"What's the point of going if you have to turn around and come right back?"

"I'll see you at one," I say, and I don't look back as I head out into the hall.

PitchBitch HQ—otherwise known as Gretchen's tiny studio apartment in the Lower Haight—may possess the most cluttered workspace on earth. The place is *all* workspace, really; there are boxes and papers and whiteboards; maps and posters are tacked to the walls and everything is golf, golf, golf. Her desk sports both a Mac and a PC, and she jokes that, while the Mac is used exclusively for design, the PC is only used for shopping and to surf for porn. As I've gotten to know Gretchen better, though, I'm starting to think that she may not be joking about the porn.

"So, I have to know," she says, facing me across the papers in our laps as we sit cross-legged on the floor. "Was it vigorous? It always sounds like he's so—"

"Gretchen! Give it a rest!" I'm laughing, but still.

"No, really, I love hearing about when he goes all crazy."

"He typically goes crazy. Like I tell you every time."

"So, it was vigorous."

"Jesus, Gretchen."

"So did anything happen, you know, while driving?" She raises her eyebrows and makes an "O" shape with her mouth.

"Stop it. No. Are you doing this just to embarrass me?"

"No, I just like hearing about it. So, something did happen while driving."

"No. Stop it! Now. Golf. Just golf."

"You're so lame, Jessica," she says, and she picks up a manila folder from the floor and starts to look through it. What I'm not telling her is that I did actually attempt going down on Josh while he was driving. It was the first day of our trip, and I accidentally knocked the car out of gear with my arm, causing a sudden roar in the truck's engine and panic in its passengers (not to mention a complete deflation of my bravado and his erection).

I did not attempt this again.

Now Gretchen is handing me papers and pictures and floor plans; apparently my next high-paying task for this golf vacation empire is to write some copy for a lodging brochure. Gretchen gives me more papers.

"There's the...yeah, that's the one bedroom unit," she says, "and you've got the pictures of the two bedroom." I must look confused as I look down into my lap. "You...yes, you do, they're right there. I only have drawings of the three and four, no photos. They aren't finished yet, or unfurnished, or something."

"They all look the same," I say.

"Yeah, I figured you could work with this. Work the angles, Jess. Hype the bedrooms. Granite counters. Upsell, upsell."

"What about the lonely wives and children, robbed of their menfolk by this wicked game?"

"Ah, right," she says. I'm handed more maps and floor plans. "There are arcades. Gyms. The day spa. Pools. Restaurants. A bar. Work it all in there. It's not all about the wicked game."

"I can come up with something, I think."

"Knew you could. How's it going with the bike clothes people?"

"They're awesome, they love me," I say. The consulting for Mike has been going perfectly. With Gretchen's guidance and the time-tracking and billing program she's set me up with, I send Mike invoices, and, in return, he sends me checks. For this, I suppose I can put up with the questions about my sex life.

"Nice."

"So nice. And they just sent me a box of like twenty sport tops."

"To keep?"

"Yep, demos. Do you want to take some? They're cute."

"Will they fit me?"

"You can take a look. The only catch is you have to fill out a product feedback report."

"I can work with that." Gretchen straightens up all the papers in her lap, lifts them a couple inches, and drops them. She does this two more times. "Should we get some lunch?"

"Oh," I start, and I pause as if I'm really considering it. "I need to get back to the studio for this scanner thing."

"Bummer."

Despite the fact that I'm really hungry, the truth of the matter is that I need to stop by my apartment to check messages and get some clothes, because yes, yes, I will be spending the night at Josh's again tonight. I'll forget about being angry, I'll forget the nagging wish to be in my own bed for a night, and I'll forget that I want to listen for Patrick's footsteps above me. I'll forget these things, and remember some others, and stay at the studio.

There is, for better or worse, a routine established with Josh. And forgetting things has become part of the routine.

It isn't a long walk to my place from Gretchen's neighborhood, and I'm relieved to see that Pat's blinds are shut as I come down the hill. The way up the stairs feels cold, and I'm sort of sad that Danny doesn't jump out of his door to pick me up or kiss me or even just say hello as I go past. My apartment, when I finally get the key to move the dead bolt so I can enter, seems dark and too quiet. The bed is made. There are no books on the floor next to the couch. If my plants could make me feel guilty for neglecting them, I suspect they would.

There's a message from Amy on my answering machine. "Where have you been, Jess?" she asks. "Call me?"

Unlike houseplants, friends can make you feel guilty for real.

There isn't much I need to take, really; some underwear and a skirt will travel nicely in my now heavy-with-golf-resort-plans bag, and I think I have some apples in my fridge that are probably still edible. I'll grab a couple for the bus ride back.

I should call Amy. I need to call Katie too. I have enough time, I think—it's only a little past noon—so I get my phone and curl up on my couch. I imagine I hear something upstairs, but it's nothing. Katie gets the call first.

"Jess Z.," she says, a little eagerly and after barely a ring. "What's up?"

"Not much. Needed to talk to you. Needed."

"I needed to talk to you too. I missed you."

"I missed you too."

"How was camping?"

"Camping was. We drove, we camped."

"Are you okay?"

"I don't know."

"What happened?"

"We drove, and camped, and got some rocks. Oh, and Josh bribed a state trooper."

"Rebel. He got away with it?"

"Very easily. Very smoothly."

"Jess, what's wrong? I can hear it."

"I don't."

"Is it him?"

"I don't know?"

"Was there sex?"

"Oh God. Much sex. Extraordinary sex. We pulled over, just for that. Rest stops. Very restful." I tell her about accidentally taking the car out of gear at seventy miles per hour—complete with an imitation of the sound of the engine and the way Josh shouted "Shit!"—and my sister laughs and laughs.

"Oh, Jessica," she says. "That's so perfect. I hate doing that. On the road, I mean. Not the gear thing. I mean, I wouldn't know."

"I doubt I ever will again."

"That's a great story, though."

"It wasn't so great at the time."

"So what is it? Is it him? Is that why you're upset?"

I don't say anything for a moment.

"Jess?"

"He's very intense."

"You mean sexually?"

"I mean, everything."

"Well, he's an artist, right? Isn't that part of the deal?"

"He gets bent out of shape about weird things."

"Like?"

"Like he doesn't like me having my phone."

Now Katie is quiet.

"I don't get it?" she finally says.

"Seriously. It started in his studio. That I guess I understand, but then like other places, you know, we'd go out, and it's not like I'm using it blatantly, or anything—"

"Come on, Jess. You're bad about that."

"No, I'm being serious. I'm not that bad, but he's always like, 'Why do you take that thing everywhere with you?' "

"Why *do* you take it everywhere with you?"

"Don't do the stupid bit with me, Katie. I need it for work. I need to call you. And it's at the point where I feel weird about taking a call, even an important call."

"Huh."

"Yeah. But it's more than that. More than phones. We got pulled over, right? And he just pays this cop two hundred dollars—"

"Two hundred!"

"Yeah, I know. He paid the cop, and then it was like, nothing. No big deal. He didn't even mention it when he got back in the car. Not because he was ashamed about it or anything, it was just no big deal. Normal. Routine."

"So, that freaks you out?"

"Not the bribe, just the way he dealt with it. He was so smooth about it. Effortless. Any other guy, any other guy I know, anyway, would have bragged about getting away with it or something."

"Yeah, I know what you mean."

"And he's never wrong about anything."

"Oh no, that posture."

"No, I'm not joking. I mean, literally, he's never wrong about anything. Like, factually. He's like an encyclopedia. I've stopped even trying to argue details with him. He's a genius like that."

"Crazy."

"Yes, so crazy. And even more, he's just, Jesus, I don't

want to say manipulative. But people do what he wants. I do what he wants."

"That's a scary feeling," Katie says, and through the phone I can hear her slurping the dregs of something from a straw, probably one of her beloved iced coffee drinks.

"It is scary."

"But a little exciting too. It's like you're along for the ride."

"Yes, Katie, that's it, that's it exactly." And this is why I love my sister so.

"But there's the sex too."

"Don't even get me started."

"Do you feel like he's making you do that?"

"God, no," I say. "I want to do that all on my own." And we laugh.

I'm five minutes late getting back to the studio, but it's no big deal. Josh and Gert are too involved with their newly assembled toy to even notice my entry. It looks like some shiny white piece of medical equipment, this scanner, with its keyboard and monitor and humming fan. There's a big metal arm extended over the table, and Josh is seated in front of its display with Gert looking over his shoulder. It takes my bag dropping by the bathroom door to make them look up.

"There she is," Gert says. "Hey, Jess."

"Is it ready?" I ask. I go to the kitchen and get myself a glass from one of Josh's nearly empty cupboards and fill it with water from the filtered carafe he keeps in the refrigerator.

"It's ready," Josh says, turning some knob next to the display. "Are you?"

"Guess so."

Gert holds my glass as I hop up onto the table. He's got a pillow there for me, and some blocks of green foam.

"We start with the knee today," he says. "You want to

take off the pants, or just pull up?" Gert says this with no emotion at all, purely clinical, and as I pull up the right leg of my pants—they're sort of baggy and I can work the leg all the way up to the middle of my thigh—I suddenly realize that this towering Dutchman is going to, over the next week or so, be viewing every dimple, pore, and crevice on my body in sub-millimeter resolution.

"Lie back, Jess. The foam is for under the knee."

"Thank you, Nurse Gert." I stay up on my elbows so I can watch what's going on.

Gert doesn't crack a hint of a smile as he places a tiny white sticker a few inches above my knee. "We being serious here now, Jess. Doc, can you give me the reference light?"

I guess there could be worse people to see me totally naked. At least he takes it seriously.

Josh presses a button in the control panel, and a dot of red light appears on the table next to me. Gert lowers the arm until it's about a foot above my leg, moves it around until the light lines up with the little sticker, and nods.

"Okay, Jess, you got to lie back all the way now. Put this on." He hands me what looks like the type of eyeshades people wear on long plane rides, and points up to a pair of lenses on the underside of the arm. "Strong lasers," he says.

That's good enough for me. I put on the eyeshades and let myself down to the pillow.

The scanning procedure, at least in this trial run, seems very, very boring. For me, at least. Josh and Gert speak of grids and reference lights; axis X and axis Y. There are beeps and whirring sounds; joy at good results and dismay at poor ones. If it weren't for all this talking, I might fall asleep.

"There's still some blur," I hear Gert say.

"She needs to be really still. Can you try not to breathe this time, Jess?" Josh asks.

Well, sure, Josh. I can try that.

After maybe an hour, it seems to be done. Josh and his

student seem happy, excited even, and again they're so distracted that I have to ask them if I can finally take off the eyeshades.

"Oh, yeah, Jess, sorry," Gert says. "Stay up there for a second, though, there's a chance we might run one more."

"Let me go find Hoffman," Josh says. "I want to see what he thinks about the resolution."

I pull off the shades and sit up, blinking at how bright the room seems. Josh takes off, leaving the door open behind him, and Gert types away at the keyboard on the scanner. There's some cheesy pop music coming from one of the other studios, and when my eyes adjust enough and I look over at Gert, I see he's just barely bobbing his head with the music while staring at the monitor.

"You're so busted," I say.

"What?"

"I saw you moving to the beat."

"In Holland boys must learn rhythm during physical education," he says without smiling or shifting his eyes from the screen. "It's compulsory."

"Uh, okay," I say. Gert may be a real-life weirdo.

Then he does look at me, and he does smile, possibly the first smile I've ever seen out of him. "It's a joke, Jess. You know, to be funny."

I'd throw the pillow at him, but I'm worried I'd break the scanner.

Josh sticks his head in the door. "It's okay, we don't need to do another one," he calls. "I'll be right back."

"You believed me," Gert says after Josh is gone.

"You're mean." I move myself over to the edge of the table to get down. Gert's backpack is there, a very hip-looking leather and chrome buckles kind of thing, and as I slide myself toward the side I accidentally knock it off the table. There's a clattering sound as it hits the floor.

"Shit," I say. "Sorry." I look down and realize what the sound was: a box of 100cc syringes has come out of the top of the pack and spilled its contents out across the floor. "Oh. Um."

The funny little bonding levity I was just feeling is gone; Gert shooting heroin is a secret I really did not want to know about. I stay up on the table, and suddenly feel very uncomfortable with the thought of him seeing me naked.

"It's okay," Gert says, coming over to scoop up the syringes and get them back into the box. He stands up with a handful of them and holds them out to me, right up in front of my face, and I recoil.

"You need some clean needles?"

"No, no."

"Jess," he says. *Chiss*. Then I realize he's pulling up the side of his tee shirt, and there's a little pager-like thing clipped onto his belt.

"What is that?" I ask.

"It's an insulin pump."

"Oh, God, Gert, I'm sorry."

"Yeah, I know what you were thinking. And I am from Holland and all that."

"Stop it, I'm sorry."

"I know you are." And he offers his hand to help me down from the table.

Spaghetti was fine for the camping trip and all, but I don't think I could handle it one more night. So I lobby for takeout; there's a Chinese place we've discovered less than a block away that has the most sublime Mu Shu crepes. I lobby hard, and win.

We eat quietly, me reading my golf resort materials and Josh the scanner manual. I've poured myself a glass of wine, but I'm feeling kind of worn out and dehydrated, and it seems like Josh is taking more sips from it than I am.

"Sorry," he says when I give him a funny look. "It looked like, you know, you weren't having much."

I think I'm turning him. Ha!

"You finish it," I say.

Josh's only response is to pull the glass over to his side of the table.

In the bathroom I strip down to my underwear. Wash face, brush teeth, don Josh's high school "scholar athlete" tee shirt that has become my sleepy-time uniform for nights spent here at the studio.

Which, as noted, has been most nights lately.

I get my folder of resort specs from the table and start up the steps to the loft and Josh tells me he'll be up in a little bit. There's a cute halogen lamp next to my side of the futon, and the pillows are of such a perfect density that I can prop myself up and not worry about slouching or slipping down. It's ideal. I lean back with my pile of photos and look at massage tables and pool slides and a restaurant right by the tenth tee.

After twenty minutes of taking mental notes on the pictures, I hear Josh climbing up into the loft. He's undressed too, down to a dark gray pair of briefs. I keep looking at my golf stuff, sort of. He has a stretching routine he does every night—touching toes, locking wrists, raising arms. Maybe it's something like yoga, but the cadence seems more like he learned it by watching a fitness show on public television. He stretches, with his back to me, and I watch the muscles beneath the skin of the lean body I've come to know.

When he's done, he turns and paces at the foot of the bed, looking at me. It's almost feline, the way he's moving. That seems like a silly way to describe it, but it's what comes to my mind. And the resort plans aren't giving me much to hide behind.

"You should take off your clothes," he says. Pacing.

I neaten up the papers across my chest and stomach, put the folder down on the floor, and reach for the lamp.

"Leave that on," he says. He's stopped moving.

I roll back to look at him. My arms are close to my sides; my legs are closed.

"Does the light have to stay?"

"Take off that shirt. Your panties. Take them off."

That ridiculous word, "panties," coming from his mouth, so seriously, almost makes me laugh. But I don't.

"That doesn't seem quite fair. What about you?"

"I'm not talking about me. Take them off."

I do, and he begins to pace again. Looking. He raises his arms over his head and stretches his neck and shoulders. My legs stay closed, and all the time he's looking.

"Roll over," he says.

"Josh..."

"Roll over. Onto your stomach."

"Josh, come on. Come lie down with me."

"Roll over."

I do it. My arm goes around a pillow and my legs stay closed, and I feel his eyes as he paces, on my back and everywhere else. And I hear him pause to slide off his briefs and clear his throat.

"Get up on your knees."

I'm shaking. "Josh, I don't know if I can do—"

"Up on your knees."

"Why?"

"Because I'm going to fuck you."

The word—*that word!*—is an explosion in the room; in my head it's like a pin going through a balloon. It's not like there was any question it was going to happen, but the statement, the proclamation...I've never heard him talk like this. I've never seen him *act* like this. And this game, this ritual, of words or bodies or anything else—whatever it is, it seems suddenly more serious and maybe a little bit frightening.

"Get up on your knees."

I do it. Clutching the pillow with my eyes squeezed shut, I do it. My butt is up in the air and he's down behind me, and I feel his hands inside my knees, pushing them farther apart. Then there's nothing. His hands on my hips, and a long moment of nothing.

My eyes are closed.

"Are you going to?" I finally make myself whisper.

"Do you want me to?"

"I don't know?"

"You do."

"Yes."

"Say it."

I take a breath and almost speak, and—did I say it?—he is, God, he is, and I'm thrown forward with an "Oh!" and I catch myself with my right arm, the arm not around the pillow, my arm is up, bracing myself, elbow at the wall and palm flat to try to hold myself steady against each of his manic jabs. Now my head is bumping the wall, too much, it's too much, he's got my hair, and I've got my left hand up now too to try to hold myself away and push myself back toward him, this man, this man, whatever he is. My hand between my legs and then back up again, it's too much, something, there's a pace or a spot or some *thing* that he gets that makes me shout, I hate that I shout, I hate that I can't shut my mouth and every time I shout he does it again, and harder.

And harder, and there's nothing, just me and this wall and this man.

Then there is shouting, and the room is back; we're both shouting. There's a frenzy, and a slowing. Arms around my waist and I let my legs slide flat. Josh rolls to my left side, his arm around me, breathing "oh, oh, oh" into the pulse in my neck.

I reach out and turn off the light.

Our breathing slows, and I grab his old shirt and my underwear and get up and scramble down to the bathroom. I leave the light off when I go in, though. I'm a little afraid to see myself, sitting there, in the mirror on the wall. Josh didn't need to ask if I did. He knows I did. The window is gone.

I can't turn on the light. I'm afraid to see my own face.

15

Over the next two days, the entirety of both of my legs is scanned in three dimensions, up and down, front and back. It didn't take long on Tuesday morning to realize that the eyeshades would be too oppressive for however long this phase of the project is going to take, so Gert ran off and returned with a pair of light stands from one of the photo studios, between which he hung a sheet with document binding clips to shield me from the deadly force of the scanner's "strong lasers."

With the sheet up to protect me, I have two options during scanning. If I'm on my back, I can read. If I'm on my stomach, I can read, or, even better, I can write in the spiral notebook I've appropriated from Josh. And in this manner I manage to compose a few stellar pages of copy for the golf resort lodging brochure.

On Wednesday night, after the last of my left heel has

been digitized and stored and backed up, Josh and I go out for dinner at a sushi place not far from my apartment. Over miso soup I delicately suggest that I may stay home—alone—tonight so I can shower in my own tub and be with my own things. He seems fine with this; we kiss before he boards the bus to take him back to the vicinity of the Academy, and I walk to my apartment.

There has been no talk of Monday night's fury, but it's been impossible to push it from my mind. Josh was his normal self the morning after, and there has been no hint that it might happen again. I don't know whether I should consider the episode to be an anomaly, or if there is some potential for reoccurrence.

I also don't know if I wish for one or the other.

I see no lights on at Patrick's as I come down my street. It is getting late, though. And at least my plants seem more enthusiastic this visit. I take a deliriously long, hot-water-depleting shower that leaves me so relaxed I don't need to resort to alternative measures to fall into a prompt and perfect slumber.

I'm confused in the morning, being in my own bed and not having to fight through a wine hangover, a condition that lately borders on chronic. It's early, and barely light, and I get the crazy notion that I can make up for my lack of recent exercise if I get up like *now* and walk all the way across the city to the Academy. Yes. I am going to do this. And maybe the fact that there's little chance I'll see Patrick this early is weighing into it, but the workout is what I'm really selling myself.

I find myself some running shorts and dig around in my bottom drawer for a tank before remembering that there is a box containing dozens of articles of high-performance women's sportswear next to my desk, so I pad over and find myself a cute top, sage green in color and sleeveless. We're going to be scanning my arms today; what could be better than a sleeveless top? In the event that I need to do something civilized, a button-down and plain skirt go into my bag along with a pair of sandals.

It takes a little less than an hour to get from my place to the Academy. It's chilly in the morning, and I'm happy I grabbed a jacket. There isn't even much traffic yet, just buses growling by and the early morning joggers and spandex bike commuters and me.

The city in the morning, with me, walking quickly through it, is surprisingly pleasant.

The door to the studio is open when I get there. Josh is gone but Gert is over at the sink and it looks like he's doing dishes.

"Hey, Gert. Where's Josh?"

"Looking for coffee."

My feet feel hot and tingly from the walk and I sit down on the floor to pull off my shoes and my socks, and just as I do so Gert shouts "Ah!" and makes a long sucking "shhhh" sound. When I stand up to see what has happened, there's Gert, standing in the middle of the kitchenette, biting his lip in a wince and cradling his right hand in his left while a trickle of deep red blood spills out and down to the floor.

"Oh God, are you okay?" I run over and grab a clean kitchen towel, trying unsuccessfully to step around the red Rorschach puddle on the linoleum tile with my bare feet.

"I broke the glass."

"Let me see it."

"It's bad," he says. I reach forward with the towel, and he offers his hand to me. "My blood is safe, Jess. I don't have anything. Ah, I broke the damn glass."

"It's okay, Gert. Let go. Let me see it."

He takes his left hand away and for a moment I see a deep smile of open red flesh where he's cut through the webbing between his thumb and palm. Then I put the towel over it and press it tight, and a spot spreads red through the cloth in my hands.

"Keep your fingers straight. Keep your thumb in close." I

wrap the towel around as tight as I can. Gert seems almost unnaturally calm. He could be in shock, but I have a feeling he's just tough.

"I think I'm gonna need some sutures," he says.

"Do you know anyone with a car?"

Just then Josh walks in, carrying a cardboard drink holder with three paper coffee cups in it. "Hey," he says, and then he sees the blood on our hands and on the floor and his knees crumple and his face goes very pale. "Whoa," he says, steadying himself on the corner of the table. "Whoa."

"Just sit down, Doc. Sit in that chair. You don't have to look over here."

"Okay," Josh says, and he sits and shakes his head. "Okay. Okay. That was just, I wasn't expecting that." He's facing away from us. "What . . . what happened?"

"I broke a glass and cut myself."

"Oh. Are you alright?"

"It's pretty deep. I think I need to go to the emergency room."

"Okay. Give me a second. Okay." Josh stands up. He still doesn't turn toward us. "I can get Hoffman's car." His color is back, but he's not looking at us or at the blood.

"I can drive, Josh," I say.

"No, no, it's alright, Hoffman, he can be weird about his car. There's only room for two. Come on."

"Hold on a second," I say, and I get a roll of reinforced packing tape from the drawer next to the fridge.

"I'll get the keys. Meet me at the north lot."

"Can you make it to the north lot?" I'm wrapping Gert's hand and the towel around and around with tape. He looks like he has a big pink club at the end of his arm.

"I'm fine. That's kind of tight, Jess. Nurse Jess."

"Yeah right," I say. "Let's go down." I walk with him to the door, tracking bloody footprints across the floor of the studio. "You're going to be okay? I need to clean this up."

"I'm okay. You don't clean all this. Call maintenance, 2212 on the phone. They have the stuff to clean the blood. And I think they got to report it."

"Alright. I'm sorry, Gert."

"No, no, my fault. Thank you. You're great." He walks off down the hall, his raised right arm the only clue that something's wrong with him.

I dial 2212 and explain what happened, and it's a few minutes before a shuffling custodial type wearing surgical gloves and a plastic face shield comes in with his big cleanup cart and starts to sprinkle some sort of powder on the floor. I go into the bathroom and sit on the edge of the tub to rinse off my feet. A voice calls, "Hello? Hello?" and I dry myself off and go back out. There's a professionally dressed woman in the doorway, about my age, with a clipboard.

"Is this where the incident happened?" she asks, and I nod. "How did you injure yourself?"

"It wasn't me. It was Dr. Hadden's assistant."

"Can I speak with him?"

"They went to the hospital."

The woman looks seriously annoyed. "You should have called us before anyone got medical care."

I'm about to ask the woman if she's joking, but she turns around and leaves the room before I have the chance.

"I am so damn tired of that woman's attitude," the janitor says. And just as he looks back down to his mop and the powdery, foaming mess on the floor, two men come in the door. They look polished, in coats but no ties, and they seem familiar in an unsettling way. They stare at me, both of them, and then, almost in unison, they look to the floor, and back at me again. It's another moment before one of them opens his mouth.

"Where's Dr. Hadden?" the one on the left asks. He's wearing square-toed shoes, and it sounds like he has a faint accent that I can't quite place.

"He took his assistant to the hospital."

"The hospital?" he asks. The other one stays quiet. "Was there an accident?"

"His assistant cut his hand." Now the janitor is watching the exchange.

"Which hospital?"

"I have no idea," I say. "The closest one?"

They look at each other, and the one on the right says something I don't hear. Then they turn away, quickly, and their footsteps snap snap snap off down the hallway. The janitor looks at me.

"Do they work here?" I ask him.

"Never seen those men before."

"Weird," I say. I hear my phone buzzing—I usually put it on vibrate for the studio—inside my bag, and when I pull it out and flip it open I see Gretchen's name on the display.

"What's up?" I say.

"Where are you? Are you watching the news? They stopped another one in Denver."

"Wait, they stopped a bombing? Another one? Isn't that, like, the third time?"

"The third, yes, find a TV."

I go down the hall, with Gretchen in my ear; I stick my head in Hoffman's always-open studio door. Everything Josh is, Hoffman is not. There's loud music from a paint-smeared boom box, and a flat screen television is on at the same time; the news channel he has on shows a circling aerial shot of maybe a hundred police cars around a van. The headline says, "THIRD DENVER BOMB PLOT DISRUPTED," and in the ticker across the bottom I read, "What Is Denver Doing Right?"

"What is Denver doing right?" I say.

"Good question," Gretchen says. "Hot cops? I got pulled over once in—"

"Stop it," I say.

Hoffman (I've never heard his first name; maybe that *is*

his first name) is a sculptor, and he's working—paying no attention to the news or to me standing in his door, apparently—with a giant pile of clay on one of his tables. There are newspapers and articles of clothing on the floor of his studio, and across in his kitchenette I see piles of dirty dishes and carryout containers. There are muddy gray streaks up to his elbows and on his face and beard, and his hair rises up from his head in a Unabomber-style coif.

There is also a cell phone clipped to his belt.

"Aren't you being scanned?" Gretchen asks.

"Josh's helper—"

"The tall guy?"

"Yes, he hurt himself, we're on hold this morning."

"So Gert cut himself?" Hoffman finally growls.

"Yes," I say, holding the phone away from my mouth while I speak to him. I raise my other hand and wag my thumb to try to illustrate the location of the cut, but Hoffman doesn't look up from his work.

"Bad?" he asks.

"It's pretty bad. He was washing a water glass, and it broke in his hand."

"Who are you talking to?" Gretchen asks.

"The dumbass," Hoffman says, shaking his head.

I step away from the door and head back to Josh's studio with the phone back to my mouth.

"Sorry," I say. "That was one of the artists here."

"No problem. How's the copy going?"

"Done, actually. I just need to type it up. Which I think I can do now, if Josh hasn't changed the password on his laptop."

"What?"

"He's weird about me using his computer."

"Ohh, yeah. Secrets."

"I don't care about his secrets, though." I'm back in the studio, and the janitor is gone. The place smells vaguely of bleach.

"Come on, you're a snoop. I'm a snoop."

"Seriously, I don't care. He only goes to Latin American Web sites, I think. All of his browser history is in Spanish."

"Ha! You've looked!"

"Well, yeah, I mean, you can't avoid it, really."

"Snoop. Mail me the copy."

"Okay."

Josh, I'm happy to learn, has not changed his password from "emmy0782." I set myself up at his desk with one of the now-lukewarm cups of coffee and spend the next half hour transcribing my handwritten text filled with word pairs like:

Spacious kitchens.

Private suites.

Luxury accommodations.

And my favorite overused combination:

Romantic getaway.

I mail the copy off to Gretchen, and since she's online almost all the time, I leave the computer on to wait for a reply. Josh's leather planner is on the desk, and peeking out of it is the dark blue corner of what looks like a passport. I slide it out of the planner—I can't help myself, really—and open it up and laugh out loud when I see the photo. It's Joshua Alan Hadden for sure, birthplace Columbus, Ohio, USA, but he looks younger in the picture and I'm astounded by the fact that he has long, straight hair hanging down over his shoulders. Every page is stamped too; places in South America, Asia, and nearly every country in the EU seem to be represented here. Additional pages had even been pasted in to accommodate more stamps.

This lithography thing must have worldwide appeal.

I know I should put the passport back, but I keep going back to stare at that long-haired photo. When I do finally put it away, though, I see there's a new mail from Gretchen that simply says, "Looks great."

Maybe this brevity is why she's so good at what she does?

I know Katie is in class right now, so I can't call her. I'd send her an instant message, but there's no client on this computer, and I don't want to aggravate Josh by trying to install one. So I shut down and fold up the laptop and set it back in its approximate original location with the thought that maybe he won't even notice I had used it. And this is good, because it isn't long before I hear Josh's voice down the hall.

"Hey," he says when he finally makes it into the studio. He picks up one of the cold paper cups of coffee and takes a sip before throwing it and the others into the trash can.

"How's Gert?"

"Gert's fine, he's home, resting. They gave him a shot for the pain, so I suspect he's fast asleep."

"And the hand?"

"The hand is not so good. He got the tendon in there. Needs surgery."

"Oh no."

"He's fine. Did you use the laptop?"

"Um. Well. I had to write some stuff for work."

"You should get your own computer."

"I have my own computer. In my home. Where I rarely am anymore."

"A laptop would solve that problem."

"You're right. And one did. Yours."

Josh looks at me, and then goes into the bathroom. He leaves the door open and the rushing sound of him peeing is like ruptured plumbing. I guess he's vigorous in that too.

"Are we scanning today?" I call over the noise of him washing his hands.

"I think scanning is off for the day."

"Then let's do something."

"Like?"

"Like something other than sitting around here. Can we use Hoffman's car? We could drive up to Marin. You could sketch wildflowers or something, and we could have lunch. We could be like a real boyfriend and girlfriend, and we could have a picnic."

Josh smirks at this, but he looks interested.

"See if we can take Hoffman's car," I say.

"I'm sure we can take Hoffman's car."

"Are you saying you want to go?"

He still has that stupid smirk on his face.

Hoffman's car, to my complete surprise, is an older—but im-maculate—Porsche convertible. It's a gorgeous day, cool but sunny, and we have the top down and Josh is driving maybe a little too fast. I've never been the sort of person to be im-pressed by cars, but strangely, I'm thrilled by this combina-tion of things.

When we started out, I considered directing us to Mario's for sandwiches to take on our picnic adventure, but that was my secret with Patrick and seems not right for the occasion. So I opt for Plan B, the Brent Deli, which has no chicken salad but is less out of the way (and, incidentally, connected to a wine store).

"Did you hear about the thing in Denver?" I ask as we drive through the city.

Josh shakes his head. "Really, how hard should it be to blow something up? You have to be a pretty big idiot to mess up something like that."

"What are you talking about? You wanted him to blow up?"

"I'm not saying that. I'm simply commenting on the guy's incompetence."

"You're so odd, Josh."

"I'm not odd. I just look at all the angles."

We're coming up to the Golden Gate, zipping through traffic; Josh is shifting and accelerating and we're talking and acting like a couple, almost. I think I've only ever acted at this. Is being a couple really just acting?

We halt for a moment at the bridge inspection station for the uniformed kid to look under the car with his mirror on a long stick, but the soldier behind him shakes his head at the traffic behind us and waves us forward and says, "Let's go let's go *let's go!*"

Josh puts the car into gear and we move on, and the tires sound different driving on the bridge. This is only the third time I've been over it since I've lived here.

"It's old," I say.

"What's that?"

"The bridge. It's old. But big. Isn't it the biggest?"

Josh looks over at me. "Biggest bridge? Like biggest suspension bridge? No, it's not. The biggest is in Michigan." He says this in the same authoritative voice he uses for all trivial facts.

"Michigan? For real?"

"It's the Mackinac Bridge. Connects the Lower to the Upper Peninsula."

"You're not kidding? It's not like the Brooklyn Bridge or anything?"

"I'm serious. Mackinac. We used to drive over it every summer. My dad and uncles had a cottage in the Upper Peninsula. Off in the woods. Right on the lake. We spent a lot of time up there. Tons of time. Every summer."

"That sounds fun."

"God, it was fun. Us, my cousins." He laughs. "You know, me and Emily..." I wait for him to go on, but the mention of his sister has pulled him back from wherever he was. We're off the bridge now.

"You and Emily what?"

"Ah, we were kids. Summertime."

"Does your family still have it?"

"The cottage? No, my uncle Charles got sick, he died, and my dad and other uncles, they thought it was time to sell it. All the kids were big anyway, nobody was going up there much anymore. It was really hard on them when Charlie died. Really hard on my dad. Charlie was the oldest."

We drive for a while, headed west, and the water, bright with the midday sun, shimmers far down to our left. "Is your dad retired?" I finally ask. I think this may be the most personal information I've coaxed out of Josh at one time.

"Nope, no, he still works." The road is twisty now, and we pass a sign saying we're in a state park. "He's a pilot for Delta."

"No way. Like, 'this is the captain speaking' pilot?"

"Yes, like that, but he isn't a captain. First officer. Like the copilot. He could have moved over to captain a long time ago, but he didn't want to give up his seniority. In the airlines, that's everything."

"That's so cool." We're parking in an empty gravel pullout.

"Yeah. I guess it is. We got to travel all sorts of places when I was a kid too. The company was good that way."

"I bet he has good stories," I say, pulling my bag and the white paper sack with our lunch from behind my seat. Josh laughs at this.

"Maybe too many stories," he says. "I've heard them all. Usually more than once."

We're up on a windy bluff looking out over the Golden Gate Bridge and the city beyond that. A small plane is flying over the city, towing a banner that we can't read.

"What is this thing?" I ask. We've walked out onto a big concrete platform, like a round, graffiti-covered patio.

"It's a gun turret," Josh says. He waves his arm out over the view of the water. "If the invasion was going to come, you know, this was where it was going to be. So they'd shoot the ships from up here. Blow them out of the water."

I walk around the circle, around Josh. "That's a big gun," I say, and sit down cross-legged to look out at the ocean. The concrete is warm and the sun is perfect, so I pull off my jacket and tie it around my waist.

"Very big."

"Why isn't it still here?"

"Obsolete. Who's going to invade by boat?" He sits down behind me and starts to rub my neck. "When it was the Soviets, it was going to be missiles or something like that. And now, now, you know, what's this big gun going to do to a guy in Denver?"

Josh has entered rhetorical mode, so I keep my mouth shut.

"What's a big gun like this going to do to a guy on a bus with a backpack?" he goes on. "We don't even know who the guy is. He could be over there. Up there. He could be right behind you. Right behind you. Who knows? So melt the guns down. Make nickels out of them or something."

"Pocket change," I say, but he doesn't hear me. Rather, he hears me, but he's not listening.

"Things didn't need to get this way. Things could have been different. Goddamn Washington." Now I really brace myself, but he leaves it at that.

I take the opportunity to get the sandwiches out, along with a bottle of wine I grabbed at the deli's package store.

"You are hopeless," Josh says as he slides around to my side and grabs the bottle from in front of me. He's smiling, though, as he reads over the label. "Do you just travel with this wherever you go? It's cold, even. Do you have ice in that bag? I want to know what else is in there."

"Bag of secrets," I say. "You probably looked in there already. Maybe when I was in the shower."

"I take offense to that remark. I am offended."

"Come on."

"I respect your personal space."

"Ha!"

"But how is the wine cold?"

"You'll just need to search my bag. But I bet you're glad I brought it. I bet you won't call me hopeless when you drink most of it."

"I bet you have a second bottle in there."

I smile and shrug. "You'll just have to find out." The truth is, there is a second bottle. I like to be prepared, especially on pseudo–boyfriend/girlfriend picnics.

"Yeah, find out, then wreck Hoffman's car. Or get pulled over."

"You can just pay him off. The cop. Or Hoffman too, I guess."

Josh lifts an eyebrow at this. "Just what are you saying?"

"I'm not saying anything."

"Sometimes," he says, "extra measures are needed to get things done."

We eat our lunch, and drink the wine. Josh asks if he can have the pickle I've left sitting on my paper sandwich wrapper, and I give it to him.

"I didn't think you were the pickle type," he says.

"I should have gotten an apple," I say. "I'm an apple type. My grandparents had an orchard by Spokane. Katie and I used to go there in the summers. Like your cabin."

"Orchards are good places," Josh says.

"They are. I loved it there."

"Are your grandparents still living?"

"No. They were old. My mom's parents. But their place is still an orchard. They got a conservation easement on it. Katie and I talk about driving there sometime. They even kept the name."

"What is it?"

"The name? Mason Farms. That was their last name. My mom's maiden name."

"You should drive there," Josh says. "With your sister." He's finished the pickle. "Want to hike down to the beach?"

"There's a beach?"

"Right down the hill." Josh points down the slope. As he

does so, a car slows on the road up behind us, and then drives on. It's the first car we've seen since we've been here.

"Is it far?" I ask.

"Ten minutes. Maybe twenty."

I gather up our mess and our bottle and stuff everything into my bag, and we start down the hillside on a dusty, narrow trail through the brush. Smaller trails branch off in different directions, but we stick to the most defined path that seems to be heading in the direction Josh wants to go. I'm walking a few steps behind him, looking at his back, and I can't help but think again of Monday night and the idea that maybe it's time for *me* to be a little aggressive for once. I pause.

"Hey," I call. "Stop. Come back up this way."

"What?"

"Come with me."

"Where are you going?"

"Just come with me, okay?"

He trots up and I lead him not quite a hundred feet into the brush. The wind brings us the smell from the ocean below, and a couple of birds hover on the current of air above us.

"Sit down," I say. "Sit. Right there."

He does, grinning because he knows what I'm going to do, and I kneel in front of him and unbutton his shorts.

"There could be people back here, you know."

"Do you not want me to?"

"I didn't say that."

I lean forward, as if I'm going to kiss him, but I don't. "Why are you smiling like that?"

"I'm smiling?"

"It's more like a smirk. I'm not going to do it if you have that look on your face."

Josh adopts a suitably serious expression and I slide myself down and get to work, feeling an outdoorsy thrill; the breeze and the sun and the tiny worry of being caught all make it seem dangerous and fun.

I use my hand and turn my head up toward him.

"Look at me," I say, almost surprising myself. I *want* him to look at me.

He bites his lip and nods. "Okay."

"Watch me." It's almost a whisper.

"Yes."

I get to work again, glancing up from time to time to meet his wide-open eyes. Then I take another little break and use my hand, staring at him, watching him watch me, but Josh makes a sudden "ah!" sound—overexcitement on his part (or poor timing on my own) has resulted in a dark wet splatter spreading down from the shoulder across the chest of my sage-colored freebie sport top.

"Um, sorry," Josh says.

"No, no," I say, looking away. "I'm sorry." Now I am embarrassed; while him watching and the threat of getting caught giving a blow job seemed daring, the thought of being seen with some guy's spunk all over my shirt is positively mortifying. I work with a deli napkin from my bag to try to clean up the mess, turning away to hide my blush, and then I put my jacket back on while Josh closes up his shorts.

"I'm sorry," he says again.

"No, really. Don't. Let's just go down to the beach." I do *not* want to be seen.

I let him go ahead so I can take a couple breaths and let the burning in my cheeks subside. Following him back out to the main trail and starting down again, composure returns and I begin to wonder if the people at Cippoletti would be interested in hearing my thoughts on the sperm-resistant qualities of their clothing in my feedback report. This thought leads to a giggle, which in turn leads to a full, unstoppable laugh as I stumble down behind Josh through the loose, dusty rock of the trail.

16

Gert stays home on Friday, and, while I'm not happy that he's hurt himself, I welcome the break. I'm not really looking forward to the fact that, as we scan higher up my body, there won't be enough room for Gert's jury-rigged sheet to protect me from the lasers and I'm probably going to need to go back to the eyeshades. I'll resist that as long as I can.

I've stayed home too, and this time, Patrick is around. I have no idea why he's not at work, and I don't know if he realizes that I'm here, as well. But from the sound of things, it's business as usual. This morning he's been standing on the landing right outside my door and yelling things down to Danny.

"Is it working now?" he shouts.

"No," Danny calls back from below me. "Still 'page not found.'"

"Hold on." I hear him run back up the stairs. Danny must be having problems with his Internet. Patrick set us all up to share the same connection, and somehow (either through generosity or forgetfulness, I can't figure out which) he's allowed me to stay online. When I hear his footsteps coming down the stairs again, I go over and put my ear to the door.

"Try it now."

"What do you want me to load?"

"I don't care, it doesn't matter. Try anything. Bring up the weather."

"Hey, that's it, you got it. What did you do?"

"Just rebooted."

"Thanks, man."

Patrick goes upstairs, slowly this time. I hear him cough as he climbs the stairs, and I hear him close his door, softly. Across the room my cell starts to ring, and I dart over and hide it under a pillow on my couch so no one will hear it.

Wait, wait. I *live* here. I can answer *my* phone in *my* apartment. I'm not hiding from anything, right?

Except maybe—I realize just as I pull the phone from under the pillow and flip it open—my mother, who appears to be the person calling.

"Mom," I say.

"Jessica, how are you?"

"I'm fine, Mom. What's up?"

"Oh." She starts with a wavering voice. "I've just been thinking about—"

"What, Denver? Are you obsessed? Can you just get it out of your head for a little bit? Can you turn off the TV? Jesus, Mom, you're going to drive yourself crazy."

"Jessica." Her voice is hard now, hard the way it would be when I got a bad grade or something in high school. "I've been thinking about your sister's party."

"I'm sorry. I'm sorry." God, I suck. "What about it?"

"Well, the party will be that Saturday night. Your sister will be coming out the week before. It would be so nice if you could come early too...."

"I cannot do that, seriously."

"Well, fine then. Jane is coming, did I tell you your aunt Jane is coming? And Alison will be here too."

"That's great, Mom," I say, and I mean it; Katie and I have always agreed that our mom's sister Jane is our favorite aunt, and her daughter, Alison, is our favorite cousin. "But what's the problem?"

"I would like to have a little bit of time with just the three of us."

"What do you mean, Mom? Katie and I are going to be there all week."

"I want to do something special."

"Like what?"

"I don't know. But I'd like it to be special."

"It *will* be special, Mom. I'm looking forward to seeing you. Really."

"I know," she says. "But just something."

"We could go out to dinner?"

"Something more than going out to dinner."

I really don't know what to say. She sounds so damn sincere. "I'll think about it, Mom. I'll give some thought to what we can do."

"Will you?"

"Yes. Serious thought."

"Thank you, Jessica. But really, how about Denver?"

"Mom."

"What?"

"Let's just not talk about that, okay? They stopped him, right? Isn't that what's important?"

"But it's such an incredible story of how they—"

"Ah, someone's at my door, Mom. Gotta run. Love you."

"I love you too, Jessica."

• • •

Josh, in an apparent continuation of our recent boyfriend/girl-friend act, suggests on Saturday that we go out to dinner. This sounds nice, but I've already spoken to Amy about see-ing her for the first time in forever. Plans are combined easily, though, and Josh and Amy, who both know about each other but have never met, seem interested in meeting and have no problem with us becoming a dinner threesome.

I've made reservations for us at Poulson's. It's a pretty nice place, and I'm using the occasion as an excuse to wear my maybe-too-formal black dress with the teeny straps. I'm really into the whole idea of this being a date, and when I see myself in my bathroom mirror in the dress I decide to go even that crazy extra step and dig around the drawer next to the sink for some lipstick.

I do have a problem, however: Josh insists on coming to my apartment and walking with me to the restaurant rather than just meeting me there. I don't really care about him be-ing here; it's just the procedure of actually getting him in that I'm apprehensive about. I feel awkward enough getting myself in and out.

Now, almost formally dressed with my hair pulled back and more made up than I've been in probably two years, I'm nervous. I keep going to my window over the street to watch for him; I'm expecting to see him coming from the direction of the bus stop, but then I wonder if maybe he'll borrow Hoffman's Porsche to come and pick me up—how embar-rassing would *that* be?

There is wine, though, always there's wine lately, and I go to the kitchen and grant myself permission to pour a full giant glass with the thought that it might help me relax. And just as I take my second long sip, or maybe the third, my doorbell buzzes and the glass is on the counter and I run over to see Josh's sandy head waiting at the front door of the building. I hit the buzzer and have my door open, and when he makes it up to my landing I rush him in to avoid any awkward situations.

"Hey, what's up?" he says. "You seem eager."

"I am. Hi." I lean forward to listen at the door for a moment, before giving him a quick kiss. "How are you?"

"I'm fine. You look great."

"You mean it?"

"I wouldn't have said it if I didn't mean it. You look fantastic. Is that lipstick?"

"Yes?" I feel my face getting hot. "I can take it off."

"No, no, leave it. It's fun. Have I ever seen you wearing makeup?"

"Probably not. Really, I can take it off."

"Leave it. Seriously."

"Come to the kitchen," I say. "Do you want some wine?"

"Do I get a glass that big?"

"This is the only big one I have. It saves me trips to refill."

"I'll share it with you."

We sit at my table, and it isn't long before I'm refilling. Josh looks fantastic himself in a dark, collarless shirt with a jacket and dark pants; he even has on nice shoes. I had no idea he was into clothes.

"I didn't know you even owned a jacket, Josh."

"Oh, you know, it is a date and everything."

"Aren't you sweet."

"I do have a confession to make." He's seems to be ahead of me already in wine consumption. I can see it in his cheeks.

"Yes?"

"I borrowed the jacket from Hoffman."

"You are sweet. I'm picturing you asking."

"I thought the evening warranted it."

"But, I have to ask, Hoffman has a jacket? And one that nice?"

"Hoffman sells his work for a lot of money. And he has a taste for fine things."

"Like the car."

"Like the car. And certain grad students."

"Zing."

"I didn't say that, did I?"

"I didn't hear a thing." I grab my goblet-esque glass and down the last sip before Josh gets it, and I pour the last of the bottle.

"Running low," Josh says. "Are we busing it to the restaurant?"

"We could, but it isn't such a long walk. I'd like to walk."

"I'd like to walk too."

Josh seems unusually animated tonight. I can't really tell if it's happiness, or something else. I might even call it affection. We finish the wine and leave—undetected—from my building, and as we're walking down my street he actually grabs my hand.

Amy is waiting for us at Poulson's. She looks great too; introductions are made and we take our table and everyone seems happy. Amy orders a martini; I haven't had one in forever and it sounds good, so I order one as well.

"Sure, I'll have one too," Josh says when asked.

"How would you like that?" the drinks girl asks.

"I don't know, how would I like that?" He looks at Amy and me. "I've never had one before."

"You've really never had a martini?" Amy asks. "Alright, you want a dirty gin martini, up. Sapphire. That's the way to start out."

"What she says," Josh says to the girl. She leaves the table, and Josh looks at us and shrugs. "New at this. Jessica is corrupting me."

"Oh, she's good at that," Amy says. "She corrupted me."

"I did not. You were corrupt well before we met. I know this for a fact."

"She's a liar, Josh. Have you figured out yet that she's a liar?"

We're having fun, joking around, and I'm pleased at the way Amy and Josh seem to be getting along. It's nice to feel for once that I can be open about the fact that I've been seeing him. The drinks come, and Josh raises his eyebrows when he takes a sip.

"Now that's—"

"That, Josh, is the taste of civilization," Amy says, and we all laugh.

"It's the taste of something, not sure what," Josh says. "But it's good."

"They make them very well here," Amy says.

"You would know," I say.

We go slowly with the drinks; we talk and laugh and order an appetizer made of tiny grilled wedges of polenta. The restaurant isn't slammed, and we aren't feeling rushed, so we order a second round of drinks.

"But there's a rule about the martini, Josh," Amy says.

"What's that?"

"They're like a woman's breasts."

"Wait, what?" He looks at me, his cheeks very red. "Martinis are like breasts how?"

Amy loves to tell this joke whenever she can, but I beat her to it. "One is not enough," I say. "But three is too many."

He looks totally blank for a one-one-thousand two-one-thousand, but then suddenly gets it and starts to laugh. "Oh, okay, okay, that's really funny. I'll remember that."

Amy taps the stem of her glass with her fingernail. "You should. Strong medicine, here." Josh nods in an obedient-little-boy sort of way. "So, I know you're an artist. Like, a printer, right? Tell me just what it is that you do."

This, of course, is the magic request, and Josh's face illuminates as he sits up straight and gives the stock ten-minute explanation of the process of lithography. He's very enthusiastic, and his explanation is animated and fun, so I don't mind so much that I've heard it a few times before. He does pause for us to order our entrees and a bottle of wine, though.

"Okay, I get all that," Amy says when he finishes, and she

seems sincerely interested. "But what does Jessica's body have to do with it? This crazy scanner, it's a scanner you told me about, right? It seems like a very modern thing to put together with this centuries-old art form you're doing."

"That's just it," Josh says. "That's exactly the point."

"But how is my friend's body involved?"

"You will just have to see how that comes together. You will see it. You will understand it."

"Is the scanning hard? I mean physically, like, for you, Jess. Is it difficult?"

"It's more boring than anything else," I say. "I'm just a prop. But we're on hiatus at the moment." I tell her about tall Dutch Gert, and how he cut himself, and Amy gasps and puts her hands to her mouth when I describe the injury to his hand.

"God, it was such a mess, blood everywhere, it was on my feet, everywhere!" Josh seems to be shrinking down into his chair as I talk about it. "The woman from the Academy was a bitch too. And poor Josh here, I think the blood was a little—"

"No," he says. "That's not right. That's not how it was." He's defensive, and looks a little angry.

"I'm sorry, Josh. I would have freaked out too if I walked in on that. And these two weird guys came in after—"

"Stop! That's not, that's not how it was."

"But they were strange, Josh. They just stood there."

"Probably some stupid OSHA guys," Amy chimes in. "Government regulation, paperwork, forms, whatever. In the event of a minor cut or abrasion." She doesn't seem to notice the sour look Josh is giving her.

"Whoever they were, they were weird."

"Sure," Josh says. "Forms. Useless forms. Sure."

Our meals come, and the wine, and Josh is silent while we eat. He does drink, though, and our very attentive waiter makes sure his glass stays filled. We're all a little drunk, and I don't pay much attention to his consumption as Amy and I talk, mostly about her work and recent breakup (it's a good thing, by the way; the guy was terrible, and she ended it).

"He sort of thought he was an activist," Amy says, stifling a laugh. "He was really just a dork. He was always trying to drag me to town council meetings and things like that. Like he could turn me, or something."

Josh sits up a bit as Amy says this. "Oh, so you aren't into participating, then," he says.

"In politics?" Amy asks. I'm throwing her a look to try to keep her from engaging him in this sort of discussion, but she misses it entirely. "I love politics, actually. But I don't participate by shouting at public meetings. I vote. That's the most effective thing. For me, anyway."

Josh nods. "I see," he says. "The ones you vote for, do they usually win?"

By this point, I'm shaking my head no, and trying to reach with my foot under the table to kick her. But she just laughs. "I'm pretty good at picking the winners," she says.

"So, these winners, are they doing a good job?"

"I think they are. Most of them."

"Sure they are," Josh says. "They sure are doing a—"

"They have an incredible flourless chocolate cake here," I say.

"—A great job," Amy says. She's not giving in. "The ones I voted for are doing a great job."

Josh straightens up and lifts his eyebrows. "Oh! Oh, yes, out there"—he gestures toward the lobby—"things are going *great*, aren't they? Things . . . things blowing up? Buses?"

"Josh," she says softly, leaning toward him and touching the back of his hand, "this is the way things are now. We just have to deal with it, right?" She straightens up and smiles, and puts her napkin next to her plate. "Excuse me. I'll be right back."

Amy leaves the table and Josh, slouching a little bit in his spiffy borrowed jacket, watches her with a sneer as she walks off past the bar toward the ladies' room.

"I cannot believe you spend time with that woman," he says.

"What? What are you talking about?"

"She's a Republican."

"I don't know if she is or not, and honestly, I don't care, Josh. She's one of my closest friends."

"She's a fucking Republican, isn't she?"

"Don't you even. Are you kidding me? Are you *kidding* me?"

"She is. I can tell. How can you be friends with that?"

My mouth has dropped open. "How can *you* sit there and suggest I should or shouldn't be friends with someone? Who the hell do you think you are?"

"I know who I am." His words are thick in his mouth. "And I know I don't need people like that in my life."

"Okay. Okay. I am leaving. Now. Not with you."

"Wait, wait." Josh puts his hands to his face. "Jess, God, I'm sorry." He takes his hands away and looks at me. "This is, I'm sorry. I did not mean that. Honestly."

"You're really drunk, Josh."

"I'm, yeah, I think I am." Now he looks sad and small.

"Okay. Just wait here, okay? Can you wait here a sec? I'm going to the bathroom. Will you be okay?"

"I'm fine." He straightens up.

I get up and head toward the restrooms, and I see Amy at the far end of the bar talking to the bartender, whom she seems to know.

"Amy, come with me a second. Sorry." I take her hand and pull her to the alcove outside the ladies' room.

"What's up?"

"Josh is drunk."

"So what? Aren't you?"

"Not like he is. He's surly. He's saying stupid stuff."

"God, Jessie babe, you know that's no biggie." I do have a little karmic room here: Amy had a date at one of our Thanksgiving dinners a few years ago who got very, very drunk and threw up. On my bathroom floor. So she owes me one, I guess, but I don't want things to get ugly.

"Why don't you just stay at the bar," I say. "We'll get the bill, and I'll get him out of here."

"No, come on, that's silly talk. I can deal with a surly drunk guy. Let's get some dessert, we'll get him some coffee, and it'll all be okay. I'm having fun."

"Okay," I say, and I go back to the table. Josh looks fine. He's sitting up straight and he smiles at me.

"That was fast," he says.

"Yeah. Are you alright?"

"I'm fine."

Amy is back in another moment, smiling.

"That bartender," she says. "Did you see him?"

"I feel like I know him from somewhere," I say. "Didn't he use to work at—"

Josh leans over toward Amy and interrupts me. "Are you a Republican?" he asks.

"Jesus Christ, Josh, don't," I say.

Amy looks surprised for a second, but she gives it right back to him. "So what if I am?"

"I fucking knew it!" he says, loudly enough that a couple people in the dining room turn their heads. "How do you look at yourself in the mirror? How do you live with yourself?"

"Josh, stop it," I hiss.

Amy leans in, and she's stabbing her finger in the air at him. "You know what? I'm not some stupid sheep. I can think for myself. I do think for myself."

"Please," I say.

The waiter is back at the table. "You ready to see the dessert tray?"

"Sure, yeah," Josh says. "Let's do a couple rich, fattening desserts."

"We'll take our check, please," Amy says.

"Here," I say, pawing through my bag like an imbecile until I can find my wallet. "Just take my card."

"So, who do you think is responsible," Josh continues once the waiter leaves, "for everything that's going on right now?"

"Josh, leave it, please?"

"No, no, I'm not going to leave it. I think it's the guys *she* put in office. It's the guys *she* voted for! Your participation."

"You don't know who I voted for. You don't have a clue."

"I know what you've done," Josh says, his eyes narrowing. "And people like you are going to get a big wake-up surprise someday—"

"You don't know the first thing about me," Amy says as she stands up. "And you're pathetic for thinking you do. You don't know anything about me. I'm sorry, Jessica. I'm sorry you have to deal with an asshole like this. I won't judge you for it, though."

Josh apologizes, again, and again, and again, on our walk back. He should be apologizing; I am furious. Sometimes he almost hangs on me for support, and other times he jams his hands into his pockets and walks ahead of me. When he isn't apologizing, he's talking what seems like nonsense.

"The terrain modeling, it can be shaded, but if you shade it, how do you, what makes the vegetation?" he says. "What pigmentation? How do I do that, Jess? God, Jess, I am sorry, I am sorry, I *am* an asshole, I am such an asshole, I am sorry."

I don't even bother trying to shut him up back at my apartment. Pat's lights are on too. My plan is to just let him pass out, and deal with how I feel about everything in the morning.

Once we're in my place, I point to the couch. "You're sleeping there," I say. He sits down and holds his head in his hands while I get him my thick fleece blanket from the chest in the corner.

"I know. I deserve it."

I go in the bathroom and brush my teeth, and I jump when I look up and see his red-eyed reflection in the mirror over my shoulder.

"What?" I say.

"Can I use your phone?"

"You aren't going to call anybody like this."

"No, really. I need it."

"What are you going to do? Call an old girlfriend?"

"No, Jess, I'm serious. I need to call Emily."

"Your sister?"

"Yes, my sister."

"Josh, I don't know. Why don't you get some sleep and call her tomorrow?"

His eyes are begging me. "Please. I need to."

"Hold on," I say, and I rinse out my mouth and turn out the light and he follows me back to the living room. I take the phone out of the cradle and hand it to him in the bare light from the street.

"It's long distance," he says. "Is that okay?"

"Josh, there's no—"

"I won't talk long, I'll keep it short."

"It's free long distance, I don't care." Does anybody charge for long distance anymore?

I go to my room and get into my bed, and it seems like a long time before I finally hear him start to dial.

"Hello, Tim. It's Josh. Yes, Josh, your brother-in-law. Damn it, yes, Tim, I know, I know it's late there. I'm sorry. Can I talk to Emily? What? Well wake her up, just wake her up!

"Emily, Em, hi, hi. I know, I know. Yes, it's late, yes. I'm sorry. I'm sorry. No, come on, you know I don't get drunk. I'm talking loud? Sorry. Better? Happy, what? Happy birthday. I'm sorry, I'm sorry I didn't call earlier. It's so hard, Emily. I've been thinking about you all day. Yes. Happy birthday.

"Did the boys do anything fun for, no, Em, come on, we need to talk right now. Don't go. Don't go. Yes, I'm going to talk about that. Speak up. Speak up. Why do you even care? He doesn't listen to you anyway. Yes, I am going to talk like that. I'm not afraid to say it. I'm not like Mom, at least I say what I'm, what? Yes, I'm going to bring her into it! Why don't you just get out, Emmy? Mom and Dad want to help you, just, wait, wait, okay?

"No, Emily, no. You keep, you keep, we need to talk about this. Mom is. I'm not going to stop! Okay, okay, okay, don't hang up, Em. I just. Okay, are you there? Okay. I just wanted to say happy birthday. Really. But talk to Mom. You need to talk to Mom, she'd help you with the kids. God-dammit, Em, yes, I'm going to talk like that. Emily? Emily? Fuck! Fuck!"

My pulse pounds in my ears in the sudden quiet, and I've pulled my comforter tight up under my chin. I couldn't help listening, couldn't get away from it, but I wish I hadn't heard any of it. Josh is breathing funny in the other room, and it takes me a moment to realize he's crying.

I wish I couldn't hear it. Slowly, it fades, replaced by his heavy, openmouthed breathing. But there's something else, something above; footsteps and doors and faucets turning on and off. The grind of a chair across the floor. I'm thinking about him up there. Picturing him. He's plucking the strings of his cello. Tuning it. He's quiet about it, but I hear it. And in my head, I can see it.

What I do next seems not like myself. I swing my feet off my bed, and I feel around on the floor with my hands for my sweatpants and pull them on. I stand, and wait, and Josh's breathing doesn't change. I wait again at my door, and then I pull it open—slowly so there's no creak in the hinges—and I slide out into the hall. With my bare feet, I pad up the stairs.

Patrick is still plucking away at his cello. My hands are pressed to the outside of his door, and my right ear is too. He picks out a soft tune, quiet, but fast, and he pauses and I hear him pluck pluck pluck and change the sound of the note with his tuning key. Then he sighs, and I hear the knock of the cello's body as he places it back into the stand.

My full weight is pressed against his door.

His chair moves again, and now I hear him typing on his laptop. He pauses, and types, and pauses again and laughs and says something that sounds like, "Danny, you dumbass." Then the chair moves and I hear the little shutting-down song of his computer. I hear his footsteps, and when I sense that he's coming close to the door, my throat feels tight and I hold my breath; I stand there and wait, and wait—*he's just two feet away from me*—and then he walks away and I breathe again. His teeth are brushed, and his toilet is flushed, and I hear bedclothes rustled and lights switched off.

My hand moves toward the doorknob, and stops. It's probably locked. Probably. I could check; it might be unlocked, and I could go in. I could check. But I take my hand away, and softly step backward, and go back down the stairs.

When I slip back into my apartment and into my bed, all that seems left is the sound of Josh's breathing. It goes on, and on, and that's the sound I fall asleep to. And when I wake up in the morning I find him with me—at my side with his arm around my waist—I hate myself a little bit because I know I've already forgiven him, and I miss him when he leaves to go home.

17

Gert is back in the studio on Monday, and, for better or worse, so
am I. Josh seems to be hiding from me behind the scanner console, and I haven't bothered to say anything to
him other than hello.

"Check it out," Gert says, holding his cast-encased
forearm out to me. "You want to write something on it?"
The cast is blue, and there's puffy batting sticking out of
the end of it along with his purple fingertips.

"Oh, Gert, I'm sorry," I say, and I hold the cast between my hands. "You have to have surgery? Are you
right-handed?"

"It's no big trouble, Jess. All I do with this scanner is
press the buttons, yeah? And surgery on Friday. I said do
it Friday so we could get the scanning done. The doc pays
for this thing by the day."

"You're dedicated. Does it hurt?"

"Sure it hurts. But I got pain pills. The good stuff." He glances at Josh and leans close to me. "You want a couple? I'm serious."

"I'm fine, Gert. But thank you."

"You just tell me when you do. It's the best for a hangover."

We're going to start on my left hand and arm today, Gert says, and he seems to think he can position his sheet closely enough to my shoulder and head that they can scan without me needing to wear those terrible eyeshades. I take my place on the table and Gert moves around like usual to set things up, except he's holding his cast up in the air so it doesn't bang into anything.

The scanning seems to go very smoothly today. Josh and Gert have their routine; they call things out to each other, Gert positions the scanner arm, Josh types and the machine hums and beeps. Then the whole process repeats.

I'm wearing shorts and a plain old blue bra as they scan me. I almost make a joke about how my bra matches Gert's cast, but I don't: it's stupid, for starters, and Gert has been regarding my body with such detachment as he works that I may as well be inanimate. I'd like to not change that.

At least, I think he's been detached. "You look like a Dutch girl, Jess," he says as he helps me roll over. "All skinny. And the freckles."

"Skinny, what?"

He taps the small of my back with his fingertip. "I can see your bones."

"You should see my sister."

"They're like twins," Josh says out of nowhere. "I've seen pictures."

"Keep the back of your hand flat on the table, Jess." Back to business. "Stretch out your fingers. Straight like, yeah, just like that. I'm going to tape your wrist down to keep you still. Will that bother you?"

"It's fine."

"You want a blanket?"

"I'm fine."

I can't lift my shoulder up now, so reading or writing is out of the question. I almost do ask Gert for one of his pills, but I do need to try to get some work done later, so I don't. The fog we had outside this morning has gone and I lie with my head turned to the side and watch the dust floating in the shafts of light coming into the room now.

By noon, my arms and hands have been completely scanned. Josh thought we'd be doing the hands in the afternoon, but Gert—even disabled—has kept things moving along. Gretchen and I had tentatively planned to have lunch, so once I have my shirt back on I go out to the hall and call her to let her know I'm free. We make plans to meet up at the Gram. I head off down the hall, and I'm just about to the door when I hear Josh calling my name.

"Hey," he says, coming up to me in a half run. "Hey." He's holding an envelope.

"What's up?"

He hands me the envelope, and I can tell there's a card inside. "Would you give this to Amy the next time you see her?"

"What is it?"

"Nothing. Just a card."

"Are you asking her for a date or something?"

"You're not very funny. Will you give it to her?"

"I will give it to her," I say. I slip the card into my bag, and he looks relieved.

"Hey, can I talk to you?"

The position I'm in here, the position of power, the moral superior, gives me a high school sophomore sort of thrill. "I have to make a bus, Josh. Can we talk tonight?"

"Do you want to have dinner?"

"I might consider dinner."

"I could make something."

"Ah," I say, and I can't help smiling. "I might consider dinner as long as it doesn't involve pasta with a red sauce."

"Oh. Well, we could get carryout, then."

"For someone so creative, your kitchen habits surprise me."

"We all have our zones of comfort."

"We do. I'll see you in about an hour."

On the bus, my curiosity is too much, and I take the envelope from my bag. The flap isn't sealed, just tucked in, and I can't stop myself from working it up and sliding the card out. There's a picture, like a watercolor, of a loose bouquet of flowers on the front. The card is plain inside except for Josh's precise cursive handwriting:

> *Dear Amy—I doubt that an apology will ever be sufficient,*
> *but my behavior the other night was inexcusable. I am very,*
> *very sorry for acting as I did, and for saying the things I did.*
> *Jessica is truly lucky to have you as a friend. Most sincerely,*
> *Josh Hadden*

Printed on the back of the card, at the bottom, it says: "Joshua Hadden—WILDFLOWER STUDY II—Chromolithograph, 2003."

Something must be going on today downtown, because the line I find upon my arrival at the Gram is out the door and up the block. I step in front of some people to peek in the door to see if Gretchen is inside, and get a nasty look from a woman in the line. As I turn back to the street, though, I see her short noon silhouette coming down the sidewalk.

"Strike out," Gretchen says.

"There must be a convention or something going on."

"It's that big antiques show thing."

"Antiques show. Right. But lunch?"

"There's Korean up the street. We'll get in there. Antiques show people are afraid of ethnic food."

We walk up the street, and, unsolicited, I start to tell Gretchen about everything going on with Josh. I know she would have asked anyway, so it's no big deal. I tell her about him getting so drunk, and I tell her about his call to his sister. We walk out of the shadow of a building into the sun and there are two soldiers with berets and guns stationed on the corner looking us up and down as we wait for the walk signal. The light changes, and just as we step into the street one of them says something that I can't hear. Gretchen hears it, though.

"Yes," she says, turning back to him. "Yes, I bet you would, you asshole." Then she *actually spits* at him and I gasp; the big gob of her saliva just misses his boot and the guy lowers his head and turns away while the other soldier, the taller one, laughs at him and tells him he's a stupid motherfucker.

"I cannot believe those guys," Gretchen says as we continue across the street.

"I can't believe you, sometimes. How do you just spit on a guy?"

"What, I should put up with that? No one should put up with that. Isn't a guy in uniform supposed to be chivalrous? Now, go on with your story."

As predicted, we easily get a table at a Korean restaurant named, with no irony, "Korean Restaurant." We order, and I tell Gretchen about the card.

"Do you have it? Let me see it." I give her the envelope and she takes out the card and looks it over. "Are you kidding me? This card isn't for your friend, it's for you."

"What do you mean?"

"I mean, he wanted you to see it."

"Why do you say that?"

"He didn't seal the envelope, for starters."

"Maybe he trusts me?"

"Yes. He should trust you. As you and I look at this card, this card right here in my hand, intended for another person. As we discuss its contents, he should trust you completely. Of course he knew you were going to look at it. Just like you look at his browser history. He did this? These flowers?"

I nod.

"It's pretty." She puts the card back in the envelope and carefully slides the flap closed, then drops it to the table. "Come on, Jessica. He doesn't care about Amy, or what she thinks. What you think is everything, though. To him."

"Hello, psychic hotline."

"It's not psychic, it's common sense." She takes some kimchi from the dainty enameled bowl between us with her chopsticks and holds it up, examining it from all sides like some lab specimen. Then she eats it in one massive bite.

"I'd like to think he sincerely feels bad about being a jerk to my best friend."

"He does feel bad. He feels like you have the upper hand. That makes him feel bad. You seeing this"—she pats the envelope on the table—"puts him back in control of things."

"You're kind of making me feel weird here, Gretchen."

"What, because I'm right?"

"Not that."

"Look, Jessica, this might not be any of my business—"

"Maybe it's not your business."

"—but I really like you, a lot. A lot a lot. And I think I can say, I mean, I've wanted to say, maybe you being with him isn't the healthiest thing? Your relationship, I mean."

"What are you talking about? And it might be going a little far to call it a relationship, I think."

"Oh, yeah. Tell me about that date you had again? Wait, was I the one who called it a date, or was it you? Road trips to Nevada? And where do you sleep most nights?"

"Stop it, Gretchen. And where is this coming from, when the first thing you pester me about every single time we talk is the sexual aspect of this so-called relationship?"

"Well, sex is sex is sex. That's nothing. It's fun. But being manipulated is something."

I haven't told her about what happened in the loft, and I certainly don't intend to now. And for an instant, I think of Gretchen and Patrick, the great unspoken thing between us. But honestly, I don't want to know anything about it.

"He isn't manipulating me, Gretchen."

"Okay, then. When was the last time you had sex?" She raises her eyebrow and waits a beat. "And I want all the details." We both laugh, and this makes the tension I was feeling disappear. I'm happy for the change in subject, anyway.

"Well," I say, making a show of leaning forward a bit. "It wasn't *sex* sex." I tell her about going to the Marin Headlands, and about our trip into the bushes. When I tell her about the mess on my top and my thoughts about semen-resistant fabrics, Gretchen laughs and laughs.

"Oh my God," she says. She's put her chopsticks down and she's covering her face. "Oh my God. I can see the campaign. I can totally see it. You need to write that for Pitch-Bitch. A big fake campaign. I can totally see it."

"For the active woman," I say. "You're active in so many ways."

"We know you get messy, active woman."

"A fabric that goes where you go. A fabric that takes it, just like you take it."

"This is so awful, Jess," Gretchen says. She rubs her eye, shoulders shaking, with her elbow on the table. "But if you don't write it, I'm going to."

Gert is asleep on the couch when I get back to the studio, and Josh is typing something on his laptop.

"Hey," Josh says, and he minimizes whatever it was he was doing on the computer. "You didn't see Amy, did you?"

"No. I'll see her this week."

"Okay. You want to wake up Gert and we'll get going?"

I look over to the couch. Gert breathes slowly through barely parted lips, and his injured arm is folded up over his chest like a big broken wing.

"Let him sleep a little, Josh. Aren't we ahead of where you thought we'd be?"

Josh shrugs and goes back to work on the computer.

I go to the kitchen to fill my water bottle. Then I go to the bathroom, and, as I'm sitting there, my phone starts to buzz. The display says "UNKNOWN CALLER" which, at this time of day, is probably my sister calling from the lab phone because she forgot her cell or her battery is dead. I have no issues with talking to my sister on the phone while sitting on the toilet, so I flip it open.

"Hello?"

"Eh, Yosh? Is there, Yosh?"

"What? Who is this?" I stand up quickly, and double-check the display.

"Yosh? Is there?"

"Yosh? You mean Josh?"

"Yosh, Yosh! Is there?"

"Hold on," I say. Josh is standing there when I go out of the bathroom, like he's expecting the call. "What is going on?" I ask him.

"Here, here," he says, holding out his hand. "It's important."

"On my phone, it's important?"

"Just, may I have the phone, please?" Feeling like I'm giving in to something I shouldn't, I hand the phone to him, and he puts it to his ear. *"Bueno?"* He looks at me and puts his free hand up to cover his other ear, then turns away and speaks in a flood of hushed Spanish. I stand behind him with my hands on my hips.

"Sí," he says, kind of urgently. *"Sí, sí, sí!"*

"Josh," I say. "Josh? What is going on?"

He waves his hand without turning to look at me, like a "keep it down" kind of wave, and keeps talking in Spanish.

"That's my phone, Josh."

He keeps talking, hunched over, taking slow steps away from me. I take slow steps and follow him. Finally he snaps my phone shut and hands it to me.

"Sorry about that," he says. "Thanks."

"Sorry?"

"Yeah, I, I mean . . . it was an important—"

I point to the studio phone on the wall. "Hello? Your studio phone? Right there? Extension whatever?"

"He couldn't call on an Academy phone."

"What are you talking about? Who the hell was that? Are you doing some drug deal on my phone? I can't *believe* you!"

"No, no, Jessica, seriously." He kind of laughs. "It's nothing like that."

"You hypocrite. You give me all this shit about me having my phone here, and then you're arranging creepy calls from some dealer or something on *my* phone? That's *my* phone, Josh. Mine!"

"It wasn't a dealer, Jess. It's, I'll tell you all about it at dinner."

"No dinner tonight. You're crazy if you think I'm having dinner with you tonight."

"Come on," Josh says.

There's a noise from the couch, and we both look over to see Gert sitting up and scratching his head with his good hand.

"Oh, boy," he says. "That was some sleep. Jess, you ready to start on the shoulders?"

I look back to Josh. "You are unbelievable sometimes," I say.

18

Josh and I speak very little over the next few days while the rest of my body is scanned. Gert does most of the work, and though I feel Josh looking at me from behind the bulk of the scanner from time to time, I ignore him. I work with him during the daytime, but at night I do not dine with him, and I do not sleep with him.

Gert is the interface between us. And as we've begun to scan my secret parts, I've let myself trust him. He's used his good hand to wrap strips of tape under and around my breasts to force them up and together for the scanner, and he's used that hand to spread my knees and aim the laser eye in close between my legs. He takes the work seriously, and he never makes jokes. Well, I've never heard him make jokes about me, anyway. I trust him.

I've stayed at my place for the past two nights. Partially because it feels nice to be home, and partially because I want to make Josh feel bad. I take the time to work on my project with Gretchen, and I take the time to write some material for Cippoletti. I savor eating by myself, and I savor drinking wine alone in bed while I read.

I return to my home, and I listen for noises, above and below.

And on Wednesday night, it happens, just as I knew it would at some point or another. I run into Patrick as I'm climbing the stairs. I see his legs, coming down, almost to my landing. Turning around would be too obvious; I'm stuck.

"Hey," he says, stopping on the landing.

"Hey?" This seems far more awkward for me than it does for him. I feel like an idiot.

"Things going well?"

"Things are, yeah. Busy. You?"

"Busy too. Crazy busy."

"Yeah."

Neither of us says anything for a moment. Patrick fingers his keys and stuffs them into his pocket, and then he clears his throat.

"Hey," he says, "we're all going out for a drink at the Palace, if you want to—"

"No, no, I have to do some work."

"You sure?"

"Yeah. It's, you know. Work."

"Oh. Well, I'm out, then. See you around."

"See you."

I think for a moment that he's going to touch my arm as he passes me on the stairs, and I brace myself for the shock of it, but he just lifts his hand in a half wave and goes by. I call Katie as soon as I'm through my door.

"I just saw him," I say as soon as she picks up. "I just saw Patrick."

"Uh oh. Like from afar? Or was there interaction?"

"On the stairs. Full interaction."

"Full?"

"No, no! Just, talking."

"Was it weird?"

"Not for him. Weird for me. I think he asked if I wanted to go out for a drink."

"What did you say?"

"I said I had to work. I feel like an idiot."

"Do you miss him?"

"I don't know?"

"What's up with—"

"Josh is in the doghouse," I say. I tell her about dinner with Amy, and the bizarre phone call.

"Creepy," Katie says. "And you're still letting him scan your bum?"

"That part is proceeding as usual."

"I have a question. Just what is he doing with all these scans?"

"Well, he's using them in some prints he's going to make, somehow, but . . . it's a good question. I honestly don't know."

The rest of the evening is spent with leftover Chinese and some lousy white wine, reviewing the digital brochure mockups that Gretchen has sent to me. The files are huge, and they're difficult to view on my smallish old monitor, but the stuff looks good and the design is well done and I feel a silly thrill at seeing so much work being built up around something I wrote.

I type up some comments to Gretchen in an e-mail, and as I'm just about to hit send, there's a general clumsy knocking around downstairs.

"Danny." I hear Patrick calling in what he thinks is a whisper. "Danny?"

It's just a little bit after one in the morning.

There's one last "Danny?" followed by the thump thump thump thump of him running up the stairs, and, wait a second, is he pausing on my floor? The moment is nothing, and he thump thumps again the rest of the way up and I hear his keys and his door opening and shutting above me.

There is water again. A toilet flushing. I hit send and close down my computer and rise up out of my chair with my right ear cocked toward the ceiling.

There are footsteps. Furniture is moved. Chair legs groan against the old wood floor.

I'm holding my breath and listening.

And, maybe with a little more certainty than the last time I did it, I stand up and go to my door.

There is no crying of hinges or creaking of steps when I make my way up to Patrick's floor, and when I'm there I halt and take a breath before I take one last step toward his door. Just as I raise my hands to brace myself so I can place my ear against the wood, the doorknob rattles and suddenly, slowly, certainly, the door opens and there he is, standing shirtless and rubbing the back of his neck with his free hand. I drop my hands and jog my right foot forward to keep myself from falling through his doorway, making a stupid face because I am so, so busted.

I'm surprised by the fact that I feel so calm. I step into the dark apartment—one step, two—and Patrick, facing me, takes two steps back and stops. We're toe to toe with the door open and a wash of blue fluorescent light behind me.

"You were at my door," he says, blinking against the buzzing glare coming in from the hall. "The other night."

"Yes," I say. "I was."

"You didn't knock."

"I know."

"You could have knocked."

"I was observing."

"Is that another word for spying?"

"No. Just observing."

"You should have knocked. You could have observed me in person."

Standing there, facing each other, my eyes are just about level with his chin. A smile breaks across his face, and I catch a hint of his boozy breath.

"Are you drunk?" I ask. My arms are at my sides.

"Maybe. Maybe a little. Not so much. Are you?"

"Not so much. Should I be?"

The smile goes, and he brings his hands forward to put them on my waist. He doesn't look stern. If anything, he looks sleepy and maybe even a little . . . sad? "You don't need to be," he says. My arms go up and around him, like a reflex.

"I don't need to be, I guess."

We move farther into his apartment, feet in sync, step, pause, step. My arms tighten, and so do his, and my chest presses into him. His cheek is scratchy with day-old beard against my forehead, and I close my eyes and tilt my head and press my face into his neck, and I smell the bar and his home and his work. Mostly it's just him I smell, there in the skin of his neck.

Patrick's lips press into my hair.

"Did you get your work done?" It's a whisper, a murmur, into my hair.

"I did my work," I say. "It's never really done, though."

"It never really is. I miss you."

"Do you?"

"Yes."

"We fit together well," I say, and as I say it, Patrick's balance goes for a second and we wobble, and then we keep each other up. "Like this."

"Yes. Like this. Do you miss me?"

I could tell him the truth and say yes, but I'm afraid if I do, this perfect moment will somehow vanish. So I say nothing; I stand and tighten my arms around him and hold my closed eyes against the line of his jaw.

"You do, don't you," he says.

I don't speak.

"I know you do."

We take more steps—slowly—Patrick leading me backward in the general direction of his bedroom. One of the windows is open in there, and the lightest breeze comes through and briefly makes his wood-slatted blinds chatter. Pat's hand is up my shirt and his palm presses warm against the small of my back, and when we take another step he staggers and I think we're going to fall but we don't, and the whole time his hand is there at my back. I laugh for a moment about the near disaster but when I look up at him I stop; his head is tilted back and his eyes are closed and his lips are barely parted. Then he blinks open his eyes and smiles and looks at me.

"Who's leading here?" he asks.

"Are you really drunk, Pat?"

"Nooo," he says. Then he smiles again. "I'm not, really."

The air moves again, and the blinds make their shivering noise. We take more steps, through the doorway into his room, then he bumps backward into his bed and sits.

"Ha," he says, more verbal punctuation than laugh. "Ha." Patrick looks up at me and his hands, inside my shirt, are resting on my waist, thumbs at the bottom of my ribs.

"Do you want to stay?" he whispers. "You can stay if you want."

I lean forward, and my cheek brushes against his own as I bring my lips to his ear.

"I—" I take a breath, "I don't think I should."

"I'm not that drunk."

"That's not it."

"Let's forget the rule, okay?"

"That's not it, either."

"What is it, then?"

I straighten up, and take his hands from my waist and hold them in my own.

"I'm tired," I say. "You're tired. I have to work in the morning—"

"Which work?" he says, a little more alertly. "Ad work or art work?" This is something I don't even want to get close to touching.

"Work work. I have to be up early."

"That never stopped you before," he says, and I can see his smile in the darkness. He lies back into his pillow and pulls his legs up onto the bed, holding my hands the entire time. "You should stay."

"No, Pat. I should go home and go to bed. And you should go to sleep."

He just looks at me for a moment, and there might be a little smile on his face, but I can't be sure in the dark. "You're right. You should probably go."

"Wait," I say. "Wait. I know what you're trying to do here." It would be so easy, and there would be so little remorse. Well, I can tell myself that now. "I could stay. I mean, we could just rest." I'd like to smile too; part of me wishes I could, but I feel weary and confused.

"Right," he says. "Rest. Rest."

"Hold on a second," I say. "I'll be back."

"You're going?"

"Just to the bathroom."

I go back through his apartment, past the still-open door and the glow from the hall, and I don't turn on the light when I go through the kitchen and into his bathroom. I see myself, my silhouette, in the mirror, and I stand there and think what I should do and what I could do, and above all what I'd like to do.

It would be very, very easy.

I could just not think about it after; and there would be very little remorse.

It would be very easy.

So I go back to the room, and see that Pat has pulled his covers over himself; his still-clothed leg sticks out from the side of the bed and his mouth is wide open and each heavy breath is just on the edge of being a snore. This makes me laugh. I'm ready, so ready, and he's passed out. Or maybe not.

"You didn't flush," he says without opening his eyes.

"I didn't go."

"Come here." He reaches his hand toward me, then pats his bed next to him. "Come here."

I can't do this. I shouldn't. But I sit on the bed and slide my hand under the sheets and onto his bare stomach and chest. And as I lean forward toward him, bracing myself against his chest, his arm comes around me under my shirt and he pulls me to him and our mouths go together all boozy and wet and breathing. He pulls me closer and I bring my knee up onto the bed, and with my left hand I'm fumbling to unbutton my pants and his hand is up the back of my shirt again. I rise up, then back down, our teeth nick and we're kissing again. Then, for an instant, I think of Gretchen. It feels so not right that I stop and sit up.

"What?" he says.

"I should go."

"Really?"

"Yes. I should."

"You probably should."

"I mean, we could just rest," I say. "We could just sleep, for real."

"You should go," he says. Maybe he's thinking about Gretchen too? His eyes are closed, and he takes a long breath after he says it, like he's really going to fall asleep. Well, fine then. He probably won't even remember this.

"Good night, Pat." There's nothing. "Pat?"

"Hmm?"

"Good night."

"Good night, Jess. I miss you."

"I know. Call me."

"I'll call you. I miss you."

I almost give him another kiss, but I get up and leave instead.

• • •

On Thursday, as Gert works over me in the studio, I try to avoid making eye contact with Josh. I mean, I shouldn't feel guilty, and I am still sort of angry with him, so why should I feel weird about talking with Patrick last night?

It was just talking, right? Nothing happened. Well, that kissing, and the near removal of my pants.

Should something more have happened?

Is just a kiss something, or nothing?

To keep it out of my head, I ask Gert what he thinks the project is going to be.

"You know, Jess," he says, "I have an idea what the doc is doing with these, but every time I think I know what he's doing, I'm wrong. So, I guess I don't know."

I'm lying topless on the table while we wait to see if Josh feels we need to re-scan the right side of my rib cage. My arm is covering my chest and my head is on a pillow, and Gert sits next to me up on the table with his cast in his lap.

"Not even a guess?"

"I have some guesses." He lifts his injured hand and scratches around the base of the cast with his left thumb.

"Oh God, Gert, your surgery is tomorrow."

"Yes. Eight a.m."

"Are you . . . do you need to do anything to get ready for it?"

"I'm just not allowed to eat tonight. They're putting me to sleep all the way."

"What do they have to do?"

"Just fix the tendon, and then another cast. Maybe another surgery."

"How long does the cast stay on?"

"Six weeks? Not so long."

"I'm really sorry, Gert."

"No, stop. It was my own fault. And it will be all fixed soon enough. More drugs in the meantime, though. And I'm pretty good at brushing my teeth with my left hand. I can do all sorts of things lefty now."

I pass on making the obvious joke. If only Gretchen were here.

Josh looks up at us from behind the bulk of the scanner. "I think we're done," he says.

"You need me anymore, Doc?" Gert holds out his good hand to help me sit up, then slides my folded tank top across the table.

"I'm just going to be cataloging these, so stay if you want, but I don't really need any help."

"I'm going to go eat, then. Eat while I can."

"Good luck tomorrow," I say. My top is back on, and Gert's holding his hand out again for me while I jump down from the table.

"You send me some chocolates while I'm there."

"How long do you have to stay? And where are you having it done?" I reach up under my top to straighten out the shelf bra in there, an act that Gert pays no attention to whatsoever.

"St. Mary's. I could leave that day, but they recommend I stay the night. I get more flowers and chocolates that way."

"Really, I hope it's fast and easy for you."

"You're a nice girl, Jess." He grabs his backpack and says good-bye to Josh, and he's off.

"Let me know how it goes tomorrow, Gert," Josh says.

I'm left standing by the table, wondering if I should make a quick exit myself.

"Jess," Josh says, not looking up this time. "You want to see what you look like?" With Gert gone, his voice seems to hang in the space of the studio. And as much as I wish I could forget it, I do feel a little guilty about last night.

"Not really? I mean, sure, I'll look."

I pull a chair over to his side of the scanner and sit next to him. On the screen is a wire-frame rendering of something; it doesn't look like a part of me or anyone else. Josh types something and the lines are filled in; he types something else and shading appears to provide relief. Whatever is on the screen looks alien; wrinkled and cratered like the surface of the moon.

"What is that?"

"It's your armpit."

"Shut up."

"No, really. Look." He spins a jogwheel on the console with his middle finger and the surface on the screen backs away and sure enough, my armpit is there in ghostly white, framed by my lifted arm and the roundness of my breast.

Josh types some more, and something new resolves itself on the screen. "I really like this one."

"It's a mountain range."

"It's the top of your foot. Left foot, when I had you point your toes up. Those are your tendons."

"Yes, yes. I see it now."

"Look at this one," Josh says. "This is one of my favorites." He types again, and I see a strange curved space; without any frame of reference I can't tell if the curve is bulging out or in. I stare and stare, and I must confess that I'm fascinated.

"I give up," I say. "What is it?"

"Right here," he says, and he reaches to me and touches the space above my right collarbone. He rubs his fingertip there, just for a moment, and it gives me a little shiver.

"From yesterday? When you had me put my hand up on my head?"

"That's it."

"That's so cool."

"Want to see more?"

"I want to know what you're planning to do with them. That's what I want to know."

"Ah. You'll see. You will see."

"You won't give me a hint?"

"Rand McNally."

"That's what you said last time. Just tell me."

"You'll see. You will."

"You suck."

"I do suck. I need to tell you something. About that phone call."

"Josh," I say, and I scoot the chair back just a little bit away from him. "I'm over it. And I don't really need that to be my business. I don't want it to be. Just don't give people my number."

"No, really, it's the farthest thing from what you think it is."

"Fine, tell me then."

"Alright. The person who called, his name's Christian. He's in El Salvador."

"That call was from El Salvador?"

"It was. Christian has been a really good friend. I lived with his family when I was a grad student, his mom is like, my second mom. They've all modeled for me. His little brother was in that PowerPoint—"

"Ramón, San Salvador?"

"Exactly. Ramón is here in the States now. But the thing is, his paperwork isn't entirely straight. And right now, he's kind of... well, he's kind of disappeared."

"Disappeared? Is he into shady things?"

"Hardly. He's a good kid, you know, here to work. But no one knows where he is. Christian's just trying to track him down. He's worried. And he wanted me to help him out. That's all there is to it."

"But why my phone?"

"From Salvador, it's a lot cheaper for him to call your cell carrier than a landline."

I think about this, and I guess it makes sense. Maybe it makes sense? "You swear you're telling me the truth?"

"Absolute truth, Jess. And I'm sorry."

"Josh, maybe..."

"Maybe what?"

"Maybe you should consider getting your own phone," I say. "For things like that."

"It sort of goes against my principles. But I will consider it."

"Good."

"You left your book in the loft, you know."

"What book?"

"The Hiaasen one."

I laugh. "Amy loaned me that book, actually."

"That figures. His picture on the back has been taunting me. I had to turn him over so he wouldn't smile at me anymore. He was rubbing it in."

"Rubbing what in?"

"Your absence."

I cross my arms. "If I go up there to get Amy's book, you're going to follow me, aren't you?"

"I might."

"And if you follow me up there, you're going to get close to me and say the words, right?"

"I could say the words, and do those things I usually do when I say the words."

"And we will undress, and probably have sex."

"That would be a possibility. After saying the words and doing the things, if we end up undressed, we may actually engage in sexual intercourse. I am currently thinking of past occasions where things unfolded in a similar fashion."

"You expect this to happen, don't you?"

"I expect nothing." Josh's straight face breaks into the faintest smile. "But I would like it more than anything."

I stare at him, with my arms crossed, for a long, long time. He stares back. It is unfortunate that, right now, compelled by the guilt over what almost happened last night, I would like it more than anything too. So I guess I'll have something else to feel guilty about.

"If this chain of events unfolds as we've described it," I say, "I'm not going to spend the night."

"Understood. But I would also love your company tonight

to celebrate the completion of the first part of this project. Scanning done. And by celebrate, I mean, there will be bottles of wine, plural. And take-out food of some exotic variety."

"Then I reserve the right, upon the completion of the act, to reconsider."

"This too is understood."

We stare at each other again, wordlessly daring the other to break. Finally I stand up.

"Well," I say, "I had better grab Amy's book before I go."

And I climb the steps to the loft.

I'm meeting Gretchen Friday afternoon, but I decide that I first should go over to St. Mary's to see if Gert is taking visitors. It isn't so far from the Academy and it's a nice day for a walk.

Yes, I completed the act last evening.

Yes, I assisted in the consumption of two bottles of decent wine and one very good bottle of champagne brought over by Hoffman when he heard us, drunk and laughing, from down the hall.

And yes, I spent the night.

Josh is busy trying to get some additional computers moved into the studio for the project, and the workers are back to dismantle and pack up the scanner. So there isn't much of a reason to stick around, and I'd really like to see how Gert is doing, so I go.

I stop at a drugstore on the way to buy a box of chocolates, and because I'm feeling goofy and I hate kitschy things like this, I buy a little pink teddy bear with a heart stitched on the chest that says: "You're the BEST!"

It takes about twenty minutes to get to the hospital. Gert Knickmann is there, says the girl at the front desk, room 516. He's out of surgery, visitors are permitted. I get an ID tag and directions to Gert's room, making no eye contact with the feeble, broken people shuffling through the halls on my way there.

Gert is awake in his room, lying in bed and talking with a plain but cute young woman seated on a chair next to him. They both look at me as I peek in the door, and Gert blinks and smiles.

"Jess, come in," he says. His voice is a little wobbly. "Come in. Angie, this is Jessica."

Angie's proximity to Gert suggests she's the girlfriend, and she stands up and offers her hand over the bed. "Oh! Jessica. You're the... You're working with Gert and Dr. Hadden? On the project?"

"Yes, that's me."

"Angie gets jealous when I come home and tell her about seeing you naked all day."

Angie slaps the pillow next to Gert's head. "Shut up. That is not true at all."

"I have found Mr. Knickmann to be a perfect gentleman," I say, smiling. "Gert, since you kept talking about them, I brought some chocolates. And a pink bear. I had a feeling you'd love it."

"Oh, Jess, you're too nice, but I was only making a joke about the chocolates. I don't eat them. I'm very happy about the bear, though." He reaches for the toy and reads it, squinting, before tucking it under his left arm. "I'm the best? I knew this."

"You are the worst," Angie says. Then she says something to him in what I assume to be Dutch; Gert laughs and says something back and she slaps the pillow again.

"She says she can take the chocolates. I say if she eats them all I won't ever want to scan her naked."

I can't compete with Gert's foreign sense of humor. "How was the surgery?" I ask.

"I think it went okay, I was asleep for it. We know better in a few days, yeah? Why don't you sit down?"

"Oh, thanks, but I don't have a ton of time. I just wanted to say hi."

"You're sweet to come," Gert says. He blinks his eyes, looking sleepy. "I suppose the doc will be too busy to come by. Tell him everything was fine."

"I will, Gert. Get better fast." I look over to Angie. "It was nice meeting you."

"Nice meeting you too," she says. "I'll walk out with you. Gert, I'm going to find something to drink. You need anything?"

"I'm fine. I just rest here with the bear."

We go out in the hall and I start to go the wrong way. Angie smiles and motions me toward her when she sees that I'm disoriented.

"It's so confusing in here," she says. "You know, Gert has really, really liked working with you."

"Gert has a good poker face. But I like working with him too. How long have you guys been, I mean, I'm assuming—"

"We're partners. It's been, gosh, it will be five years in September. I went to Delft for my undergrad. In the Netherlands. That's where we met."

"Are you Dutch?"

"My mother is. We were back and forth when I was a kid, there and here. But yeah, that's where I met Gertie. Did you know he studied architecture? It's strange, five years. Five years and it seems like nothing."

"I'm lucky if a relationship goes five months."

"It's terrible that I'm asking this, but are you and Dr. Hadden like, together? I mean, Gertie has mentioned it, but he never really... God, I'm so sorry, this is none of my business."

"No, it's fine. And yeah, we are. I think?"

"What's it like? What's he like?"

"It's, well, it's interesting."

"I bet. Dr. Hadden is kind of, he's, hmm..."

"Yeah, he is," I say, and we laugh.

"I'm just asking because Gert, he and the doctor, it's a—"

"How does Gert feel about him?"

"Don't ever tell him I said this. Gert, I mean. Or Dr. Hadden, either, I guess, but I think Gert is really intimidated by him."

"Really?"

"Yeah. Gert thinks he's crazy. But he also thinks he's a genius."

"I would agree. On both counts."

"Gertie is talking about maybe going to the U.K. to work with him more. Dr. Hadden asked him if he'd be interested." We've stopped in front of a bank of vending machines, and Angie digs through a little pocketbook looking for change.

"What do you think about that? Would you go?"

"Oh, yeah, I would. London is great too. It's nice to see Gert get all excited about something. But Dr. Hadden is so intense." She plugs her coins into one of the machines and gets a bottle of water.

"He is," I say.

"Hey, I should get back. It was so nice meeting you. And thanks for coming. I know it made Gertie really happy."

"I'm glad," I say. "Do you think it would make him mad if I called him 'Gertie' back in the studio?"

"You could call him that, and he'd probably laugh. If the doctor called him that, he'd search for hidden meaning."

I guess I'm not surprised to find I'm not the only one who looks for hidden meaning in Josh's actions.

19

Over the next few weeks, the studio changes from looking like a radiology lab to a computer lab to something defying description; giant flat-screen monitors stand around the perimeter and the interior is now filled with slabs of rock and sheets of paper. An old-fashioned printing press stands in the very center of the room. Josh, more often than not, wears a heavy rubberized apron and surgical gloves, and Gert, also aproned, has a ridiculous plastic bag held over his new cast with a rubber band.

The project becomes a twenty-four-hour operation. Shades stay down, almost always, on the big sunny windows, and a fold-up cot appears in the corner. Gert's backpack is usually stashed beneath it.

Textbooks with titles like *Elements of Cartography* and *Mastering the UNIX Command Line, Volume III* sit on the computer desks. The monitors are enormous, like miniature movie screens, and although sometimes I see the ghostly white scans of my body across them it's more often a bouncing ball screen saver. Jugs and buckets of chemicals and inks sit around the tables and fill the studio with a new, caustic smell. It's vaguely acrid, almost like vinegar; the scent creeps up in my nose and lingers in the top of my sinus and it invades my clothes and my bag and I always worry that I stink like a darkroom after I leave.

Josh, when I visit, has perpetual stubble and dark rings below his eyes. Some days he has ink smeared on his cheek or neck or forehead. When he finally does notice me he seems surprised; he blinks and gives a little shake of his head, as if the real me has sprung up from the 3D me he sees all day on his monitors and shouted "Boo!"

"Would you turn around and lift up your shirt?" he asks one day when I come through the door. "I need to see your lower back." This is how he greets me.

I pull my shirt above the waistband of my skirt and turn around for him, and I look over my shoulder and see him cocking his head as he stares at the small of my back. He says okay, okay, then he nods and pulls off one of his gloves to chew the nail of his ring finger before going back to one of the tables to pick up a pad of paper. He makes a note about something, or maybe a sketch. Gert works on, silently, while this happens. He's always working.

I usually ask if I can bring them anything when I come. Can I get you something to eat? Something to drink? They wave me off. To be honest, I don't feel so welcome in the studio anymore. I haven't spent the night since...well, I honestly don't remember.

I think I might be taking this a little personally.

Professionally, though, the time away has been a good thing. Cippoletti and the golf resort are both going like crazy. I write and I write—magazine ads, brochures, and copy for radio spots—and somehow I manage to keep Mike, the Italians, and Gretchen all happy. Thankfully, Gretchen is the only one of us who deals directly with our masters in golf land.

My mother calls too, during this time, almost daily. Plans for my sister's going-away-to-the-South-Pacific party have become concrete; a barbecue is set for one week from Saturday with family and friends, and two days after that we're going to drive out on the peninsula to eat at a seafood restaurant and stay at a bed-and-breakfast for our special mother-sister-sister time. My dates to travel up there have been set, but my mom—who has some special voodoo method for finding cheap airfares—is waiting until the last minute to buy my tickets.

"It's almost time," she says during one afternoon call. I'm sitting in my bay window and watching the street as we talk. "It's very close."

"They're so cheap right now, Mom, why not just go ahead and get them?"

"This fare will be ten to fifteen dollars less in two days. I'll buy them at the right time, you don't need to worry."

In her frugal nature, I'm beginning to understand what drew my parents together so long ago.

"I appreciate that you're paying for these, really, but I'm happy to get it myself, Mom." I seriously am; salary-wise, I'm doing better right now than I ever have in my adult working life.

"No, no, Jessica. This is my special treat for you girls. For me too."

"You *will* let me get the B and B. I'm not joking."

"Oh, Jessica, it's enough trouble that you're coming up."

"I'm paying, whether you like it or not."

"We can talk about it."

We get off the phone, and I go to the computer to try to write some more. Katie has left me an instant message while I was on the phone that says, simply: "SCAN MY ASS."

I can't even think of a response for this, so I just type: "you win, K., today and for always. go easy on caps lock." I get her away message when I send it, though; she must be off teaching now or something important like that. So I write. It's a piece about the Cippoletti tops; a serious piece with no mention of bodily fluids. As I work, there's a knock at my door, and I jump because I think for an instant it's going to be Patrick.

"Jess, are you there?" It's Danny's voice. I open the door and Danny comes in and holds me in a long hug.

"Where have you been, Jess? I've missed you."

"I missed you too, Danny. I've been turned into a work of art, I guess."

"You've always been a work of art. A piece of work, at least."

"Ha."

"I was worried my big brother services would no longer be needed."

"You're always my big brother, Danny. Forever and ever."

"I know it. Is your computer working? I can't get online."

I point to my desk with a sweeping move of my arm. "My workstation is yours."

Danny sits and brings up his e-mail. "You plug straight in, but I'm using wireless. It always dies on me. I don't know what I'm supposed to reboot up in Pat's place. All those wires."

"I don't know anything about it. But he'll be home in an hour."

"No, he won't. He's in Singapore right now."

This is news. "For real?"

"They're doing a demo of their project. Asian launch party. I think he's in Tokyo tomorrow, then he's back Tuesday."

"I didn't even know."

"Now you do."

"How did the launch go here?"

"You can ask him yourself when he gets back. I'm not going to be your proxy, Jessica. That's stupid."

This gets me a little huffy. I cross my arms and glare at Danny, which is a pointless act because, despite all my angry nose breathing, he refuses to turn around and look at me, and even if he did I doubt he would care. So I go to the kitchen and adopt a new strategy.

"It's five o'clock," I say. "Wine time. Do you want a glass?"

"Even if you make me drunk," he calls back, "I'm not talking about Pat."

"Damn you, Danny! You're impossible!"

"Sure," he says. "I'll have a glass."

An hour after Danny has left, I'm tipsy and nursing my goblet with Amy's book in my lap. I'm reading without really reading, sitting in sweatpants just looking at words with my hand in my shirt on my stomach; I'm tired and a little drunk and thinking maybe, maybe, I'm going to go to bed early tonight.

There's a knock at my door and the first thing I think is how I'm happy my computer is still on so Danny can quickly check his e-mail and get the hell out of here. The knock comes again, softly, and I move my wineglass so I won't kick it over and put my book on the floor next to it.

"Hold on a second," I say, and walk across the space of my living room. "Hold on."

Josh is at my door; he looks jangly and his eyes seem ready to pop out of his head.

"What are you doing here?"

"It's done, Jess. We finished."

"How did you get in?"

"The prints are . . . we got the last one done an hour ago." He steps into my place and holds me by the shoulders.

"How did you get into the building?"

"You didn't see the note."

"The note, what?"

"You'll see the note. Who's your neighbor downstairs?"

"Danny?"

"With the dark hair. From the party." He kisses me, and his beard is rough on my chin. "It's done. The prints are done."

"That's great, Josh. Thank you for telling me. I'm exhausted, though. I was getting ready for bed." He's pushing me—gently—into the apartment, and I'm letting myself be nudged back.

"They look...it's incredible."

"Maybe I can see them tomorrow?"

"No, no, the exhibit. At the Academy. Week from Thursday. That's when you can see them." We're at my couch; Josh pushes me back so I'm sitting down and he kneels on the floor in front of me. I think I hear my wineglass tip over.

"I am really, really tired, Josh."

He takes my sweats by the waistband with both hands and pulls them down. I cringe as I lift my hips a bit to facilitate this action, but he doesn't see it.

"Could we maybe do this tomorrow?"

He's kissing my stomach.

"Damn it, Josh."

Now I'm grabbing a pillow. He goes to work; I'm too self-conscious to peek and see his face down there, and the lamp is too far for me to reach and turn off. At least the blinds are closed.

When it's done, he doesn't need to ask "Did you?" It's fairly obvious, at least to me, that I did.

Josh stands up and stretches his neck. He stares at me sitting there, and I'm coming back to earth and wondering how I can get my sweats and do I need to wipe up spilled wine on my floor?

"Come by the studio tomorrow," he says.

"Where are you going?"

"I need to help Gert finish cleaning things up."

"You're really leaving?"

"It's a mess."

"Can I take care of you? Just stay for a little bit."

"I need to get back." He leans down and his kiss tastes like me. He kisses me a second time, and then his face gets that look of just remembering something.

"Can I use your phone? Fast."

"You don't need to ask."

He dials the phone and stands facing my bookshelf with his fingers pressed to his ear. I get my underwear and sweats back on, and yes, there is a wine mess, so I go to the kitchen to get some paper towels.

"Hey, Emmy, hey, it's Josh, maybe you guys are out or in bed or something, I wanted to call and say, it's done, Emily, it's done! I want you to see it, I'm going to try to get some pictures from the opening, God I wish you could be there. And, um, hey, you know I talked to Mom, please, please call her, she's got, she *wants* to help, Emily, she's there for you, she and Dad have room—" Josh suddenly stands up straight and looks at the phone. I'm on my knees wiping up the spill that has migrated under my couch.

"I think it hung up on me." I stand up, paper towels in hand, and he gives me another kiss.

"You can stay, really."

"I'm going back. Come see me at the studio."

He leaves, and I go to the bathroom and brush my teeth and turn out the lights and climb into bed. Tonight, falling asleep is hard.

I'm craving good coffee—a latte or some other overpriced hot drink—in the morning, so I dress myself and have a glass of water and a multivitamin and head down the stairs to brave the hipsters at Tommie's Coffee Shop. Danny, the little geek, is getting a newspaper from his box out front.

"Late night visitor?" He rolls up the paper and swats it into his hand a few times.

"Shut up," I say. "Give me a little warning next time before you provide access to any late-night visitors in the future, will you?"

"Provide access, what?"

"Didn't you let Josh in?"

"I didn't let anyone in. I heard someone run up the stairs, and I heard you talking."

"Stop it, you're messing with me."

"I'm not. Come on, Jess, I wouldn't just let someone in. It was Josh?"

"You really aren't saying this just to freak me out?"

Danny shakes his head, and I am, seriously, freaked out.

I try to call the studio on the way to the coffee shop, it rings and rings, but no answer. I call the Academy back and ask for Hoffman's extension this time, and he picks up on the second ring.

"Nah, he's not here," Hoffman says. "He took my car about forty minutes ago."

It's nice enough to sit outside at Tommie's, so I do; this also gets me away from the dreadlocked guy who stared at me the whole time I waited for my latte at the counter. I stare at my phone, as if somehow just looking at it will guide me to getting in touch with Josh so I can ask him what the hell is going on. And as I look, the display lights up and it starts to vibrate in my hand. The number on the display is from the 617 area code; I know this is Boston, but the number isn't Katie's.

"Hello?"

"Jess Z." It is Katie. "What's up?"

"Lots. Where are you calling from?"

"New phone. New provider."

"I thought you could keep your number?"

"You can, if you want tall doctors to call you every *twenty effing minutes.*"

"You ended it?"

"It's an ongoing process."

"Congratulations?"

"Thank you, I think. I might not have initiated the breakup if I had known it would be this hard. I could have just ignored him on the boat. But I wanted to do it like a big girl. What's up?"

I tell her about Josh coming over, and everything that happened. I tell her about Danny not letting him in.

"What the hell?" Katie says. "That's creepy."

"I know."

"I think you need to end it too."

"I know. Thank you. I needed to hear you say it before I let myself think it."

"It's just a weird picture you've painted. The whole time. So how do you do it?"

"Well, there's a show next week, I guess, with the stuff he made from my scans. I haven't even seen the prints yet. Do I do it before that?"

"A gallery show?"

"I think so."

"Featuring your bum?"

"Stop it, I'm trying to be—"

"Wait until after the show. Don't have sex with him again. See the prints. Don't lose your will."

"That's what I should do?"

"That's what you should do."

I thank Katie and we say good-bye, and I program her new number into my phone.

I have my second opinion. And I know what I will do.

There is serious fog on the night of the opening. Gert has called to make sure I'm coming; yes, he says, it's a dress-up kind of thing, and yes, there will be an open bar. The news about the bar pleases me. I can fortify my will for free.

Since his visit, I haven't seen or talked to Josh once. I

haven't gone to the studio, and he hasn't come to my apartment. I'd like to think that he suspects something is up, that something is going to happen, that I'm going to stand up and say this can't continue. I'd like to think that, but I might just be imagining it.

I have gotten back into the habit, over the past week, of using the chain and the dead bolt on my door. From behind this wall of paranoia I've made for myself, I often hear Patrick; going up, coming down. He yells things to Danny. Danny yells things back. They've been hanging out a lot lately, without me. As I put on my black dress for the opening, they're yelling things again.

"You ready yet?" Danny shouts. "We have twenty minutes before they start."

"Almost, almost! Jesus, Danny, those guys never start playing on time."

I wait for them to leave, and with my low-heeled shoes and my bag and a funky knit shawl I'm almost out my door, but then I stop and go to my shelf and get my road atlas. I flip through it, not really looking at anything in particular, wondering if I should bring it along. But instead, I just slide it back into its place among my books. Then I head out the door and off to the bus stop. The fog feels kind of lovely, and in a strange way I feel like the mist and the dark are bolstering my courage for what I'm planning to say to Josh.

Maybe I'm building it up to be a bigger deal than it is. Maybe he'll shrug. Maybe this was nothing. Maybe I was just part of the project, a prop, and will be treated as such.

Or maybe, as I'm kind of secretly hoping as I sit here in this humming bus, he'll flip out and throw a tantrum.

The gallery is close to the Academy, just off campus, and as I walk up to it I see people inside and a giant sign, suspended from the ceiling, that says: "JOSHUA HADDEN: *The Physical Atlas.*" Below the big sign is a smaller one, a detail of what looks like a greenish hiker's topographic map; there are lines and marked elevations and named roads, and as I step through the door, staring up, looking and looking more, I suddenly realize:

That's my left arm, slightly bent, at the crease inside of my elbow.

There are maybe twenty-five or thirty prints hanging around the walls of the gallery, and many, many more people. The room is filled with a general talky hum, bits of laughter and conversation rise from time to time punctuated by occasional flashes from a camera. Just at the edge of the crowd I see Gert, smiling and taller than everyone around him and looking handsome in a dark coat and shirt with no tie. Angie stands next to him, her arm looped through his injured wing, and when she sees me she smiles and beckons me over.

"Hi, hi," she says. She has a glass of white wine and Gert, who doesn't stop his dorky grinning, holds a cocktail glass.

"Jess," he says.

"The prints are incredible," Angie says. Then she leans close to me and speaks softly in my ear. "No one knows they're you. The secret's safe with us."

"Thanks," I say. "Gert, good work."

"Thank you, Jess."

I walk around and look at the prints. They are incredible. They are *me* too, and as much as I want to look at them, I also want to look away.

The sound of voices gets louder as I make my way around the room; I see Josh talking to some people with notepads and cameras. He looks great too; clean shaven and bright eyed in a coarse-yarned charcoal colored sweater. His face lights up when he sees me, and he walks away from the interviewers to come and put his arm around me.

"Jess," he says, squeezing me. His cheeks are red like the glass of wine in his hand. "Jess! Do you like them? What do you think?"

"They're terrific, Josh. They are, really."

"What's up?"

"Nothing, what?"

"You just seem..."

I look at him, and then I lean in and crane my neck up and talk into his ear. "I don't want people to, you know, know that *I'm* the one in the prints." It's true, kind of.

He takes his arm from my shoulders. "So you don't want me to be close."

"Exactly."

"I completely understand." He smiles. "Completely." I draw in a breath to begin the inevitable "hey can I talk to you later on" bit, but he nods at me and raises his eyebrows in a way that's not subtle *at all* because he's drunk, and he turns back to a woman with a notepad.

There will be time for that talk, I'm sure. So I look for the bar, and as I make my way through the too-close people I pause and look at myself on the walls.

In one print, my lower back is bisected by an interstate highway and a network of bright red and blue roads.

In another, the bumpy margin of my nipple has become a national park.

Here's another, my shoulder, with a cross-hatched trapezoid marked "Restricted Entry—Government Research Area."

I look at another as I walk by, just a glance. There are more roads, maybe on my stomach, the upper part? I go past, and then I stop and go back. There's something about it, something that brings me back, and in a rush I look from side to side and think and gasp—that's it *that's it!*—the blue line curving up the middle of my rib cage is identical to the interstate that goes to Spokane, the line Katie and I traced a hundred or more times through our atlas to the dot we made with the neatly lettered words: "Grandma and Grandpa Mason's Farm."

I'm smiling at this. When I look up, I see two men have joined me to look at the print, but they quickly turn and head toward the bar, as if they realized they were interrupting something.

"Wait," I say. I'm pretty sure these are the same two guys from the studio, the day Gert cut himself. "Hey?"

I follow through the crowd, and when I finally get close to the bar the two men are not there. I do want a drink, though, so I ask the bartender for a glass of whatever red wine he's got. He tells me the apple martinis are very good, and since I have orchards on my mind now, I say sure. The drink is kind of green-colored and has a pretty, thin slice of apple floating in it. It's delicious too, in a candied, drink-it-too-fast sort of way.

I wander around, looking, getting used to my close-up, listening in on people's conversations. There's a couple talking next to what looks like a map of a lake.

"It's her navel," the girl is saying. She draws out the first syllable, like *naaay*vel. "He filled it in with the blue color. You can't see the actual belly button part."

"Navels are symmetrical," the guy says. "That is a seriously asymmetrical lake."

"Most navels are symmetrical. But not all. Some are not."

"Yeah, let's check," he says, and he makes a joking grab like he's going to lift up her shirt and she laughs.

"Stop it!" she says.

I make an orbit of the room, then another. I say hi again to Gert and Angie. Hoffman shows up and doesn't say a word to me. I'm standing by the print of my lower back when he sees me; he looks at the print and looks at me and nods like he understands that I don't want to be recognized, and he makes no acknowledgment of me again after that.

I stop at the bar again to trade my empty glass for a full one. The voices in the gallery get louder; there's more laughter, more noise, more bared teeth. People are getting drunk and having a good time. I'm getting drunk and not having a very good time at all. Gretchen and I had talked, earlier in the week, about her coming with me, but today I called her and told her she shouldn't bother, the opening would probably be a bore. I didn't tell her the real reason: I was afraid she would somehow make me lose my nerve.

On my next lap, it looks like Gert is being interviewed. He has to lean down so the woman can hear him, and he holds his cast across his chest while he gestures with his good hand. Angie stands next to him with a look of supportive false interest, but steps over when she sees me hovering.

"Having fun?" she asks. "Don't lie."

"Are you?"

"I was, an hour ago." She brings the back of her hand to her mouth to hide a yawn. "I'm sorry. I'm tired. I have to work tomorrow."

"What do you do?"

"I'm a high school teacher. Physics and math."

"A girl geek," I say, and Angie smiles, so I know I haven't offended her. "Summer school?"

"Private school. Goes year round."

I'm tired too, and it shows as I stand there with my paper-thin apple slice, completely unable to come up with any additional chitchat. It doesn't seem to bother Angie, though.

"Are you staying for the whole thing?" she asks.

"I kind of have to," I say, and Angie says "ah" like she completely understands, even though she doesn't understand it at all.

"Do you want another drink?" I ask. "I'm going to break the martini rule."

Angie starts to ask about this rule, but just as she begins to speak there's an abrupt change in the sound of conversation in the room; people are suddenly quiet, they look back and forth to each other and there is murmuring and a repeated sound like, "Miami, Miami, it happened in Miami, what happened in Miami?" And, just as quickly, it seems as though half the people in the room have taken out cell phones and flipped open glowing displays; breaking news,

news alerts, news by text message, text from my cousin who lives in Miami, it was Miami.

Angie looks at Gert and then back to me. "What happened?" she asks. Gert leans down to see the reporter's phone; she holds it to her side to share and he squints to read it.

"Car bomb in Miami," Gert says to Angie, and the taste of bile and sickly sweet apple comes up in my mouth. I glance around for a bathroom.

A man with a goatee and a tight black shirt looks up from his phone. "Nope, backpack," he says. "It was a backpack in a club. Possibly two backpacks. Many casualties."

Everyone's an expert. My mother, I'm sure, is right now in front of a television in her robe and slippers.

The buzz goes out of the room like water draining from a bathtub as people start to leave the gallery. They stop to talk to Josh before they go and he nods in an understanding way and shakes their hands, one by one, as they leave. I go and stand by Josh at a discreet distance, listen to the early-departure apologies mixed with declamations of his brilliance. He understands, he understands, thanks so much for coming, thank you.

"What can I do, Doc?" Gert asks. He's come over too.

"Nothing, I don't think we need to do anything."

"Same plan for tomorrow? Will anything change?"

"We'll still set up. Go ahead and pick up the truck in the morning."

"Alright, Doc. I'm getting Angie home."

"Good night, Gert. Thank you."

I wait with Josh until the last people are gone. We aren't far from the bar, and I'm startled when I hear the shattering sound of the bartender dumping a bus tub of ice into the sink; I'd figured he'd already left, but he's got a cell phone to his ear and is urgently speaking into it.

"You try Dannica again, and I'll try James," he says as he loads some bottles into a box down at his feet. "I don't know if they go to that club. I don't know."

"Hey," Josh says to the guy. "Any chance I can get something before you leave?"

The bartender looks annoyed at this. He crouches down and comes back up and puts a half-filled bottle of vodka on the bar, followed by a full one. "Take care of yourself, dude," he says. "They're yours anyway. I have to get out of here."

Now it's just us, and I'm trying to keep the feeling of sickness from rising up in me. I wait for Josh as he hunts around to find the light switches for the gallery, I wait while he looks for the keys, I wait while he fumbles with the keys in the door. There is still fog in the dark as we walk back to the Academy. It's not even midnight yet.

"I'm sorry if that was boring," Josh says.

"No, it was—"

"It was turning into a good party too."

"There were—"

"There's a satellite show this weekend, private show tomorrow." Josh has his courier bag, and he lifts the flap with a Velcro rip and pulls out the half-full bottle. "I'd like you to come to the private thing tomorrow. Here, have some."

"No thanks, Josh, I'm really—"

"People seem surprised, or something." He drinks from the bottle. "At this Miami thing."

"It's always a surprise," I manage to slip in.

"It's never a surprise. This is here, Jess. It's forever. Wake-up call."

We're on the campus now, and we pass a group of people talking under a light. "Miami, Miami, Miami," they say.

"They're surprised. Like it's a surprise."

"Josh, can I talk to you?"

"These people need to wake up. Wake up!" he yells, and I wrap my arms around my stomach.

We climb up the stairs in the studio building. Hoffman's door is wide open and his TV is on, but he's not there. Josh walks in and I follow because I'm too scared to do anything else.

"Look at this shit. Look at it!" It's cable news; an aerial shot of a building. Flames shoot from the windows and police lights flash around it.

"Thank God for helicopters," I say, but he doesn't hear.

Josh holds the bottle to his mouth and tips it up and takes one gulping swallow, and another.

"This is forever!" he shouts.

"Josh."

"People need to wake up. Wake up! Wake up!" He jumps up and sits on one of the tables next to an amorphous sculpture. I take a couple steps backward toward the door. The text crawl at the bottom of the screen says sixty plus dead, many missing. Many unaccounted for, and I blink and try to focus on the words. Josh slouches, holding the bottle between his knees. He shakes his head and holds his hand out in the air, out toward the TV screen.

"Look at this shit. It's about time people... they're, they're surprised by this?"

I take some more steps, quietly, and I'm in the hall. I'm bordering on drunk, and I'm crying. I'm scared. I go down to Josh's studio and the door is unlocked; maybe seeking refuge here is crazy but I go in. I can't handle a bus ride now. Will the buses even be running? In the fog-light oozing in through the windows I see Gert's cot, and I sit on it and dig for my phone. Katie will know what to do.

All circuits busy. All circuits busy now. Circuits are busy.

Of course all the circuits are busy, Jess.

I really, really need to go to the bathroom; I run in and hitch up my dress and sit in the dark with my knees tight together and my hands full of dress and I pee quickly because I'm worried Josh will come in and who knows what? I'm an idiot for coming here. I turn on the light and the faucet and splash cold water on my face, and when I shut off the water my attention is caught by something shiny on top of the medicine cabinet; it's a key on a leather fob and when I take it down to look at it there's just *something* about it that makes me start to shake. I get my own key from my bag and I know even before I line them up that the little valleys and ridges are identical, but when I see it for sure I feel like I can't breathe.

How did he get this? How?

I throw the keys—both of them—into my bag and flip off the light and try to compose myself. I'm tired and drunk and scared. I go back to the cot, the cot feels safe, there's a blanket folded on it and I pull it over myself and lie down with my knees pulled up. I can't go anywhere else. I can't face going outside. It's an hour—maybe two, maybe three—before I hear Josh come in and my skin goes cold with sweat; I see his shadow stagger and bump hard into the table and he goes "uh!" like the wind is knocked out of him. He goes into the bathroom and I close my eyes against the shock of the bright light, he doesn't flush and the light goes out and I hear him haul himself up to the loft. I hear his body hit the bed. I hear his breathing, steady and nasal.

With this sound, I force myself to calm down.

And somehow, I sleep.

20

In the bare dawn, I wake to the sound of snoring. I have to think for a moment, process the snoring and the cot and why I'm wearing a fancy black dress, and it's several minutes before the flash comes and I remember everything. And I think maybe I could leave now, but I don't. I'm not ready to go outside by myself, not ready to go home and pack for Katie's party. And I still need to talk to Josh.

I must fall back to sleep, because the next thing I see when I open my eyes is that it's much brighter and Josh, with wet hair and wearing a robe, is standing next to the cot.

"Why did you sleep down here?" he asks.

"I was drunk? You were still at Hoffman's when I got here, anyway."

"Okay."

I sit up and pull the blanket around my shoulders. "What time is it?"

"Quarter 'til eleven."

"You're serious?"

He holds his watch in front of me so I can see it.

"Do you want to take a shower before we go?"

"Before we go?"

"Set up at the Fay Gallery. It's across town."

"Josh, look at me. I need to get home. I need to clean up. I need to talk—"

"You have clothes here. Jeans and a couple shirts. Take a shower, and we'll go."

"Can we get lunch? Can we talk?"

"There isn't a whole lot of time."

"I'm starving."

"We can pick something up. Take a shower."

Josh gives me a stack of clothes I didn't even know I had here, and I go in and lock the bathroom door and sit in the bottom of the tub with the shower on. I try to remember everything I had scripted for myself for this "talk"; everything that seemed so clever I can't recall, and what I do remember just seems dumb. I want to ask him about the key, but even thinking about it makes me afraid. The hot water feels good, though. There's one good thing today, at least.

Gert is in the studio when I come out of the bathroom. He says hello, but nothing else, and he gets to work packing things up for the show. He and Josh look over some papers spread out on one of the tables, the same one that Josh slammed his hip into last night.

"Okay, Doc." Gert nods. "Okay. I see you there." He picks up a big flat box, supporting it from underneath with his cast, and leaves without saying anything else.

"Are you ready?"

"I'm...Josh, I'm going to die if I don't get something to eat. And I need to talk to you."

"Alright, we can get something. Where should we get something?"

"What is the gallery? Where is it?"

"It's on Taravel. We're taking the 54 bus. Taraval and Fourteenth."

Mario's is on Taraval. "I know a place," I say. "We can take the bus all the way there." I get my things and put them in my bag, and when he isn't looking I grab the canvas grocery bag I got for Josh that, to my knowledge, he has never used. If he won't use such a nice bag, I'm going to take it back.

"You can leave that stuff here," he says. I don't think he noticed me stuffing the grocery bag in with my dress.

"I need to do laundry. What are you doing with that pack?" Josh has Gert's trendy backpack on his shoulders, and he looks ridiculous.

"Gert left this. He needs it."

On the bus, I almost say something. Almost. A couple times. My mouth opens, but nothing comes out. This bus is packed, people are close, and it feels like the wrong time. Josh just faces forward with the hip leather pack in his lap, and I have to tug his arm when we get to the stop for Mario's.

The lunch rush hasn't quite started, so it doesn't take us long to get through the line to the counter. I order a chicken salad sandwich, like I used to with Patrick, and I ask Josh what he wants.

"Just get whatever," he says.

"Well, what do you like?"

"I don't care. Just get something."

"Such as?"

"Just order something."

"Josh," I start to say, feeling like I might burst into tears, "this is exactly why I . . . ?" But he's already stepped away to wait out on the sidewalk.

"Do a second chicken salad," I say to the kid at the counter.

Josh looks at his watch while we wait. And after we get our sandwiches, wrapped in white paper, we go out and he starts to walk back up to the bus stop.

"Wait," I say. "Wait. We need to sit."

"We need to go."

I was feeling nervous, but now I'm angry. "Five minutes, Josh. Sit, and eat, and listen to me. Five minutes."

Josh turns back to me and sits down at one of the sidewalk tables. It's gray outside, and cool, and no one else is out here. Perfect. I sit down and unwrap my sandwich, and take a deep breath.

"Josh, I—"

"We really, really need to go."

"I need to talk to you."

"We're going to be late." He won't look at me, and he hasn't unwrapped his lunch.

"I need to tell you something."

"Okay. I have to go. Come if you want." I can see the muscles in his face tighten and relax as he clenches his jaw before standing up and walking toward the bus stop.

"What is your problem?" I say, my voice cracking like I'm going to cry. I wrap up my sandwich—I haven't even taken a bite of it—and follow him. "I'm asking you, what is your problem? Why won't you listen to me?"

"I don't think you understand how important this is."

"I don't understand how important this is? Are you serious?"

A bus pulls up and stops with its air brake hiss, and I consider storming away but I want him to hear me out and I step on and swipe my pass. I take the seat across from him. There aren't as many people on this bus.

"Why won't you listen to me? You know what? You have never listened to me."

Josh doesn't say anything, and the bus starts moving.

"I'm nothing but your subject. I'm like, I'm like, like a still life." I am crying now, and I hate it. "Why won't you even look at me?" I yell. He may not be looking at me, but some other people on the bus are.

"Jessica, this is very, very important."

"I am important! *I* am! Right here! Why don't you ever listen to me?"

"What?"

"Exactly! That's exactly it!" I turn and yank the stop cord. "I don't want to see you. I don't want to talk to you. This is done. Use the scans, whatever. Don't ever talk to me again."

"Wait, Jess, what? What are you talking about?"

I pull the stop cord again, and the driver looks up in her mirror and says, "I hear you, girl, I hear you, you just hold on." An Asian man three seats in front of Josh looks extremely irritated.

The bus barely slows down to a stop before the doors swing open.

"There you go," the driver says. "You get yourself out and settle down a little."

I grab my bag. "Don't call me. Don't see me." Josh looks at me like I'm talking to him in a foreign language.

"Wait, Jess, wait."

"No," I say, and I climb down out through the rear set of doors to the sidewalk and hope, hope that Josh does not follow me. I reach in my bag for my phone and look for my sister's new number on the speed dial as the doors finally fold closed. Just go, go, please go.

I find the new number and press send, and the phone is to my ear just as the bus groans and starts to pull away from the curb. There's a ring, and a ring again.

I did it, Katie. I think I did it.

A ring again, and the bus is moving.

Then there is a brightness and a thump that hits me in the chest, and a clatter and a howl and a rush of air.

My phone is pulled from my hand and I'm falling to the ground.

I'm on the ground.

And then there's nothing.

PART

3

21

The first thing I'm aware of, after who knows how long, is the ringing. Not like a phone, or a bell, really, but a shrill tone, a squeal, a siren that doesn't go away. Putting my hands over my ears does nothing, so, after a while, I give up.

The next thing that I'm able to notice, as I open my eyes and blink the room into focus, is my bag, lying like a deflated beach ball right in the middle of the floor, encircled by a halo of loose change, a mint tin, some tampons, and my checkbook. A mini-pack of tissues left over from my cousin Tricia's wedding is over by my bookshelf.

Perhaps most important, my butt—and the couch underneath it—is cold and wet.

These three things have me at my limit. Sitting here, curled in a wet spot at the end of my couch with a scream in my ears and a mess on the floor is enough; I'm not going to bother finding anything else out for the time being.

But there's something else forcing its way in. Over the scream there's a thumping, banging sound. At the hazy edge of my vision, it looks like my door is moving. The chain is engaged, though, and the door can only move so far. Something red and black—it looks like a beak—pokes in up by the chain.

Maybe a giant parrot is breaking into my apartment?

Suddenly the door swings all the way open, and I cower down into the couch cushions. It's not a tropical bird, but Danny, standing there, holding a big pair of bolt cutters. Behind him stands Patrick, along with two men in suits, and behind them is my landlord. There's a woman next to him too, tallish and plain, I think I know her maybe? Her hand is over her mouth and she takes a step back and I can't really see her anymore.

They come in, all of them except the landlord and the woman. Their mouths are moving, but their words don't make any sense, the voices delayed like in an old TV movie where the sound has gone out of sync.

"Jesus, Jessica."

"Jessica. Jessica."

"Mr. McAvoy, sir, I'm telling you, don't go over there until we've had a chance to talk to her. Don't go over there."

"Why don't you step the fuck off?"

"Danny, calm down."

I can't tell who is talking, so I close my eyes and put my hands over my ears again. I feel something touching my knee and I recoil even further, but when I open my eyes I see Patrick crouching next to me. Back at the doorway, Danny has puffed himself up in front of the suits and looks like he's ready to swing the bolt cutters at one of them.

"Jessica, I'm here." The voice makes it through the scream in my head.

"Mr. McAvoy, don't do that. Don't touch her. Do not speak to her. Please."

"Jessica."

"I'm warning you."

"Can you talk to me? Can you say something?"

I blink at Patrick, and he blinks too, again and again. Then I see him sniff the air, and he touches his hand to the couch and the seat of my pants. And then, like it's nothing, he slides both arms under me and picks me up and carries me into my room.

"Jessica, I'm sorry. You're okay. You're okay. I'm sorry."

My eyes are closed again. I'm weightless.

"Mr. McAvoy—"

"Goddammit, I'm just getting her into some dry pants, okay?"

Over the noise in my ears, I can hear his voice breaking.

"Danny, can you do something with that cushion?"

My eyes stay closed as I'm placed on my bed, and I squeeze them shut tighter at the feel of hands unbuttoning and pulling off my jeans. Underwear too.

"I'm sorry, Jessica. I'm sorry. I'm fixing this."

"Mr. McAvoy!"

"Your sweats, Jess. Where are your sweats?"

Patrick finds them without my help, and he pulls them on me, warm and, better still, dry. I keep my eyes closed even while reflexively lifting my hips. Then I'm weightless again, but not moving, just held tightly.

"I'm sorry."

It's a whisper.

"I'm sorry."

"Mr. McAvoy! We can have you arrested—"

We move, and I open my eyes as Patrick eases me down into the old recliner in my living room. One of the cushions, the one I was sitting on, is gone from the couch.

Another whisper, close to my ear.

"I'm not leaving."

"We'd like you both to step out of the room."

"Bullshit. Why don't you try to make us, asshole."

"Danny, relax. Calm down."

"Out of the room, please."

"We'll wait in the hallway. Door stays open."

"Mr. McAvoy, we can't—"

"Jesus Christ, look at her. What do you think you're going to get out of her? Can you just let her rest?"

"That isn't an option for us right now. This is all developing—"

"Then the door stays open."

They're all looking at each other, and Danny is still holding the bolt cutters.

"Alright. Wait in the hall."

"Try to be quick."

"It's going to take as long as it takes, Mr. McAvoy."

Patrick and Danny back themselves into the hall, facing me the whole time. One of the suits, the taller one, starts to close the door and I feel panic in my stomach, but Danny holds out his arm and stops the door from closing all the way. The other suit comes close to me and kneels down and starts to move his mouth.

"Jessica Zorich? Is your name Jessica Zorich?"

I can only stare at him. The disconnect between his mouth and his voice is making me queasy. I know you. Do I? Do I know you from somewhere? Behind him, the other suit brings chairs from my kitchen. They both take a seat in front of me, and I try to disappear into the recliner.

"Are you Jessica Zorich? Is that your name? Can you nod for me? Can you indicate yes or no?"

I manage to nod, but the space in time between his lips moving and the sound hitting my brain is getting to be too much, so I close my eyes and cover my ears. But some things still come through.

My name is——.

And this is Agent——.

We're with the DHS.

Must be very difficult for you.

Investigation.

Bombing.

Investigation.

Something, a different sound, makes me open my eyes. The tall one is pulling the elastic from around a bulging accordion file, and he lifts the flap and starts to look through the papers inside. More words come as I watch him.

Concentrate.

Important.

Concentrate.

"Miss Zorich, we need you to concentrate. We need to ask you some very important questions. Can you help us? Can you concentrate for us?"

I just look at them.

"Okay. Good. Miss Zorich, did you board the Muni bus line 54 yesterday morning around eleven-forty?"

The bus. Josh. Oh God. We fought. Was it yesterday? What time is it now?

I nod.

"Alright. You got off the bus almost ten minutes later, close to the intersection of Taraval and Sixteenth. Is that correct?"

We fought, didn't we?

I nod again, and the tall one leans closer.

"Miss Zorich, did you know something was going to happen on that bus?"

I'm honestly not sure what *has* happened.

I shake my head, and the way they're looking at me makes me feel a little scared.

"Jessica, did you know that an explosive device was going to be detonated on that bus after you got off?"

"Did you know something was going to happen?"

"Is that why you exited the bus?"

"Did you know it would be blown up?"

Explosive?

Detonated?

Blown up?

Josh?

I want to speak, to tell them about the argument we had. I know, though, that if I open my mouth, the only sound that will come out is the screeching in my head. So I keep it shut.

I want to ask what happened, but all I can do is shake my head.

I put my hands over my ears again.

"Jessica, we'd like you to look at some pictures. Tell us if you recognize any of these people, okay? Can you look up, up here, look at me, please. Have you ever seen this man before? How about him? Him?"

The tall one flips through a stack of glossy black and white photos. They all seem familiar. A black woman. An angry Asian man. And the last one.

"This person?"

It's Josh's passport photo, the one with the long hair. I can't stop looking at it, and it doesn't stop looking at me.

"Do you know this man?"

"Joshua Alan Hadden?"

"Did you board the bus with him?"

I'm nodding, nodding, keeping my hands over my ears and trying to blink away the blurriness that's filling my eyes and overflowing down my cheeks. I can't force it out, not the blurriness or the screaming or their words, so I pull up my knees and close my eyes. They keep talking.

Associates in Britain.

Associates in El Salvador.

Panama City.

Berlin.

No, no, no, I don't know about any of this!

"Do you have any knowledge of Mr. Hadden's experience with chemicals?"

I open my eyes. Well, there was everything in the studio.

"Had you ever seen Mr. Hadden handling explosives?"

What?

"Jessica, this is a photograph of an industrial detonator. Did you ever see something like this in Mr. Hadden's possession?"

What are you trying to say?

"Was Mr. Hadden carrying a backpack or a bag yesterday? Did you notice anything unusual about his clothing? Did it seem unusually bulky?"

With this, my mouth fills with rotten bile. I cough once, choking, and then I spit watery puke down the front of my shirt and start to sob.

"Come on, Jesus Christ, that's enough. She's had enough."

What are they saying? This can't be for real.

Patrick stands next to me now, and the two men rise from the chairs.

"Do your search and get out of here. She's not going anywhere. She's gone through enough. Please. Guys, come on. I told you upstairs, there's no way she knows anything about this. Just do whatever you have to do and go."

They speak to each other, the suits, and the tall one goes out into the hall and comes back with a pair of big plastic toolboxes. He opens one of the boxes and pulls out some rubber gloves that he squeezes his hands into while the other one goes to my computer and turns it on. Danny comes over with a wet towel and gives it to Patrick, who kneels down and cleans up the front of my shirt.

"I'm sorry, Jess. I'm sorry."

The one with the gloves walks around my apartment with a stack of white gauzy pads. He takes a pad and wipes it over my things—my dresser, my bookshelf, my shoe—then drops it into a plastic bag that he labels with a Sharpie and ties off before throwing it into one of the open toolboxes. The other one has hooked a cable from a little gray metal box up to my computer, and he's typing something on the keyboard. He waits and he waits as a light on the gray box flickers, then he turns off the computer and unhooks the box and whispers something into his partner's ear before leaving. A moment later, the other one snaps off his gloves and drops them into the open toolbox. He latches the lid, then rises up and hands a card to Patrick.

"Please call if you have any questions."

Patrick says nothing, and finally the suit picks up the toolboxes and walks out the door. Danny goes over and shuts it behind him, and the sound of the lock clicking into place feels like it might be the first clear thing I've ever heard.

22

I don't know when it turned to night, but now it's dark in my apartment. Patrick has been coming and going all afternoon, trying to get me to drink water, taking me on an unproductive trip to the bathroom, putting a blanket over me, asking if I'm okay. Telling me I'm okay. Telling me he's sorry.

I want to answer, but I can't. There's that screaming sound in my head, for one, and it's taking everything else I've got in me to not think about what I might have seen. So I sit in the recliner, with my afghan over my legs. If Patrick is here, I don't know it, and if he's gone, I'm not sure how long he's been away.

All I know is that it's dark in my apartment.

The sound of my door opening makes its way into my head, but I don't bother to look at first, then a light comes on and I see that Gretchen is standing with

Patrick in the doorway. She comes over to the chair and looks down at me and forces herself to smile.

"Jess, I'm so glad you're, I tracked down—"

She stops and presses her lips together and turns her head away, and then she takes a breath and looks back at me with wet eyes.

"I got ahold of . . . Oh, Jess."

Her face falls apart into tears and she runs off, and I can hear her crying in my bathroom. It's a distinct noise coming from back there, little snotty yelps. I've never seen or heard Gretchen crying before. As the sound goes on, Patrick lowers himself down next to me with his hands on the arm of the recliner.

"Gretchen called your doctor. She's on her way here right now to take a look at you. We want to make sure you're . . . she's going to check to make sure everything is alright."

Now Gretchen is back, sniffling, and she kneels at my other side and takes my hand.

"I'm so glad you're okay."

There's a new sound, not so unlike the screaming sound that won't stop in my ears, and Patrick gets up to buzz open the door downstairs. A moment later I see Miss Nakamura, the nurse practitioner I've seen for my annual ever since I moved here. She looks at me, and I think she can tell I'm trying to smile at her. She has always insisted that I call her Elaine, but, with regard to our professional relationship, I like the formality of using her last name.

"Jessica. Hi. Hi." She puts her bag on the floor and crouches down and strokes the back of my hand. "You're here, honey. You're here. You see me, yes? You hear my voice?"

I'm trying to smile at her, I really am.

"I want to take a look at you."

Miss Nakamura puts her hands to my cheeks and looks into my eyes. She presses my stomach and feels my neck, and then she takes a blood pressure cuff from her bag and wraps it around my arm. In my head I can hear my pulse and my breath and that scream that won't go away, and I wonder if she can hear all of that too, through her stethoscope. When she looks into my ears, I wonder if she can see it.

"I want you to sleep. I'm going to give you something to make you sleep a little bit. Do you need to go to the bathroom?"

I manage to shake my head. I'm made of dust inside now.

"Can we . . . is there any way you can help me get her into her bed?"

Patrick comes to my side and his arms come under me, and once again I weigh nothing as he lifts me into the air. Gretchen darts ahead to pull down my comforter and sheets before I'm eased down onto the mattress. I try to work my mouth to say thanks—to say *anything*—but it isn't happening. Not yet.

Miss Nakamura sits next to me on the bed and rolls me to my side and pulls down the elastic of my sweatpants. It's cold on my skin where she's swabbing me with alcohol.

"Little stick, here."

There's a pinch on my butt and a hot tingle that radiates down into my flesh, and Miss Nakamura gives the spot a pat before pulling my sweats back up.

"This will make you sleepy. You don't need to fight it. I want you to rest. Rest. I'll be back tomorrow. I'm going to leave some medicine with your friends. Just rest, honey. Rest."

She touches my cheek and turns out the lamp next to the bed, and then she's gone and I hear more voices.

"Thank you so much. Thank you."

"Obviously, she's in a pretty serious state of shock. Physically, she's all there, but it looks like her left eardrum has a little perforation. Okay. You take these, they're similar to Valium. Give her two in the morning after she wakes up. You don't need to ask if she wants them, just give them to her. I'll be back tomorrow sometime between eleven and noon. Give her food if she wants it, keep trying to get her to drink something, water, juice, whatever. Stay with clear liquids. I think

I've got your, yeah, I have your number. Call me if anything serious comes up."

I hear my door close, and then lowered voices.

"Do you want me to stay?"

"I'll be okay."

There's a pause. A kiss?

"You'll call me?"

"I will."

My door closes again, and as it does, my eyes close too.

As I sleep, I dream of tiny pieces of paper blowing through the air like leaves. Pieces and pieces of paper, an autumn of confetti tossed up and caught by the wind.

Then I open my eyes, and it's over.

The room is still dark, and as I lie there, staring up at the ceiling and the patterns of light cast up through my blinds from the street, I hear breathing beyond my own. I'd be startled if I wasn't so relaxed, and when I turn my head and let my eyes adjust further I see that Patrick has moved the recliner next to my bed and is now asleep on it.

He's on his side with his knees drawn up, his hand under his face with his mouth wide open. He looks like a little boy there, his face soft and blank in the bare light. He's sleeping and breathing. And I know I love him.

I'd go to him, curl up behind him, press my face to the back of his neck and sleep next to him if my body wasn't lead right now. It's all I can do to turn my head and reach toward him with my heavy hand. I look, and look, barely touching him, before I'm asleep again.

Patrick is gone when, in the daylight, I open my eyes. The recliner is gone too, and I wonder if maybe I dreamed him being there, just like the tiny leaves of paper. The screaming in my ears seems not so bad today, but I feel a headache coming on. Feeling anything, though, seems thrilling.

Hunger too, is exciting. Like: I'm *starving*. This is even more thrilling than my headache, because I know I can do something about it.

I push myself up, and into a sitting position. There's a moment of dizziness, but it passes, so I swing my legs to the floor and stand. Another little spin in the head comes and goes, but I know I'm doing okay.

Patrick isn't in the living room, and the recliner is in its normal spot. A cushion is still missing from my couch, though, so I'm sure I didn't imagine all that. And when I get to my kitchen, I see the big foam block from inside the cushion sitting on my counter and the unzipped cover soaking in some dead suds in the sink.

I'm blushing because I peed on my own couch.

I find three of Patrick's matching blue Tupperware containers in the refrigerator. The one closest to me is filled with some kind of pasta with red sauce, and as I look at it I start to cry. Then I hear my door open and close.

"Jessica? Hey, Jess—" He comes into the kitchen. "You're up?"

"I think I need something besides spaghetti," I say, gently closing the refrigerator door.

"Oh God, Jessica." He's to me in an instant, his arms around me, pulling me close to him. "You're talking," he says. "What do you...are you hungry? What do you need? Anything, anything."

"I don't know," I say. My head is resting on his shoulder. "Could I maybe just have a piece of toast?"

"Yes, yes. Anything you want," he says. "Here, sit down. I'll get it."

"With some peanut butter on it?"

"Anything. I'll be right back."

He runs off, and I can hear him moving around above

me up in his own kitchen. Then he's back with a plate with two pieces of peanut butter–slathered toast and a glass of what I know must be organic and expensive apple juice.

"Thank you," I say.

"It's fine," he says. "It's okay." Patrick has a prescription pill bottle in his hand too, and he shakes a couple tablets from it out onto the table. "I want you to take—"

"I know, I heard her last night."

"You heard?"

"Yes." I take a bite of the toast. "This might be the most perfect thing I've ever tasted, Pat."

"You've got to be starving."

"Yes."

"Does your ear hurt?"

"I think so. It's ringing."

"Do you hurt anywhere else?"

"I'm getting a headache."

"These will help that," he says, and he slides the pills toward me. "Do you..." Patrick swallows, and pauses for a moment. "Jessica, do you know what happened?"

"I can't think about it now."

"Okay." Patrick watches me as I put the pills in my mouth and take a big drink of the juice. It too is perfect.

"But if you need to, when you want to talk about it, I mean, when you're ready, I'm here."

"Okay," I say. "Thank you. I do have a question, though."

"What's that?"

"Do you know how I got back here?"

"I have no idea. Your door was locked, Danny got here before I did. We could hear you inside. So, no, I don't know."

"You could hear me?"

"You were crying."

"Oh," I say. I take a bite of the second piece of toast and put it back down on the plate. "I think I might want to lie down again."

"Do you want me to carry you?" Patrick asks. "Or can you walk?"

"I can walk," I say, and we get to our feet, and now I do manage to smile. "I did like it when you carried me, though. You're still pretty strong, skinny boy."

Patrick says nothing, but he puts his arm around me as we walk to my room.

I'm awakened, sometime later, by the feeling of someone sitting down on my bed.

"What?" I say as I blink my eyes open. "Oh, hi, Miss Nakamura."

She smiles. "So you decided to start talking again, huh?"

"You're supposed to tell me I can call you Elaine."

"You can call me whatever you want," she says, and she checks my pulse at my wrist. "Did you have something to eat?"

I nod. "And the pills," I say.

"Good. Those are some pretty impressive black eyes you've got."

"What?"

"Have you seen yourself in the mirror?"

I haven't, and I shake my head no.

"Don't be startled when you look. How do you feel?"

"I'm kind of sore."

"I'm not surprised," she says. "You have a big bruise on your lower back. I have something for you for that."

"Big bruise?"

"I think you were knocked down."

"Knocked down."

"By the explosion."

"The bus blew up, didn't it?"

"Yes."

"Did everyone die?"

"I don't know, Jessica. You didn't die."

"But everyone on the bus?"

"I don't know, honey. We can find that out later."

Neither of us says anything for a little bit. Finally I nod and say, "Okay."

"Do you want to sleep a little more?"

"Yes," I say. "Wait, do you mean another shot?"

"We can do another, if that worked for you." She reaches for her bag at the foot of the bed. "You want me to get one ready?"

"No. No, thank you."

"It's not a bother, Jessica."

"I just don't want to be that sleepy. The pills are fine."

"Alright. You just let me know." Miss Nakamura holds the bag in her lap. "You're alright?"

"I think so."

"That's good. You can call me if you need me."

"Okay," I say. "Thank you."

"How long ago did you have those pills?"

"This morning. Like, hours."

"You want more? You ready to rest some more?"

"Yes, please."

"Let me get you a cup of water. I'm going to give you a little something for the pain in your back too."

"Miss Nakamura?" I ask. "If Patrick is still here, would you see if he has any more of that juice? It was the best."

"I'll see what I can do," she says.

The next time I wake up, my head feels better but my body is worse. My back hurts almost too much to sit up, and by the time I finally pull myself together enough to stand, my stomach muscles feel as though I've been punched.

Maybe I should have opted for the shot.

The blinds in my room are closed, but it feels like it must be afternoon. I have no way of telling for sure, though, because the clock radio is missing from my nightstand.

I need, I need, I *need* to call Katie, like right now. She must know what happened, certainly she's heard, but I need to talk to her. The last memory I have of my cell phone is when I was dialing my sister, and I don't think I've seen it anywhere in my apartment since I've been back. And this is a problem: I only had Katie's new number in my cell's speed dial and didn't commit it to memory. If I can't find the phone, though, I can look at my cellular statement on the computer and call her from my landline. Perfect.

Except, maybe not so perfect. When I finally shuffle like a stooped old woman into my living room, I see that my cordless is missing from its base, and the message display alternates flashing the words "MEMORY" and "FULL." And my computer, when I bend down enough to press the power button, seems totally dead. The amber light on the monitor just blinks at me like some kind of silent jeer.

Damn that guy in the suit!

So I lower myself to the one cushion left on my couch, and wait. Patrick seems to be checking in fairly regularly, so I close my eyes and slip into the easy half sleep that comes with the lingering effect of Miss Nakamura's pills. It isn't long before I hear the key in my door, and I keep my eyes shut.

"There she is," I hear Patrick say.

"Jess?" my sister says, and my eyes snap open and I sit up straight over the protest of my stiff and painful muscles. "Jess?"

The soreness in my back is forgotten and my skin goes tight with goose bumps as I rise up to face Katie; standing there in the doorway her hair seems darker than the last time I saw her and she looks tired. In truth, she looks older than I remember. I walk to her with my arms held forward.

"Jessica," she says.

Then I try to push her back into the hallway.

"Jess!" she says, her expression changing from relief to alarm. "What are you—"

"What are you doing here?" I scream. *"What the fuck are you doing here?"*

You are not supposed to be here. Not here! Not where things blow up and people are killed and broken glass is scattered in the street. Not here, not here, no no no *no!*

"Jessica!" she shouts as she pushes me back. "What are you doing?"

"Get out of here! You're supposed to be on your way to the boat!"

Where it's sunny, and safe, and things don't explode.

Katie wraps her arms around me and pushes me back inside. I trip on my own feet and we crumple to the floor. On the way down I see that our mother is standing next to Patrick, looking through the doorway with her hand over her mouth.

Landing on the floor hurts my back and my head, and the way that I land on Katie's arms knocks the wind out of me.

"Ouch," I say with a cough. This really, really hurts.

Katie doesn't let go. "I'm sorry," she says.

"I don't want you to be here. It's not—"

"Shut up. Don't be like Mom."

"Mom?" I call. "Mom? Katie, please, this really hurts."

Our mother kneels next to us and pulls Katie's hair out of my face. She touches my cheek and holds my hand before bending down to kiss me. Katie pulls her arms out from under me but doesn't get up, and that's how we stay: a big, red-haired knot on my living room floor, long after Patrick has brought up their bags from the street and gone away.

23

We sit, Katie and I, on the cushioned end of my couch with an afghan pulled up tight around our necks. A two-headed monster. The only thing different from the million other times we've sat like this is that now, because of the soreness in my back and neck and ear, I've asked Katie to sit to my right side instead of my left. It feels strange, like how lacing your fingers together the wrong way feels strange, but still, it's comforting. With my sister here, I am almost myself.

We tried to turn on the TV but got only static, so we've been sitting and talking about nothing important. Nothing involving explosions or dying. Right now, I'm telling her about my neighbor in the building next door. We can see his messy bureau through his open blinds.

"He's pretty boring," I say.

"Is he ever naked?"

"He's always dressed. The people who used to live there were much more interesting. It was this crazy Romanian guy and his family. He yelled at them all the time."

"Yeah," Katie says, as if it's entirely normal to yell at your family.

"His oldest daughter was beautiful. He yelled at her the most."

"Because she was so beautiful?"

"Maybe. Patrick gave her violin lessons while he was unemployed."

"Did the guy ever yell at Patrick?"

"Don't know. We'll ask him."

Mom has been very quiet, doing something in the kitchen for the last hour or so. Once in a while she looks out at us, then disappears again.

"Was it hard to get a flight here?" I ask Katie.

"We drove," she says.

"You drove? You're kidding?"

"We left as soon as Patrick called Mom."

"He called you?"

"As soon as he knew what was going on," Katie says. "He hitchhiked back here from his office. Did you know that? He kept us posted."

All I can do is shake my head. He hitchhiked from Mountain View?

"Are you going to miss your boat?"

"I'm not so worried about the boat right now, Jess. But I called the Woods Hole people to tell them what was going on. Mom drove pretty much nonstop. We only took a break once, for a little bit, south of Portland."

"To sleep?"

"To freak out. Mom was speeding."

"Excuse me," our mother calls from the kitchen. "I was driving responsibly."

"Mom, you were going almost ninety."

"That's an exaggeration, Katie."

"The car wasn't going to take it," Katie says. "We needed to stop."

We hear someone running up the stairs and jangling keys outside my door, and Patrick comes in carrying two big grocery bags with green, leafy things poking out of the tops of them.

"Hey, guys," he says, then goes straight to the kitchen.

"Oh, Patrick, thank you so much," we hear Mom say.

"The leeks were a little ragged, I tried to get the best-looking—"

"No, no, these are perfect. How much was it all?"

"I've got it, don't worry about it."

"No, please—"

"Seriously, Maureen, don't worry about it."

Hearing Patrick call Mom by her first name makes us both giggle. He comes back into the living room with a glass of water and his other hand cupped to hold what I'm assuming are some of my pills.

"What are you two laughing at?" he asks.

"You," I say.

"Call her Mo," Katie says. "All our friends in high school called her Mo. She likes it."

"Katie," Mom calls, in a very Mom-like way. "Enough."

Patrick shakes his cupped hand like he's about to throw a pair of dice. "Ready for your dose?"

"Yes," I say. Then I turn to my sister. "You want some too?"

"What are they?" she asks.

I shrug. Honestly, I don't know what they are, and I don't particularly care, as long as they work. "Bring two more. Katie needs some too."

Patrick gives us a funny look, but then he goes back to the kitchen and returns with two additional pills. Katie sits up and the afghan falls off us as she takes the glass of water from Patrick and holds it up for me to sip with my pills before taking her own.

"Pat," I say. "You hitchhiked here from your office?"

"I, ah . . . I got a ride pretty quick." I can tell he doesn't want to talk about it, and he turns away before I can say anything else.

Patrick sticks his head back into the kitchen. "Just pound the ceiling if you need anything, Maureen."

Katie and I snicker again.

"See you guys in a little while," Patrick says as he starts for my door. "I have to do some e-mails."

"Oh, hey, that reminds me," I say. "Can you take a look at my computer when you have a chance? Those guys did something to it. It won't turn on."

"That was me," Patrick says. "I took the power cord."

"What? Why?"

"Just, you know, the news, you didn't need to see it. Yet."

"Is the fact that my TV isn't working related to this, somehow?"

"I disconnected the cable box too."

"And my phone?"

"Upstairs. It was ringing nonstop."

"Did you take my clocks?"

"Elaine didn't want you fixating on time. That was her idea."

"You took my watch off me too, didn't you?"

Patrick smiles.

"He's very thorough," Katie says.

Patrick smiles again and opens the door. "I'll be down later," he says. Then my door closes and he's gone.

"I think he did the right thing," Katie says as she pulls the afghan back up over our shoulders.

"Whatever."

"What do these pills do?"

"They're sleepy pills," I say. "You feel like sleepy Jell-O."

"I can handle sleepy Jell-O."

We lean into one another, looking out the window as we listen to Mom working away in the kitchen. Running water, cabinets opening and closing. My good knife—a gift from Patrick last summer—tapping and scraping on my maple cutting block. I have no idea what she's making in there, but whatever it is, I'm so happy she's cooking. Dinner by Mom is a much needed anchor in reality right now.

"Do you think Dad will come?" I ask.

Katie snorts. "With Wilma? God, I hope not. Is it always foggy here?"

"There are sunny days," I say. "And it rains. In the winter it rains a lot."

"Is it a nice rain?"

"I love the rain. Sometimes there's rain. Sometimes there's nothing."

"Do you want Dad to come here?" Katie asks.

"Honestly? No."

"Didn't think so." Katie rests her head a little more on my shoulder. "Has he called? I wonder if he even knows."

"I have no idea. The volume control is on the handset. I can't hear messages without the phone."

"I'll go through them for you tonight," Katie says. Then she yawns.

"Patrick had better bring my phone back. And the computer cord. And everything else."

I smell something cooking, and there's a new sound coming from the kitchen; brushing, or scrubbing.

"Katie?" Mom calls. "Would you come in here for a moment?"

"I'm kind of resting right now." I feel her move closer to me. "Jess and I are resting."

"Just for a second. I need your help."

Katie mumbles something I can't quite hear as she gets up, but I do understand her when she says "Whoa, sleepy Jell-O!" before stumbling toward my kitchen. I close my eyes and rest my head on the back of the couch.

"Can you help me look for cleaning supplies? Or ask Jessica where she keeps them?"

"Mom, do you have to do this right now? Why don't you just come out and sit with us?"

"I've already started straightening up, she doesn't have anything in here, I can't believe she doesn't—"

"Will you just take a break? We've been going like crazy for days, do you always have to be doing something? Take a break. Please?"

"Katherine," Mom says, and the way she says my sister's given name is like a splash of cold water in my face. "If I do not keep myself busy, I am going to *fall apart.*" Those last two words sound like they have been squeezed from her body, and they hurt me as much, I think, as it must have hurt her to admit them.

Neither says a word for a long time, and all I hear is water running in the sink.

"Is falling apart such an awful thing?" Katie finally says, and the quiver in her voice makes me think she might fall apart herself. "You're allowed to break down, Mom. We've all earned a breakdown here, I think."

"Please," Mom says in a voice I can barely hear. "Please. Just find out where she keeps her paper towels. Ask her if she has any scouring powder."

The look on Katie's face, when she returns to the couch, is a mixture of fear, resignation, and sorrow. I imagine it's a lot like how my own face must look.

"Did you hear her?" Katie asks in a low voice.

"It's all in the bathroom," I say. "In the green metal locker behind the door. Down on the floor."

Katie goes back, and I hear her rustling through my things in the bathroom. Mom seems pleased with whatever Katie's brought her. Maybe she's just happy that she has raised a kid who keeps cleaning supplies in her home.

"Thank you," she says to Katie in almost a whisper. "Thank you."

Katie slips down by my side, and we don't speak after she

pulls the afghan up over us again. Mom is Mom, I'm thinking, and I know Katie is thinking it too. Poor Mom.

I'm listening to Katie's slowing breaths and the occasional stainless-steel gong sound that comes from my sink as it's being cleaned. Maybe I doze. Maybe not quite. My sister's head feels heavy on my shoulder.

"Katie," I say, despite the fact that I think she's passed out, "was I sleeping with a guy who blew up a bus?"

"No," she says. I guess she wasn't passed out after all.

"Are you sure?"

Katie sits up a bit. "Wait, what are you asking me?"

"I don't know."

"Do you think Josh blew up the bus?"

"I don't know. Maybe?"

"Whoa, wait, Jessica, why are you thinking this? Where did this come from?"

"There were some men yesterday. Like detectives or something. They just asked me some questions that made me wonder."

"Jess, you've been living with the guy—"

"We weren't living together."

"Practically cohabitating, then. For months. Do you really think he could have done something like that without you knowing?"

"Probably not."

"Would he have?"

I really want to sleep now and forget about this. "He was always talking to weird guys," I say. "In Spanish."

"That doesn't mean anything. I mean, seriously. If someone was going to do something like that, wouldn't you know? And what about his project, the scan thing?"

"What about it?"

Katie looks at me. "If you were dedicating your life to making something like that, would you work and work and work on it and then one day, just... boom?"

"I guess not."

"Really, do you think he could have?"

"No," I say.

"Good," Katie says. "I don't think he could have, either."

Her head goes back onto my shoulder, and we are quiet. This is just what I needed to hear, but there still isn't much relief as I feel Katie fall into an easy sleep.

24

My kitchen table only came with three chairs, so Patrick brings down one of his own when he joins us for my mom's dinner. A casserole dish, which I had forgotten I even owned, sits steaming in the middle of the table on a folded dishtowel, bubbling with some cheesy-looking contents that smell like, well, home. Like Sunday nights, in our kitchen back home. Katie would be reading, and I'd be doing homework. Mom would listen to classical music on public radio and make a casserole.

Exactly what I need right now, I think.

Patrick has pulled my table into the center of the room to make space for his extra chair. It's a little cramped, but comfortable. He's across from me, Katie is to my left, and Mom is to my right. My back hurts so much now that I'm sitting straight up, and I've found that if I keep my chin lifted, the soreness in my neck is eased.

"Would you have some wine, Maureen?" Patrick asks. "I could grab a bottle if you'd like."

"I don't think we need any, thank you," Mom says.

"This is great, by the way," he adds. I know he's just being kind by saying it. He's a snob with food just like he is with everything else, but Mom doesn't know that, and she purses her lips and cocks her head and almost smiles. She's never been good at taking compliments.

"I might have a glass," Katie says. "If it's not a hassle for you."

"No, no," Patrick says, starting to rise from his chair. I can tell he wants to win Katie over. "It's not a problem—"

"I don't think we need any," Mom says again, this time with a little more finality.

"Well, this part of the 'we' would like some, Mom," Katie says, lifting an eyebrow.

"I know you've been taking those pills with your sister, Katie. Do you think drinking alcohol on top of them is such a good idea?"

"I only had a couple, Mom. And I think I can make my own decisions, is what I think," Katie says. She and Mom stare at each other, and then they both look at Patrick. I feel bad for him—if he goes and gets a bottle of wine, all the points he's gained with my mother today will be lost, but if he doesn't, he'll be on Katie's bad side.

Honestly, I'm kind of with Mom on this. I'm really—*really*—not ready to be drunk, either, and I'd like to avoid even the temptation. And maybe it isn't such a good idea for Katie to drink after those pills today? I'm pretty sure she had a third.

Am I turning into my mother?

"Maybe we could have some later, if we still feel like it," I say.

"*You* are not having *any* later, Jessica," Mom says. I am programmed from my childhood to respond in a huffy way to a challenge like this, but I don't. She's right, anyway.

"Later is maybe a good idea," Katie says. I'm glad, for Patrick's sake, that she's backed down.

"What was the name of the Romanian guy who used to live next door?" I ask.

"Nick," Patrick says between bites. "Big Nick."

"Did he ever yell at you when you gave, what was her name, Julia? The oldest one. Did he ever yell at you when you gave her violin lessons?"

"He didn't need to yell. He didn't need to say a word, really. That guy scared the shit out of me." Katie smiles at this and glances up at Mom, and Patrick looks suddenly embarrassed. "Oh, sorry, Maureen."

Mom is unfazed. "You teach the violin?" she asks, leaning in and looking sincerely impressed. I think she might have a crush on him.

"I'm, ah, it was a side job thing. I needed some work. I really play the cello."

"That's lovely!" Mom says. "Do you play well?"

"I—"

"He plays very well, Mom," I say. Patrick doesn't notice that I'm smiling at him. Just smiling about anything is good enough. Mom is smiling at him too.

"I always wished I knew how to play the cello," she says, and I know Patrick has scored big, big points with Mo.

Patrick works at reconnecting the cables behind my TV stand while Katie and I wait for the computer to come up. Mom, who doesn't seem to approve of me seeing any news about this so soon, has gone for a walk—only agreeing to go alone after Patrick convinced her that crime in our neighborhood is, in fact, very rare.

Katie sits to my right with her hands on her knees, and she leans forward as I type in my password.

"You sure you're ready?" she asks.

"Do you think I'm not?"

"I think you are. I mean, I would want to look."

"I do want to look."

Patrick pushes himself up from behind the television and closes up his pair of pliers before twirling them and jamming them in his pocket like a gun into a holster.

"I don't know if I would want to see it so soon," he says. "I mean, if it happened to me."

"Well, it didn't happen to you," I say. "I don't even remember it. I want to see."

"I think you're totally ready," Katie says.

The browser loads up and I go to the cable news page, and I close my eyes and bite my lower lip because I have no idea how I'm going to react when I see what they have posted. Katie makes a little "ha!" sound and I open my eyes and see not a picture of a smoldering bus, but a map and a headline reading, "Tennessee Floodwaters Threaten More Homes."

"What?" I say. Katie doesn't say anything. There's news about the Nashville flood, and a few headlines about the bombing in Miami, and some golf tournament, and an Alzheimer's disease drug, and a recipe for heart-healthy fish. No buses. I scroll down the page a bit, and my sister points to the screen.

"There it is. There."

The headline in the "National" section says, "SF Suicide Bombing Leaves Questions, Few Answers." I almost click on it, but stop.

Will I see Josh here? The passport photo with the long hair?

I take a breath and click, and Katie leans in close to me as the page comes up. The picture isn't a picture at all, just a generic graphic of an explosion over the words "DOMESTIC TERROR." The name of the bomber has not yet been released, the story says, because of the ongoing investigation. It goes on to say that the improperly assembled bomb didn't detonate all the way, and only nine people were killed.

Only nine. Well, that's lucky, isn't it?

Maybe this is why my bus is not so newsworthy?

There are links to stories about some of the victims, and a photo gallery from the bombing, but I don't click on any of them. Thankfully, I don't see anything with my name. I'm just about to go to search on Google for other pages about the whole thing, but I see a link at the bottom of the page that makes me stop. Katie sees it at the same time.

"RELATED:" it says. "New York exhibition goes on for artist killed in suicide blast."

"Go there," Katie whispers. "Click it."

I do as she says, and this time, when the page loads, we see Josh. And I start to cry.

"That's him," I say. The picture is of Josh in an apron, gesturing while he's talking. It takes me a moment to remember it was one of the images from the presentation he gave at the Art Academy. The first night.

"It's okay, Jess."

"We were fighting. I mean, kind of. We argued. I argued. I was trying to break up with him. He wouldn't listen." I look over my shoulder to see if Patrick is still here, but he isn't in the room anymore. I don't want him to be here right now.

"I understand, Jess."

"I was trying to end it. He wouldn't listen to me."

"I know. It's okay."

"He never listened to me. But he didn't deserve that."

"It isn't your fault."

"He didn't deserve it, though."

"No one deserves it, Jess."

I sob for a while, and Katie puts her arm around my shoulders. It dies down and I'm almost through with it, but I look at the screen and see his picture again, holding his ink-stained hand out, palm up, talking with a half smile in front of the trees changing color through his studio window, and I fall into shaking sobs again. Each gasp makes my back hurt, and I want to stop crying, but I can't.

"It's okay," Katie says, and only then do I realize my strong little sister is crying too.

I click on the gallery link in the story, and another window comes up with a bigger version of the picture of Josh in his studio. I scroll through the images, there's some of his older stuff, flowers and things like that. There are no genitals. Then there's one of his new ones.

"That's my shoulder," I say with a sniffle.

"Your shoulder has a lot of roads."

"Yes. That's how he saw it."

"It really isn't your fault, Jess."

"I know. Thank you. I don't want you to go."

"I'm right here."

"No, I mean away. I don't want you to leave me. But I want you to be on your boat."

"I've been thinking about maybe not going."

"No, no, Katie, you have to go. I didn't mean that for real. You have to go. You have to."

"My flight is Thursday. I switched it so I can leave from here."

"I'll go with you to the airport," I say.

I turn back to the computer to search for pictures of my bus. The crying is over for the time being; now I'm feeling analytical. I type "taraval+bus+bomb" into the image search page, and this combination is a winner: the very first result is some person's photo blog with maybe a hundred little thumbnails from just after the explosion. The guy writes that he lives right above where it happened; apparently he was home and taking a shower and he heard a boom and when he came out in his towel his windows were gone and his floor was covered with glass and there was a bus on fire in the street. So like any smart person would have done, he grabbed his camera.

We go through the photos, one by one, starting at the beginning. There are images with flames, and broken glass, and blankets and trash all over the sidewalk and road. There are pictures of the smoking bus with blackened seats, and when Katie sees me spending too much time trying to make out the dark unfocused shapes on board she puts her hand over mine and makes me click back to the thumbnail page.

We pick and choose a little more. In one picture, some policemen are holding up a dirty striped blanket to hide something in the bus. There's another that shows a man with gold teeth and blood on his face. A woman is yelling. Two men talking. Papers in the street. We scan over the images.

"Click on that one, here." Katie grabs the mouse from me and clicks. "Oh my God, it's you," she says with a gasp. It's actually a whole series, six or seven photos, of me sitting on the ground with my bag and a half-wrapped sandwich in my lap, looking off with a blank, stupid expression on my face. There's a bystander next to me, just a regular pedestrian, in some of the pictures. He's pointing to something and maybe shouting for help, and in the last two there's a medic-looking woman trying to talk to me with her hand on my shoulder. It doesn't look like I'm saying much back to her.

"Katie, look," I say. "It's my phone!" It's on the sidewalk behind me, still flipped open, about six feet away.

"I have a feeling it isn't there anymore," I add, and when I look to see if Katie laughs at my dumb joke I see that she has her hands covering her face and her shoulders are shaking. This sets me off once more, and we sit again and cry with our arms around each other.

"I can't believe you weren't hurt, Jess. I can't believe how close it was."

"I know," I say. "I know." But I really am having a hard time comprehending it.

"I think I'm not going to do the boat."

"You have to do the boat."

"I want to stay here with you."

"I'm making you do the boat."

"I don't know."

"Let's take more pills," I say. "We can calm down. Go to sleep."

"What about Mom?" Katie asks.

"What about her? Do you think she wants pills too?"

"No, no. Shouldn't she be back now?" I realize that it has gotten dark outside, and Mom isn't normally the explore-a-strange-city-in-the-nighttime type.

"Call her from your cell."

I go into the kitchen to get the pills and water, and have a momentary freak-out when I can't find them in the cupboard above my range hood before remembering that I left them in my bathroom. In the other room, it sounds like Katie got ahold of Mom.

"Yes," she says. "Yes. Are you okay? He is? Really?" A pause. "No. Yes, I've been crying, Mom. No, it wasn't the news, we're just kind of emotional. Okay. I love you too. We may be in bed already. See you in a little bit."

I go back to the living room and hand my sister two of our little magic sleepy pills. She's shutting down the computer.

"She's okay?" I ask.

"She's walking with Patrick. He went and found her."

"You're kidding," I say, but Katie shakes her head.

"That was a gentlemanly thing to do," she says, and I roll my eyes.

"Maybe," I say. "He does things like that, sometimes."

"Do you love him?"

"I don't know? I did. I think I still do?"

"I know you do," Katie says. "I think Mom loves him too." We look at each other and laugh, then we both sniffle and I wipe my eyes with the back of my hand and we take turns drinking down our pills with the water that I've brought in a big plastic cup.

We go to the bathroom and get ready for bed. I floss and wash my face while Katie pees, then we trade places. I take one of the other pills too, the ones Miss Nakamura left for my back, and Katie says no at first when I offer her one, but she changes her mind and takes it.

We're side by side in bed when Mom comes home. I can tell that she's trying to be careful about making noise when she closes the door, but she doesn't need to be.

"We're in the bedroom, Mom," Katie calls to her.

"I'll be there in just a minute."

When she comes, she sits on my side of the bed. Mom touches my face, then she puts her hand to Katie's cheek too.

"My girls."

"Mom," Katie whispers.

I can't say anything. If I try, I know I'll lose it. My mother, my nervous, insecure, petty mother, has become a mountain of strength. Maybe she's been like this all along. Has Katie known this? Am I so stupid? All my life I've seen her as nothing other than frightened and nagging, and I suddenly hate myself for it.

"Sleep, girls. Sleep. Sleep well."

Mom leaves, and we listen to her as she gets ready for bed. Water runs; bags are zipped open and shut. Then a new sound, like furniture moving, and Mom calls:

"Jessica honey, can you tell me how this couch opens up?"

I swallow and hope my voice will come. "It's not a pull-out, Mom."

There's a silence. "It's okay," she finally says. "I can sleep on your chair."

"Mom?" I say. "Will you come back here with us?" My chin is shaking as I say it.

"There's room," Katie adds.

Mom doesn't answer, but she comes back to the side of my bed. Katie moves over and I work my sore body to the middle of the mattress, so our mother can slide in under the covers beside me. She takes my hand.

"I'm so sorry, Mom."

"Sleep," she whispers.

25

I'm alone in my bed when I wake up to daylight. My back is a little better, I think, but my stomach feels so upset when I sit up that I think for a moment that I'm going to throw up in my own lap. The queasiness passes, though, and I get myself to my feet and make my way out to the living room where I find Katie sitting at my desk. My phone is up to her ear, and she's writing something on a legal pad.

"I'm at sixty-six," Katie says.

"What?"

"Sixty-six messages so far."

"Seriously?"

"Yes. And someone has called pretty much every time I put the phone down. The ringer is off, but watch." Katie presses a button on the phone and holds it in front of herself, and it's only about ten seconds before the display lights up and flashes.

"Who is it?" I ask.

"Unnamed caller."

"Don't answer, then."

"I haven't answered any of them."

I lean forward and look at Katie's pad, but I'm having a hard time making out what she's written there. "Has anyone important called?"

"Not sure," she says. "Is CNN important?"

"Not to me," I say. "Anyone else?"

"Do you want to just look at the list?"

"Not really. Not yet. Did Dad call?"

Katie laughs. "Twice, actually. From Idaho. And he sounded genuinely concerned. He'll be calling back sometime."

"Sometime, right. Where's Mom?"

"Kitchen."

I go to my kitchen and see that Mom is sitting at the table with a newspaper and a cup of coffee, the scent of which sets off both a deep craving and a flip in my stomach. Mom looks up at me and smiles.

"You went out and got a newspaper?" I ask.

"Patrick brought it down before he left for work."

"I think Patrick is trying to impress you," I say, and I ease myself down in the chair across from her.

"If he's trying," Mom says, "it's working." She gives me a half smile, then her look turns more serious. "You are lucky to have a friend like him."

Now I'm wondering just what they talked about on their walk last night.

"Mom," I say, "our friendship is a little, complicated?"

"Don't think I don't understand." She folds the paper. "How are you feeling today?"

"Better, but I have a stomachache."

"It's those pills." She's reassembling the paper, section by section, in proper order. "Do you want me to run out and get you something for it?"

"I'd like some ginger ale, I think."

"I'll go get some if you just tell me where."

"I feel like I need to get out of here. Will you walk to the store with me?"

"I will, but are you ready to take a walk like that?"

"It's just up on the corner. Some air would help."

"Get yourself dressed, then."

Mom follows me to the living room, and I make my way into my bedroom to hunt for a pair of jeans and maybe a sweater. I pull up the blinds in my room to try to get an idea of what the weather is like, but looking out at the clear sky and my street down beneath it feels like looking at the surface of some newly discovered planet.

"Katie," I hear Mom say, "your sister and I are running over to the store to get something for her stomach." Katie starts to say something, but Mom keeps going. "Will you stay here in case anyone calls?"

"I—"

"Thank you."

Miraculously, I find some clean jeans, and I opt for a fleece pullover over the same tank top I slept in last night. I slip sandals onto my feet, since I'm not sure if I could bend down enough to tie any laces and I'm too stubborn to ask anyone else for help. It's only the MacGyver store, anyway; that's close enough for sandals.

"Okay, Mom," I say.

"We'll be back soon, Katie." Katie gives me a "what the hell?" look that Mom doesn't see.

Descending the flights of stairs is not too painful, and once we're on the sidewalk I'm so surprised and pleased by the warm morning that I pull off my fleece and knot the sleeves around my waist as we start up the hill. Just breathing this outside air has made my stomach feel better already.

"Why didn't you want Katie to come?" I ask.

"I just wanted a chance to talk. You and me talk."

"About?" Mom shrugs, and I lead us over to the other

side of the street to stay in the sun. "What about your walk with Patrick last night? I'm assuming you want to talk about Patrick."

"I want to talk about you."

My street seems a little too clean, and the day seems a little too bright, but I'm drinking in the air and the warmth like they're some kind of wine.

"What about me?"

"You are my daughter," Mom says. "My strong, intelligent, beautiful—"

"I think you're talking about Katie," I say.

Mom lets out a long sigh. "Jessica, your whole life, ever since you were a little girl, you have been incapable of seeing yourself outside of someone else's shadow. Usually your sister's." She takes my hand as we walk on for a few steps. "I feel like that's my fault. I feel like it's because of something I did wrong."

"Mom—"

"No, no. Jessica, I'm not saying this to make you feel guilty. I'm not being... I'm just not. I'm telling you this as a woman who wishes she had done a better job raising her two girls. I wish I could have helped you feel more confident. That's my fault. I'm telling you this like I would tell one of my own friends. I'm sorry I didn't help you more that way."

"Mom, stop it." I think I'm going to start to cry.

"No. Listen to me. When we were driving here I... I know this is going to sound corny, or silly, but I knew you were okay. I *knew* it. I mean, we had no idea what was going on, just that, this thing had happened, and you were involved. We couldn't find out anything more than what Patrick had told us, and that wasn't much. But I knew you were okay. I just could feel it. I wasn't worried. No, I mean, I was so worried. But I wasn't worried that you were gone. I was worried about you feeling alone and scared. I was worried that you needed something to eat. I was worried that you needed someone to take care of you."

I am crying now, and the only thing I can think is that I wish I had my sunglasses to hide it.

"As it turns out, you have someone who does a very good job of taking care of you. I shouldn't have worried about that so much. But I didn't worry you were gone. I knew you weren't, because you are the strong daughter. You are the smart daughter."

"But Katie is the smart one," I manage to say in a wet croak. "Katie is the one who's going to get a Ph.D."

"So what, Jessica? So what? Fine. Is that really how you measure it? If that is what you think you really want, and I don't think it is, go back to school. Go back and finish your master's and get your Ph.D. You would accomplish it easily. Pick a school and your father will pay for it, as he is obligated and more than willing to do. He would be proud, I'm sure. He might actually give a damn about it. But do you know what it would mean to me?"

"What?"

"Absolutely nothing. I'd still worry about you. I might address you as 'Dr.' when I called you, though. Maybe."

This makes me laugh, and I wipe my nose with the back of my thumb.

"But aside from that? Nothing. I'll love you and worry about you just the same. And I'll still feel the same way. You are my strong and smart daughter." Mom squeezes my hand.

"Is this why you didn't want Katie to come with us?"

"I'm not telling you anything that Katie doesn't know herself. But you wouldn't have listened to me if she was here."

Something is taped up in the window of Joe's apartment as we come up to the crest of the hill, and as we get closer I see that it's a "FOR RENT" sign. Someone has added the word "IMMEDIATELY" with a Magic Marker above the phone number.

"Joe is gone," I say.

"You knew the person who lived here?" Mom asks, and I nod. "Where did he go?"

"I don't know. He may have gotten evicted." Mom just shakes her head.

We turn the corner and go back into the shade, and Mom rubs her fingertips on the small of my back. "Do you know the real reason your sister is going to get a Ph.D.?" she asks.

"Because she's brilliant?"

"She is brilliant. But that's not why. It's because she's scared."

"What do you mean?"

"Your sister is an academic for the same reason your father was. She's too afraid to try anything else."

"Do you really think that's true?"

"I thought it was true enough to divorce him for it. But your sister, it isn't ingrained in her yet. There's hope. This boat trip could be a very good thing for her. Maybe she'll meet a boy. Maybe she'll do something crazy. Maybe she'll act a little bit like her big sister."

"Mom, I can't believe I'm hearing you talk like this."

"Maybe she'll move to some island in the Pacific for a while. Wouldn't that be fun?"

"She was talking about not going—"

"Yes. This is the part of her where she's very unlike your father. She wants to take care of you."

"We've always taken care of each other."

"I know. Can I tell you something?" We're in front of the MacGyver store now, and I stop and nod. "I was always a little jealous of how close the two of you were when you were kids. Those summers you drank so much of your father's so-so liquor and watched movies."

"You knew about that?"

"Jessica, come on. I'm your mother. Did I yell at you when I found you two passed out on that musty couch? It happened more than once. Of course I didn't yell at you. I tucked you in."

I feel a flush coming up in my skin, and I love my mother in a way I've never felt before.

"I was jealous, Jessica. At that time, me, by myself with two teenaged daughters, how much did I wish I had a friend I could be drunk and giggly with? Do you think I didn't listen to you girls laughing and laughing down there? I almost came down to join you. More than once."

"You should have," I say.

"No, I shouldn't have. Not at all. That time was for you and your sister. But I wasn't bitter about it, Jessica. Ever. It made me happy that you had each other. It makes me very happy now."

"Oh, Mom."

"I've wanted to tell you these things for a long time."

"Thank you. But Katie—"

"We need to make sure she goes on her trip."

"We will," I say.

Inside the store, Nabil is working, as he always is, and today he's watching a bass fishing tournament underneath the omnipresent gaze of Richard Dean Anderson. Nabil doesn't look up when we come in, just murmurs, "Hello." The indifference makes me smile; being ignored tells me that—mostly—everything is okay in the world.

Katie has finished going through the messages when Mom and I get back home, and I can tell by the look on her face that she's dying to know what Mom and I talked about. The funny thing is, I'll tell her. Later. For now, though, I just sit down next to her at my desk.

"What was up with that?" Katie whispers as she looks over her shoulder to watch Mom go back to the kitchen.

"She was just making sure I was okay."

"Are you okay?"

"Do you think I am?"

"We're probably on the same level of okay-ness," she says. "You and I. Do you want to see who called?"

"I don't think I can deal yet. Did anyone sound really urgent?"

"They all sounded urgent, Jess. You were nearly blown up."

"Figures," I say. A conversation with a "survivor" is only inches away from an *actual* brush with death.

Katie holds up the suddenly illuminated phone.

"MG Communications? Do you want to take it?"

"Yes. Wait. No. I can talk to them later."

"Okay." She puts the phone back on the desk. "What did you talk about? Really."

I'm trying to keep my voice low. "She wants you to go on the boat trip."

"She's been all enthusiastic about it. Even before this thing with you."

"I want you to go too."

"Why should I go?"

"Honestly? I want you to be safe."

Katie glances back to the kitchen. "She told you to say that, didn't she?" Just as she speaks, the display on my phone lights up again. "Unnamed caller," she says.

"Leave it. And no, she didn't tell me to say anything. But I might be turning into her? I'm the one who wants you to go to be safe. She wants you to go to be happy."

"Weird."

"Is it?"

Katie just stares at the unlit phone.

"What day is your flight?"

"I moved it again while you guys were out. To Friday. That's the latest I can go, or I miss the boat. Literally."

"Mom and I will take you there."

"I don't know, Jess, I could stay here with you—"

"And do what? Take care of me?"

"Yes."

"Katie, look at me. I'm fine." I hold out my arms. "Look. Me, one piece. I'll probably start work again on Monday."

My sister sighs. "I think you're being a little ambitious."

"Come on."

"I think you're still in shock."

"Great," I say. "Now who's turning into Mom?" I'm a little scared, though, that she might be right.

"Maybe we're all turning into Mom." She doesn't sound very nice when she says it.

"Stop it. We need to calm down. Let's take some more pills." That should fix everything, right?

"I need a break from the pills." The phone lights again and Katie holds it up close to her face. "David Hadden? Dublin, Ohio?"

"Did you say Hadden?" I feel a pressure in my chest at the mention of the name.

"Yes. David—"

"Answer it," I whisper. *"Answer it."*

Katie presses the button. "Hello? No, this is her sister, Katie…Oh, I'm so…I'm so sorry." Katie's eyes look wet and she blinks a few times. "She's okay. She's doing okay. She's actually right here…Let me…No, it's okay, let me see if she can talk. Just a second." I can see how hard my sister is trying not to cry as she holds the phone in her lap with both hands. "It's—" she starts, then she pauses for a second to get herself together. "It's Josh's mom. She wants—"

"I'll talk to her," I say, and Katie holds the phone out to me. I take a few breaths before I put it to my ear and say hello.

"Jessica, this is Alice Hadden. Josh's mother." There's something to the way she speaks, the timing of her words, that ties her to Josh; hearing her normal-sounding voice beneath the burden of her loss makes me lose it. Katie breaks down too, and she gets to her feet and goes off to my room.

"I'm so sorry, Mrs. Hadden," I manage to say. I'm sorry.

"Jessica, we are sorry too. For you. And thank you."

"We were...I was arguing with him right before...I'm so sorry."

I can't tell if Alice Hadden is crying; she seems much more composed than I am right now. "We saw the thing about you on the news," she says.

"Yes," I say, even though I have no idea what she's talking about.

"And the investigators who came to talk to us the first time, they knew your name too."

I squeeze my fist when Josh's mother mentions this.

"You were very lucky," she goes on. "Were you hurt badly?"

"I'm more...just shaken? I'm bruised more than anything, I guess."

"Right away we realized you were the Jessica he told us about. He wrote about you often. In his letters to us."

"He did?"

"He did. He was a letter writer. Our son hates...he hated e-mail. These letters. I'd like to show some of them to you."

"I don't know if I could handle that, Mrs. Hadden."

"You can call me Alice. And you should see them, when you're ready. You meant so very much to him, and to his work—"

"Please, Mrs. Hadden, Alice, I can't, this isn't the time for me to hear this, I don't think."

"I'm sorry."

"No, I'm sorry," I say. I think I am still in shock. I think I need my sister here.

"Jessica, I need to ask you something. My husband and I, we'd like to ask you to join us at Josh's funeral service this Saturday. You meant so much to him."

"I'm sorry but—" Do you tell a grieving woman that you were trying to break up with her son before he was killed? Do you tell it to yourself?

"I know it's so soon, and you have gone through so much. You might not feel well enough to come."

"I'm fine, but I don't know if I can get the flights and everything—"

"We can help with your travel, we can take care of that. My husband works for the airline. And you can stay with Josh's sister. At our daughter's house."

"I could just get a hotel, I wouldn't want to bother—"

"No, no, please, she's offered. They have plenty of room. She gave us your number, actually."

"She did?" Then I remember the times he called her from my apartment. She must have had it in her caller ID.

"I understand if this is too soon, though, if you're not ready."

I take a long breath and try not to think. "I'll come," I say.

Patrick has been oddly absent through this day of message checking and call returning and general emotional ups and downs. By the time Mom has slipped tonight's meal into the oven—another casserole, lasagna, I think—he still hasn't shown up. Mom has made enough for all of us and him too, and she thinks we should call to ask if he'll join us. Of course she wants him to join us. I want him to join us too.

"I'll go up," I say.

"We could just call," Katie says.

"No, it's okay. I'll go up."

I know he's up there; I've heard his footsteps, and all day I've been listening for the thump thump thump of him running down the stairs on his way to see us. But no thumps, no Pat. I'm ready for a solo trip out of my apartment, anyway. I need to tell him about my upcoming trip to Ohio, and the surprising encouragement my mother gave me when I told her I was planning to go. Katie didn't seem so excited about the idea. I need to tell him a lot, I guess.

It's a reflex for me to go to my dresser to look for Patrick's key before going upstairs, and it takes me a moment to remember throwing his key at him, and another moment to feel stupid about it. I'll ask for it back. Katie seems sulky, looking up from her book and watching me run my hand over the dusty top of the dresser. Maybe I'm imagining it, the sulkiness, but she doesn't say anything to me when I say "Be right back" and go out my door.

It's a lot easier, with my back, to climb up steps than to go down them. And as I make it to the top of the stairs, I hear some sort of orchestral, string-heavy music coming from inside Patrick's apartment. I have to knock twice before he hears me, and he looks surprised when he sees me at the door.

"Hey," he says. "Hey." He scoots over to the wine crate where his stack of stereo equipment is perched and turns down the music, and beckons me in with his hand. "What's up? You want to sit?"

"You moved your furniture."

"You haven't been up in a while."

"That's not true," I say.

"What?"

"Nothing," I say, and I ease myself down to the couch. "Sorry."

"No. Don't say that. What's up?"

"Mom made dinner," I say, and Patrick laughs.

"I'm invited?"

"You know she adores you."

"Well it's good that somebody does."

"Shut up," I say, and I pinch the side of his back above his hip as he sits next to me.

"Ouch! Jess, Jesus, aren't you supposed to be messed up right now or something?"

"I am messed up. But I mean it when I say *shut up*. What are you listening to?"

"Gavin Bryars. He's the composer."

It's getting dark in Patrick's apartment. "It sounds sad," I say. "The music."

"It's called *The Sinking of the* Titanic."

"Well, that's pretty sad, I guess," I say, and this makes me giggle for no particular reason at all.

"You are messed up, but I forget, were you this weird before the bus thing happened?"

Being teased like this, by Patrick, right now, is the most perfect thing ever. It doesn't feel forced, or awkward, or wrong. Just perfect.

"I don't remember any of the bus thing. Maybe it didn't happen at all."

"None of it? Really?"

"I saw pictures of myself after, so I guess I was there."

"One of my guys at work said they mentioned you on CNN the first day, but he didn't see anything after that. The lucky passenger."

"CNN left me a few messages. I didn't call them back."

"You're a human interest story. A face on the tragedy."

"I was arguing with Josh. Then I got off the bus and tried to call my sister. Then I was home. Poof."

"Poof."

"Yeah." I trace the pattern on Patrick's couch with my fingertip, noting how much more comfortable it is than my own.

"You were fighting?"

"I think I broke up with him. I was trying to break up with him, anyway." I laugh, a little forced "ha!" laugh. "I was trying to break up with him for a while."

"I know." I look at him, and he says, "Gretchen told me."

"Oh, right, your girlfriend the spy."

"She was never my girlfriend."

"Uh huh."

"Did she tell you we were dating? If she did, she was lying."

"She never . . . I guess she never said anything."

"Did you ever ask her?"

"Why would I ask that?"

"Did you?" Patrick has sunk down into the couch with his feet up on his low coffee table. He's close to me, but not touching.

"I guess I didn't want to know. I mean, I wanted to ask her, I guess. Sometimes. I wanted to ask how you were doing, how the launch went."

"It went okay. Better than okay."

"I tried to ask Danny about it. He wouldn't tell me anything. Where is Danny, anyway?"

"He had to go to New York," Patrick says. "He wanted to stay. I promised him I'd take good care of you." He puts his hands over his eyes, and I think he's going to say something else.

"What?" I ask, but he keeps his hands on his face and shakes his head. "Okay. I'll ask something. Did anything ever happen with Gretchen?"

He lets his hands fall away and we look at each other.

"Nope" is all he says.

"Really?"

"Is it important if it did or it didn't?"

"It's not my business. I'm sorry." Then I laugh. "I still want to know, though."

"If it had been up to her, something would have happened," he says. "But it wasn't. And it didn't. And that's all I have to say about it."

The slow dirge music ends, the *Titanic* is sunk, and it seems really dark in the apartment. But I don't mind. I can smell Mom's dinner from downstairs.

"What is she making tonight?" Apparently he smells it too. "Wait, let me guess. Something baked in a casserole dish?"

"You don't have to come down if you don't want to. She loves you, though."

"Do you?"

The question gives me a little jolt. "Do I what?"

"Do you want me to come down?"

"Oh. Yes. I'd like you to."

"I will, then."

"We have a few minutes."

Patrick rubs his eyes again. "I have a question. About not remembering stuff."

"Seriously, Pat, it's like a fog."

"No, I mean, about me not remembering stuff. Those nights you came up here. You were outside my door two times. And the second time you came in."

I keep a straight face. "You're making it up," I say. "You're having dreams."

"I saw, like, the shadow of your feet under the door."

"Your imagination," I say, even though I'm starting to laugh.

"You did, you came up here, and I opened the door—"

"Dreaming."

"—and you came in, we walked in here. I was backward—"

"Did not happen."

"And I was, in my room, you told me to call."

"Maybe that part happened."

"Shit, Jess, I felt like an idiot, you told me to call, but I was..."

"You were what?"

"I was scared, Jess."

"Scared? Of what?"

"Of what you'd say."

"What do you mean?"

Patrick straightens up a little bit. "What if I called and you were like, um, what?"

"You should have just called."

"I couldn't just call. I wanted to sleep with you that night."

"Did you dream that too?"

"Stop it. I'm being serious. But you were with Josh. I couldn't call. I was just...I was scared. I felt like an idiot."

"No," I say. Patrick is quiet; he just slouches down into the couch.

"Are you okay?" I ask.

"Yeah." His hands cover his eyes.

"Anything else?"

"No. Yes. Work, just work. My boss has asked me to lead a new development team...." He keeps rubbing his eyes as his voice trails off.

"That sounds like a good thing, though."

"Yeah, well, I guess. We'll see." He takes his hands from his face and looks at me again. "So, just what happened with Josh?"

"Pat, please. Didn't you ask Gretchen?"

"Maybe I didn't want to know, either."

I suddenly feel very sad. The feeling sneaks up on me, like it has, off and on, all day. I don't want to cry in front of Patrick, not now, not when being next to him feels so normal and ordinary. I need normal and ordinary. I don't want to ruin it. But I think I'm going to cry anyway.

"I thought I loved him. I mean, there were times I thought that. I never, I never said it, though. I don't think I ever really felt it."

"Don't feel guilty about that."

"He never listened to me. It was like, he was so wrapped up in his art, or his opinions, or politics, or whatever..."

"He was that way, wasn't he."

"And now, now I'm terrified that..."

"That what?"

"What if he did it, Pat?" I whisper.

"Did it, you mean...did the bus? Like he *did* that?"

I nod.

"Oh, come on, no...there's no way, Jess, no way. No. Just, no."

"But what if he did?"

"Jess, I knew him. That just, he couldn't have...that wasn't in him. He didn't do that. He couldn't have done that."

"Are you sure?"

"I just don't think ... He had his art, Jess. He had his convictions. I don't think killing people was in him. That wouldn't have been art. He had his facts. Art. Opinions. He was certain about things."

"Yes, he was certain," I say. "He was so sure of what he thought, the way he saw things, he never really expected anyone to disagree with him. And if they did, if I did, you know, he never listened." Now I'm crying. "I hated it. It made me hate him."

"You're allowed to hate people, Jess. Even people who die."

I just cry for a while, feeling stupid, and Patrick carefully puts his arm over my shoulders. I want to lean into him, but the pain in my back keeps me sitting up straight and I hope he doesn't read it as me being distant. I think he understands.

"I'm going to his funeral," I say. "In Ohio. I'm flying there on Friday."

"That's ... Jesus. Are you ready for that?"

"Is anybody ready for anything, really?"

"Good question," Patrick says. "Do you still hate him?"

I think about this for a moment. "Maybe. But I respect him. And I want to meet his mom and dad. And his sister. I think she hated him. I'm staying at her house."

"You are messed up," Patrick says, and the lightness of the way he says it makes the sad feeling dissipate.

"I know," I say, and now I smile. "Mom is taking us to the airport Friday. Katie leaves for New Zealand then too. Can you pick me up Monday afternoon?"

"I'm sure I can borrow Danny's car."

"Thank you. Can I ask you something?"

"Hmm?"

"Can I have my key back?"

Patrick frowns when I ask this. "What, the key I have to your place?"

"No, no, my key to *your* place," I say, and even in the dark I can see he's relieved.

He takes his keys from his pants pocket, jangles them, and then works one deliberately from the ring.

"You sure you want it?"

"Yes," I say, and he places it in my hand. "Thank you. Hey, wait, how did you get a new key to my place?"

"There was a spare one in your pants. I found it when I helped you change."

This makes me feel sick to my stomach. "Josh made that key," I say. "He made it without asking me."

I feel like I'm going to cry again; this damn feeling comes and goes like waves and I grab Patrick's hand to try to hold the feeling off.

"God, Pat, you knew him too—"

"We weren't super close. He knew Joe from way back, though."

"Joe, what happened to Joe? I saw the sign, did he get kicked out?"

"Joe got his shit together and went back to work. He's in Sacramento."

"You're kidding me?"

"I'm not."

"Josh didn't really blow up the bus, did he?"

"I just don't think he could have."

"Okay," I say, and I take a deep breath. "Can I tell you something, Pat?"

There's a knock on the door and we both jump as my sister's muffled voice says, "Are you guys coming down? Mom just took dinner out of the oven." Neither of us heard her coming.

Patrick stands up, and takes my hand to help me to my feet. "Not now," he says. "Don't tell me anything now. Tell me when you get back."

26

Patrick leaves early Friday morning to run—literally—to his company's satellite office here in the city to pick up Mom's car. They have a parking garage, and Patrick worked some deal with one of the attendants—probably involving the exchange of soft drugs or expensive wines—to let him park it there for the week.

Katie's flight for Auckland leaves just before ten, and my own flight is something like an hour and a half after that. We're going to the cellular store to get me a replacement phone, then Mom will take us to the airport, wave good-bye, and drive back to Seattle as one of her daughters flies far west, and the other goes not so far to the east. And she'll be happy about it. This is my prediction.

Katie seems to have turned back into herself after being sulky over my walk with Mom. I'd say I've turned back into myself too, but I don't feel like I can exactly put a finger on just what "myself" is. But things feel normal, at least, with the two of us.

My sister has taken over the floor of my living room to repack for her trip. She's only allowed one duffel bag on the boat, she's told me, along with a laptop and a day pack. So, sitting cross-legged and surrounded by her things, she's consolidating. I manage to work myself down into a sitting position next to her. Some scientific-looking devices are sitting on top of her laptop bag, and I examine what appears to be a shiny stainless-steel measuring cup set. It's a series of nesting rings, each one with a progressively finer mesh screen inside.

"Is this for . . . for sifting sand?" I ask.

"Mmhmm," Katie says, without really looking up. "They're graded. Sometimes I catch little bugs in with the sand."

"Do the bugs screw up your results?"

"They have no impact on my research. They are cool to look at with the microscope, though."

"You have a microscope?"

Katie gives me an exaggerated "duh, of course I have a microscope" look, and we both laugh.

"What is that for?" I say when I see Katie put a fleece pullover into her duffel.

"It might get chilly at night."

"You're going to the South Pacific, though."

"New Zealand gets chilly. Rainy. It's winter there now."

Mom sticks her head out from my bedroom, where she had been putting away the clothes that she washed for me in the coin-op at the bottom of our stairs last night.

"I think you should bring the fleece," Mom says.

"See?" Katie sticks out her tongue at me when she says it.

"It's practical," Mom says.

Katie pokes at the fleece in her bag. "Mom says it's practical."

"I have something for you to take," I say, and Katie cocks

her head and gives me a funny look as I go to my bookshelf; when I pull out the road atlas her mouth drops open.

"You still have that?"

"Of course I still have it," I say as I hand it to her. She laughs when she sees our names on the cover, and she laughs again when she flips to one of the pages.

"Oh my God," she says. "The trip we planned to Texas—"

"You wanted to follow the theater teacher guy."

"*You* wanted to follow the theater teacher guy. I wanted to follow the theater student guy."

Katie looks through some pages and laughs again, then lifts the atlas up and looks beneath it as if she expects to find something there. "This doesn't really, you know, cover where I'm going."

"You can take it," I say. "If you want. It might just be fun to look—"

"No," Katie says, and she thumbs the book open to Ohio for a moment before closing it. "You should take it with you." And she hands it to me.

Patrick is back, and when he peeks in at us sitting on the floor, he nods and says simply, "Ready." He's pulled Mom's car up on the sidewalk in front of our building, and he ferries our bags down to it—one trip, two trips, three—and Katie walks at my side as we go down the stairs. I'm feeling even better today; the stiffness in my back is more like a memory, and descending the stairs feels almost easy.

Mom stands next to the car with a tissue clenched in her right hand. Patrick slams the trunk closed, then comes and puts his arms around my mother.

"Thank you," she says. "Thank you." Her eyes are wet. Pat gives Katie a hug; she opens her mouth as if she's going to say something, but just ends up shaking her head.

"Have a good time on the boat," Patrick says, and now Katie nods.

Patrick stands in front of me, and Katie and Mom get into the car. My arms are at my sides.

"You're okay?"

"I don't know?"

"You're okay. Call me when you're there?"

"Yes."

Patrick reaches to me and touches my left arm and strokes my shoulder. Then he kisses his fingertips and presses them to my mouth.

"Call me," he says, and all I can do is blink and say

Yes.

Patrick stands on the steps of our building with his hands in his pockets, and I watch him from the passenger window as Mom drives out over the curb and onto the street with a thump.

"Tell me which way, Jess," Mom says.

"Left up here. Stay left. Get on 101 South, and we'll see the airport signs."

"Are you going to have time to get your phone and still make it through security?"

"Oh, shoot. We can go ... Ah, forget the phone." Josh did well enough without one, didn't he? "I don't need it. I'll take care of it when I'm back."

The Cincinnati airport, where I lay over after my long, boring flight from SFO, seems completely populated by frat boys and boob-job blondes and thick-bodied families coming home from some theme park vacation. I've never been to the Midwest before, but I may as well be on another planet. And the stares, the stares, I feel like everyone is looking at me, the frat boys and the fat women; I remember my black eyes and wonder if they know I'm the one who made it off the bus?

Does anyone even care?

The gate for my flight to Columbus is close, and I proceed there immediately—no magazine, book, or coffee shop—as my punctual mother has trained me to do. I'm looking forward to sitting down and trying to make myself invisible, but the monitor says "SEE AGENT" and when I do see the agent I find out that, due to mechanical trouble, we are waiting for a replacement plane and won't be taking off for another four hours. Now I'm wishing I *had* gone to the phone store this morning so I could stand now amidst the constellation of businessmen and college kids and call someone too and say sorry, sorry, I'm going to be a little late.

I should call Emily, though, who is supposed to be picking me up. It would be the nice thing to do. I have her number written somewhere, and I dig through my bag and eventually find it scribbled on the back of my itinerary along with Alice Hadden's number and the airline's number and some other unknown number I don't even remember writing down.

Emily does not pick up when I dial from a pay phone, and I leave a borderline coherent message about the plane being delayed or late or changed and well I'm just going to be late and I hope you get this message. In the event she doesn't get it, though, I try Mrs. Hadden, who does answer.

"I'll get ahold of her," she says. "You were nice to call."

We're about to say good-bye, but there's a hesitation, an opening, and I ask what I'm really wondering. "Mrs. Hadden, are you okay?"

"We're doing fine. We are." In her voice, there is something of my own mother. "Are you?"

"I don't know?"

"I understand," she says. And in the way she says it, I believe it.

I try to wander and watch the coming and going; the fat, sagging faces, the elderly conveyed on electric carts, the tee shirts from chain restaurants. I'm feeling too obvious, though, with my black eyes, so I make my way back to my gate and try to make myself one with a torn vinyl chair and an abandoned magazine.

It's dark outside when we finally board the little commuter plane, and I watch the lights underneath us as we lift into the air. We're hardly up before we come back down again into more orange lights. The airport in Columbus is quiet and I'm surprised when I pause in the nearly empty terminal to move my watch back and see that it's almost eleven o'clock. There's hardly anyone at security when I walk through, just a couple bored soldiers and a cornrowed TSA woman slumped down in her chair, texting someone on her phone. She doesn't look up as the handful of passengers from my turboprop walk past her.

I follow the overhead signs to baggage claim, towing my little roller bag behind me, and before I've rounded the concrete pillar, I see Emily next to the first carousel. Even though she's facing away from me I know it's her—she has the same shoulders as her brother, and her hair is the same straw color but longer, down past the collar of her shirt. She's shorter than me, and delicate-looking. A white-blond child is asleep on her shoulder, and she rocks very slowly from side to side as I approach them.

"Emily?" I say, and I'm shocked by how much she looks like Josh when she turns to me. His nose and the eyes are there, the eyes especially; maybe her mouth is a little fuller in the lower lip, but he's right there in her face.

"Jessica. Hi." She looks like she's going to say something, but instead she shifts the little boy up higher on her shoulder. I catch a glimpse of his openmouthed slumber.

"I'm sorry it's so late," I say. "I hope you got the message?"

"I did, thanks."

"No, thank you for picking me up. I didn't check any bags, so . . ."

"Let's go," she says.

I follow her through some automatic doors out to the parking garage and the night air feels warm and damp and the first thing that comes to my head is that the air smells like dirt and sex.

"Who is this with you?" I ask.

"This is Caleb. He wanted to stay up to meet his uncle's friend."

"Oh, I'm sorry. Sleepy guy."

We come up to a big white car, it's something between a minivan and an SUV, and when Emily repositions her son to get her keys from her bag I see that her hands have slender artist's fingers. No great surprise, I suppose.

"Can I help you? I can take him."

"I've got it." Emily presses a button and the car chirps and flashes before the door on the side magically hums open, and she works her sleeping little boy into his car seat while I stand and watch. Then she withdraws and straightens out the front of her jacket and touches the wet drool spot on her shoulder. She looks at me, and I look at her, and at that very moment I want to ask her everything, everything there is to know about her brother. I want to ask if *she* thinks he could have done it. But I don't.

I snap down the tow handle of my bag instead.

"Should I put this in the back?"

"Sure," Emily says. "Sure." She presses another button on her keychain, and, with no chirps, the rear hatch of the van swings open.

27

It takes me a moment to remember where I am when I open my eyes in the morning—there are peach-colored walls and nice clean carpeting and a tidy computer desk with matching dresser and nightstand. A benign guest room. In Josh's sister's house. Emily's house. And her husband's, whose name I have forgotten on this sunny morning.

The place is mostly silent as I rise and dress, a condition I ascribe to some sort of reverence for the upcoming events of the day, but as I make my way out of the room toward the scent of coffee, I begin to get the feeling that the quiet of the house is more like a permanent fixture—as much a part of it as the pale yellow walls in the hallway or white painted chair rail in the dining room. Emily is in the kitchen, and the black dress she's wearing makes her body look more slender and her skin seem paler than when I met her last night. She looks at me with an almost-smile, and I see Josh's face in the expression.

"There's coffee," she says. "Mugs are up above."

"Thank you," I say. "Can I do anything?"

"I'm fine. There's half-and-half if you need it."

"I'm okay." And this is the extent of our conversation on the morning of her brother's funeral. Maybe she's grieving. Or maybe she just never talks.

I get myself some coffee and stand at the sink, looking out the window into the treeless neighboring yards of the houses around us. I'm about to say, for the sake of saying anything, something about the fact that every single yard I see seems to have the same matching wooden swing set with a yellow plastic slide and canvas awning, but there's a noise and at my side is a little blond boy, older than the one last night, wearing a white polo shirt buttoned up to the collar. His face is rounder than his mother's.

"Are you my uncle Josh's girlfriend?" he asks. I can see a broad gap in his front teeth when he talks, and there's something contemptuous in the way he says the word "girlfriend."

"Well, yes, I—"

"Justin, stop it," Emily snaps. "Please go wait in the front room." Justin slinks off, but looks back at me from the hallway for a moment.

"Justin! Go to the front room." Emily looks at me and makes the almost-smile face again. "I'm sorry."

"Kids are kids," I say.

"I'm sorry."

There are more footsteps, heavier ones, and Emily's husband, thick-faced and scowling, comes into the kitchen. He's wearing a dark suit that may have fit better sometime in the past, and I see his eyes go up and down over me before he turns to Emily.

"Let's get in the car," he says. These are the only words he speaks to us before going back off down the hall. "Justin!" I hear him call. "Come on, bud, let's load up! Caleb, let's go!"

"Tim?" Emily calls. "Tim?" But he's already gone.

I take a big swallow of my coffee, then another, and pour the rest down the sink, and Emily takes the mug from my hand when I try to rinse it out.

"Don't," she says. "I'll get that."

"It's not a problem."

"Really, I'll take care of it." She places the mug in the bottom of the sink and guides me by my elbow to a door, and when we step into the garage I'm shocked by the sudden humidity and stink of gasoline and lawn clippings and trash cans. I stand back as Emily buckles her kids into their car seats in the big white car, and I stop her when she starts to climb up between them in the backseat.

"Why don't you sit up front?" I say.

"You don't want to be back here between these two."

"I can handle kids. You sit up front."

I squeeze my way over the younger one, Caleb, and into the space between the two car seats. As we back out of the garage, I catch a look at their second car, a tan sedan of some sort. I know nothing about cars, but I do see a bumper sticker that says, in thick blue lettering, "WE VOTE PRO-LIFE."

Katie, if she were here, would combatively bring this up. I will certainly not bring it up. Not today.

Caleb is to my right, looking at me. And Tim, even though he's wearing sunglasses and probably thinks I can't tell, keeps peering at me through the rearview mirror. He's creeping me out.

"You were kind of sleepy last night," I say to Caleb. He holds out his hand, but doesn't smile.

"It was a late night for Caleb," Emily says, twisting to look at us. "That was a special thing, going to the airport."

Caleb blinks, but says nothing.

"You don't talk much, do you," I say.

Justin, to my left, leans forward. "He just doesn't want you to know he had a pee accident in his bed last night," he says. He's sort of smiling as he says it, and his mean gap-toothed smile grows when sweet little Caleb's lower lip goes out and his eyes fill up with tears.

"It's okay," I whisper to him as I squeeze his bony knee. "I understand."

I can tell that Justin hates me for saying this, but this is not a problem because I'm already beginning to hate this bratty little kid right back. More troubling, though, is the look I get from Tim in the mirror.

We drive away from the houses, into more trees. The spaces are older, storefronts are older, and we slow to join a line of cars turning into an older parking lot in front of a brick building surrounded by big trees. I see the words "Memorial Gardens" on the sign as we go past.

The funeral is outdoors, held in a place that seems—appropriately enough—to be designed exclusively for the pur-purpose of hosting funerals. Chairs are arranged, there's a table set up with coffee and Styrofoam cups and bottled water, and the people arriving segregate themselves into two main groups: a gathering of family to the left, populated at the center by a cluster of tall, lean men, gray at the temples but still bearing a resemblance to Josh, and a younger group of friends to the right, more casually dressed and speaking in low voices. There are a lot of people here, but Emily and her husband and children don't seem to align themselves with either group, and I feel seriously awkward standing with them, so I make my way toward the table to grab a bottle of water for some cover. As I do this, though, a man from the younger group comes toward me. His head is shaved and beaded with perspiration and he's wearing two small hoop earrings, and I gasp when I make the realization that this is my old high school friend, the giver of my bedroom-hanging lithographs, Greg Murrant.

"Oh my God," I say.

"Jess Zorich," he says, and he wraps me in a respiration-stopping bear hug. "How are you? I heard you might be here."

"You look so good, Greg." It's the first thing I think to say, and I feel like an idiot for it. "I'm sorry."

"No, you're nice. You haven't changed. I'm so glad you're okay."

"Thank you."

"When I heard what happened, I thought, oh Jesus, but then I saw the pictures of you online—"

"I don't think I can talk about this, Greg. I'm sorry."

"No, don't. Stop. How's Katie?"

"She's good. She's in the Southern Hemisphere."

"That's awesome," Greg says, and he asks for no further clarification.

"You always liked Katie better," I say.

"Not true. Actually, there really was no better or worse. Both Zorich sisters were equally unattainable by us mere mortals."

As Greg is saying this, I see a woman go to Emily and give her a hug, then hold both of her hands as they nod and talk. Tim stands off a bit with the boys. Then Emily points to me and the woman looks in my direction and nods, then they embrace again and she walks toward me.

"That's Josh's mom," Greg says.

She comes to me, a middle-aged woman, built like her daughter but carrying herself with certainty like her late son. "Jessica," she says, and when I nod she takes me in her arms and says "thank you, thank you. I'm so sorry. I'm so glad you're okay."

"No," I say, and for the first time today I feel like I might cry. "I'm sorry for you. I'm sorry for Josh."

"He cared for you so much."

"No. Mrs. Hadden, don't. Please."

"He really did."

"No, really. Please." I wipe the corner of my left eye with my fingertips and see that Greg has slipped back into the knot of Josh's contemporaries. Among them, I see two familiar-looking, dark-complected men—are these the same

ones from Josh's studio?—but Mrs. Hadden pulls me away
before I can look at them for very long.

"Wait," I say. "Those guys—"

She doesn't hear me. "I'd like you to meet my husband at
some point," she says, gesturing off toward the group of tall
relatives. "He's very happy you could come."

"I appreciate your help and everything, bringing me
out."

"It's nothing. He's having a very hard time with this. And
the investigators, whatever they are, they keep coming and
coming, can't they just leave us alone for a day?"

"It must be hard." What else can I say, really?

"David was reading Josh's letters last night."

"I was surprised to hear he was such a letter writer."

"I think he liked how it felt old-fashioned. I think he sent
us one e-mail when he was a graduate student, and that was
it. Always many letters, though."

"An anachronism."

"So many letters. Many letters from this summer. He
talks about you in—"

"Mrs. Hadden," I say, and my stomach tightens so
sharply I feel like I may puke at her feet. "I feel terrible saying
this, now, right now, I know this must be the most impossible thing to deal with, today. But, there's all this uncertainty,
and . . . you need to know that my relationship with your son,
I mean, he is, he was the most incredible person and so gifted
and all that, but our relationship was not—"

"Wasn't the most stable thing?"

"You could say it that way."

"I know."

"You do?"

"He wrote many letters."

"About that?"

"About everything. He was very excited about this project he did, with you, and the maps."

"It was," I say, "unlike anything I've ever done before."

Alice Hadden smiles at this, a sad, tired smile.

"Those prints, his last project, the ones of you, they're beautiful," she says. Then she turns and looks at her daughter. "Is everything going well at Emily's house? She made it to the airport at the right time?"

"Yes, and thanks for giving her the message." Mrs. Hadden keeps looking toward Emily, and I say nothing for a moment. "You have cute grandsons," I finally say.

"They are good little boys. And you met Tim?"

"We haven't talked much."

"He's not much of a talker. Did Josh ever tell you anything about Emily? Or Tim?"

"I don't think Josh liked your son-in-law very much."

"That is an understatement. I was a little surprised that Tim even came. If you hadn't been staying with them, maybe he would have kept Emily home too."

"I know Josh loved your daughter," I say.

"He did." Now Mrs. Hadden's eyes fill. "Yes, he did. And I wish I knew, I wish I knew why they . . . Here, come with me. I want to show you something." She takes me by the arm and guides me to a table covered with framed pictures, and she picks up one of the frames and holds it up between us. "Look at them. My babies."

I take the frame and look; the colors are washed out and there's a crease in one of the corners of the print, but it's of Josh and Emily as little blond children. They're on some beach of rounded pebbles, right at the margin of the water and the shore, both of them smiling, and Emily is down on her haunches in a frilly pink one-piece, touching her hands to the ripples beneath her as Josh struggles, wide-eyed in his droopy green swimming trunks, under the weight of a big round stone he's holding up under his chin.

"My babies," she says again. Then someone touches her on the shoulder and she blinks and says, "Oh! Jean. Thank you so much for coming," before she turns back to me and says, "Excuse me, Jessica."

I nod and turn back to the table of pictures. A big mounted print, one of the wildflower lithographs, stands on an easel nearby, but all the rest are photographs. All the pictures feature Josh in some way, sometimes with his parents, sometimes alone, or with friends, or with Emily. There's one of a group of people posing before a Ferris wheel, Josh at the center. It's the ones with Emily that fascinate me the most, though. I pick one up, a tall picture in a heavy wooden frame of Josh in a graduation gown, smiling and talking to someone out of the frame as Emily stands at his side and looks up at him. Her arm is looped through his, and she leans into him, hanging on to him, listening to whatever it is he's saying.

In another, teenaged Emily is holding some sort of certificate, some sort of award. Josh stands next to her with a stern look, but he's making rabbit ears behind her head.

The last one I look at, the one I can't put down, must have been taken up at the cabin Josh told me about. He and Emily are jumping from a tall dock, cannonball-style, into a deep lake below, and the big suspension bridge stands off in the haze at the horizon. Every wavelet reflects the setting sun with a flash, and I see the perfect arc they both make through the air into that lake of orange sparks. Emily holds her knees tightly up to her chest, looking terrified and exhilarated, and Josh, who has launched a little sooner, has let go, is opening up, preparing to slice into the electric water. His arms have spread wide and his mouth is open in a shout.

I look at this photo and realize I'm waiting for both of them to hit the water. I know it won't ever happen, but I keep looking, as if the picture is going to magically become a little movie in my hands and I'll get to hear them scream as they finally splash into the lake.

"Jess," a voice says. *Chiss.* I turn and look up and there's Gert with a brace on his hand, wearing a dark sport coat and possibly the saddest expression I've ever seen. His eyes are ringed in red and he's got some stubble, and when I grab him to give him a hug, I pick up a general beery smell and the whiff of stale cigarette smoke.

"Are you okay, Gert? Is Angie here?"

"She's back home. She sent some flowers. There is always the teaching."

"Gert?"

"I'm not so good with all this, Jess."

"Have you been drinking?"

"I was out with those guys"—he points to a group of people, and I can see Greg Murrant's bald head in with them—"last night. Some of us just kept going."

"I want you to stay with me, Gert."

"I'm not doing so good with the doc's funeral."

"I'll take care of you, Gert." This is good. Taking care of Gert will give me cover. And it would be the nice thing to do. So I slip my arm into his and gently pull him along, and in this gesture we take care of each other.

"How is your hand?"

"Painful. Therapy is painful. Did you know there are hand therapists?"

I think for a moment that Gert is setting me up for one of his straight-faced jokes, but the fact that he looks like he's going to fall apart at any moment makes this seem doubtful.

"I didn't know that."

"There are. Mine is especially cruel. But she says the hand will work like it did before."

It is just at this moment that I realize we are standing next to Josh's casket. People mill around it, paying no special attention. It's as if it's just another table for pictures or water bottles. There's a spray of white flowers across the top, and I'm horrified to find myself wondering what he looks like in there. Is he resting, posed peacefully? Is he an approximation, reassembled from collected parts?

Gert sighs. "I saw him, Jess. There, in the bus, after it happened." He must be reading my mind.

"Oh, Gert," I say. "Wait, you were there?"

"We were setting up, at the gallery. It was only a block away, you know. And when we heard the boom, it was just something, something I know, I know exactly what happened."

I can't say anything to this. I just look up at Gert as he stares at the casket.

"So I run there, it's not far, just follow the smoke. Stuff all over the ground. And the bus, you know, all the windows are gone, I go right up on there, and see him. He's dead, the doctor is dead."

"Gert."

"He doesn't look sad, or afraid. He doesn't look in pain. He just looks, I guess he just looks surprised."

Now I feel tears on my cheeks, and I'm not sure if Gert's holding me up or if I'm holding him.

"Really surprised. Sort of calm. But not living. I check for his breathing, but it's not there. I don't look at anyone else. I can't look. So I get out of the bus."

"Gert, do you think he . . . ?"

"No, Jess. No way."

A jowly man in a dark suit is silently ushering people to the rows of chairs. As he comes toward us, slowly waving his arms to herd us along, Gert reaches into his coat and takes out a folded piece of paper.

"I don't know if you saw this," he says, and he hands me the paper. "But I wanted you to see if you hadn't." I unfold the paper and gasp: it's a pair of photos, printed from some Web site, it looks like, of Gert picking me up from the sidewalk and carrying me away.

"Did you take me home?" I ask.

"I did. You were confused. You were talking nonsense. Just nonsense. Gibberish. Your sister's name. Josh's name. Nonsense. You didn't know who I was."

"Gert," I say.

We go to some seats in one of the back rows, and I keep

my arm in his as we sit down. "I picked you up, and you hung on to me like a baby."

"Thank you, Gert."

"You were shaking. I was shaking. Everything was so loud. There were sirens. People yelling. You kept saying something about your phone."

"I lost my phone."

"I lost my backpack. I saw it in there too."

"I'm so sorry, Gert."

"It's just a backpack."

"No, I'm sorry about everything. I'm sorry that you saw everything."

"Seeing it isn't so bad, Jessica. I see it, and I know it's real."

"I understand."

He looks at me with his bloodshot eyes. "Do you know that it's real?"

Do I?

"It doesn't seem real, sometimes. My back hurts, and that's real. My ear hurts, and that's real too."

"My hand hurts," Gert says. He holds it out, encased in a blue fabric brace with Velcro straps, and I take it between my own hands. "It's funny. I have a hard time remembering cutting my hand. Was that real?"

"You were so calm."

"No, you were calm. That's what kept me calm."

"See? You remember." As I say this, I see Gert smile for the first time today.

"We got to your place," he tells me. "Somehow you tell me how to get there. I'm crying so much, you know, it's too much, thinking about the doc. We climb the stairs, I'm dying on the stairs. You're heavy for such a little girl. And when I get you in, it's like, you go crazy, screaming, screaming, and I'm crying like a baby, saying, 'Jess, Jess, calm down, you got to calm down.'"

I'm biting my lip and closing my eyes as he tells me this.

"You're screaming, 'Get out! Get out!' You know, like crazy. I think I got to take care of you, but I think you are gonna hurt yourself screaming like that, or maybe hurt me. So I step outside your door, kind of hold it so it doesn't latch, thinking maybe you will calm down, calm down, and I can come in and help you. But you run over and push the door to close it, you know, bam! I can hear the locks click click as you do them, and I'm saying, 'No, Jess, no!'

"So I don't know what to do. No one is in your building, I knock at all the doors, no one. I'm going crazy. So I walk home, you know, people are just looking at this crazy tall guy in the street, walking and crying and pulling his hair. But then Angie, you know, she has some sense—"

"Angie," I say. "Angie was at my door. When they came in."

"Angie has some sense. She calms me down. She asks where you live, how to get in. Somehow I explain it."

"She was there."

"She was there. She calls me and lets me know she got in, someone let her in. She lets me know Jess is okay."

"Thank you, Gert."

"We all do the same."

"Thank you so much."

Now most of the people are seated, but I don't see Emily and her family anywhere among them. Toward the front, though, a few rows ahead of us, I see two of the tall men helping a third to his seat. He's sobbing and can barely stay up on his feet, and I'm pretty sure it's Josh's father. The men support him on either side—they must be brothers, Josh's uncles—and when they sit down they put their arms around him. Josh's mother follows, and one of the uncles moves over to give her his place.

The jowly man stands before the seats and the people, just to the side of the coffin, and says some things I don't listen to. He talks about Josh, his art, his life, but I don't really hear him. I hold Gert's injured hand while he says the words. A young cousin is introduced, and he gets up to say more words in a quiet voice. Another man gets up to speak, a friend, and another. Greg Murrant gets up, and talks, and even though I'm not listening to his words, I hear that he speaks in a strong and confident voice. He tells a story that makes everyone laugh, and even though I don't understand what he's saying I go ahead and laugh too to hide the fact that I'm lost in fog. Finally, one of the uncles gets up, the one who made room for Alice Hadden. He goes in front of everyone and speaks in a cracking voice, and I manage to understand that he's telling a story about Josh, as a teenager, helping to build something at their cabin in Michigan. He was building a porch, Josh was, and hit his thumb with a hammer.

I'm missing the significance of this, somehow.

There's a wail from in front of me, and heads turn discreetly and I look myself to see that Josh's father has completely fallen apart; he's slumped forward with his head hanging down and Mrs. Hadden is leaning in close to him and rubbing his trembling shoulders with her hand. The uncle standing up in front of us can't speak anymore, and he rubs at his eyes with a handkerchief. Gert watches all of this too. And as we watch, wanting to see and not wanting to see, an elderly man rises from his seat in the front and walks to Josh's father. His shoulders roll forward in a severe stoop and his face is wrinkled like a dried-up apple, but I can still see he has Josh's eyes as he makes his way down the row.

Everyone watches him.

He stands in front of Josh's father and puts his crooked old hands on the sobbing man's shoulders, and he leans down and says something. He says something, and says it again; Josh's father nods without looking up and the old man squeezes his shoulders. I can't hear what he's said but the look buried in his ancient lined face seems to say

You will endure this.

Josh's father nods.

You will.

The man goes back to his seat and the uncle clears his throat, and I feel like I've been holding my breath the entire time.

"You can understand," the uncle finally says, "that my brother has had a very hard time today."

The uncle sits down and the jowly man begins to speak again, and as he does, I look over my shoulder past Gert and see that Emily has walked off with Caleb. She's holding his hand as the little boy tugs at the bough of an old pine tree. She turns back and sees me watching her, and I feel for a moment that we are trying to say something to each other in our heads.

We try, anyway. But I don't know what it *is* exactly that we're saying, and after a little while Emily turns back to her son and the pine tree.

After the service, there's some talk of a reception, but I don't feel much like going. Josh has been lowered into the ground. Gert and I mill back with everyone else to the line of parked cars, walking silently, arm in arm. Just in front of us a man—there's something familiar about him—shuffles along in a tailored suit, shoulders stooped.

"Joe?" I say. The man perks up and turns around to face us. It *is* Joe, but he hardly looks like I remember him; his hair is styled and he's wearing expensive clothes. He has designer glasses on too, and his eyes are red and weepy under them.

"Jess," he says. "Jess. You're here. I didn't see you. Are you okay?"

"I'm fine, Joe. How are you? This is Gert Knickmann."

"I know Gert. How's your hand?"

Gert holds up his brace and nods his head from side to side, but doesn't say anything. He looks like he's about to cry, and he lets go of my arm and walks away.

"This is hard for him," I say.

"I'm glad you're okay, Jess," Joe says. He grabs my hand and squeezes it, then starts to turn away, almost like he's embarrassed.

"Wait," I say, holding on to him. "Joe, wait. You look great. You're in Sacramento? Things are going well for you?"

"I got my shit together, if that's what you're getting at."

"That's not—"

"I was a train wreck. I know it."

"Stop. Please. You're doing fine now, right?"

"You want to know something?" Joe looks back toward the casketless bier, now surrounded by empty chairs and a couple men with trash bags. "It was him," Joe says, and I gasp.

"What?"

"It was him, Jess. He was the one who told me I was fucking up. He was the one who said it so I could hear it. And he was right. I was bottoming out. He made me...he *made* me get my head straight. So I..." Joe pauses and swallows hard, and then he reaches into his pocket for his phone. He flips the thing open and presses some buttons with his thumb, and then he waits for a moment before handing it to me. "Have you seen this? That's the guy who did it." His voice cracks as I stare at the picture and story on the tiny display. "That's the fucker who killed him."

SF BUS BOMBER IDENTIFIED, the headline reads.

"How do you scroll this?" I ask.

"Right here."

His name was Andrew Li. He was twenty-three, born in the U.S., living in San Jose. He was a nobody. He was recruited. He put on the backpack and blew up the bus. No one knew who he was.

"It wasn't Josh," I whisper.

"What? Of course it wasn't...It was that son of a bitch. He killed Josh. He almost killed you." Joe takes the phone from me and snaps it shut, then he takes off his glasses and rubs his eyes. "I gotta go," he says. "I'm glad you're okay." And he walks off toward the cars.

It isn't hard to find Gert towering over everyone else in the crowd, and when I move toward him, I see he's talking to the two dark-complected men. They're wearing suits, and they watch me as I approach.

"Who are you guys?" is the first thing I can think to say.

"Jess," Gert says, "this is Christian, and his brother, Ramón."

"From San Salvador?"

"Yes," Ramón says. He has a narrow, handsome face. "We're very sorry for you." Christian says something to him in Spanish. "My brother is very sorry too."

"You guys were always showing up...I thought you were..."

"Ramón and Christian did a lot of work with Josh," Gert says.

"Josh told me something, you were...missing?"

Ramón rolls his dark eyes and makes a *psh* sound. "These guys," he says, "Christian and Josh, they worry too much about me." He doesn't speak with much of an accent at all. "Like, they can't call me for a couple days because I lose my phone charger, and they think I'm running away to Canada or something. I was in *Oakland*. Big brothers, man."

Christian follows this, and then he looks at me. "Yosh is like, he is brother. He help us. You know? And my...my mama..."

"Our mother's heart is broken," Ramón says. "He lived with our family in San Salvador. She called herself Josh's second mama."

"I'm...I'm so sorry" is all I can say. They speak together in Spanish again.

"We go now, Gert," Ramón says. "Good luck to you. Good luck, Jessica." They walk off, and Christian claps his hand on his little brother's shoulder as they go.

"Why didn't you ever tell me who those guys were, Gert?"

"You never asked."

We walk again, through fewer people now and the sounds of cars starting up and driving away. I see Tim and Emily and their children standing by their big wagon. Tim has his arms crossed, staring at me over the grassy lawn.

"Will you come to the reception?" Gert asks.

"I don't think so. Gert, it wasn't Josh."

"What?"

"It wasn't Josh. He didn't blow up the bus."

"Of course it wasn't, Jess. The doc couldn't do something like that."

"Did you ever wonder, though? Even for a second?"

Gert tilts his head, but says nothing.

Dinner that night at Emily and Tim's is a mostly silent affair, just like the entire day with them has been. Maybe the silence has something to do with the events of the morning, but I don't really get the feeling this is much different than any other night here. Tim and Justin talk about peewee football, or something, and Emily sits next to Caleb in his booster chair and spends a lot of time helping him eat the leftovers she's reheated for dinner.

Other than Justin's girlfriend comment this morning, nothing has been said about Josh here all day, and it's sort of unsettling. I want to say something, anything, find out what the hell is wrong with these people, but I'm too polite and I feel like saying anything would be like standing up and screaming or smashing a glass on the floor or something jarring like that. So I sit, and I watch Caleb struggle against the washcloth Emily wipes over his messy face.

"Come on, guys," she says. "Let's get ready for bed. Say good night to Daddy, Cale. You want to say good night to Jessica?" He shakes his head no and buries his face into Emily's shoulder.

"I don't want to say good night to her!" Justin shouts, and he runs off down the hall. Tim smirks at this.

"Okay," Emily says. "I'll be back after I get this little boy down to sleep." I stand up and start to gather plates, but Emily shakes her head. "That's alright. I can get all this later."

I continue to get plates and load the dishwasher, and Tim sits and stares at me as I do it.

"Are you done?" I ask as I reach for his plate. He just shrugs. I get the casserole dish and start to scrub it out in the sink.

"Do you normally put this in the dishwasher?" I ask, but Tim just shrugs again. "I'm sorry," I say. "Is something wrong?"

"Nope," he says.

"I know you hated Josh. But he didn't do it. Did you know that? It was on the news. It wasn't him. So if that's the reason you're being so—"

He rises and walks away, and I hear a television turn on in some other room.

Is this man for real? I am furious, and barely keeping myself from following and telling him exactly what I think. I start to clean to calm myself down, just like my mother would do. I wipe down tables and countertops, and chip burnt-on cheese from Pyrex. I need to get out of here. There must be a hotel by the airport. I finish and wipe everything down again, and head to my room and wish I could call Katie *right now* to tell her everything, everything about Josh, and everything about these crazy people. Emily comes toward me down the hall from some other bedroom, and her face has the same sad, tired look it has had since I first saw her last night.

"Are they asleep?" I ask.

"Justin is fighting it, like he always does. Do you need anything? Towels are under the vanity, if you haven't found them already."

"I'm fine. Thanks for dinner. I wasn't sure where to put the casserole dish."

"You really didn't need to clean up."

"Well, your husband wasn't doing anything."

"Pardon me?"

"Is he always like that?" I ask.

"What are you saying?" Emily's lips go down to a thin line and her cheeks turn red and she almost shakes for a moment. "Just what exactly are you saying to me?" She grabs me by the elbow and pulls me into the guest room and shuts the door.

I have touched, I think, the proverbial nerve.

"How dare you," she says. "How *dare* you talk to me in my house like this."

"Emily, it was your brother's funeral this morning. Hello? Don't you get a break?"

Now she really is shaking, and her whole face is red. "How we conduct ourselves in our own home is none of your business. None." Emily keeps glancing at the door. She isn't quite whispering, but she never really raises her voice.

"Look, I'm sorry. I'm sorry. I really appreciate you letting me stay here, but I think I'm going to get a hotel or something for tomorrow night. Maybe it's the best."

"Yes. Maybe."

"I'm sorry."

Emily looks like she's going to walk away for a moment, then she turns back to me.

"You do realize why my mother had you stay here, don't you? She was afraid I wouldn't go. That we wouldn't go. She knew if you stayed here and we had to take you, we wouldn't have any excuse not to go."

"You didn't want to go? Did you think he did it too? Blew up the bus? He didn't, you know."

"I never, ever thought that."

"So you wouldn't have gone to your own brother's funeral?"

"Basically my mother used you—"

"You didn't answer my question."

"—just like my brother probably used you. They're a lot alike that way."

Ouch. "Emily, you don't know anything about Josh and me."

"I know just as much as you know about him and me. So nothing, really."

"But I know everything," I say, for no reason other than to be spiteful. But this has touched something too; Emily looks very startled. Almost afraid.

"What?" she says.

"Nothing. Really." And suddenly I'm very curious about whatever it is she doesn't want me to know. Probably as curious as she is about finding out if I really know it. Neither of us asks, though. We stand in silence.

"I'm sorry," Emily finally says.

"No, really, I'm sorry. I'll find a hotel in the morning."

"You're welcome to stay here. Please stay."

"About Tim," I start, "I didn't mean to—"

"He's . . . just don't. Ignore him. You can stay. Please."

"Can I use your phone? For a long-distance call?" I think of Josh asking me the same question and almost laugh.

"Of course you can use the phone." She points at an old corded phone next to the computer monitor, and I see a little picture of that suspension bridge, framed on the desk behind it.

"Is that the bridge in Michigan? The picture?"

"Yes."

"With the weird name."

"The Mackinac Bridge."

"Can we go there?"

"What?"

"We could drive there tomorrow."

Emily laughs at this. "No, we can't," she says.

"Why not?"

"For starters, it's like eight hours away, or more. That would be a two-day trip, at least. We have church tomorrow, and then I have to watch the kids Monday, and take you to the airport. If you stay."

"I'll stay. But we should go see the bridge."

"It's too far to just pop up there. There's no way."

"Could your mom watch the kids?"

"I think my mom is a little busy with other things right now. You could go there. Rent a car or something."

"If I went, I'd want to go with you."

Emily gives me a funny look. "Why would you want to do that?"

"To talk about your brother, maybe?"

Emily gives me a long look, then a little boy call of "Mommy!" comes from down the hall. "Oh, Justin," she says under her breath.

She nods toward the door. "Sorry, I have to—"

"I understand."

Emily leaves the room, and I grab my bag to hunt for the scrap of paper with the Haddens' number on it. I grab the atlas too; Michigan, like California, takes up two pages and I have to turn the book sideways to look at it. The Mackinac Bridge, connecting the Upper and Lower Peninsula of the state, is up at the top.

The phone seems clunky and brittle and old, and I punch in the numbers and feel the odd tug of the cord as I hold it up to my ear with my shoulder. The phone rings and rings, and I'm so prepared to get an answering machine that I don't even think to just hang up. By the time the notion of just putting the thing back on the cradle hits me, Mrs. Hadden picks up.

"Jessica," she says. "Is everything alright? Thank you again for coming today."

"Everything is fine," I say. It's not at all, but why bother her with that? "How is Mr. Hadden doing?"

"He's much better. Some times are better than others."

This I understand completely.

"I wanted to ask, would it be a big problem for me to go back home on a different day? With the flights?"

"Probably not, it's all standby anyway. Why do you ask?"

"I want...I want to go up to see that big bridge. In Michigan."

"You what?"

"Josh had told me about it. The bridge. So I want to see it."

"My husband's family had a cabin up there—"

"Josh told me about it."

"That doesn't surprise me. Our family spent, oh, he just loved it up there. But it's quite a drive."

"I know. I want to see it. I have another thing to ask."

"Yes?"

"I want Emily to come with me. Can you watch her kids?"

Josh's mother doesn't say anything.

"Mrs. Hadden?"

"You really want to do this? You are serious?"

"I do. I am. Can you watch them while we do it?"

"Of course I can watch the boys. I would love to have the boys. This wasn't her idea, was it?"

"No. I asked her about it. She didn't seem to think it was possible. Can you make her do it?"

"She's an adult, it's her decision."

"But you're her mom."

There's a pause, and then Mrs. Hadden draws a quick breath. "Are you doing this because of Tim? Are you going to talk to her about him? Do you think you can talk to her? I can't get anywhere with her. You could be the one to finally talk some sense, if you think—"

"I just want to go see the bridge, Mrs. Hadden. Maybe we'll talk about other things too."

There's a pause. "Is she there right now?"

"She's getting one of the kids back to sleep. Maybe call here in ten minutes."

"I will."

"Make her go with me."

"We'll see what she says."

I hang up the phone and sit on the bed, and as I sit I look at the computer and think maybe I should check my mail and see if Katie has sent anything yet. So I get up and power on the computer and it's old and slow and takes forever to boot up, just like my own back home. I don't even know if they have Net access, but the home page—something about daily prayer for sports fans—loads right up. I don't really look at it, but when I start to type in the address for my e-mail, I think well, what could it hurt, and I peek in the browser history in hopes that maybe I'll see something I can tell Emily about. But there's nothing but prayer and faith and football, the weather, and home-schooling resource sites. Nothing. This lack of dirt makes me hate Tim even more, and I continue on to my e-mail.

There isn't much in my mailbox when it finally opens up. Gretchen writes: "Hi, are you okay are you okay are you okay??!!" She misses me and she's crying every night like a dork, she writes, because she's worried about me and she wants me to come back. She wants everything to be normal and she wants us to go to lunch at the Gram and laugh about stuff. She tells me the golf people wanted to send me flowers so she gave them my address. She really hopes I'm okay. I almost smile when I read it.

There's an e-mail from Patrick that says—a little more subtly—the same, he hopes I'm doing alright, he's thinking of me, and he doesn't even know if I'll be checking e-mail. I respond and write: "Am checking e-mail. May stay a couple extra days. I'll keep you posted."

Just as I hit send, the phone rings, and the harsh mechanical bell sound makes me jump. I can actually see the telephone shake on the desk with each ring. Emily picks up and I can hear her talking down the hall.

"Hi, Mom," she says. "Hi. Yes. Is Dad doing...I was going to call, I just got Justin back down..." A door closes, and I can't hear her voice anymore, just the constant mumble of the television in the living room.

The only other e-mail I have is from Cooper & Greaves, announcing some "Get Ready for Fall Fashion" promotion. No matter how many times I unsubscribe, their mails keep coming, and typically, the copy is atrocious. I read, and mentally edit, and think how I'd never let myself write such awful copy as this, ever.

Thinking this, thinking of work, thinking of writing even about things I hate like tops and jackets and closeout bathing suits, makes me feel very, very good. It's like fog breaking to blue sky.

A door opens, and I hear quick footsteps, and Emily is suddenly in my room, steaming.

"What did you say to her?" she asks, shutting the door behind her.

"Who? What did I say, what?"

"My mother, you called my mother. Don't do this stupid act with me. What did you say to her?"

"I asked about going home on a different day."

"And you talked about Mackinac."

"Are we going?"

"What did you say to her?"

"Are we going up there together?"

Emily crosses her arms, not looking so angry now. "You aren't telling me what you said." She sees the atlas on the bed, and picks it up. "How old is this? This is...that road isn't even there anymore, it's the interstate now."

"You're not telling me if we're going."

"Yes. Yes. Okay? Yes. We're going. Alright? Now what did you say to her?"

"Seriously? When?"

"Tomorrow. After church. We'll drop the boys off at my parents' house, then we'll go. We'll stay the night somewhere, and get to Mackinac on Monday."

"Do I need to rent a car?"

"We'll take Tim's car."

"Will he be okay with that?"

"It doesn't matter what he thinks. It's my car too." She looks to the door and seems a little embarrassed that she's saying something assertive. "I'm going to talk to him right now. What did you say to my mother?"

"I said I wanted to go up to see the bridge, and I told her I wanted you to come with me. That was it."

"You are just like them. You're manipulative."

"That's funny, your brother actually said I was just like you."

"He said what?"

"He said you and I were a lot alike. He said we were naïve. Well, he sort of said that. More or less."

"So typical!" Emily opens the door. "I'll be right back." She goes down the hall, and I go to the doorway in an attempt to hear her conversation with her husband. There are no raised voices, though, just the television. And in a few minutes, she's back.

"Alright," she says. "We're taking Tim's car. It gets better mileage."

"I can pay for gas."

"Fine, you can pay for gas." She almost looks like she might smile. Maybe. And in this almost-breaking smile, I see her brother's face.

"We're really going?" I ask.

"Yes."

"Can I do anything to help you get ready?"

"I don't think so. Maybe just help me with the kids tomorrow while I pack."

"I can do that," I say. "I'll see you in the morning, then."

She looks at me, still on the edge of a smile, and starts to back out of the door. "Good night," she says. And she pulls the door shut as she goes.

I want to tell Patrick about this trip. I pick up the phone, mentally calculate the time difference between here and the West Coast; it's just after six there, so there's an okay chance he will have just gotten home. I dial his number but get an error, then feel like an idiot when I realize I've left out the area code.

"Jess?" he answers after I redial. Second-ring pickup.

"How did you know it was me?"

"I'm pretty sure you're the only person I know in Ohio right now."

"I didn't know if you'd be home."

"I've actually been home for a while."

"Did something happen there?"

"No, nothing like that, I just had another interview for that project manager thing at our office in town."

"Another? Is that good?"

"I guess it's good. They seem pretty interested."

"That's great?"

"I guess so."

"But what else?" I ask. "There's something else."

"It's in Tokyo."

I feel my chest squeeze at this, and I say the very first thing that comes into my mind. "I'll go with you."

"Jess, come on."

"I'm serious, I will. I'll go with you. Anything. Whenever. I'll go."

"We'll talk about it."

"I will."

"Okay."

"Is the rule over?"

He lets out a little laugh. "We can talk about that too."

"I sent you an e-mail."

"I saw it. What's this about staying longer?"

"I'm going on a little road trip with Josh's sister. I'll let you know when my new flight is. I can take the shuttle if you can't pick me—"

"I can pick you up. Just tell me when."

"I miss you, Pat."

"I've missed you too. Lots."

We say good-bye and hang up, and when I go to shut down the computer I see that there's a new message in my inbox, just six minutes old, and the subject says "HI FROM NZ." I can't click on it fast enough. It's a short mail, and it says: "JZ—On the boat in Auckland. Feel lost. Feel alone. I love you.—KZ"

I hit reply and look at the screen and think for a moment, and then I type

"ME TOO."

I look at this, and I look, and then I tap the backspace key again and again and again until those two words are gone. Because maybe I don't feel that way. Then I think for a bit and I type

"I LOVE YOU, KZ."

And I hit send.

28

The road north of Columbus is rural and absolutely flat. There are fields and farms and woods, and no hills to speak of. Green leafy trees, and rows of crops. Red barns, and satellite dishes.

"Does it ever bother you that there aren't any hills?" I ask Emily. She's been behind the wheel of the midsize Chevrolet with the pro-life bumper sticker since we left.

"I've never really known anything different. Are you bothered by mountains?"

"Well, no," I say.

"There you go."

I stayed home this morning to pack my things and take a shower and check my e-mail while Emily and Tim and the kids went to church. I'd hoped to see a reply from my sister, but there was nothing. When everyone was back, I played with Caleb and his snap-together blocks while Emily packed their things for a stay at Grandma and Grandpa's house. Tim said nothing to me the entire time.

The drop-off at Emily's parents' place was smooth and the kids did not cry; Alice Hadden and I chatted in the driveway while Emily went inside to see her father and the boys chase each other around the yard. Mrs. Hadden and I stuck to small talk (though I could tell she wanted to talk about more), and when Emily came out of the house her eyes were red like she'd been crying. She kissed her children and her mother, and they'd all waved when we pulled out into the street.

An hour later we pass a stinky oil refinery in northeast Ohio. Later, handsome white minarets tower over soybean fields as we approach the most incongruous, beautiful mosque in the middle of nowhere.

"They built that right around when I was born, I think," Emily says. "I always wanted to go inside."

"We could stop. Do you want to stop?"

"No. I do not want to stop."

We find a grocery store in Toledo to get some things to eat. I buy bottled water and apples and deli sandwiches, and Emily seems to approve of my choices. She acts like she does, at least, but she doesn't eat very much as we sit in the car in the parking lot and have our lunch. Then we're back on the road again, crossing into Michigan. There's a heavy silence in the car, and I talk, and talk, to try to fill it. I talk about Katie and her boat, and I talk about Gretchen. I tell her about writing advertising copy.

Through all of this, Emily says nothing.

We drive through Detroit, through road construction and heavy traffic. Emily holds the wheel with both hands. We stop to pee and to fill up the car. I pay for the gas.

We go on, north of Detroit, and the traffic eases somewhat. We drive over a tremendous bridge spanning a river in a place called Zilwaukee.

"What kind of name is that?" I ask. "Is it Indian or something?"

"The people who founded this town intentionally called it that so immigrants would come here to work. Instead of going to Milwaukee."

"You're kidding."

"I'm not."

"Do the Haddens have like, an authority gene or something?"

"What do you mean?"

"I mean, you said that just like Josh would have said it. Like it's an absolute truth."

Emily lets out a little sigh at the mention of her brother's name. "Unlike Josh," she says, "I've always been able to recognize that some facts are useless."

I laugh at this, because it's completely true.

"He filed every bit of trivia away like a treasure," she goes on. "Not for himself, though. Well, I guess they were for himself in a sense, he kept facts around to use against other people as he saw fit."

I nod at this.

Now past the town ripping off Milwaukee, the traffic eases, and the countryside is rural again. There are hills, too, rolling hills with fields and trees and deep red barns and silos, and seeing all this makes me happy. We drive in silence, rolling along, and pass a sign announcing an upcoming twenty-seven-mile-long construction zone.

"Every road in this state has been under construction for my whole life," Emily says.

"They're dedicated to continuously making improvements?"

"They're dedicated to wasting time. It's the union effect."

"That's a very Josh-like statement," I say. "Sort of on the other side of the ideological spectrum, but Josh-like nonetheless."

"Stop," Emily says. "Stop. No more talk like that. Please."

Emily is quiet for a long, long time after this. We enter the construction zone, and the road squeezes down to one lane and the car buzzes from driving on the shoulder rumble strip we've been forced onto. I feel Emily looking at me, though, again and again and again, and I can tell she wants to say something.

"What?" I finally ask.

"I want to know what he told you," she says.

"What do you mean?"

"Yesterday you said you knew everything."

"I don't know everything."

"What did he tell you?"

"He didn't tell me anything."

She's quiet again, and when I look over at her I see tears rolling down her cheeks.

"Are you okay?" Emily shakes her head. "Emily, what's wrong?"

"He told you, didn't he?"

"Told me what?"

"About—" She holds her breath for what seems like a minute, and her face is bright red. "About the abortion," she finally coughs out.

"Whoa, whoa, what? I mean, I know your husband didn't like him, and he almost punched him, and he talked to your mom about you leaving him, I think? But I didn't know anything about—"

Emily is really crying now, and she's all over the road. "He told you I had an abortion, didn't he?"

"Emily, he didn't . . . I didn't know anything about that."

"He told you, I know it." The car knocks over a couple orange traffic markers, and swings back into the lane.

"Why don't you pull over, Emily. Emily?"

"I knew he told you."

"Can we pull over?"

"Damn it, I knew it!"

"Fines doubled in work zones, Emily. Please pull over? Now?"

She sobs and sobs, and the car swerves from left to right.

"There's a ramp, Emily, there's a ramp. Please get off here. Exit ramp, here. We can stop, and talk." I'm almost ready to take the wheel myself, but she steers us over through her sobs and we roll up the ramp and coast to a stop at a farm road. Emily puts the car in park and her whole body shakes as she holds her face in her hands.

"I know he told you," she whimpers through her hands.

"He never told me that."

"Seriously?"

"I'm serious."

Emily drops her hands and looks at me, and her face is a wet mess. "Well, I had one. I did. And I don't care what you think of me."

"Honestly, I don't think anything." I open the glove box, and just as I suspected, there's a box of tissues in there, like there should be in any car that regularly ferries children around. I pull out the box and hand it to Emily.

"I don't care what you think of me," she says again.

"Emily, I am not thinking anything about it. It happens to people. I'm not holding it against you. It's not a big deal." I don't know if that was the right thing to say, because suddenly Emily falls into a new round of sobbing.

"It *is* a big deal," she says.

"Do you want to talk about it?"

"Let me, let me calm down." Emily wipes her eyes and blows her nose. "He was the only one who ever knew. Josh was."

"Was it, was it Tim's?"

Emily laughs at this, a bitter sort of chuckle. "God, no. I was seventeen. My boyfriend didn't even know."

"Your parents?"

She shakes her head. "My dad would have freaked out."

"Whose dad wouldn't have?"

"I didn't know what to do. I was terrified. And Josh, Josh, my big brother..." She wipes her eyes again. "I don't know if you can understand this. I told him. He was my best friend."

"I do understand."

"He took care of everything. He made the appointment. He drove me to Cleveland. He paid for it. We stayed at his friend's apartment after, and he took care of me."

"You did the right thing," I say.

"No," Emily says. "No." She bites her lip and shakes her head. "After, after I did it, I realized I made a mistake. But Josh kept telling me, and telling me, that I did the right thing. And the more he told me that, the more I realized I did the wrong thing."

"You feel like he pressured you into doing it."

Emily nods, and cries, and covers her face again.

"I'm sorry," I say, and I reach over and touch her shoulder. "I'm sorry. He could convince people."

"I flipped out," she goes on. "I graduated, and went to college, and I hated myself. I had this secret, you know? And I hated myself for it. And the more Josh tried to help, the more I convinced myself that he made me do it. I got crazy. I got militant. I started protesting at clinics. I thought that would somehow fix my bad decision."

"I can see the logic. You were confused and upset."

"There are weird people in that group. The protest types."

"I bet."

"But there are some nice people too. Sincere people. Tim was one of them. And the more time I spent with him, the more I hated my brother."

"I think you were okay to be angry at him."

Emily breaks down again, and whispers, "No, no. There was something I forgot."

"What?"

"There was something I made myself forget. When I told Josh I was pregnant. I called him, he was at school in Chicago. I was freaking out, it took me like an hour before I could get myself to the point I could tell him. And after I did, he told me to stay calm, stay put, and he borrowed a car and drove straight back to Columbus. He told our parents he came back for some lecture, or something."

"He could be smooth, like that. And he was good at borrowing cars."

"You don't even know. But he calmed me down. He was like, 'Emmy, you have some options. You can end it, or you can keep it. You could give it up for adoption.' And this is the part I forgot. This is the part I made myself forget. He said whatever I did, whatever I chose, he'd support me. He'd help me, no matter what. That's the part I put out of my mind."

There's a change in the sound of the idling car, and Emily blows her nose. I don't say anything.

"In my head, I wanted to keep it. I really did. I know it's crazy, but there was a little part of me that was almost, maybe excited?"

"I can see that," I say.

"But I was terrified my parents were going to kick me out. I mean, I was seventeen, right? Josh tried to tell me that they would probably be really supportive, but the only thing I could see them doing was kicking me out. All I could imagine was my dad going crazy and my mom screaming at me. But Josh said even if they did, he'd take care of me. He'd make sure I had a place to live. I mean, he was just saying that, now I know my parents wouldn't have kicked me out, but he was really ready to do those things.

"But there was one thing he told me I had to do. One thing. I had to tell Mom and Dad myself. If I was going to go through with it, if I was going to keep it, I had to tell them. He was like, 'I'll be there with you when you do it, but you're the one who has to tell them.' And that's what it came down to. I had an abortion because I was too scared to tell my parents. Josh made it easy for me with his support. He made me feel strong about what I chose, and then I blamed him for it. He didn't talk me into anything. But I made myself believe he did. I regretted making the choice, and I made myself believe it was his fault that I did it."

"I understand," I whisper, and my voice breaks when I say it.

"So I went to college. They were active there, you know, it was easy to get wrapped up with them, and I started protesting. I started seeing Tim. I never told him I had one. I could almost believe it never happened, and those times I couldn't make myself forget, I made myself believe that Josh forced me to do it. So I lived this hateful life. We'd drive around in a little bus, we'd go to these clinics, and I would scream at girls going inside. Like, six a.m., and I'm screaming that some girl is a murderer. Sometimes they'd put jackets over their heads or whatever to hide from us. But sometimes they'd look at us. Sometimes I'd see a girl going in, and it was like I was seeing myself. And it just made me scream louder. I'd hate the girl like I hated myself."

"Did you really hate yourself?"

"I did. And Josh was the only one who understood that. He understood it in a way I couldn't, you know? I was inside it, I couldn't see it like he could. And when he'd try to bring it up, I just, I guess I just closed him off. And I made Tim hate him too, you know, all I had to say was that he was a liberal, pro-abortion, virtually a socialist, and that was enough. And the art too, that was over Tim's head, and just another reason for him to think Joshua was virtually a criminal. They got into it, a couple times. Like, really into it. I thought Tim was going to take a swing at Josh once."

"He mentioned that before."

"A couple years ago, actually, I guess three, I was really pregnant with Caleb, I was huge, Josh had just gotten back from South America and he came to visit us. He and Tim were really going at it, *really* going at it, and it was starting to get ugly. I don't even know what they were talking about, probably politics or something, but it got to where Tim was standing over Josh and pushing him in the chest with his fingers. I came in and I was like enough, enough, you're going to wake up Justin. I really didn't want Tim to hit Josh or anything. So

I took him into the guest room, the same room you were in, actually, and I was like, just leave it, please? And he looked at me and he said, 'I should just tell Tim everything, right now.' And at first, God, I laughed at him, I was like, 'I don't think he would even believe you.' And he kept looking at me, just calm, that look he had, and he goes, 'Too bad I still have all the paperwork and bills. He might believe that. And if he doesn't, I bet Mom would.'"

"What did you say?"

"I didn't say anything at first. But the way he said it, I knew he was serious. And at the moment, it was like, like breaking through the ice on a frozen lake. I was shocked awake, and all of a sudden I saw this lie, this whole lie I had built my life around, I could see it from the outside. But then I was terrified, like *terrified*, I knew he was serious and I was down on my knees and crying and begging him, begging him not to say anything."

"Emily, I'm so sorry."

"So, I don't know. He pulled me up and sat me down. He told me I was killing myself, living like I was, hating myself like that. He understood it. And for the first time, I guess I did."

"What exactly did you understand?"

Emily laughs. "Okay, well, for starters, I married someone out of self-loathing. I married Tim so I could keep hating myself. How's that for clarity?"

"I'm sorry."

"Don't apologize. I'm sorry that I'm telling you this."

"Did he ever give up the secret?"

"No. But I was always scared he would. Especially when he called drunk."

"I know what you're saying."

"That night, in the guest room, he promised me he wouldn't. But he said I had to do something about fixing the way I was living. About fixing my life. And if I didn't, he'd reconsider his promise."

"So what did you do?"

"Well, I had Cale a couple weeks after that, and everything was crazy, new baby and all that. And Tim, believe it or not, is a pretty good father. So I had second thoughts. But Caleb got bigger, and Josh kept calling, and he'd give me little reminders about my promise to him. Little hints. I hated him for it, but at least I realized he was right."

"So?"

"So I talked to my mom, I sort of floated the idea of what if I just came and stayed at the house with the boys for a while? You'd have thought I had just told her she won the lottery or something. I mean, she was thrilled. She never had a good feeling about Tim, but she never really said anything outright. I guess moms just know things like that?"

"I think they do," I say.

"But now Josh is gone. No one is going to find out what happened, right? So I could just go back to business as usual."

"But are you going to?"

Emily starts to cry again. "I don't think I can."

"I don't think you should."

"I can't. But the boys, I don't know."

"But one thing," I say. "Now I know everything. I could tell your mom, or your husband."

Emily wipes her eyes and looks at me. "You could, I suppose. But I know you won't."

The funny thing is, I know she's right.

We find a hotel in a small town near a military base, and when we settle in to the austere room with two double beds there's a feeling of something like relief. Emily sits on the bed closest to the bathroom and takes off her shoes while I look out the window and spy what looks like a Chinese restaurant, and maybe a pizza place and a beer and wine store in the strip mall next to the hotel's parking lot.

"Does Chinese food work for you?" I ask.

"Chinese food is fine."

I run over and order us carryout. Emily has asked for sweet and sour pork, but I won't hold this against her. While I wait for the food to come up, I walk down and happily find my metal-capped table wine at the beer store. Two bottles are purchased, and I slip them into the big paper bag with our food and stroll back to the hotel. Emily looks like she's fallen asleep, but she opens her eyes and sits up as I shut the door.

We sit on the floor to eat. I go for the cheap, splintery chopsticks; Emily wisely opts for a plastic fork. I procure two plastic cups from next to the ice bucket and bring out one of the bottles, and Emily gives me a barely convincing "no, no, well, okay" look before I pour.

I am pleased to see, in an oddly comforting way, that Emily's cheeks turn red as she drinks. She takes a big swallow, and I do too, before asking what I've wanted to ask all afternoon.

"When do you want to leave him?"

Emily puts down her fork, and wipes the corners of her mouth with a dainty gesture that would be cute if it weren't so perfect. "Is there ever a good time to do something like that?"

"Maybe before your kids are too old?"

"Please," she says, and she takes a long swig of wine and tucks some of her hair back behind her ear. "Please. When you put it like that, it seems impossible."

"What do you mean?"

"The boys. It's going to be devastating for the boys."

"Kids adjust." I consider, for a moment, telling her about my own parents' divorce and how well I adjusted to it, but then I don't, because, now that I think about it, maybe I'm not that well adjusted at all.

"I know my mom will help. And my dad will be happy. Caleb will wet the bed, and Justin will hate me. But my mom will be there."

"Josh would be very pleased to know you were doing it."

"He would, wouldn't he? I have a question."

"Ask?"

"Was my brother always . . . was he very serious with you?"

"You mean like, serious about his art? Or more like—"

"I mean in general. His attitude."

I think about this. "I'd say yes. He was pretty serious. He was pretty into his art."

"He was totally into his art."

"But sometimes he could be really affectionate. And sometimes . . ." I almost start to talk about the times with him in bed, but I realize this is *not* Gretchen I'm talking to. But Emily has picked up on it.

"Like when you . . . did . . . you know . . ." Her face turns red as she says it.

"He was very affectionate."

"Was he funny?"

"What, during sex?" Emily's face turns a deeper shade of red when I say this.

"Oh my God, no! I mean, just, did he laugh about things? Did he make you laugh?"

"He had a dry sense of humor, I guess." Considering this, I realize I have no memory of him just laughing out loud. He had a little laugh he would make, like a puff of air through the nose, but that was it. Hoffman made him laugh like that.

"He used to be . . . he loved jokes," Emily says. "Practical jokes, that kind of thing. He pulled off big pranks."

This is news. "Really?" I ask.

"Yeah, sometimes kind of mean stuff, they put a lawn sprinkler in this guy's living room once. And he stole a Ferris wheel when we were in high school—"

"A Ferris wheel? He *stole* it? Was that the picture at the funeral?"

"Yeah, like, from a carnival company, they fold up and fit on a semi truck. He put on a jumpsuit and smeared grease all over himself and he walked into the office and told them he had to take it to Toledo for inspection, and they just gave him the keys."

"How does he talk people into things like that?" I say, then I correct myself. "How did he?"

"He was good at it. And he talked like twenty people into helping him set it up. He had the manual, and they set it up overnight in front of our school. Then when everyone came the next morning, there it was, just going around and around in the teachers' parking lot. He wouldn't let anyone ride it, though. He was too afraid they put it together wrong. So I guess he was kind of responsible. Even when he was being an idiot, he was responsible."

"I can't see him doing anything like that. I mean, I guess I can? Did he get into trouble?"

"He talked his way out of it, like always. He never got into trouble. The carnival people thought it was..." She takes a gulp of her wine and blinks. "Jessica, my brother stole their Ferris wheel, and they thought it was funny. They all came and took pictures before they took it apart and drove it away."

"That's—"

"Yeah. He did things like that all the time. But then, you know, after everything happened, the, you know...he just kind of changed. Like it went out of him. And after I married Tim, it really went out of him."

"Tim. Right. So when do you do it?"

"When do I what?"

"Leave?"

"When? When." Emily sets her cup of wine on the floor next to her and folds her hands in her lap. "How about, two weeks from today. There. That's as good a day as any. My parents will have had time to deal."

"Will you tell them you're going to?"

"Maybe I'll tell my mom."

"Good."

"You can't tell her, though. You can't tell her we talked about this."

"I won't."

"Promise me."

"I told you, I won't."

"I want you to promise me. I want you to say, 'Emily, I promise I won't tell your mother.' "

"Emily, I promise."

"Promise what?" She's a little drunk. "I need to hear you say it."

"I promise I won't tell your mother."

"Good. Thank you. Are we out of wine?"

"There's another bottle."

"I've had enough. But I'll have more." She laughs, with her head tipped back and her teeth showing, and I wonder if this is what Josh looked like when he laughed.

I pour us both some more, and we drink as we unwrap fortune cookies.

"I think I got yours," I say. "It says: 'The journey of a thousand miles begins with one step.' "

Emily holds her little slip of paper up close to her eyes. "You will be rewarded for your patience and understanding," she reads. Then she giggles and says, "In bed. Maybe I did get the right one."

We're too tired to finish the second bottle. Emily takes a shower and I lie on the bed and watch some show about people who risk death while fishing for crabs in Alaska. She's in there forever, and by the time she comes out in her tee shirt and flannel pajama pants, I'm too damn tired to take one myself. So I go in and just brush my teeth and floss and when I come back out I find Emily passed out and snoring. The crab fishing show, incidentally, is over, and I turn off the television and the lamp between our beds.

I'm a little drunk, but sleep isn't coming to me. I could go to my bag and get one of my remaining pain pills, but I know a better remedy, and even though I can't remember the last time I did it, I'm pretty certain it will work. So I tune out the snoring and get to work. I'm almost there when suddenly Emily's voice nearly makes me jump.

"I think I know what you're doing over there," she slurs. "Just try to be a little more quiet." Then she starts to snore again.

I'm mortified. Even Katie never busted me like this. And it's at least another hour before I finally start to fall asleep.

The drive on Monday is a little different. We've got our secrets now, we've bonded, and with this between us the conversation is no longer forced. There's no mention, thank God, of my waking Emily up last night, so maybe (hopefully) she doesn't even remember.

We actually aren't saying that much as we roll along, just listening to an '80s station, sometimes singing, sometimes talking, sometimes thinking. We chatted over coffee this morning too, which was great, but now I'm starting to feel the effects in my bladder.

This interstate pushes through thick green woods and over rolling hills. There isn't much traffic. There are billboards here and there, advertising tourist shops, hotels, restaurants.

"I need to pee," I finally say.

"I'll stop when I can."

We pass a blue sign announcing a rest stop in three-quarters of a mile and I almost cheer; my legs are crossed and I can hardly take it any longer. I groan out loud, though, when we get to the exit, because it's covered by a barricade with a sign that says, "CLOSED FOR EXTENDED MAINTENANCE."

"It's that highway union," Emily says.

"I don't care what it is. Just pull over. Anywhere. Please."

She pulls onto the shoulder and I practically dive out of

the car; I run down a little embankment and into some trees and drop my shorts and squat and feel sublime relief. Then I feel like an idiot when I realize I've managed to spray the inside of my right shoe, and Emily sees it immediately when I get back in the car, and she laughs at me.

A sign says "Mackinac Bridge, 7 miles."

We finally see the towers of the bridge pushing up into the blue sky over the trees as we head up the interstate, and I must confess I am a little excited about this. I give Emily some cash to pay the toll, and after the soldiers look over and under our car and the gate raises up, I turn off the stereo so I can better hear the weird hum beneath us.

"I always used to worry our car would blow off this bridge when I was little," Emily says. I laugh at this, and then she says, "But then I read that a car did blow off here a few years ago."

"Are you serious?"

"It was a Yugo."

"You're messing with me."

"I'm not, I swear."

"Well, I guess it's a good thing we're in a Chevrolet. It's like a selling point. These heavy, union-made cars never blow off bridges." Emily laughs at this, and I do too.

It really is a beautiful structure, and I decide right then that blue-gray and green are far better colors for a bridge than the rust-orange of the Golden Gate. I suspect no one will ever ask me for my opinion on this, though, so I sit and listen to the hum. Then we're over, and I'm sad for a moment until I realize we get to drive back over on our way home. The soldiers on this side wave at us as we roll by their station.

"There's a little beach up here," Emily says. "Like a park. We always used to stop and have lunch there."

"Let's go there," I say. "Wait, stop at this gas station."

"We're fine on gas."

"I want to see if they have a disposable camera."

Emily pulls into the parking lot of the minimart, and I run

in and find a disposable digital camera. Then we're off again, and it's only a few minutes until we're in a gravel parking lot ringed with picnic benches and shady trees. The breeze off the lake is almost chilly, but the sunshine cuts through the cold as we walk down to the beach. I've got the little plastic camera in my hand, and Emily is a few steps in front of me.

"Don't look," I say, and when she does look, I take a picture of her with the lake and the big bridge in the background.

"That's going to be a great picture," Emily says, and she pulls a face of mock disgust.

"It will be. I'll e-mail it to you when I get the disk."

There's a beat-up official-looking truck close to the beach, and a man in green coveralls is kneeling down next to it with a wrench, working on some water-valve-type thing sticking up out of the sandy ground.

"Excuse me, sir?" Emily asks. "Would you take our picture?"

The man works his way up to his feet with a groan and dusts off his hands on his work clothes. He doesn't say anything, but he holds out his hand for the camera.

"It's the clear button," I say. "You don't need the flash."

Emily and I stand next to each other. She smiles, and I smile. The man snaps a photo, and then he takes another with the camera oriented vertically.

"Nice picture," he says. "Nice picture."

We thank him and walk off to the edge of the water. We look at the bridge, and the waves, and the colored rocks in the beach. We don't say much. Emily walks, and I follow, and we come to an informational plaque next to a bench.

"Opened in 1957," I say.

"Yes."

I keep reading, and as I do, I start to laugh.

"What's so funny?"

"Josh was wrong."

"What do you mean?"

"This isn't the longest suspension bridge." I don't know why I'm laughing like this, but I can't really stop.

"I could have told you that. The longest one is in Japan." Just as the plaque says.

"He was wrong. He said it was the longest. He was wrong!"

"He wasn't always right about everything, Jessica. But he sure acted like he was."

"He did," I say. "He did act that way. But this time he was wrong."

"You seem to like that."

"I do." I say this, and I smile. "I do."

After the park, Emily and I grab some lunch at a funky little sandwich/trinket shop in the town by the north end of the bridge. The man working there seems grateful for our presence; tourism here, even in the middle of the summer, seems nearly dead.

Emily wants to go visit her family's old cottage after we eat. It's only about an hour to get there, she says, and since I don't really have anything else to do, I tell her I'm in.

We don't say much as we drive. The road winds through a thick evergreen forest interrupted by stands of white-barked birch trees, and Emily leans forward and looks almost excited as we zip through them.

"There's a curve just up here," she says, "where you can see the bay. Josh and I would like, compete. Who would see the water first. It's almost, there it is, there it is!"

We come around a curve and, for a moment, the surface of the big lake shines up through the trees.

"We're almost there," Emily says. She slows at one of the dirt roads headed off to our left, and then she shakes her head and speeds up. "Oh, shoot. It's been a few years. I never actually drove here myself. And there used to be a sign, oh, Jess, it's still here!"

We slow and turn in front of a hand-carved sign that says "CEDAR LANE." Peeling hand-painted signs with very Anglo-sounding family names hang by hooks beneath it. Andersons. Brainerds. Smiths. No Haddens. The gravel crackles beneath the car and it's suddenly darker as the trees close over us, and Emily smiles and leans close to the wheel and looks up, out through the windshield, at the trees.

"It's right down here," she says. We pass some tidy cottages, A-frames and log cabins; porches with wind chimes and screen doors. The lake shows in blue-green flashes between them as we drive by. There's a woman tending some tomato plants in a plot next to her driveway. She waves as we go by, and I wave back.

"I don't know who that was," Emily says as we go around a curve. Then she looks surprised. "Oh! There it...Wow, they built a garage, that wasn't here when we had it." We pull up to the garage; it's painted barn red and there's a high-end SUV out in front. Emily parks next to it.

It's hot in the clearing in front of the garage. Emily seems almost reluctant to step out of the car, but she does, finally. She looks at me and smiles almost nervously, then she turns down to the direction of the lake.

"Hello?" she calls. There's no answer, just the hum of summer insects. "Hello? Let's just, I guess we could just go down."

Emily walks, and I follow. We climb down wooden steps, down a slope through the trees, and they lead to a perfect little cottage, also barn red, built up on the bank above a wide rocky beach.

"Hello?" Emily peeks in through an open, screened sliding door. She's smiling. "Hello?" There's a radio or something on inside. "It's exactly the same. It hasn't changed. Different furniture, I guess. The kids' rooms were back there. We slept out on the deck sometimes, if it was warm. This is...these trees are bigger. We used to...Josh got stuck up in that one..."

She talks, breathlessly, on and on and on. Every rock, every tree, every breaking wave carries some memory for her.

"...That hand pump, it never worked. Let's go down to the lake, my gosh, the water is so low this year!"

I follow her along a short trail through tall grass, and down some more wooden steps to a rocky beach. "The water used to be like, up here when we were kids," Emily says, making an imaginary level at her waist with her hand. "We never had to build the dock out that far." There's a little boy off to our right looking up at us from the miniature mountain of stones he's been piling up. A plastic orange sand pail sits by the stones. Emily walks over and crouches down next to him.

"Is that your cottage up there?" She points, and he shakes his head no. "Do you know the people who live there?" He shakes his head again, and Emily stands up and shrugs and laughs a little uncomfortable laugh. I just stand and watch her. Then she sees something pulled up to the top of the beach, and tied to a tree is an old aluminum rowboat, battered and faded green. She points at it.

"That's our old boat!" she says, and takes a couple steps toward it. "Josh and I, oh my, we'd go, he rowed me all over the bay in that boat. All day, we'd just talk and talk..."

Her smile goes; her hand, though, still points at the dented-up boat.

"I could have..." she says.

Her hand drops.

"Why didn't I..."

Then she breaks down. Completely. Her palms come to her temples and she presses them there, then she runs her hands back over her hair and she shrieks. The little boy gets up and runs away; his orange pail is left behind.

"Why didn't I just listen to him?" She sobs. Emily faces me, her hands closed into clenched and shaking fists. "Why didn't I listen to what he said?"

This is something I cannot answer.

"Why didn't I?"

Then she comes to me, into my arms, and I hold her as she shakes and sobs.

"I can do it. I can," she finally says.

"Yes," I say. "You can do it."

"When we get back. I'll do it when we get back."

Emily pushes herself back away from me, and rubs her nose and her eyes.

"Why didn't I just listen?" Then she covers her face.

"It's okay," I tell her.

I could have.

Why didn't I.

"It's okay," I say again. "It's okay."

But I don't really know that it is.

We drive through Tuesday and spend the night at another nothing hotel, and we get back to Columbus late on Wednesday. The lights are out at Emily's house. She's not picking the kids up until after she takes me to the airport tomorrow, so we don't have to worry about that little detail. Once inside, we find there's a message on the answering machine from Mrs. Hadden telling us I'm on standby tomorrow at 7:35 in the morning, and, through the miracle of time zones, I should be back at SFO at 10:48 a.m.

We whisper good night to each other in the kitchen before I go to the guest room to call Patrick and leave him a message with my flight information. There's a tap at my door just as I'm hanging up, and Emily comes into the dark room and takes my hand.

"Thank you," she whispers.

"Are you going to do it?"

"I think I can do it."

We say good night again, and once I'm in bed I have no trouble falling asleep, then it seems like no time before I hear Emily making coffee and I'm awake again and pulling some clothes from my still-packed bag to get dressed and going.

It's just before dawn when we get out the door on our way to the airport, which should give me the required two and a half hours to make my way through security. Emily has loaned me a travel mug for my coffee, and we don't really say much as she navigates the minivan through the pre–rush hour traffic. We come to the airport and zoom up the ramp to arrivals, departures, pickup, and drop-off, and I put the mug into the van's drink holder as we pull up outside the Delta counter. A couple of soldiers are talking to each other at the curb.

"Thank you, Emily," I say. "Thank you for everything." When I look at her, though, I see her chin trembling. "What's wrong?"

She shakes her head. "I can't," she says. "I can't do it."

"You can. I know you can."

Her face becomes composed again, and she closes her eyes and shakes her head. "No," she says. "No. My boys, they need their daddy. They need a daddy and a mommy."

"You need to do what's right for you, Emily. They aren't going to be happy if you aren't."

"He's a good man, he is, really, he loves those boys."

"But think about you."

"No, you don't understand. They need a daddy. What could I do? Just a mom for those two boys? I'm sorry. I'm sorry."

"It's okay."

"What would they do without their daddy? I don't think you can understand."

"I . . . Just do what you need to do, Emily."

I step out of the car and grab my bag, and say good-bye and shut the door.

29

My flight from Columbus to Cincinnati is nearly empty, and, from the looks of the gate, this last flight doesn't seem like it will be very full, either. My seat is toward the back of the plane, so I'm allowed to board early and watch the dazed and tired people find their seats. No one else has come back to my row, but I'll wait like a good girl until we're airborne before I slide out of my assigned aisle placement to the window where I can look down on the world.

A fat woman comes down the aisle, wrestling her bag forward with each step she takes, and as she gets closer I can hear a swishing, crinkling sound like she has some sort of plastic girdle encasing her body beneath her dress. She gets to my row and looks from her ticket to the seat number placard above us, then down to the ticket again.

"I'm sorry," she says. "I'm in A."

She smells vaguely of lilac, like my eighth-grade English teacher.

But still, I wanted to be alone in the row with my thoughts. Damn her.

I give her a false smile and get my bag from the floor so I can step out of her way, but she waves her hand at me to stop.

"Oh, honey, you can tell me no, but, would you be interested in trading places? A window seat can be an awfully uncomfortable place for a big old lady like me."

"It's no problem," I say, and now I really smile. "I'm happy to." Well, how about that? I slide over, pulling my bag after me and kicking it forward to make room for my feet. The woman raises the armrest and settles down into her seat.

"Woo boy," she says. "Boy. This humidity." She pulls the safety instruction card from the seat back in front of her and uses it to fan her face. She opens her mouth like she's going to say something, but just closes her eyes and lays her head back and sighs.

"Almost home," she says.

Yes. Almost home.

We taxi out, the attendants say the things that they say and the little video plays, then we're up, up, and Ohio and Kentucky and the river and everything else falls away. I press my forehead against the window and look, and as I do, I fall away from myself.

There are roads down there. And rivers and cars and houses and baseball diamonds.

There are roads. And visible demarcations, fields and irrigation systems, different crops. Watered lawns. Green parks and dusty brown cities. Semi trucks and interstates. Maybe Josh saw the world like this all the time.

His family is down there.

The fat woman is sleeping with her mouth open, and I turn my face closer to the window frame.

I'm still down there, I think, covered in roads and boundaries. But I'm up here too, watching myself.

There are trucks. Recreational vehicles. Rolling slowly.

Things are built up, and things fall apart.

Lines are traced. Voyages are planned and taken.

Fathers and mothers and children.

There are hills and mountains, and more mountains, and I haven't moved over the hours. Then we slow, and fall, and I see the bay, and my city. I see my neighborhood, I think. Maybe I see my house.

Am I down there too?

We move out over the ocean, and the plane makes a big, wide turn, and I am looking straight down at the waves underneath me. The mid-morning sun is low and each crest flashes silver, silver, until it crashes into the rocky beach we're flying over now and turns to foam. The rocks are broken into sand, and each grain of sand, eventually, is broken down further.

And as each grief crashes into us, we are broken too. We are rendered down and broken apart, like rocks into sand. Maybe some scientist could determine our ages by the size and number of pieces into which we've been broken? Maybe she could look at our pieces and measure the weight and impact of every grief and joy and agony.

Maybe.

We slow down further; there's a rush of air over marshes and lights and red spinning radars just beneath us. Then asphalt and a thump and we're down and home.

People stand up.

Rules are made, and abandoned.

The fat woman thanks me for the seat and leaves.

I'm the last one on the plane.

From my bag at my feet, I take the crumpled scrap of yellow legal paper that I've used to keep track of all of my flight information. I look at the phone numbers I have written there. Josh's sister, Emily Channing. Josh's mother, Alice Hadden.

I fold the paper in half and leave it in the seat back

pocket. And then I reach to my bag again and pull out the atlas. The taped-up first page has torn more on this trip; the shock of movement after living for so many years on my bookshelf has left it hanging by barely a staple. I thumb through it, and there's a flash of yellow color toward the back, at Washington State, that catches my eye. It's a sticky note in the center of the page, and on it, in a familiar hand, is scrawled:

I needed to get in to make a copy of your map. Thanks for the key. JH

I could laugh about this, or cry, but I do neither. Instead I fold the atlas shut and look at my name, and my sister's name, printed there on the wrinkled cover.

Then I put it in the seat back too, and leave.

Walking, again, right now, it's like nothing. I should still be looking down. Going up the jetway is like floating. And these people, these loud, misshaped people, I could float above them, if I wanted to. I could float above the people, and the strollers; the conveyor belts and the luggage carts, the wheelchairs and the laptop computers. I could float above it all, if I wanted to, looking down at myself.

But I don't.

I stay on the ground and walk; past stairs and security, past the soldiers and their berets, right on by the X-ray machines and the bomb dust sniffer and the opened suitcases. I go past all that, and see him there, standing at the screen announcing arrivals and departures, looking up with his arms crossed and his short hair and his tight tee shirt. He's rolling his big shoulders and rubbing his chin, looking at the display for my flight and the words "on time." When he sees the words, and the rush of people, he turns and looks for me. And when he sees me, he lifts his hand and smiles.

Patrick finds a parking space in front of our building, and carries my bag up the stairs for me. I follow behind, slowly. My back doesn't hurt so much anymore, and climbing the stairs seems much easier. I just want to take my time. He unlocks the door to my apartment, and stands back for me to enter. The blinds are closed, and it's warm inside.

"You want something to eat?" he asks.

"Not really feeling it," I say.

"Want to just sit down for a bit?"

I nod, and go to my couch. Patrick puts my bag in next to my bed and starts out the door.

"Where are you going?"

"I just figured—"

"You can sit too," I say. "If you want."

He comes down next to me, and when I hold out my hand, he takes it. Our fingers lace together. And in that feeling, that perfect feeling of our hands and fingers pressed together, I want to tell him everything. I want to tell him about Josh, and his sister, Emily. I want to tell him about tall, crazy Gert. I want to tell him about bridges and funerals, and most of all, maps. More than anything else, I want to tell him about myself. I want to tell him that I know what things look like from above now. There's so much I want to tell him, because I know he'll understand.

I look at him, and open my mouth.

What. What is it, Jess? What?

I needed to be close to you.

I knew you'd understand.

ACKNOWLEDGMENTS

Making a book is a mostly solitary venture, but I'm grateful to have received invaluable feedback as I wrote it from Michael Hodes, Carolyn and Bret Winkler, Cynthia Clausen, Jennifer Beastrom, Eve and Geoff Lynes, and Hillary Berry. Amy Fulwyler's comments over several revisions were especially insightful, and I always looked forward to hearing them. Thanks also to David Renner for his help in a particularly tough spot, as well as to Kendra and Korin Deyarmond, and to Mary and Jim Leversee and everyone at RMR for their support. Thanks too to Jack Scovil, for his great help and confidence in my work. To Kerri Buckley, I am grateful beyond words for your enthusiasm, sharp wit, and general editorial brilliance. It's a joy to work with you, and this book has benefited immeasurably from your marks.

Most of all I'm grateful for the love and support of Julie, Birch, and Axel, and only hope I can give the same in return.

© David J. Swift

ABOUT THE AUTHOR

SHAWN KLOMPARENS lives in Jackson Hole, Wyoming, with his wife and two children. He is currently at work on his next novel.

Visit www.shawnklomparens.com for more information.